Don't Quit Your Daydream

ADRIAN J. SMITH

EREKA PRESS, LLC

Don't Quit Your Daydream

Darlin', don't quit your daydream

It's your life that you're making

It ain't big enough if it doesn't scare the hell out of you

If it makes you nervous

It's probably worth it

Why save it for sleep when you could be living your daydream?

~ LILY MEOLA ~

Darlin', don't quit your daydream.
It's your life that you're making.
So it ain't big enough if it doesn't scare the hell out
of you.
If it makes you nervous
It's probably worth it.
Why save it for sleep when you could be living your
daydream?

—JOEY MROLA

CHAPTER

One

"I'M AN ENTREPRENEUR."

Oh, God, she's going to give me her whole life story in one elevator ride. Laura squeezed a little tighter on the paper coffee cup and glued her gaze to the crack at the bottom of the elevator doors. Maybe if she didn't say anything this woman would leave her alone and shut up. She had six floors until she could escape, but she did not want to talk to some millennial who thought they could own the world one side hustle at a time.

"I just moved into the co-op building because I needed some office space. What do you do?"

Cursing inwardly, Laura tensed. Now this *millennial* expected an answer. Perhaps she could pretend she was deaf and heard absolutely nothing of what this bubbly woman said, except that wasn't ethical. But it wouldn't be the first time Laura had walked that line—all the issues in the office were her fault from when she had failed to make the right decisions, and now she was left to suffer the consequences. The coffee cup burned the pads of her fingers, but she wasn't about to move or give any sign that she'd been paying attention to the young brunette next to her.

Even if she couldn't help but notice the energy that surrounded her. It was electric, as if she was on fire and ready to go in an instant in whatever direction the conversation went. Laura pursed her lips, narrowed her eyes, and tried to ignore the vibrant life next to her. Her brown eyes were so soft and warm, as if nothing had tainted her sweet life yet. Laura's stomach swirled as she listed inward before pulling back with a wave of annoyance. She wouldn't allow herself to be tempted by doe eyes and sweet smiles.

She was so young. *Is she even a millennial?* Perhaps she was on the older side of Gen Z. That would ruin Laura's day. They were getting younger and more naïve with each passing year. Had she ever been like that? Did it matter? Laura guessed this woman would end up on her ass and out of the co-op contract before the first six months were up. There was no way she could afford it anyway.

Why is the elevator running so damn slow? Laura raised her gaze to the buttons on the right side of the doors. The sixth floor was the only one pressed. Were they going to the same floor? That was just perfect. Laura wouldn't be able to avoid the child in her presence if that were the case. She closed her eyes and a whiff of something fruity reached her, taking over her senses. Laura raised her coffee cup and drew in a deep breath to erase it, letting the bitter beans do their work. Keeping her silence, she waited for the elevator to swallow her whole.

"What company do you work for?"

She's pressing, Laura thought. She wasn't going to be able to avoid the conversation. Clenching her jaw tightly and sighing, she dared a glance over. The *girl's* brown hair was pulled tight into a ponytail, little loose short hairs framing her face. She had big curious eyes that were far too innocent. Her T-shirt was loose and had a flare of writing across the front that read *Unstoppable Today.* Her outfit ended with skintight yoga pants with mesh running up the sides. It fit her bubbly personality for sure, the sleek curves of her body that highlighted her youth and health, her pert breasts that probably didn't need any help staying up where they belonged.

Still, Laura would never dare to wear such casual clothing to an office even when she had been younger, and if she dared try something now Rodney would have her head. She hated working with him, but she was stuck with it, unable to find a way out. "I'm sorry. Are you talking to me?"

"You're the only other person in the elevator." She grinned, her straight white teeth showing off in the dull light of the elevator like she didn't have a damn care in the world. She belonged at a beach sipping cheap beer, not in an elevator to a business building. Laura envied that casual relaxation, something she had never managed to attain. "So, yes, I'm asking you. I'm Skylar."

Great, she even has a ridiculous name. Will this elevator go any faster? Laura pursed her lips, staring at Skylar's extended hand and refusing to take it. She resisted the urge to wrinkle her nose and faced the front of the elevator again. She would ignore Skylar and her perky self if it was the last thing she did. It was rude, but they wouldn't ever see each other again, so it would be fine.

"I guess you must be rather busy," Skylar stated, her tone dropping at the end.

Laura didn't mistake the ounce of hurt. She knew she was the cause of it, but she honestly couldn't bring herself to do anything about it. She wanted nothing to do with this Gen Z entrepreneur who knew nothing of the real world. Everyone had to learn through their own struggles and mistakes, and she didn't have the time or the energy to teach *Skylar* how to avoid making the same mistakes she had. Her hand burned from the coffee cup, but Laura refused to switch hands again. Finally the elevator dinged that they were at their floor. Without hesitating, Laura strode out of the machine and took a sharp right to walk toward her office.

As soon as she was out of sight, she switched her coffee into her free hand and shook out the pain from the burn. That would come back to bite her in the ass later, just like everything else in her life did. Squaring her shoulders, she stepped precisely in her heels to the office that she hated coming to every damn morning but did it anyway. She had no other options and couldn't bring herself to find a new job.

The sign on the main door had been her idea fifteen years ago, and Rodney had agreed to it at the time, but she'd been unable to convince him to update it. Apparently, there was too much cost associated. Despite her repeated efforts to keep the business running smoothly, he routinely shut down her ideas. It was exhausting.

She'd gone from being pivotal and necessary to being ignored and shut down anytime she tried to make a change. Rodney took the credit for her work and routinely took the better parts of their job. Laura had shut down over the years, not pushing for anything and becoming the silent partner. She hated it, and she hated that she'd let herself become that.

The first set of offices were a bustle of energy and people. It was good to see her staff working when they should be and not just when she was in the building. Perhaps the only good thing about this job, and wasn't that saying something? She went around the central desk where her two office administrators were stationed and made her way to the back of the building and toward her sanctuary.

Rodney's lights were off, which meant she was the first one in even though she was running a few minutes late. Her arrival had been hindered by the long elevator ride she'd endured. Clenching her jaw, Laura fished around in her purse for her key, sliding it into the lock and pushing open the door.

Laura stepped into her office and dropped her keys and purse onto her desk, setting the coffee next to her computer. This was her home away from home, the one place she felt the most comfortable and uncomfortable in the same breath. Her shoulders dropped from the tension they'd had as she'd come into the office, the scent of the potpourri she kept on a shelf instantly easing her. As soon as Rodney arrived, she would feel that tension come back, but for now she had her peace.

She hated working there. Every damn day was exactly the same, but she supposed that was what she'd signed up for when she went to school. Routine was what she lived and died by. But it wasn't the work that bothered her so much as the man she worked with. He was someone she could live without—and had even tried to when they'd been in the midst of a divorce.

"Laura!" Rodney's light tenor voice filtered through the main office area and into her personal office.

Laura tensed, her back rigid at the sound of her name. She hated that she still did that when he was around, that she hadn't been able to school that response after two decades of working with him. She didn't bother looking up, making sure everything was set at her desk the way it should be so she could begin her day.

"Laura," Rodney said again, coming to stand at her door. He flicked the light on, which she had forgotten to do in her haste for comfort. "Didn't you hear me calling you?"

"No," Laura stated firmly, grabbing her purse and shoving it into the bottom drawer of her desk as she prepared for her workday, still not raising her chin to give him the time of day.

"I was trying to get your attention as soon as you got off the elevator."

Bristling, Laura paused in her preparations. Was it too much to ask to be able to get to her desk and get situated before he tried to remind her how the office revolved around him? She kept her tone cool and distanced, the conversation an inconvenience for her. "I'm sorry. What did you need?"

She didn't exactly want to ask him that, but she didn't see another choice. The sooner she paid attention to him, the sooner he would get out of her office, and she could get started on her workday. She needed the routine to set her back on her feet, the gentle lull of reading reports and projections. Putting her hand on her hip, she looked into Rodney's brown eyes as he stepped into her office fully and shut the door behind him. That stopped her. This must be serious if he was doing that.

"You were late this morning," his tone had lost the chipper humor he'd had a moment before.

"It happens," Laura's answer was clipped, and she added in her mind, *and only by seven minutes.* She didn't regret a moment of it. He didn't need to know why she was late—no one did.

Rodney looked put off, and she was glad to have caught him off-guard. It was the one defense she had against him still, and she would always keep that in her back pocket. "Anything serious?"

"No." Laura put her burned fingers on the desk and leaned forward, hoping the stoic move would send him on his way. She wasn't his concern anymore, and she didn't want to be stuck in that same cycle they always seemed to repeat. "You're late as well."

"I am." He sighed and ran his fingers through his hair. "Jennifer couldn't get the kid ready on time, and so I had to step in because she begged me to, and Grayson was giving her attitude again. I don't know what is up with him in the mornings lately. She makes one simple request like telling him to get dressed for school and he throws an entire fit about it."

"Sounds like a seven-year-old," Laura mumbled, dropping her gaze to the top of her desk. She always cleared it of papers and work every night before she left, needing the clean start each morning when she came in. "This is the third day this week you've been late, however."

"I know." Rodney brushed a nervous hand through the back of his hair. "Thanks for covering for me."

Laura frowned. She would always cover for him, and unfortunately, he knew that. She was compelled to even if she hated it. She wanted to hate it, wanted to put some more damn distance between them, but she just couldn't make herself. They had relied on each other for too long, and Rodney was the only one who knew all of her demons.

"Anything major on the agenda today?" he asked, as if she'd had a moment to sit down and look at their calendar.

Laura mentally ran through the list, hoping she remembered exactly what the schedule looked like since it was still currently shoved into the top drawer of her desk. "Just the usual, I think."

"Good." Rodney put his hands on his hips before pulling at the tie at his neck nervously.

Laura's fingers itched to fix it now that it was askew, but that wasn't her job anymore. She straightened her back and looked him over. She prayed he would take the hint she was about to give. "We really should get the workday started."

"You're right," he said, stepping toward the door.

"Try not to be late tomorrow, Rodney. I don't want to explain to the team why you can't show up on time, but they get written up for being late."

He at least had the decency to blush like a scolded little boy. She'd said the words softly, but if he was late the next day, she'd likely add a bit more vehemence into her tone. Her annoyance levels were already high that morning, and she pitied whoever entered her office to speak with her—Rodney aside. She could hold her tongue with him, mostly.

"Thanks for covering for me, again. I know it's been a rough start to the school year for Grayson. I just wish I knew what I was doing."

"I'm pretty sure that's the exact point of parenting. You never know what you're doing, and as soon as you figure it out, something changes."

"You're right. I can see why you never wanted kids."

Laura's heart gave a sharp tug. That hadn't been the reason, not really anyway, but it had been what she'd let him believe after giving up. She had, at one point, wanted kids and a family and the white picket fence, and she'd been on track to achieve those goals, until her ex-husband had considered her a cold-hearted bitch who was ice in the sheets and ditched her for the pretty young thing he had on the side. Cold washed through her at the thought, and she made an extra effort to school her features when she looked back up at him. She had to remain untouched by his words.

"If you'll excuse me, I have a list of people I need to meet with today."

"Right. Want to grab a lunch?" As usual, he missed her inner turmoil, though he'd never been in tune with her to be fair. He'd never tried.

"Not today, I have a meeting already scheduled." It was a blatant lie. If he looked close enough, he could see through it, but Laura knew he wouldn't. He never looked that closely at her.

Rodney left her alone, thankfully shutting the door automatically behind him. She never left it open, preferring the quiet isolation she had created for herself. Sure people came and went throughout the day, but largely she sat by herself going through reports and predictions in order to do her job to the best of her ability. Rodney often came in, asking for advice or for her to check his numbers, which was an annoying habit he had never been able to break, not since college when he would find her in her dorm room and ask for help with his homework.

Some days she wasn't sure why she was there still. Plopping into her chair, Laura undid the button on her blazer and relaxed for the first time since stepping into the elevator that morning. Curse Skylar and her damn bubbly personality, her absolute freedom from a past full of painful moments. Laura had been that way once, before she'd gotten married, but the ability to be carefree had swiftly been pulled from under her feet. Laura wanted nothing to do with a Gen Z who thought they owned the world and didn't understand the complications it came with. She'd had enough of that when she was the new kid on the block in the business, and she'd run into her fair share of problems with that attitude.

Skylar would have it beat out of her someday, just like Laura had all those years ago when she'd first started out in business. So many unrealized hopes and dreams for the future. Laura pulled out her calendar to check over her schedule for the day, then she turned on her computer and compared it with the online scheduler that her office assistant kept for her. As predicted, they matched perfectly. She took great pains to make sure that happened, and it gave her a quick rush of pleasure to have this in place at the very minimum.

Laura sighed heavily and rubbed her temple. She needed a change. The constant back and forth with Rodney over petty things weighed on her, and she was tired of being the underling to his obtuseness. She needed to make a change. They'd been in business for twenty years and it was time to revamp, not just the business but also her role in it. She had to bring them to the next level. Then and only then would she be able to prove to Rodney that she was worthy of being a co-owner, that she had more to contribute than keeping track of the damn schedule.

Closing the online calendar, Laura pulled up the reports one of her junior analysts had brought her right before the end of business the day before. She needed to go through it with a fine-toothed comb before making any decisions as to the accuracy. She would spend the next hour on it and nothing more. She didn't have the time to spare on people who couldn't do the background before they handed her information.

CHAPTER
Two

SKYLAR PUT her business and her life on the line to work at the co-op building. Success was her only option, and she'd been born with a mean streak of determination she'd never willingly give up. She'd needed to get out of her brother's basement in order to land herself new jobs that would let her fire the only client keeping her business afloat at the moment—her ex-girlfriend. Her lips curled upward at the thought of finally being able to break that last lingering connection between them as she closed her computer for the day and rolled her shoulders.

Caffeine vibrated through her veins from one too many coffee meetings she'd scheduled that afternoon. But it had all been worth the effort even if none of the companies or people had signed with her. Her name was out there, her business was on the radar, and they would eventually come seeking her. She had to believe that—her brother, Brady, had always told her to look on the bright side of things and to find the silver lining.

Still, perhaps she did have one too many cups of coffee while on the run. She'd spent more time out of her office that day that she had in it. Smiling at the thought, she swiveled in her chair and stared at the mass of boxes she had stacked in the corner. She really needed to figure that out.

Skylar hadn't rented the room in the co-op building for the purpose of being a storefront. She had always wanted to hang onto some of the products she had helped create and market in order to show them off to the next client and create a network. It would also show people who met her just how diverse and good her work was. They would want to hire her in seconds after being there.

But not currently. Now, it was an utter mess. Boxes stacked, the rug she'd purchased to cover the floor still rolled and standing in the corner, and the only thing she had managed to set up was the desk so she could work. While it had been a good idea to have that as her priority at the start, she really needed to make the time to deal with the rest of it. What was the point of having an office for clients to visit her in if it was such a disaster that she'd be embarrassed for them to show up?

With the thirty minutes she had left before she had to leave, Skylar started on organizing things so they would at least seem somewhat presentable. She needed a place where she could bring a powerful woman like the one she'd met in the elevator that morning, where she wouldn't mind stepping in to discuss business. Skylar's lips twitched as she thought of that woman, the suspicion she'd looked at Skylar with. That was someone Skylar would love to meet when it came to networking and working together, someone who really could turn her business around for the upcoming year if she could land herself a contract.

As much as she wanted to dream of how to make the right connections to grow, Skylar didn't have the time. After finishing some cleaning, she stopped and gathered her things. Right now she needed to stretch her back muscles and leave to meet up with her brother for dinner.

Since being in the office, she saw less and less of him, and that was an actual problem to remedy. Skylar put her laptop into her backpack and slung it over her shoulder as she stared around her office. She still couldn't believe the space was hers. She'd been in it for almost two weeks and was so much happier having her office there than at her brother's. She needed the emotional space, but the stress of paying rent was more than she ever thought she could manage.

Stepping out of her door, she put her hand on the glass. Getting a decal for it would have to move up the priority list. No one would know she was there if she didn't tell them. Rolling her shoulders, she looked up and headed down the hallway.

Since she'd been looking at the small office to rent, she'd noticed that one company sprawled the majority of the floor. She'd been told they'd been there for twenty years and were their best clients. Frowning, Skylar stared at the door and the *blah* logo they had covering it. "Solace" was etched into the glass in big bold letters which said anything but solace. It said bold and not much else. Frowning, Skylar cocked her head and tried to see inside, but the glass was opaque. She wondered if that was where the woman from the elevator had gone.

She had been cold and standoffish to say the least, but it wasn't the first time Skylar had dealt with someone like that. They either came around or they didn't, but if Skylar could convince her to at least give her the time of day, then perhaps she could land herself the biggest client yet. These offices took up the majority of the floor, and Skylar was curious about them. She'd have to dive into some research to see if she could sway the pretty brunette.

Stepping into the elevator, she wondered if it would be possible to start up a campaign to redo their logo and their business to make it fit better with the name they so clearly had chosen. She leaned forward to press the button for the bottom floor when a hand shoved through the closing doors to force them back open again.

Skylar lifted her chin and stopped short, her breath leaving her lungs in an instant. The brown-haired beauty was back in the elevator with her. She was smaller than Skylar, petite where Skylar had curves in abundance, but she wore that same hard look she had before, as if her features were cast in marble. A timeless beauty that drew Skylar to her this time as much as it had the last time they'd landed themselves in an elevator together. She wanted to know more, and it caused a bubble of nerves to spin around in her belly that she couldn't possibly control.

"Just perfect," the woman muttered before stepping all the way inside and facing the elevator doors without a second glance in Skylar's direction. Skylar couldn't tell if the comment was because the elevator had been there or if it was because she was in it. Either way, she determined she was going to push through and at least try to break through that thick layer of ice.

Skylar pursed her lips and hit the button for the main level, assuming they were both heading that way. It would give her time to observe and learn, which, if she was going to land herself a client like this woman, she would need to do. She almost asked what floor this woman needed but worried such a simple question would earn her even more venom and worsen her chances at a contract. Straightening her shoulders, Skylar chastised herself.

Lifting her tone into a lightness she wasn't sure she possessed, Skylar said, "I'm sorry, I didn't ask. Were you going to the lobby?"

Those ice blue eyes turned on her and a shudder ran through Skylar's spine—a shudder filled with a sense of dread, hint of fear, but also intrigue. This woman was a fortress, one surrounded by a large moat, used to getting her way, and one who would challenge Skylar's ability to pull out information. But she was up for it. She'd worked with hard clients before, and if this woman truly was part of Solace, then she would have a hand at potentially landing Skylar her biggest client ever.

"Yes." The clipped answer stung the air.

If this woman was going to remain so aloof, then Skylar would have to work twice as hard to make a connection with her. It would be good to challenge herself and perhaps she could learn a new skill in the process.

Keeping her tone jovial, Skylar set her shoulders and took

another chance. "Oh, good, here I thought we were going to have to stop on every floor on the way down."

The glare she received for the semi-joke was outstanding and had certainly been practiced. It rivaled even the best glare from a toddler or a teenager. Skylar had to work hard to hold the smile and giggle, but she knew that would likely push the connection she was trying to make into the impossible category.

Skylar smiled, as brilliantly as she possibly could. "What is it you do for work, Ms. ..."

A thin eyebrow raised up as shoulders stiffened, and she slowly twisted to face Skylar. Unprepared for the full force of that look, Skylar's stomach turned to knots. This woman was stunning, an understated beauty in precision and intensity. Skylar held her breath and waited for the inevitable comment that it was absolutely none of her business, or better yet, that she should just shut up and let the elevator ride continue in silence. Even if she was given that command, she wasn't sure she'd be able to follow through with it.

"I *work* for a living, unlike entrepreneurs."

Skylar's lower lip quivered, and her eyes widened. She nearly took a step backward, but she stopped just in time. "Sorry?"

"Must you apologize for everything?" The vehemence was back. What the actual hell was wrong with this woman? Maybe she'd had such a shit day that she was taking it out on the world. Skylar knew she'd had her fair share of those days.

Skylar wanted to look away from those ice eyes, but she couldn't force her gaze to move. Something swirled behind the look the woman gave her, something that was filled with—something. Gosh, she wished she knew what it was, but there wasn't only ice in the gaze, as much as this woman might want there to be. In fact, she knew it intuitively. This woman put up a front to keep the world out. *Just what is she protecting?*

"I apologize for what I see fit to apologize for." Skylar raised an eyebrow right back and had a squiggle of satisfaction roll through her at the surprise now reflected in those beautiful eyes.

"I think you were trying to insult me. If you were, you should probably be the one apologizing, not me."

Shock rang through the woman's features as her lips parted slightly, the lower one full and teasing a pout, and her shoulders tensed as her gaze narrowed. Skylar was pleased with the reaction. If she was a betting woman, which she was, she would surmise this woman was in charge of Solace. She was certainly someone who held power and authority well, knew how to use it and keep it. Skylar wished she could give off that impression most days, but her laid-back demeanor had never allowed for it.

Holding out her hand, Skylar waited to see if she would take it this time. "Shall we start again? I'm Skylar Ross. I own several different businesses, but my main business right now is Warehouse Thirty-Three—a marketing and coaching enterprise."

"What kind of name is that?" Her tone was sharp, and she still refused Skylar's extended hand, which Skylar kept in place to make it as awkward as possible. She was curious how long this woman could hold out before giving in to social conventions.

"It's a long story about the name."

She snorted. "I would never trust marketing of a multi-million-dollar firm to a wet-behind-the-ears kid dressed like you."

Skylar had to bite back her laugh. This woman didn't hold back. Everything she said was to weasel her way under Skylar's skin, and each time she tried, Skylar let it roll off her shoulders as if she wasn't affected—mostly because she wasn't. She'd heard it all before. This woman didn't know her, and she certainly could only judge on superficial things at this point.

"Okay, boomer." Skylar tried to hide her smile in her shoulder as the elevator doors slid open. She stepped out of the door and walked straight toward the front doors to the office building, not even giving Ms. Solace a second glance. Though she could feel the icy glare the entire time.

It took a few seconds for the clack of heels on the tile floor to reach her ears, and Skylar broke out into a full grin as she pushed open the door and then stood there with it against her back, the door wide open to the stairs that would lead down to the parking lot. She waited for Ms. Solace to figure out what was happening with a sense of impending glee in her chest.

Ms. Solace was halfway through the lobby when she stopped short, her chin lifted while she stared Skylar down. Skylar only responded with a smile and by theatrically moving her hand outward, indicating she was holding the door for the great queen who owned her floor.

"Ma'am," Skylar bowed her head slightly, mostly to cover the laugh that wanted to escape at how put off this woman looked, but also to show she was fine with no answer.

With a huff, Ms. Solace walked through the doorway. She hitched her purse higher on her shoulder and barreled through without another look in Skylar's direction. Skylar let her go, admiring the fine way she walked down the cement stairs in four-inch heels, and the swish of her ass as she went.

Skylar stared out into the fading sunlight of the Denver skyline and smiled at herself. She normally wouldn't have played those games with anyone, but something about Ms. Solace—and that was a good nickname for her until Skylar could learn her actual name—pushed her to do it. Perhaps it was the way to get through to her eventually, but this one would take patience.

As the sun dipped below the horizon, Skylar stepped down the stairs and out to her car in the parking lot. She turned on the audiobook she had started that morning and took a moment to refocus her mind on it and away from Ms. Solace. She needed the time on the drive to relax and center herself. Car drives to and from places were the small amount of serenity she found and allowed herself. Skylar wasn't someone who stopped or even slowed down well.

With her hands on the wheel, she pulled out of the parking lot and drove home—well, to her brother's rental house, since she lived with him still. She had to remedy that eventually. As much as she adored that he allowed her to stay with him since she had moved out there, two years with him was plenty. His fiancée had moved in a year before, and they were in the midst of planning their wedding. Skylar wanted nothing to do with it.

She was happy for him, yes, but planning a wedding that wasn't hers when she'd thought she would get to do that with her ex was a different story entirely. She'd planted all her dreams for the future in that one relationship, and it had shattered her in the end, landing her on her ass to build up herself once again. As soon as she was on their street, Skylar prepared herself for the conversations she didn't want to have. That was the real reason she'd found an office to rent. She needed space. They all did. It was why she needed to succeed and land herself a client big enough to pay her rent. Failure wasn't an option.

CHAPTER
Three

THE ECHOING "OKAY BOOMER" rang through Laura's ears. She hated that *Skylar*—her name was now a curse—had been able to get under her skin so damn quickly. No one had ever managed that, especially a pretty young new kid on the block. Usually, it took years for it to happen.

"I wasn't sure you were going to make it." Camryn pointed at Anna. "She even placed a bet on it."

"Perfect," Laura muttered, taking a seat at the restaurant table and snagging the glass of wine that was waiting for her so she didn't say something she might regret. They would all know just how unhappy she was soon enough, though at the same time, they seemed obtuse about it lately.

She had been the first one to get divorced. They'd sided with her at the time, anger resolving into nothing because it was easy to be angry. It was much harder to sit in the grief. While Laura had wanted the divorce, it still stung when those papers were signed and when she'd moved into an apartment all her own—the first time she had ever lived alone in her life.

Laura sighed, ordering her food as soon as the waiter came over. She crossed her legs and eyed each of her friends. They went way back, years of time spent together as they went through school.

"Isla has a girlfriend," Lynda announced loudly to the table, blossoming as she talked about her stepdaughter, the one she'd struggled with for so many years.

Always suspected that. A murmur echoed in response, and Laura kept her mouth shut. Lynda had been devastated when Patrick had died suddenly and hadn't wanted to date afterward. They were very similar in that regard, both opting to focus on work instead of personal lives. She appreciated Lynda's forward and focused nature.

"She's finally trusting me again," Lynda said a little more quietly, as if once the words were released into the atmosphere, it would make them untrue.

Anna reached around and patted Lynda's hand. "I'm so glad about that."

Laura clenched her jaw. The answer was a pat one and didn't really give Lynda an opportunity to expand, but that was Anna. *Never one to talk about someone other than herself for very long.* Laura finished her wine, and when the waiter walked by, she flagged them down and ordered a whiskey sour. She needed it after dealing with the princess in the elevator. She wished she could focus on her friends instead of being distracted by *Skylar*.

"Teagan's flunking out of college. I'm not sure what to do about it." Anna sighed heavily into her drink.

Ah, there it is. Laura had waited, knowing it wouldn't be long, and she was satisfied that her prediction had proven correct. Camryn and Joni leaned in to console her, more than they uplifted Lynda. Laura shot Lynda a pitying glance and smiled when her drink was set in front of her.

"She's so smart, but she keeps getting hung up on boys."

Laura withheld her snort, but just barely. Anna had been the same when they were in college, though she would likely remember it differently. Anna had gone from boy to boy while she tried to find the right one to marry. They had all seen how that turned out, though again, Laura could have predicted that. She'd known he was not a one-woman man from the start. Much like her own ex. Laura frowned at the memory. She'd been thinking about him in that capacity far too much lately. It was time to put a hard stop to it.

"She's spending more time with Brent than in her classes and doing her homework."

"You can't control an adult," Laura stated firmly, not adding in the other two cents she really wanted to give, which had to do with parenting prior to a child growing up and that if Anna had spent more time doing that than trying to find husband number three, Teagan would be a different kid.

Anna raised her gaze and glared at Laura from across the table. "What do you know about parenting?"

"Nothing," Laura mumbled into her drink as she downed half of it in one gulp. She would need her food soon if she was going to drive home. As far as her friends knew, she didn't want kids. She hadn't wanted to be a parent, and she was nearing fifty, so all bets were in, and they won. No children were in her future—that ever-present ache sharpened, and Laura had to look down at the tabletop to gather herself. "You know what? No. Lynda did an amazing job raising Isla and Aisling who weren't biologically hers, thrown into the deep end of parenting in the midst of crisis, and yes, she's had problems with her girls, but Isla is talking to her again. That's a huge feat and something that should be celebrated."

Lifting her glass and tilting it toward Lynda, she raised an eyebrow with a slight twitch to her lips. That was one way to get the attention off Anna and back where it was rightfully deserved.

"So let's toast to Isla and her girlfriend."

Lynda's eyes lit up. She raised her wine glass and slowly, with Camryn's pushing, everyone else at the table followed suit. The alcohol that flowed down Laura's throat didn't burn this time but had the sweet taste of success.

Her mind drifted back to that elevator as their food was set in front of them and her friends continued their conversation. She hated that she was so distracted by the young woman in the elevator, as if she'd never seen a young woman before who was full of confidence and wiles. She shivered as Skylar's warm brown eyes reached the front of her memory. She'd been so drawn to them.

Laura focused on her meal, but every time she closed her eyes, she saw Skylar staring at her with that satisfied smirk on her face. She was so damn young that Laura had been taken a bit aback by her audacity in pushing the conversation toward antagonism. Normally young adults were too afraid of her to do that. Still, the "okay boomer" stung, though Laura wasn't completely sure why. No one else had managed to get under her skin like that.

She wondered just what kind of upbringing would churn out a woman like Skylar. *Probably a typical two parent house with two point five kids.* Laura sneered at the thought. Skylar would have been handed everything in life in order to blatantly do nothing for work and have daddy's money to rent office space in a co-op building. It was an assumption, yes, but one Laura was happy to make until proven otherwise.

That had to be it. It was the only logical conclusion because Skylar didn't come off as someone who had to scrape by in her mother-in-law's house so she could afford rent on an office building. Camryn caught her attention, leaning close to exclude the other women, still chatting away, her focus on Laura. "What are you so deep in thought about?"

"Nothing important," Laura answered and reached for her new drink, her hands shaking and her cheeks heating with embarrassment at having been caught so distracted. Setting the drink down, Laura distracted herself from Skylar. "How is everything going with you, truly?"

"Decently well, I think. There are always ups and downs, as you know, but we're working on it, which is what's important."

Laura couldn't fault Camryn. She was the only one of the

group who had managed to stay married to her first husband, although Lynda was widowed and likely would still be with Patrick if Laura's predictions stuck.

"What about you?"

"Same as before." Laura gave a short answer not wanting to dive deep into her life. She never wanted to do that, always trying to hide away from the problems she faced and the fact that in the twenty-five years since her marriage and fifteen years since her divorce not much had changed in her life outside of that. She kept her head down, worked, and followed the preset routine that she'd ironed out decades ago. It was easier that way, even if it was harder at the same time. The draw for connection with others was strong, which was why she continued to meet up with her college friends, but she couldn't let them get too close, otherwise they would see the way she would fail them.

"I'm not sure if I believe that." Camryn winked and grabbed her own drink, keeping her voice low so as not to disturb the others. "You seemed unsettled coming in here tonight."

Laura's stomach tensed at the thought that she hadn't managed to keep her disturbance well-hidden. It was one thing for her lifelong friends to notice something was up, but Skylar had also managed to do it. Perhaps her age and weariness with the complications at work really were weighing on her. Clenching her jaw, Laura rapidly debated what to say, the options flicking through her mind in an instant. "I don't know why you would think that. Rodney is an ass as normal, and I'm still taking on most of the work."

Camryn hummed, her gaze locking on Laura's. "That doesn't usually distract you to the point of absolute silence when Anna goes on one of her rants."

Laura's lips parted in surprise before she clamped them shut. "I'm tired of playing that game with her."

"Are you?" Camryn raised an eyebrow. "Because you always feed into it."

"Maybe I'm trying to turn over a new leaf." Laura gave her a pointed look, still ignoring the rest of the conversation going on around them.

"That *would* be new for you." Camryn chuckled lightly. "But what were you thinking about when you got here? Your cheeks were all rosy like it was someone—"

"It was no one. Just an incident in the elevator on my way from the office." Laura held her fork over her food, trying to decide what she wanted to start with to distract herself. "Nothing I haven't dealt with before, and if it continues, I'll speak with the building manager over it."

"Someone trying to proposition you?"

"Something like that," Laura mumbled and kept her eyes glued to her plate. The "okay boomer" echoed in her mind again, the sweet sing-song way Skylar had said it, the quirking of her lips as amusement hit her. She'd been teasing. That was what bugged Laura so much. It hadn't been a simple accusation, which she had received before, it was a tease, a flirt. Frowning into her plate, Laura took a bite.

"Is that all that it is?"

"Yes," Laura answered, glancing up at Camryn to seal the deal that there was nothing else. She had practiced that look so many times that it came naturally to her. Camryn must have bought it because she nodded slightly.

"I'm glad life is treating you well, then," Camryn answered, but it seemed disingenuous. Which perhaps it was. Laura should throw her a bone about the depths of her unhappiness, but unraveling that would be a monstrous feat, not to mention Laura wasn't sure she'd be able to pick herself up again.

Laura listened in on the rest of the conversations at the table, her mind automatically drifting back to the damn elevator. If she didn't work on the topmost floor, she'd certainly be taking the stairs for the next week if only to avoid Skylar whenever she came and went. Sighing, Laura pursed her lips and finished her drink.

She needed to go home, hide away, and rest so she could

prepare to talk to Rodney in the morning. The entire day she had felt off-kilter, careening through the moments to the point she couldn't keep up with what was happening. It had all been because of *Skylar*, the perky bubbly woman in the elevator who had shattered her ability to focus for the entire day.

She was nearly fifty years old, and she shouldn't be distracted by some woman who came in and threw her more than one curve ball in the span of twenty-four hours. Holding back her sigh, Laura kept herself together. She wasn't in a place where she could analyze this, not that she was sure she wanted to anyway.

Laura downed the rest of her whiskey sour and ordered another one. One more wouldn't hurt, and they'd certainly be there at least another hour catching up. They did only get together once a month, and Laura was going to soak in the time with friendships while she could. They needed each other.

CHAPTER
Four

LAURA PARKED in her usual spot, the lot empty that early on a Monday morning. She pushed the button to turn the engine off and rested in her seat, head pressed back into the leather headrest. There was a clenching in her chest that was unexpected—and unwelcome. Her dinner the previous Friday with her friends had done nothing except show the cracks in her life she had been ignoring. She didn't have a partner to complain about. She didn't have kids to worry about. And her job? While it was contentious working with Rodney, it was stable and non-dramatic. Which was exactly the way she liked life.

Right?

Grabbing her purse, Laura slung it over her shoulder and picked up the to-go cup of coffee she treated herself with every morning. It was still steaming hot and perfect. Sliding her heels onto her feet, Laura grabbed the door handle and pushed open the door.

As soon as she was in the crisp autumn air, she stopped short. Parked no more than one spot over was *Skylar*. The name was a curse in her head at this point. Skylar had plagued her thoughts since the elevator ride Friday evening. Laura stood still, not wanting to alert Skylar to her presence, though she didn't see how that was possible, considering they were the only two in the parking lot and they needed to get to the same floor.

Slamming her door shut in a burst of frustration, Laura immediately stalked toward the front doors to the building. As she passed Skylar's car, Skylar lifted her head up with a backpack in her hand. Laura wrinkled her nose. If there was anything to make her seem young, that was it. That and the yoga pants and the loose T-shirt that read something. Laura squinted, trying to make out the words, but it was next to impossible without her reading glasses or being closer. Forced to recognize her age—and being stuck in the same place she had been for the last half-century—Laura cursed inwardly.

When Laura raised her gaze up to Skylar's face, she realized belatedly that she had stopped walking and was staring right at Skylar's chest. Heat rushed to her cheeks, and her body went rigid as a wave of pleasurable anticipation coursed through her.

Skylar cockily walked around her car and held the strap of her backpack over one her shoulder. "Good morning, Ms. Solace."

Cold washed through Laura, her palms sweaty and tingles running up and down her back. She hadn't been called that in fifteen years. Fear ran through her at the thought, at being shoved backward in time to a world she hated living in. Skylar's smile faltered as she came closer. Laura schooled her features and planted a stone-bitch look on her face.

"My name isn't Solace," Laura stated firmly, heat in her tone from anger she hadn't anticipated finding its way to the surface.

"I'm sorry." Skylar lowered her voice to nearly a whisper as she stepped up right next to Laura. "The name of the company you work for is Solace and since you've refused to tell me your name, I resorted to calling you that."

Laura snorted slightly and clenched her eyes shut for a brief moment. She never would have expected her decision to with-hold her name would result in being called something she despised. Pursing her lips, Laura dropped her gaze down to

Skylar's shirt, finally reading the fancy scrawl across her pert breasts.

Do Good Recklessly.

Right, as if anyone ever had that mindset when it came to business and succeeded. She'd believed it once and had been burned more times than she cared to admit, so she'd given up on being purposely kind when it didn't suit her. Laura's fingers burned against the paper cup, a stinging reminder of the first time they had met in the elevator, and she feared she would experience the same fate this time. Giving in, Laura squared her shoulders.

"My name is Laura Finch, and I don't work for Solace. I own it."

"Oh!" Skylar's eyes widened in surprise.

Satisfaction hit Laura that she'd managed to pull that one over on her. "I own it with my partner, Rodney Solace."

She had to stop. There was no reason for her to be giving out that information. Why would she do that? Biting the inside of her cheek, Laura stared back down at Skylar's chest and the damn words scrawled across it. *They will come back to bite me in the ass, won't they?*

Skylar started walking toward the building, and Laura reluctantly followed, decidedly annoyed that they would be sharing yet another elevator ride up to the sixth floor on a morning she couldn't keep her mouth shut when she wanted to.

"How long have you been in business?" Skylar asked.

Debating whether or not to answer, Laura kept quiet. Skylar could easily figure out the answer by looking at their outdated website, which Laura was getting close to embarrassed to send to clients. Rather than sending the eager young woman there, Laura answered. "Twenty-four years."

"Damn!" Skylar's eyes went wide. "I'd love for my business to make it that long."

"I'm sure you would," Laura muttered under her breath as they started up the cement stairs.

Flashing her badge at the door, Skylar reached forward and opened it, holding it for Laura to walk through. The last time Skylar had done this it was with a whole different attitude. Laura shuddered, remembering the not-well-contained grin forming on Skylar's lips. "When's the last time you updated everything?"

Laura turned on her sharply. "What is *everything*?"

"Your logistics, your website, your logo, your branding—everything you use for marketing purposes. I had noticed the other day that the logo on the door seemed a bit dated, and I was just curious."

A bit was a kind way of saying it. Rodney was convinced that if they kept it that it would eventually come back in style, the way nineties fashion was ironically chic again, but Laura knew it wouldn't, and their website, while mostly functioning, was a disaster when trying to navigate. But change came as easily to Rodney as moving a mountain did to a child. Though she wasn't going to tell Skylar any of that.

"We have people for that."

"Oh, I'm sure you do. I was only asking for research purposes."

Right. I'll believe that one over Rodney's dead body. Laura jabbed her finger into the button to call for the elevator. They stood in awkward silence, Skylar clearly not sure whether she had offended Laura, and Laura was relieved to have finally reached that level with the impossibly bubbly girl.

They stepped into the elevator and turned to face the door. Skylar pushed the button, and Laura gripped her coffee tightly, burning her finger pads again. Why did she always do that lately? The worst part was it had happened the last time in the elevator with this very same woman, and Laura again refused to move or show any sign of acquiescing to her pain.

"I could always help if your people wanted an extra opinion. It's actually what my business does, revitalizing companies in terms of their online presence and promotional materials. I also do logistical and structural coaching." Skylar lifted her chin as Laura raised her gaze.

Impressed, Laura took her time answering, letting the silence linger between them to make it harder for Skylar to know what she was thinking about the confession. She was sure she was a job to Skylar, a big client that could put her business on the fast track to earning.

"That won't be necessary." She almost added a thank you but managed to stop herself in time. That would not be a good thing, and it certainly showed signs she was becoming too weak. Rodney would have a field day with this if he saw it. Just the thought made Laura cringe. He liked to exploit her weaknesses like that, always had.

Skylar shifted slightly, coming in one step closer. Laura wanted to back up, move to keep the bubble of space around her perfectly balanced, but at the same time, she didn't want to give Skylar the satisfaction. "Well, the offer stands if you would like. I'm not hard to find."

"I'm sure someone like you doesn't even know what an actuary is. How could you begin to create materials for us that would be useful?" The blank look that flashed across Skylar's eyes told Laura exactly what she needed to know. Skylar had no idea what an actuary was. "Next time you should do your research before you pitch a proposal."

"I'm not pitching a proposal," Skylar defended. Immediately, her tone lightened. "I was simply offering a hand with something you might need help with. There are plenty of others out there who do what I do, if you wanted to hire them, since your team is clearly missing the boat on updating."

Laura wrinkled her nose at the comment. She didn't have a marketing and PR team. She'd lied. Full out. And no matter how many times she'd brought up the idea to Rodney, he had nixed it. She hated that he had the power to do that, yet she didn't have the power to just get done what she felt was a necessary thing for their company to survive the next twenty years. Their website was pathetic and said nothing. They were nowhere on social media, and anyone who was under the age of fifty wouldn't likely find them. They were on the cusp of something big, and yet, he held them back at every step.

"I think you missed the boat on a lot of things," Laura muttered, raising an eyebrow at Skylar with anger in her gaze. Skylar was so similar to how she had been twenty-five years ago —young, bold, and willing to take risks. Frustrated because she was stuck at Solace right where she'd been when she started, her anger grew. "I'm not some rich business owner you can try to proposition yourself to. It's insulting."

Skylar's lips parted in surprise, but the doors opened on their floor, and Laura left without a second glance. She made her way into her office, setting her coffee down and putting her purse in the bottom drawer. Starting her routine for the day, Laura stopped immediately and let out a huge sigh, collapsing into her chair. She'd been an ass, but what else was new?

Wallowing in self-pity for one minute, Laura started on the day's work. The office was always this quiet in the morning, which was in partly why she liked arriving that early.

"Laura!" Rodney's sing-song voice irked her.

She tensed as soon as he entered her office, and despite the fact she was on her second cup of coffee that morning, it was far too early to deal with his antics. "Glad you made it on time this morning."

Rodney at least had the decency to frown. "If the boss doesn't have the privilege of being late sometimes, then what's the point of being the boss?"

Laura raised her gaze sternly at him, ready to retort, but he held his hand up to cut her off.

"I worked it out for this morning. Be happy with that."

Bristling, Laura shifted around some papers on her desk and grabbed her lukewarm coffee cup. She really should have drunk that faster than she had. Leaning back in her chair, she looked him over. He did look better this morning, less harried and frantic, than he had the last few weeks, so perhaps he had figured out what was going on.

"We have a lot of work to do today," Laura commented, hoping it would shoo him out faster.

"You do," Rodney countered. "I have a meeting with a potential new client."

Laura frowned. He hadn't been taking her on those lately, and she wasn't sure why, but broaching that topic wasn't something she felt quite ready for. She couldn't let her lingering anger over the elevator conversation taint what would need to be a tactical conversation with her co-owner.

"Make sure to talk us up since people are noticing how out of date we really are." Skylar might get under her skin, but Laura was thankful for this bit of ammo provided by her.

Rodney at least had the decency to look offended. "What do you mean?"

"Other residents of the co-op are noticing how out of date our signage and website are, amongst other things. You really should let me update it, you know."

Rodney frowned. "Who mentioned it?"

"Some bubbly Gen Z girl in the elevator." Laura sneered at the memory. That was the worst way to pitch anyone a job. Her shoulders tensed just thinking about the charged interaction. "She came right out and asked if we needed help, as if we're too old to know what to do."

Laura scoffed and took a sip of her coffee.

Rodney frowned, his brow knitting together. "We're not old."

"Certainly not," Laura quipped. "Hardly."

She smiled at him, genuinely, for the first time in longer than she cared to admit. She'd been so unhappy with life that she'd forgotten what it felt like to smile. Rodney grinned, shaking his head before he laughed. "Jennifer tells me I'm old all the time."

Laura stiffened, her entire countenance changing in the instant reminder of what the man in front of her did with *that* woman. Jennifer was quite a bit younger than they were, which had been a point of contention when Rodney had announced he was marrying her, and of course, he had done it in front of the entire office instead of being considerate and telling Laura in private. Everyone had seen her reaction that day, when the dam broke.

"You *are* old." Laura could say it, even if she didn't mean it. Rodney had a whole year on her and reached fifty first. She had given him a nice gift, not even one teasing him for his age or for being over the hill. Still, she knew she couldn't expect the same when her birthday rolled around—if he even remembered it this year.

"I am not," he joked, his tone lightening.

Laura hadn't meant to take the conversation that direction. She pursed her lips, her jaw clenching, and set her coffee cup down on the desktop. She could always feign having a lot of work to do, but she knew he wouldn't listen to that excuse anyway. He never did. "What potential client are you meeting with today?"

"EarthBound Exotica."

Laura jerked her chin up at that. "I'm sorry?"

"They're an import-export company, I swear."

"Sounds like something else entirely," Laura commented and took another sip of her tepid coffee. She frowned at it, knowing she'd need to replace it with something. However, her daily treat had turned out to be a cause of stress that morning, which annoyed her.

"I know." Rodney put his hands up. "I swear I researched what they did before I agreed to a meeting with them. I was just as confused."

"And people say our company name is confusing." Laura said it quietly, hoping Rodney hadn't heard her, and since his hearing was going with his age, she was in luck that day.

"I have a lunch meeting with them, and I'm bringing Henry and Landon to make our proposal."

Those two were Rodney's favorites, and he always brought

them whenever he had a meeting like this. She wished he'd give a little more thought to diversifying who they brought, especially to a company that likely worked with diverse clients. Saying nothing because she didn't want to add an argument with him to her plate that morning, Laura nodded. "Let me know how it goes."

"For sure," Rodney answered and pulled at his shirt sleeves under his jacket. It was a nervous habit of his that he'd never broken, not that he tried. Laura had noticed it from early on and had never even commented on it. "We need this account."

"It would be nice to add to our current accounts, but I don't think it's a need." Laura stared up at him.

Rodney shook his head. "No, we need it. We have three projects ending in the next two months, and we'll need something to replace them with."

She knew all this, but still, the amount of worry he was exerting was something she wasn't used to seeing. She would let him worry about that one for now. She had work to do and reports to read and hot coffee to obtain.

"Let me know," she repeated, dismissing him with the comment.

Rodney nodded at her, pulled at his sleeves again, and finally left her office in blissful quiet. Laura's stomach churned as the flash of his face etched into her memory, the worry all over it. He'd never looked quite that worried before, not about the business anyway. She stared at the closed door in quiet, working through every possible reason he could look that anxious. She could figure it out if she had enough time and direction, but he hadn't given her either. The tepid coffee she had sipped moments before threatened to come back up. No matter what happened, they needed a plan to fix whatever was broken.

CHAPTER
Five

SKYLAR TRIED all morning to concentrate on her current project, but it was next to impossible. She kept wandering back to that simple moment in the parking lot when she swore she had broken through some of the walls Laura had in place, though that could have just been wishful thinking. However, it was the first time Skylar had managed to get a name out of her elevator companion.

Laura Finch.

And what a name it was. It sounded like a powerful name that a stoic woman would have. Skylar shifted in her rolling chair and bit her lower lip. Though they had gone right back to the cold and aloof that had been Laura's norm since they had first met. Curious about that and where it came from, Skylar had pushed, but she'd only found resistance.

With her pen between her fingers, Skylar doodled on the notepad she always kept next to her desk. Laura did have a point, however. She had no idea what an actuary was, but it did answer one question. Or at least it would in the future as soon as she did some research. Leaning over her computer, Skylar typed into the search bar and waited for results.

Squinting at the screen, she pursed her lips and read it again.

So Laura dealt with risk and management in terms of business finances. She'd probably think the worst of Skylar's businesses. Skylar sat back in her chair and shook her head. No wonder Laura was so standoff-ish. She'd outright said she was a new business. Laura had probably done a quick judgment on her and determined she would fail.

The sinking feeling in the pit of her stomach hit harder than she expected. A stranger's opinion of her business rarely affected her, but for some reason, Laura's mattered. Laura was someone who knew what she was talking about when it came to businesses, so surely she would be able to tell if Skylar was full of shit or not. Right?

Groaning, Skylar rubbed her hands over her thighs and moved back to the search screen. She spent the next hour learning all about actuarial science and just exactly what someone does when they work for a company like Solace. It was all interesting, but that devastation in the pit of her stomach grew bigger by the minute, and she was pretty sure it was going to swallow her whole.

"Sky, what's up?"

Jumping out of her seat, Skylar put a hand to her heart as she spun around and stared at the propped-open door.

"Chill out!" Brady said, giving Skylar an odd look of amusement and concern.

"You scared the crap out of me." Skylar took in deep, steadying breaths while she waited for him to come in. She hadn't realized she'd been so engrossed in her research that she hadn't noticed anyone outside or the five text messages from him telling her that he was coming up to bring the lunch she had forgotten to grab from the counter.

He held up the lunch bag and raised an eyebrow at her. "Your lunch?"

"Right. Thanks." Skylar stepped forward, taking the cold bag from him and gripping it tightly in her hands, still not ready for normal conversation just yet. Calming down from this one was going to take some time, no matter how unintentional the scare was.

Brady furrowed his brow and collapsed onto the small futon Skylar had him help drag in when she'd finally gotten the keys. It wasn't the best setup, but it would do for now. Which reminded her, she still had all those damn boxes to go through.

"You didn't have to bring my lunch, you know. I could have just grabbed something."

He grinned at her. "What are big brothers for?"

"Free room and board." Skylar laughed lightly as she shoved her lunch into the mini fridge she'd kept from her college days. "Which, again, seriously thank you for that."

"Hey, it's not totally free. You pay your share."

"Yeah, yeah." Skylar rolled her eyes and crossed her arms. It was a debate they'd had many times throughout the years, but when she'd graduated college, she hadn't wanted to live with anyone but him. The constant drama from college roommates cycling through the apartment was more than she cared for. Living with her brother was a safe bet that the drama would be less and the stability great. That, and there had been a room for her office, which she had loved until his fiancée came into the picture.

"Sky?"

"What?" She raised her gaze to meet his.

"What are you thinking about?"

"Nothing in particular. Did Mom and Dad say if they were coming for Thanksgiving this year?"

He shrugged. "I think they might go to Jaz's."

"I need to call them."

"Yes," Brady stated firmly, giving her a hard look. "You do."

Skylar frowned. She was probably the one who talked to their parents the least. It wasn't because she didn't want to—it was because she was always working. Skylar tried to avoid that land mine of shame. She barely had time for her brother, which meant she had even less time for their parents or sister, not to mention friends. Friends she would love to hang out and spend some time relaxing with. Instead, she was always trying to find the secret sauce for her businesses, going into business with her friends to the point they became coworkers. She loved having the counterpart to work with, the sounding board to bounce ideas off of. It was a curse in her life, that was for sure.

"Sky, what are you thinking?"

"Nothing," she muttered and folded her hands together. She had to learn to do this on her own and stop relying on those around her so much. There were so many answers she could give him, but she knew he didn't have the time or the emotional capacity to deal with her problems, not now that his focus was on his fiancée, and rightfully so. Though the adjustment to that had been tough, she wanted to support it.

"*Sky.*" This time her name came out as a chastisement.

When she looked up at him, he held her world in his gaze. "What's going on?"

"I hate that I don't talk to them more often." Sadness filled her chest like she hadn't expected it to—it was tinged with regret.

"You're the one who can change that, you know."

"I know."

"Look." Brady leaned forward, folding his hands. He was the perfect image of their father anytime he was going to give them a lecture, a serious love talk as he would call them. Skylar couldn't stop the image of the two of them doing this together, and her lips curled upward into a smile. "You're the one in charge of your life. If you want to make changes, then you're the one who has to do that. If you want to talk to them more, you have to make the phone calls and start the change. Then they'll call you more."

"I know," Skylar answered again, grinning at him as he barreled through without listening to her agreement.

"If you want to have friends, which I know you've said you

have none, then you need to find them. You're the only one who can do that."

Chuckling lightly, Skylar nodded. "I know, Brady. But this is one of those things that is easier said than done, and while I've worked at it, it's still hard."

He glanced up at her and gave a single nod. "So long as you know."

This was why she loved him. He would do anything to support her, from giving her room in the house to being the reminder that she was in charge of her life and her own happiness. "Join me for lunch today?"

"Can't." Brady shook his head. "I'm meeting Callie for lunch today."

"Right. Got to take care of your woman," she teased, but there wasn't an ounce of honest joy in it. She missed having him to herself, and while she was glad he had found someone to love and who loved him, that left her uncertain of where she stood and what her future would look like.

Brady grinned proudly, which was the only answer she needed.

Skylar laughed. "I'll see you tomorrow morning before I leave, then."

"For sure." Brady slapped his knees and stood up. "I'll let you go, but remember, you want friends, you go find them."

She saluted her brother. "Got it."

After Brady left, Skylar found she was able to focus on the work at hand. She spent the rest of the day hunched over her desk, creating a mockup for Solace as soon as she had finished her other proposal and emailed it off.

By the time she looked up, the sun had fallen below the horizon. She hadn't even realized how much time had passed. Stretching her back, Skylar paced around her office a few times before stepping out into the hallway to stretch her legs even more. She walked the entirety of the floor, stopping in front of Solace's main doors the second time and putting her hands on her hips and pushing to stretch the muscles again. She would need to do an extra round of yoga in the morning to wake up and make sure her muscles weren't sore.

Stepping past the door, she walked to the end of the hall and stared out the large floor-to-ceiling window that overlooked the parking lot. Laura walked confidently from the building to her car. Skylar frowned. She was probably going off somewhere with a partner or friends, the workday done at a normal time for her.

How Skylar longed for that, to be able to leave at a natural time and spend the rest of her hours with people she loved and loved to be with. An uncharacteristic frown reached her lips, but she didn't try to get rid of it either. She would have to expand that circle of loved ones, however. Her breakup with her ex had done a number on those she called friends, many choosing her ex's side over hers. It had been hard since then. That hurt more than anything.

Laura stood by the passenger side of her car, sliding her purse and briefcase onto the seat before she came around and grabbed the handle. Instead of getting in, however, she turned and faced the building. Skylar's breath caught in her throat, but she knew Laura wouldn't be able to see her through the tinted windows. That was the entire point of them, right?

Biting her lip, Skylar stayed put to see exactly what she was doing. Laura stayed perfectly still, her chin raising to the sky, her long dark tresses catching in the slight breeze. Skylar could have sworn Laura was looking directly at her, but that was impossible, wasn't it? Shuddering, she found herself wrapped up in curiosity about this woman.

She had such a hard exterior, and Skylar was damn sure it was there on purpose. Over the years, Laura must have worked to build it up and make it even thicker. Any woman in business would have to on some levels—Skylar certainly had, though she could probably use a few more of those layers if she was being honest.

Finally, Laura opened the car door and slipped inside. Within a minute, she drove out of the parking lot and up the hill that would lead her to the road and home. Skylar's eyes prickled with tears. While she loved Callie, it had been stressful after she had moved in. With all the wedding planning and every conversation being about the wedding, Skylar had found it so damn difficult to be home, especially alone with her.

She longed for a place of solace where she could sit and be completely at peace. But she knew at this point in her life that was next to impossible to find or create. Sighing, Skylar went back to her office and stared at it. Since Brady was working that night, Skylar would be left alone with Callie. With the loneliness she had been struggling with all day rearing its ugly head again, she knew she couldn't put herself in that conversation and survive it well. Focusing on the office, she pulled out boxes and started the long process of putting everything together.

It wasn't avoidance, she told herself. It was being practical.

CHAPTER
Six

LAURA SHIVERED. Leaning back in her chair, she crossed her arms and turned to face the window behind her. The sun shone brightly outside, but she knew the fall air was crisp and would sting her cheeks as soon as she stepped outside. It was the time of year when the weather liked to trick her like that. Much like whatever Rodney was up to lately.

She had seen the same numbers he had. He wasn't wrong when he said they were in trouble and needed new clients to come into their business. There had been a decidedly sharp decline in new clients in the last two years, but they had been trending that way for easily the last ten. Laura played with her pen on her desk, flipping it over and over between her fingers.

Earthbound Exotica was a Hail Mary that would keep them afloat for a little while longer, but it wasn't going to solve any problems. It wasn't going to fix what was broken. Rodney actually paying attention to it meant it was bad enough to have him worried, and he didn't handle stress well.

Picking up her cell phone, Laura stared at it, very nearly calling Camryn or Lynda, whichever one she could get ahold of first. They would at least listen to her, but she still wasn't sure what to say or how to describe what she was feeling at the moment. Melancholy wasn't quite it. Divorcing Rodney had been the best decision for the both of them. He didn't have to hide his cheating any longer, and Laura was free to dive into work and ignore relationships, something Rodney had claimed she was already doing anyway. She hadn't ignored him at all, but she had put distance between them when the doctor had told her it was impossible for her to become pregnant. Guilt ate away at her belly for that one, still, and she hated herself all the more for it.

The door opening startled her, but it also told her who was there since only one person would come in without knocking first. *Rodney.* She almost didn't turn around, not wanting to think about what he needed when her thoughts had taken such a move toward the past. She had been doing that far too much lately, analyzing what she couldn't change. Frowning, Laura closed her eyes and centered herself. She could at least change the future. She also knew Rodney would be more annoying if she didn't deal with him immediately, Laura faced him.

Rodney sat down in the chair across from her desk, crossing one ankle over his knee and sliding down slightly. *Oh, so this is going to be a long conversation.* Laura inwardly cringed, knowing she had more work to do than she had time in the day and that she'd likely end up leaving late if this conversation was going to take longer than necessary.

"We need to let someone go," he stated, his voice far calmer than it should be.

Laura had suspected this conversation would come up closer to the end of the year when they dove head-first into finances to get a lay of the upcoming year. Their situation was becoming dire.

"Why?" Laura clenched her jaw, wanting his answer before she gave hers. Their financials had been in the black—barely—for the better part of the year, but that was also the problem. They weren't increasing their profit and thus wouldn't be able to keep up with their employees into the next year. They were barely surviving and the prospects she had hoped for in terms of increasing their profit margin were slim. It had been part of why she'd wanted to update their company's marketing strategies to begin with. It was the one place she could point to and say they were failing.

"You know why." Rodney had an edge of anger in his voice, which was unexpected.

He must be far more stressed than Laura had originally thought. She'd seen him floundering, but for him to admit there was a problem was a new level of anxiety.

"Tell me," Laura pushed. She wanted him to say it out loud. Perhaps that would force him to look at the idea of rebranding rather than avoid it. It would cost money, but if Laura could do the bulk of the work like she had in the beginning, then it wouldn't be too much of an investment, other than her time.

Rodney raised his gaze to meet hers, a challenge in his eyes. He always did hate it when she forced him to say something he was avoiding, didn't he? Another reason their divorce had been for the better.

"We can't afford it."

"And what shall we do about that?"

Rodney sighed heavily and ran a hand over the back of his head. "We need to make some changes. I think weeding out where we're weak would be for the better."

"We can certainly lay someone off, but who would you suggest? Someone who is paid enough to cover two positions? Perhaps we can cut Jana."

Rodney's eyes went wide, and he shook his head slowly. "Cut my admin? Why would we do that?"

"Because Greta can easily cover both positions. We've shared admin before." Greta could do that, they both knew it, though it would tax her hours significantly, and Laura wasn't sure it was the best solution. However, her choice of suggestion wasn't because she thought it was the best solution—she wanted to know what Rodney's reaction would be.

"Not Jana. I'd prefer someone who isn't cutting it."

Laura resisted the scowl and folded her hands in her lap as she eyed him. She knew at this point Rodney was fishing for one person in particular. "And who isn't making the cut?"

"I don't know. You look at the data more often than I do."

Interesting he would admit that, but Laura kept that thought to herself. Eyeing him carefully with a direct stare, she waited to see what he would say next. Sometimes with Rodney, letting him fester was the easiest way to get information.

"Isn't there someone in accounts receivable?"

Laura pursed her lips, still saying nothing and letting her silence linger through the room. There were certainly one or two people she felt they could stand to lose in their company, but accounts receivable was not where she would pluck those people from.

"I think we should spend some money to earn some money," Laura countered.

Rodney glared. Laura was surprised, thinking he would take it slightly better than he had, but perhaps he really just wanted to get whoever he was fishing for out of their business. "I just said we can't afford to keep our people and you want to spend money?"

"Yes," Laura answered precisely. "I want to rebrand and bring our company into this decade. We need new marketing methods, and we need to make sure we're keeping up with the times."

"No."

"What do you mean *no?* You want us to shrink back into the nineties when we started this company?" Laura hated the hurt in the edge of her tone. Their marriage may have failed, but the one thing they had succeeded at was the business, and that was something she wasn't willing to give up. To go back into the corporate world and work for someone else wouldn't be in her best interest.

"I don't want that." Rodney narrowed his gaze. "Why do you twist my words like that? You always do that."

And they were right back to where they started in college. Petty arguments where everything was her fault. Laura seethed, straightening her shoulders as much as she didn't want to. She couldn't control the reaction. "Then what do you want, Rodney? Because we need to do something drastic in order to keep our company afloat. We won't die out today or even next month, but if the data is right, not changing will be the death of us. We know that in any business. We're maintaining the status quo right now, and that's unacceptable."

Her entire body vibrated with energy she hadn't felt in far too long. This had to be the straw that broke his back. He had to realize she wasn't wrong. The numbers were dire, and they were her area of expertise. He could schmooze all the clients he wanted, but if they weren't up to date and ready to bring in new clients, they would never succeed. Laura looked him directly in the eye, about to bring home her point. She stopped short. Rodney leaned in, his hand firmly on the desk.

"That's why I want to lay some people off." He always saw the easy way out, didn't he? And he would make her be the bad guy and lay them off, the damn dynamic she had willingly walked into once and upheld for years coming back to haunt her fully. For once she would like to be the one who got to shoot the shit with their employees.

"How many people?" They were back at that conversation again, and Laura hated it. She'd given in one more time to her prescribed role. Cursing herself, she stayed put as she lost her gumption.

"Enough."

"How many people do you want to lay off?" Laura pushed, needing to know how many lives she was going to make miserable that week.

"One or two."

"Which ones?"

"Hannah."

Laura's stomach sank. She had suspected Rodney had fallen

back into his old habits of cheating, and Hannah was exactly his type—petite, brunette, eyes of steel, and younger than the last few. Her heart thundering, Laura strove to remain as calm as possible. "Who else?"

"Just Hannah."

"Are you done with her?" Laura lifted her gaze to meet his, hoping he understood what she wasn't asking, what she didn't want to ask. But she had dealt with his cheating before.

"I'm not having sex with her if that's what you're implying." His cheeks reddened, and his jaw hardened. Laura used to be able to read him easily but right now she couldn't. She never could when it came to this. His defenses had come right up, but that would be natural, and she was left to parse out what was truth and what was lie.

"It is." Laura stared him down. His left eye twitched, and that was her sign to not believe him one bit.

"I'm not having an affair. I wouldn't do that to Jennifer."

He would do that to her, however. Laura kept her mouth shut as that age-old pain consumed her for the brief second she allowed it to. And as much as she suspected he had done it to Jennifer in the past, she could never prove it. Raising up from her seat, Laura leaned over her desk, pinning him with her gaze. "You better not be having sex with an employee, Rodney. I don't give a rat's ass about an affair, but when it comes to *our* employees, you keep your hands off them, and unless you can prove that Hannah needs to be let go for good reason, she's staying."

"You're not rebranding this company."

Jerking her chin up a little higher, Laura clenched her jaw to keep from saying anything she might regret. "We need to do something. You're not an idiot. You can see how bad this is."

"You're not doing anything except what you should be doing, which is building a proposal for a new client. That client will keep our finances going if we land him."

Rodney was right about that. A new client would help them out, but she was once again stuck doing all the work while he received the glory. Her heart sank, once again unable to push an agenda on him that would truly make a difference in the long run.

"Do you hear me?" Rodney asked, making his point again.

"I understand how a business works." *Probably better than you do.* But she didn't add that part to her comment. Her internal thoughts rarely helped when said out loud.

"Good." Rodney stalked out of the office and shut the door behind him.

They were equal partners, but for too long, Laura had allowed him to have more control than she did. She'd kept herself busy with the day-to-day work and less with the dreaming and talking. He was good at that most of the time, but he had been distracted these last few years since Grayson had hit toddlerhood. This was the time she was going to have to step in and force her hand into an area Rodney thought was completely his. But her livelihood was at stake as much as his, if not more. She had built her life around Solace, and she wasn't willing to give it up so easily.

Laura deliberately relaxed all the muscles in her body, at least as much as she could, and then pulled up the employee files on the computer. She wanted to know exactly why Rodney was out to get Hannah fired. Her file revealed nothing, so Laura sighed. This was going to require a much more personal approach when she dug for information, something she wasn't fond of doing. She lacked the tact to be able to do it, whereas Rodney or even Skylar would be perfect for that kind of recognizance.

Where did that thought come from?

Laura turned around to look out the window of her office again, steepling her fingers together. Skylar wasn't a part of her business plan, although her bubbly personality would make it easy to use her as an under manager. Her ideas weren't awful either. They did need an update on their website and graphics in order to continue reaching new clients. Laura could hire her after eating crow, of course. Huffing, Laura spun around in her chair and dug out the proposal she had attempted to work on all morning.

She stared at the papers for another twenty minutes before giving in and starting on what she really thought would help save their profits. *Rebranding.* She imagined Skylar standing in front of her, her light brown hair pulled back in a ponytail that had loose strands flailing about by her ears. Something that was so uncontrollable about that, which seemed to fit the younger woman perfectly. Laura's lips curled at the thought of Skylar before she caught herself and straightened out again. New businesses weren't where she wanted to put her money. They were so damn risky, and she was sure Skylar could understand that.

Huffing again, Laura closed her eyes and imagined her face. Gen Z and millennials, while they weren't the ideal contractors to hire, were potential clients. It might just take one to show her how to reach them. Solace had a handle on the older businesses and how to attract them, but as they grew older and sold out, they would need to appeal to the younger generations, as much as that made Laura's stomach churn.

If she could hire Skylar, or someone like her, then they could come in and rebrand the company, bring them up to date in terms of technology, and then they would appeal to everyone who was out there. At least until there were newer cultural changes she had to keep up with. Laura frowned.

Skylar could sit at the table in her office and work on all the details while she kept up with the day-to-day that she couldn't miss out on. Laura's gaze meandered over to that table, the chairs pushed in nicely. It had been used at one point for her and Rodney to work on problems together and occasional meetings with other employees, but it hadn't been used in at least three years. It had sat empty, but she could envision Skylar there now, with her ponytail falling against her back, her head bent as she typed away on a computer, her gaze completely focused on the screen. It would be the perfect place for Laura to observe her in action.

"Ugh." Laura threw her pen onto the top of her desk. She didn't want to be thinking about Skylar. She wanted to know what had crawled up Rodney's ass and put the bug in his ear that Hannah needed to be fired. Thus far, that was a decision she absolutely disagreed with.

Glaring at her door, Laura looked at the proposal that was due at the end of the week. Work was her priority, not some fantasy of rebranding that would never happen if she couldn't get Rodney on board with the idea. With her pen back in her hand and her fingers poised over her notepad, Laura went to work.

CHAPTER
Seven

THE MAN who stepped into the elevator with Skylar was finely dressed, the yellow of his shirt making his skin look tinted in a sickening shade of puce green. His gray eyes met hers, and he immediately looked away before looking back with a pleasant smile on his lips. As soon as he faced her, Skylar's heart thudded.

"Headed to the sixth floor?" he asked, his voice upbeat in a way Skylar didn't expect.

"Uh...yeah." She pulled her lower lip between her teeth and held her hands together in front of her. The button had already been pushed, so he could easily see that.

"I'm Rodney Solace." He turned, holding his hand out.

Skylar eyed him carefully as she shook his hand, looking him up and down. His belly was slightly rounded, and his jacket was a bit tight. "I had wondered who the other owner was."

He grinned broadly. "I see you've met Laura and survived. And who are you?"

"Skylar Ross. I own Warehouse Thirty-Three." The more they stood together, the more comfortable she became. He didn't push any boundaries, and she was curious, not only about him but about the mysterious Laura Finch. He didn't push her away like Laura did either, which made it far easier to talk to him about potentially working together. With him, Skylar had hope of landing a job. This might just be her way in.

"Interesting name for a company." He held onto a briefcase, but his eyes never left her face. "It's good to meet you."

"It's a long story." Skylar smiled, bringing in as much charm as she possibly could. He seemed like a man who needed his ego stroked a little, which was something she could certainly accomplish.

"I'd like to hear it some time, but what does Warehouse Thirty-Three do?"

This was perfect. She could segue into how she could help him without even needing to try to find her way into the conversation. "Oh, I'm a marketing firm. Specifically, I focus on rebranding and revitalizing companies who are in a dip and need some rejuvenation to keep going. I do that by coaching businesses."

"Oh?" Rodney cocked his head at her. "That sounds like interesting work."

"It is. I enjoy it. It's very rewarding work." Skylar kept her smile plastered on her face, though that wasn't hard to do either. It came so naturally to her.

The elevator doors opened, and Rodney stepped out first, holding his hand against the door to keep it open for Skylar. She shifted her backpack on her shoulder and gave him a shy smile. "Thank you."

"I'd like to talk to you more about your business someday, but I've got a meeting and I'm running late. When are you done for the day?"

"Oh, um..." Skylar tried to remember her schedule, but for some reason, staring into his gray eyes, she couldn't. "I can just call your office to set up a time."

"Do that. Please." He held his hand out for her, and Skylar took it. "It was good to meet you Ms. Ross. I look forward to speaking with you."

Rodney turned toward the offices and walked away. Skylar stared at where he had stood for another minute before walking into her office and shutting the door behind her. Joy bubbled inside her, working its way through her body to the point that it was going to burst from her. That had gone amazingly well.

She sobered a moment, her smile faltering as Laura's ice-blue eyes came to mind. So that was Mr. Solace—he was far more pleasant than Laura. He must do all the front facing work and Laura did all of the background work because if she was speaking with clients, it would likely end in disaster. She had zero people skills.

Skylar smiled at no one but herself as she pulled her laptop out of her backpack and put it on her desk. Perhaps she did have an in with Solace after all, and maybe she could land herself her biggest client yet. Then again, would she want to work with Laura? If she worked with Rodney, at least what she had seen of him so far, she could probably handle it. He seemed nice enough up front, but that didn't necessarily mean he would be in the long run.

Huffing, Skylar turned on her computer. She could get ahead of the game. She didn't even have a proposal for them, or an offer to send a proposal yet, though she had been working on that one in her spare time—who was she kidding, when she couldn't concentrate—and the proposal she wasn't supposed to be working on was nearly done already. If she could just land confirmation, she could nail this job. She knew it.

Skylar opened up her email and stared at the one at the top of the list. The invoice still hadn't been paid from that last job she'd done. She read the email, even though she knew what it was going to say. Fear hit her hard. She needed another job to make up the income she wasn't getting from a job already completed. At least until she could figure out how to take these jerks to court for it, which would cost more money and time she didn't have. Since wallowing wasn't something she wanted to do that day, Skylar straightened her shoulders. She would finish her proposal for Solace and make an appointment with Rodney that day.

～

Skylar walked the halls with a mug of tea in her hand, stretching the muscles in her back and her thighs. She'd been sitting most of the day, unable to make any connections or to network other than with Mr. Solace himself that morning, which had been rather unexpected.

She should at least give it a few days, right? She didn't want to come off as desperate—even though she was. Working for Solace would put her business in the exact direction she wanted it to go. It might give her the opportunity to leave her ex-girlfriend's business behind and focus on what she wanted, but until she had more revenue from Warehouse Thirty-Three, she was stuck working with Trina.

She stopped short at the far window at the end of the hall. Laura Finch—in the finest dress that ended mid-thigh with black nylons and four-inch heels, her hair around her shoulders blowing slightly in the breeze, stood with her back to the building and stared at her vehicle. Skylar crossed her arms and observed, for the first time, Ms. Laura Finch without anyone around her.

Laura didn't move. She stood stoically, a few feet from her vehicle until suddenly she stepped forward and kicked her tire. Skylar nearly choked on her tea as she sipped it. Well, that was unexpected. Laura gripped the purse on her shoulder tighter but still faced her vehicle. Skylar suddenly wished she could see her facial features. What would pure anger look like on her? It had to be better than the constant annoyed sneer that graced her any time Skylar was in the vicinity.

"Who are you underneath all that animosity, Ms. Laura Finch?" Although, Skylar preferred to think of her as Ms. Solace still. It suited her better.

When Laura kicked the tire again, Skylar gave in. She walked directly to her office, grabbed her backpack, and shoved everything she would need for the night into it. Leaving her newly made cup of tea on the desktop, she locked the doors and headed for the elevator. The ride down was suddenly quiet.

What will I even say to her?

Skylar had no idea why she was going out there except seeing Laura in a mood she'd never exhibited was more temptation than she could resist. She could also chalk it up to making a turning point if they were actually going to work together now that Skylar had a better in with Solace. If Rodney hired her, they would have to find a way to be around each other that wasn't all antagonism.

As the cold air hit her face, rejuvenation swelled within her. She could do this. She could take another chance to build a connection with this woman who so clearly wanted the world to stand back in her wake. It would be a job that Skylar would love, one she could use as a reference in order to propel her business forward into the upcoming year. She wouldn't worry about unpaid invoices ever again if she could land herself this one job.

The soles of the tennis shoes she'd had for four years were soft on the ground as she walked closer. Waves of annoyance and anger rolled off of Laura. Skylar wanted to do nothing but smooth those ruffled feathers and ease whatever was bothering her. It was an uneasy feeling, and Skylar questioned it. But something in the pit of her stomach told her Laura wasn't the person she wanted everyone to believe she was. Putting her backpack over both her shoulders, Skylar straightened, stepped right up to Laura, and stared down at the offending tire, which was flat.

"That sucks," Skylar said before she could bite her tongue.

Laura jerked with a start and growled.

The sound shocked Skylar, but she probably should have expected it. This wasn't an ideal time to tease anyone, and certainly not a grumpy business owner. She should have chosen a wiser entrance to this conversation. The growl rolled through her, rumbling through her chest to the pit of her stomach and did something damn funny to it. This perfectly made-up woman wasn't so perfect after all. The frustration, the base reaction, was such a joy to witness because it meant Skylar was right. There was more to Laura Finch under all those layers.

"Run over a nail or something?" Skylar asked, keeping her tone light. What was she supposed to ask? She had to say something, and Laura, as always, wasn't giving much by way of conversation. "You know, I have a friend who can come fix this. He does roadside repairs all the time, and I'm sure if I call, he could be here in a second."

"Hardly necessary," Laura's voice was low, still full of anger, though Skylar swore she detected a note of embarrassment.

Turning and lifting her chin, Skylar looked directly into Laura's ice-cold gaze. It was there—the embarrassment—though she was damn sure Laura would never admit it to anyone, including herself. Skylar had to work to hold back the curl of her lips into a smile.

"It wouldn't be a problem at all. He literally does this for his job." Skylar put her hands in front of her, trying hard to come off as non-confrontational, when all she wanted to do was grab Laura by the shoulders, shake her, and make her come to her senses.

"No," Laura answered simply but firmly.

"Your choice." Skylar shrugged, and finally Laura moved to look into her eyes. Skylar held her gaze, as if she could silently speak into her mind that she would help her—all she had to do was ask. They held eye contact, longer than Skylar ever expected Laura to be able to do, especially when she was not the one in control of the situation. "Are you sure?"

"Yes, of course, I'm sure. Don't be ridiculous."

Skylar couldn't resist the curl of her lips this time. The way she sounded so disturbed was amusing.

"I don't need you," Laura added at the last minute in her unnaturally ruffled moment. Her look was direct, firm, and it sent shivers of an entirely different nature down Skylar's chest, through her nipples, and straight between her legs. Laura's intensity sizzled.

Skylar's smile faltered. She hadn't meant to impose. Laura's body was so rigid and tense that Skylar worried one hit to the right spot would shatter her. But God, that look. It did unnerve things to her insides in a way she hadn't felt since Trina.

"I didn't say you did," Skylar answered, sliding in a step closer even though she feared Laura would take her down with the move.

She was taller than Laura by a good inch, even with those four-inch stilettos. Still, Skylar didn't want to make her feel as though she was boxed in, but she did want to make her point very clear.

"I'm only here if you want help, but I have connections to get your car fixed and going so you can at least get it to a shop without paying a tow truck."

"I can afford a tow truck."

Skylar laughed slightly at that. "I have no doubt you can, Ms. Finch. I meant that if you wanted assistance, I know someone who can help. But I can see that my connections aren't wanted here."

Laura said nothing. Skylar stayed there for another minute before tightening her hand into a fist. Disappointment washed through her that Laura wouldn't give her even a moment of breaking or a small crumb to work with.

"Well, I guess I'll get going." Sighing, she moved toward her car and slipped behind the wheel. With her engine running, she almost made one more plea to convince Laura to take her helping hand, but the look in Laura's eyes told her it would be fruitless.

"What is wrong with that woman?" Skylar mumbled under her breath before putting her car into gear and pulling out of her parking spot. She still had work to do, which she could finish up in the office in her brother's basement or in her bedroom, but she'd left because she thought she could help.

In fact, every time she thought she could help or get an in with this woman she was pushed in the complete opposite direction. Skylar gripped the steering wheel as she pulled out onto the road and tried to relax. She was only trying to be nice and helpful. *Why can't Laura see that?*

One moment they were making headway and the next Laura was pushing back and putting up even more walls between them. Skylar couldn't figure her out. Surely they weren't that different, were they? Surely they could be on friendly terms, couldn't they?

After she parked, Skylar let herself into the house and started toward the basement office. Brady's voice caught her attention, but Callie's voice echoed through the kitchen into the entryway as well. She stiffened at it as she walked farther inside. She had forgotten coming home early would throw her right into the conversations she didn't want to have.

"Hey," Brady greeted. "How was work?"

"Not bad. I need to find a new client soon, and I've got a few proposals out, so I'm hopeful." Skylar wasn't about to tell him how dire the situation really was. She could at least protect him from that for now.

"Yeah?" He raised an eyebrow at her and glanced at Callie.

"Yeah." Skylar shifted her backpack over her shoulder. "I've got a bit more work to finish up."

She was already planning on adding in customer service training to the proposal she was building for Solace. If Laura was any example, then the rest of the team needed it, and it would at least help focus her mind to build up the potential training, even if it was never implemented. She could use it somewhere else, she was sure.

"Hey, Sky, I had a question for you." Callie's higher pitched voice reached her ears, and she came around the corner of the kitchen with a wine glass in her hand.

Skylar had to work hard not to wrinkle her nose at it. Callie loved wine, and since she had moved in, Skylar had been forced to drink a variety even though she hated it. She much preferred hard liquor, or even beer if she had to drink something other than liquor.

"Yeah, sure, what's up?"

"I was wondering if you wanted to be a bridesmaid. I know Brady would love it, and I would too."

Skylar stiffened, but she was grateful she managed to hold back the tears that usually threatened to spill anytime this topic came up. She had known the question was coming. Brady had given her a heads up, and she still hadn't come up with an excuse as to why she could say no. She had wanted it to be her asking Callie that, the image of her and Trina standing together and committing to each other in front of all their family and friends.

Skylar cringed. That wasn't going to happen, and this was what she was left with. Callie still stood in front of her, waiting for an answer. "Yeah, I'd...uh...I'd love that."

"Yay!" Callie's entire face lit up, and as much as Skylar hated talking about the wedding, she was glad she could at least make one person happy that day, since her attempts with Laura had failed so miserably.

Callie came up and wrapped her arms around Skylar's shoulders, tugging her into a hug. Reluctantly, Skylar hugged her back. It was the first time since her breakup that another woman had touched her, and even though it wasn't in the same way, it still felt so odd and out of place. She wanted to feel that physical connection with someone who loved her romantically, have arms wrapped around her in comfort and in passion. Skylar moved out of the embrace as quickly as she could and nodded at Brady.

"I'm going to go finish up my work for the day. Don't wait for me for dinner. I'll scrounge." Skylar couldn't bring herself to look at either of them in the eye.

"Got it."

Skylar escaped to her bedroom, shutting and locking the door behind her. As soon as she was inside, she flopped onto the bed and closed her eyes, tears stinging and her chest tightening. It shouldn't still hurt this bad, should it?

CHAPTER

Eight

LAURA SET the folder on the top of the desk and stared at it. It wasn't her usual form of work, but she had researched and put in the hours to create a proposal for Rodney, something he would never expect but something she knew needed their attention. This time had to be different when she argued for it. Gathering herself, she gripped the folder hard in her hand and stood up.

She wasn't going to let him fall into his old ways and run her over with his bullheadedness. She was going to stand up for herself and make a clear, decisive argument for why they needed to address this part of their business. It was true that both of them were getting older, and their ability to connect with the current businesses around would be a struggle, but they couldn't afford not to. She had to make that clear in a way he would understand, and push through the rest of the crap he flung at her.

She'd already checked the online calendar and knew Rodney wasn't busy at that moment—not that he ever really was. She straightened her shoulders and strode out of her office, across the hall, and to his. Knocking four times in rapid succession, Laura opened the door without hesitation and stepped inside.

Rodney's office could not be more opposite from hers. He had light from floor to ceiling windows on two of the walls. His desk backed up to them, so there was no way to look at him without the view outside. Laura ran her fingers along the smooth paper in her hand, using it to center herself.

She was about to do something she had never done before—she was going to push for what she thought was necessary. Rodney glanced up at her, his graying hair spiked up that day. His suit jacket had been abandoned on the back of one of the chairs in front of his desk, and he was hunched over something.

"What do you need?" he barked.

Immediately, Laura tensed, and her defenses went up at his tone. "We need to talk."

Rodney let out a little snort. "Usually when women say that to me it's in an entirely different context, though I don't suppose that's the way you mean it."

He did glance up at her at the end for that one. Laura pursed her lips and raised an eyebrow, the jab at their former relationship stinging more than she expected it to and in a way she wasn't quite ready to deal with yet. He had been doing a lot more of that lately, and the old wound wasn't healing over as quickly as it used to either. Refocusing on the task at hand, Laura said, "Our business is floundering."

"So lay someone off." He was so damn flippant sometimes, expecting her to have solutions to problems he didn't want to admit existed. Except he had admitted this one, which was why she even thought there was a potential he would listen to her proposal.

Laura sighed heavily. "I'd rather keep people in their positions, if possible. It makes for easier transitions later. And laying someone off doesn't solve the issue of income or the downward spiral we've found ourselves in."

"Transitions?" That *would* have his attention. Rodney sat up straight before leaning back in his chair, folding his hands over his stomach as he stared at her, vexed.

"Yes, for when we need to hire new staff. It's easier to have them trained by someone who already knows the position." This wasn't where Laura wanted to start the conversation. She knew in his mind that he wasn't anywhere near the stage of bringing in more employees because of the reality of where they currently were.

Rodney closed his eyes slowly before opening them again. "Why are you here, Laura?"

Stepping forward, Laura dropped the folder onto his desk right in the middle of all the papers he'd been leaning over seconds before.

"We need to align our business model to the changing times. It's crucial for us to be agile and change up some of our processes and marketing." There, she'd said it, the simplistic hook that she wanted to grab him, that she knew had to persuade him to listen to her.

"This again?" Rodney sighed heavily, but he did snag the folder and flip it open. That was something, at least. If anyone else had come in here with this idea, he would listen without the attitude, but since it was her, she knew she had to fight her way through it.

Laura squared her shoulders, determination in every breath. This had to work. "Yes. It's important."

He said nothing as he looked through what she had done on the proposal. Laura held her breath, willing him to accept it so they could start working. With all of the proof on the paper, he had to see the folly in the current situation. He had set up the business to run as if it was built in the fifties, and while it had worked for them for now, it wasn't going to work for them in the long run, not anymore. They needed to do something else. It was plain and clear on the paper he just finished reading.

"This is horse shit, Laura." He closed the folder and slapped it onto the desk. "You don't understand how to do marketing."

She knew she wasn't the expert when it came to marketing, but they had done all right in the beginning when they had started. She always thought she could learn to do anything that she needed if she was given the right amount of time, but in the last twenty years, she had been so focused on growing the business through clients and good work that she'd forgotten to continue learning. Diving deep into rebranding and marketing to convince Rodney had shown her how out of touch with the reality of it she was. She could not afford to do that any longer.

"We don't need any of it." Rodney shook his head.

"We need all of it and more. We're old, Rodney. We need help to figure out how to reach younger generations because they're the ones forming the current business world." Laura leaned over his desk, planting her fingers on the top of it and looking him directly in the eye. "I'm concerned we'll begin a much quicker decline into death if we don't do this."

Rodney eyed her. "Right now, you're supposed to be working on a proposal for EarthBound Exotica. Where is that?"

Laura bristled. "I've almost completed it."

"Then do that. If we don't land ourselves new clients, we'll fail to pay our employees."

"One client, even a well-paying client, isn't going to solve the issue. It's a stopgap. It'll buffer the finances for a time, but we're not finding enough new clients. We're becoming irrelevant." Laura balked at her own words. If Solace ceased to exist, what was left of her? She had poured everything of herself into this, and if it was gone...she couldn't even bring herself to complete that thought. Laura clenched her jaw, her teeth compressing on each other so tightly that she had to back off because it hurt.

"I need you to finish that proposal. I have to leave early today."

"What?" Laura tensed, brought back to the conversation from the chaos her mind had taken her to. "Why?"

"Jennifer needs me home for something or other."

"Unacceptable. I can't keep filling in your hours because you have to leave." She seethed. This was just another one of his tactics to distract her, she knew, and she'd fallen right into the trap like she did every time.

"You don't have a family, so I don't expect you to understand. You never wanted to." Rodney locked his gaze on hers, his look hard and mean.

Laura's lips parted in surprise at the vehemence in his voice, at the obvious poke into the one place he of all people should know hurt. This was the main reason why she still hated working with him. He took her weaknesses and shoved them in her face for the world to see. He made her feel ashamed that she hadn't measured up to his expectations. She had never managed to become who he wanted her to be. This was just one more example of that.

"So because I don't have a husband and kids, I have to work all the hours you don't want to?"

"Hardly." Rodney eyed her carefully. "But since you don't, you have the time to finish that proposal."

Laura scoffed, not believing they were even having this conversation. "What's going on with Jennifer? It can surely wait."

"It can't." He glared, and Laura knew she wasn't going to get more of an answer than that. "And just a reminder, I'll be attending a funeral Friday, so I won't be in the office most of the day."

Of course, he was taking the entire day off for it. Laura clenched her jaw shut to keep from saying anything else that might get her into deeper trouble.

"We meet with a new prospective client Monday, so I want you to have a portfolio ready for them." He went back to the work he'd been doing when she entered his office, obviously dismissed.

"Just use the current one." Laura wasn't going to put up with this. She had put so many hours into building that plan to convince him they needed to do something drastic, and he wasn't even going to give her the courtesy of listening?

Rodney shook his head. "Not for this client. They need something catered to them."

She couldn't fathom anyone who would need that. "Who is it?"

"Sandy Landers."

Laura tensed. They had gone to school with Sandy, and she had been one of the few students in their class to succeed. She had a multi-billion-dollar business and consistently worked with other businesses to build them up and take them over. Landing her as a client would keep them afloat for a long time, but she and Sandy hadn't exactly gotten along in college either—not that Laura got along with many people in general.

"What's she looking for?" Laura asked.

"I don't know yet. I have a lunch meeting with her and thought I could float her some of our information."

"So she isn't even a potential client and you're having me waste time on that instead of something worthy of our time and effort?" Laura tightened her hand into a fist at her side, trying to figure out what game Rodney was playing. One minute he acted as though he had the client in the bag and the next she found out it wasn't even a meeting to discuss business. She never understood this side of things, at least in practice, and Rodney certainly was the right man for that job.

"Everyone is a potential client." Rodney handed back the folder she had brought in. "You should have figured that out by now. Get me that proposal for EarthBound Exotica and the portfolio for Sandy. This isn't something I want to discuss anymore."

Devastated, Laura said nothing as she walked out of his office and right back to hers. What was she supposed to do with all of that? She sat heavily at her desk and stared at the folder she had spent hours preparing and had been shut down in seconds. Swiping it off her desk, she dropped it into the trashcan and tried to ignore the hurt that wanted to bubble up in her chest. If he wasn't going to pay attention to what was happening, she would have to push harder or find another way around it. She wouldn't let his failures become hers.

~

It was dark by the time Laura managed to gather her things and head out of the office door. Rodney had left hours before, as had every other employee. Laura was about to shut off the lights, but the cleaning crew came in, so she left them on. Nodding at them, she walked out the front door to Solace and stopped at the elevator. Weariness slipped into her bones from the day, from her confrontation with Rodney, from her hopes being dashed in one quick pile of shit.

Perfect day.

Laura sighed and pressed her pointer finger into the button to call the elevator up to her floor and leaned heavily against the wall next to it. She needed to get home, pour herself a stiff drink, and sink into a good book that would keep her busy until she couldn't keep her eyes open. Then she would wake up early and start the day over again, likely working the same hours she had that day, which would leave her exhausted by the weekend.

She was just about to step into the elevator when the sound of feet moving swiftly on the carpet caught her attention. Looking up, she saw Skylar coming toward her in a rush. But she stopped as soon as her eyes lit on Laura's face.

"Oh," Skylar said, her lips forming into a circle before a frown covered her features.

It was probably the first time Laura had ever seen her unhappy about anything. Displeasure rolled through her at the sight of sadness in Skylar's gaze, though it was quickly masked, and her full lips pulled tightly into a smile. Laura was always the person to cause that kind of reaction with others. When she and Rodney had first started Solace, they had played to their strengths, but now, with Skylar in front of her, she didn't want to be that person any longer. She wanted the smiles and excitement, the easy conversations and small talk.

"Good evening. Leaving late, I see," Skylar started again, as if her sudden exhortation hadn't happened.

"As are you," Laura commented, eyeing Skylar carefully as they stepped into the elevator. Something was different about the girl today, and Laura couldn't quite put her finger on it, but she discovered an incessant urge to find something she hadn't expected. Still, she managed to resist.

"I usually work this late," Skylar stated.

Laura paused at that. Just the day before, Skylar had left at the same time she had, and while it was later in the day, it wasn't *this* late. Laura let the elevator doors shut before she leaned forward and pressed the button for the main level. She said nothing in response, not quite sure what to say, but she was curious why Skylar would work so much and when she found time to be a young woman out in the world. She had to stop that kind of thinking. It wouldn't be good for her to get caught up in Skylar's life, and she definitely wasn't interested in it.

"You're normally done before now, though, aren't you?" Skylar's inquisitive nature won over the silence.

"I am," Laura answered quietly, exhaustion seeping into her bones. It would be so nice to have what Rodney had, someone to talk to when the day was crappy and emotions heavy. Though she wasn't sure a near stranger in the elevator was the person of choice for that conversation.

"So why are you leaving so late?" Skylar turned toward her, opening space for conversation.

"I had a proposal to create for a client." Not that Skylar needed to know that, but again, her quiet countenance and that damn look she'd had on her face when they'd run into each other at the elevator had done Laura in. She wanted to know—needed to know—what was behind that gaze.

"Funny, I was doing the same thing."

The connection struck Laura as slightly ironic. Their businesses worked similarly, the need for clients and contracts in order to thrive. She didn't comment on it, however, buckling down on just living in the presence of another person who might understand the need for late hours.

They exited the elevator together—Laura first. Walking through the empty lobby, she shuddered. The cold air from the start of fall was going to hit her hard, and of course, she had forgotten a jacket that morning. She stepped out of the building and stopped short. She didn't have a vehicle. Skylar followed her movement, giving Laura a confused look before she faced the parking lot.

"Car not fixed yet?"

"No," Laura mumbled, whipping her phone out of her pocket. Of course, Skylar would bring that back up. Camryn had said she would give her a ride home from work that day, but it was late, and Laura wasn't entirely sure she would still be up for it. Sending a quick text to find out, Laura waited by the front doors, the damp chilly air surrounding her body.

"I can give you a ride if you want."

Laura focused on Skylar, on the honesty in her face, the earnestness in her voice. She was genuinely trying to be helpful, and Laura should take her up on that offer. Yet, she hesitated. She couldn't push past the block in her chest to say yes. Shaking her head in a must softer decline than the previous day with the offer of help, Laura stared out at the nearly empty parking lot. "My friend will come and get me."

"Are you sure? I'm here now, and then you don't have to wait." Skylar was everything Laura needed in that moment, but for some reason, she couldn't shake the thought that to give in would be a weakness. The last time she'd relied on someone, she had failed the relationship. She couldn't allow that to happen for a second time.

Laura slid her gaze over to Skylar, and again she was struck by just how young this woman was. But that look, when they'd met at the elevator mere minutes ago, filtered back through her mind. Something was there that Laura wasn't able to read.

"I'm sure. Thank you." Laura bowed her head slightly, showing a sign of acquiescence even though she wasn't giving in to the offer of help.

"All right. I guess I'll see you around then."

Skylar walked away without another word, and the cold in Laura's bones wasn't just from the weather. She stood at the doors to the building, watching as Skylar got into her SUV and started the engine, keeping her eyes glued to the vehicle as she pulled out of the parking lot and drove up the small hill to the hotel parking lot so she could get to the street. As soon as the SUV was out of her sight, Laura frowned.

What was all that about?

Not just Skylar but herself. She'd never wanted to accept an offer of help more than she had in that moment. She could never just let herself be vulnerable, could she? She'd been taught from childhood that it was weakness, but standing there in the cold night with the slight breeze cutting into her skin through her clothing and open jacket, she had to admit it wasn't. Skylar wouldn't keep offering, she knew that much.

Her phone buzzed in her hand, and she knew what it would say already. Camryn was already busy with late night things. Laura put in a request for a ride share and went inside to wait. Loneliness edged its way into her, taking over her heart and her chest, then her stomach and her entire body. She stared out in the dark parking lot and cringed. What had she done with her life?

CHAPTER
Nine

SKYLAR'S STOMACH was a bundle of nerves as she stood in front of Solace's main door. She'd met with almost all the other businesses in the building and had put up signs by the doors and on the bulletin boards. Most people were on board with her crazy idea, which was great, but she hadn't heard a single word from Solace in the week the information had been out there.

She needed to talk to them in person, because from what she knew of them, they wouldn't pay a lick of attention to a flier and would only notice if there was a direct conversation. They seemed old-school like that. The handle was cold against her skin as she pushed the door open. The interior of the office was a hushed bustle, which was odd.

The walls were painted a nice beige with newer furniture inside. Cubicles were off to the far side. Right in front of her was a large desk with two people sitting there, and two monitors for each of them. She hoped it wouldn't be difficult to get past them to Rodney—he definitely was the one Skylar wanted to talk to about this project. Not Laura—she would probably shut Skylar out simply because of who she was.

"Can I help you?" A woman in a smart blazer with her hair

pulled back into a tight bun asked, eyeing Skylar from the large desk.

"Um...yes. I was wondering if I could speak with Mr. Solace."

"Do you have an appointment?"

Skylar's palms sweated. "No, but I can set one up if that would be easier."

She pulled up a calendar on the screen in front of her. It looked filled to the brim with things. Skylar's stomach sank. She'd never get a meeting with him that week, and next week it might be too late to join in. She was just about to speak when Mr. Solace stepped out into the hall and caught sight of her. He raised his eyebrows in her direction and stepped closer to the desk.

"Ms. Ross."

"Mr. Solace, I was just making an appointment to come and speak with you."

"You don't have to do that." He held out his hand toward the door he'd just come from. "I have a moment now."

"Sir," the woman interrupted, spinning in her chair. "Ms. Finch—"

"Can wait," he stated and stayed still.

Skylar tentatively walked toward the office, not quite sure what silent battle was happening or what argument she had just stepped into, but she was going to take the opportunity while she could. She wasn't going behind Laura's back to land herself a much-needed job because Rodney had offered for her to come in there, but it still felt squicky. She couldn't shake it either, and with each step toward Rodney's office, it got worse.

He kept the door open, which Skylar was grateful for. If Laura walked by then, she could be included, and Skylar couldn't be blamed for going behind her back. This could very well be the connection she needed in order to land herself an actual client in Solace later on down the road.

Nothing they were going to talk about couldn't be shared,

and she preferred to have the open exit when she could and to not hide anything of the professional capacity in which she was there.

"What did you want to discuss?" Rodney leaned against the desk, sitting on the edge of it casually.

"I wasn't sure if you had seen the flyers, but I'm planning a building-wide trunk-or-treat in the parking lot the weekend before Halloween. I thought it'd be a good way to promote all our businesses at once and get people to the area so they would know where to find us. Some network marketing, you could say."

"Sounds like a good idea. My wife loves to take my son to those kinds of things."

Skylar nodded and handed over a piece of paper with the information on it. "If you want to participate, I just need to know how many vehicles will be participating."

"I'll put it out to our workers and see if they're interested."

"You're allowed to hand out promotional material." Skylar didn't add in that she wondered if they had any, but she was genuinely curious if they did. It would help form more of what she needed to focus on in a proposal, if she could ever get that far in the relationship.

"I'll make sure we have some. Jana can put it together. I'm not sure if I'll be there with a vehicle, but I'll bring my son."

"How old is he?"

"Seven." Rodney sighed, a smile tugging at his lips.

"Do you have any other children?" Skylar knew she was prying but making those personal connections was sometimes the way to get the in, and she wanted an in. Laura certainly wasn't going to be that person for her—if anything she'd be the opposite—so she had to work her networking magic on Rodney.

"No, just the one. I got started late. Jennifer and I have talked about having more, but it's been a struggle."

"I'm so sorry." Skylar frowned slightly. "My sister struggles with fertility. They've been trying for six years."

"We've been trying since Grayson was born. He was a fluke according to the doctors."

"A blessing for sure," Skylar added, folding her hands together in front of her. "How long have you two been married?"

"Fourteen years now."

"Wow." Skylar shook her head. What she would have given to have a relationship with someone last that long. "You must work hard at keeping your marriage alive."

Rodney paled slightly, his cheeks tightening. Skylar wasn't sure what she said to make him do that, but clearly it wasn't a comment he was comfortable with. She needed to get confirmation of his participation and get out of there quickly before she made any other steps in the wrong direction. "Well, if you want to join in, I'd love to have you."

"We will. I just have to find someone who is willing."

"Right." Skylar pressed into her toes, ready to turn around and leave now that she had what she wanted.

"Willing for what?" Laura's icy voice washed over Skylar.

A shiver raced through her, and Skylar raised her gaze to meet Rodney's, not sure if she should turn around and face Laura. Surely it was about to turn fiery in an instant. Holding back her wince, Skylar moved. "I'm planning a trunk-or-treat in the parking lot. We'll all use it as marketing and to get people to the building. It's a simple thing, but it should help get our names out there."

Laura snorted, her eyes rolling in the process as she stood perfectly still and in complete control of the room now that she had entered it. "What an obtuse idea."

Skylar's stomach dropped at the idea that Laura would think she was stupid in any way. It was a bit lowbrow by Laura's standards, she was sure, but feet on the ground was how she had built her business from day one. "It'll get some name recognition going."

She couldn't pinpoint why she felt the deep need to defend herself. Normally, she would have walked away. Laura had shown no sign of being interested in anything Skylar was doing or any of her ideas thus far, and she didn't understand why she wanted that to be different each time they spoke.

Laura's voice lowered, barely above a whisper as she spoke. "If you didn't even know what an actuary was, why would anyone trick-or-treating know?"

Skylar's lips parted in surprise, and Rodney said nothing as he eyed the both of them. It didn't matter. What mattered was, Skylar was working her ass off, making kind gesture after kind gesture, and yet Laura refused to even acknowledge that Skylar was anything other than a nuisance. Flexing her fingers, Skylar shot back, "It's a cheap way to do some basic marketing. You're free to join in or not." Then, with a level of spite that surprised her, she tacked on, "But I suppose you would need a working vehicle first."

Laura's gaze snapped up at that. Rodney furrowed his brow, finally saying something. "What's wrong with your car?"

"Nothing," Laura snapped. "I had a flat and had to call for a tow."

"You could have borrowed my extra car."

Laura's face pinched, and a small amount of victory rose in Skylar's chest. She was at least making headway and poking back where it stung, and she just found another of Laura's weaknesses —though it was all in the same vein. Asking for help would be her undoing.

"It's unnecessary. My car is fixed."

Rodney looked defeated, which was odd. Skylar furrowed her brow at the interaction, trying to read between the lines, but without more context as to how the two of them worked together, she was left in the dark.

"Ms. Ross' idea is one we shouldn't participate in." Laura crossed her arms and raised an eyebrow in Skylar's direction, disdain all over her face. Skylar had just shot herself in the foot.

"I think it's a brilliant idea, actually," Rodney interjected.

"Jennifer takes Grayson to a lot of those events, and they get the word out about businesses."

Laura scoffed.

Skylar stood completely silent, watching the ping-ponging back and forth between the two of them and trying to keep up with the argument that was happening under the surface.

"It's not the clients we want to attract."

"You never know who is going to show up to these things, Laura."

Skylar stiffened, the use of Laura's first name had an edge to it that she couldn't name, and Laura herself tensed at the sound of it. Laura glared at Rodney, her hands tightened into fists at her sides, and she cocked her head slowly in his direction.

"Oh, don't give me that look. Weren't you just talking about some new ways of marketing?"

Laura's lips parted, as if she was going to make a retort, but then suddenly she turned on Skylar, as if remembering she was still in the room with them. Skylar wanted nothing more than to slip out of the room unnoticed and escape from that part of the floor, maybe even the building, so they couldn't come find her until she gathered herself together again.

"Do you have the proposal yet?" Rodney interjected.

"That's what I was coming to speak with you about," Laura answered tersely. "I didn't realize you had *company*."

"It's not company."

Skylar was about to speak and make her exit known if only to escape, but Rodney barreled right over her.

"We were talking business."

She could tell Laura wasn't pleased with that response, as if it was only an excuse, but that was all they had been doing. She wanted to make that clear, wanted her to know there was nothing else going on, but she wasn't even sure how to begin that conversation without offending her even more.

"I'm just..." Skylar reached for the desk and grabbed the flier.

"Here. This is the information you'll need if you decide to participate."

Handing the paper to Laura, Skylar turned to Rodney and nodded in his direction. "Thank you for the time, even though I didn't have an appointment."

"Anytime, Skylar. I mean that."

Laura looked like her head was about to explode. Skylar tried to scoot around her and make for the door, but Laura blocked it. As soon as she got close enough, Laura dashed her hand out and gripped Skylar's wrist tightly. Heat seared at the touch, burning Skylar in a way she didn't expect. For some reason, she wondered if she was Laura's lifeline.

"It's a stupid idea," Laura repeated, but she wasn't looking at Skylar—she was looking directly at Rodney. It made Skylar think the comment wasn't about her but something else entirely.

"You might think so," Skylar dropped her voice, hesitating slightly, "but if you don't want to participate, that's entirely up to you. The building has already approved it, and I have at least twenty vehicles and companies signed up. Just think about it."

Laura shifted her gaze from Rodney to Skylar. Those ice-blue eyes looked hopeless. It jarred Skylar enough to stay put. The urge to comfort Laura was overwhelming, but she needed to maintain her distance and keep her head in check. This woman had just called her idea stupid, out loud, and had been trying to dismiss her since, but the iron grip on her wrist said something else.

"It's pointless," Laura tried again.

"You're free to think that," Skylar stated simply, keeping all anger out of her tone. "If you don't mind, I have work I need to get to."

Laura's grasp immediately released. Skylar resisted the urge to rub her wrist. She glanced at Rodney who seemed as confused as she felt. Skylar stepped away from Laura's reach and finally got to the door.

"Let me know if you decide to join."

"Will do," Rodney called after her, not taking his gaze off Laura.

Finally free from the tension in that office, Skylar said goodbye to Jana at the desk and walked right out the door. "Solace" was anything but what was in that office. With what she had just witnessed, she wasn't sure she wanted to work with them anymore. Something in the way Laura had clung to her had been achingly desperate.

As soon as she was ensconced in her office, the quiet stillness of the air enveloped her. It was so different from what she had experienced as soon as Laura had entered the room. Before then it had been cordial and fine, but Laura's energy—Skylar had to take a deep breath at the thought—it was chaotic.

Hours passed before Skylar was able to find her focus again. She worked on some marketing for a couple different potential clients before she dove into the work that needed to be done. By the time she was ready to finish up for the day, she opened one more file—the unofficial proposal she was making for Solace. Adding in leadership training and conflict management seemed an absolute must now, and thanks to Rodney's dig, she had a direction to go with demographics to aim for.

Still, she wasn't sure why she was working so hard on something that had no potential to become a reality, especially if Laura had any say in the matter. Her stomach clenched at the thought of Laura, once again wondering what exactly had happened in that office. It was clear Skylar wasn't in the know about something, but she also wasn't sure she wanted to be.

Closing up her office for the night, Skylar packed up her backpack and left the building. She was the last vehicle to leave, meaning Laura was already gone, and she hadn't heard from Solace whether or not they would be participating in the trunk-or-treat at the end of the month. Trying to brush off the disappointment, Skylar got into her car and headed for the house. She'd talk to her brother about it when they had a chance—he was always a clear mind to her scuttled thoughts.

She wasn't even sure she'd take the job, even if it was offered. As desperate as she was for the income, for the recognition that she could work with a bigger company, the dynamic between Rodney and Laura was charged. It would be a challenge for anyone coming in there to navigate their way through it. But she still needed the income and the client base. Warehouse Thirty-Three depended on it.

CHAPTER
Ten

LAURA'S NERVES WERE FRAYED. Rodney had stuck her with dealing with the proposal that morning because he hadn't even had time to look it over, and while she knew the paperwork like the back of her own hand, she still hated giving presentations and talking to people. Rodney was so much better at that than she was.

Juggling her briefcase, her coffee, and her jacket all at the same time, Laura stepped out of her vehicle. She tried to shut the door with her hip and missed. Dropping her briefcase to the asphalt, Laura cursed as she reached for it in a jerk, spilling her coffee all down the front of her new, white blouse.

Heat seared her skin, and she hissed as it spread over her chest and onto her belly. Immediately, she clenched her fist and jaw, trying to hold back the pain and the scream of discomfort that wanted to expel from her lips. She wasn't sure how she managed it.

"Oh my gosh! Are you okay?"

Wincing at Skylar's voice, Laura tensed even more, really not wanting anyone to see her in the state that she was in. She needed to be able to fix this without the added embarrassment of anyone seeing her in this weakened state.

"Ms. Finch, are you okay?" Skylar reached forward and grabbed the lidless cup, setting it on the ground before taking Laura's jacket in her hand. "Did it burn you?"

"No," Laura managed to croak out, though she wasn't sure how much truth was in the word. Other than the burn from the hot beverage, the burn from her embarrassment was over the top.

"Are you sure?" Skylar gripped Laura's forearm, her fingers pressing in lightly against the damp material and into her skin.

"I'm sure."

"Then breathe," Skylar commanded.

Laura dragged in a breath of freezing air, the sudden cold hitting her precisely as she needed it to. It felt heavenly compared to her wet chest. Glancing down, she noted the coffee had gone all over her white button up, but she had somehow managed to miss her skirt. Straightening her back, she took another long assessment of her body now that the shock was wearing off. She had definitely burned her skin, and she could only hope it was a slight burn and nothing too serious.

Skylar still held her forearm as she shifted and raised her gaze to meet Skylar's worried eyes. "I'm fine, I promise."

"Sure you are." Amusement flashed in Skylar's look before she schooled it. "Do you have another shirt?"

"No," Laura sighed. "I'll have to go home."

"I might have something you can wear."

Laura furrowed her brow. "I doubt anything you have—"

"Will be fancy enough?" Skylar challenged her. "Don't doubt me, Ms. Finch."

A thrill ran through Laura at the sound of her name. She'd missed it the first time, so caught up in the shock of spilling her drink, but this time, she caught every intonation in her name as Skylar said it. She almost missed being called Ms. Solace now, although the reminder of her ex-husband wasn't something she wanted, the nickname was highly appropriate.

"If you'd let me finish..." Laura looked Skylar directly in the eye. "I'm not sure you'd have anything that would fit."

Skylar bowed her head slightly, a gentle pink rushing to her cheeks that suited her so well. "You might be right on that, but we can at least try it, can't we?"

Laura's lips parted as she almost accepted the offer, but accepting the help would be a weakness, wouldn't it? She hated asking for assistance, but in a case like this, she didn't have time to drive all the way home for a new outfit before coming back and making the meeting. She needed an alternative plan, and Skylar may just be the unexpected solution.

"Yes," Laura answered finally, suddenly wishing that Skylar would stop holding her arm as if she was going to fall over but not wanting to lose the physical touch she'd forgotten she craved.

"It's in my office. Come on." Skylar bent down and grabbed Laura's briefcase, holding it tightly in one hand. Laura wasn't used to someone else taking charge of an emergent situation. It had always been left to her to sort out, and a small thrill moved through her at the idea that this time not everything was on her shoulders.

Laura took her jacket and slung it over her arm as they walked, not wanting to put it on and potentially ruin it too if she was going to need it to hide whatever hideous dress shirt Skylar came up with.

"Do you ever relax?" Skylar asked as they stepped into the elevator.

Laura turned on her, very aware of just how tightly the blouse clung to her curves now that it was damp and chilly instead of hot and burning, and the fact that her bra was soaked through as well.

"Of course, I do." Laura pursed her lips. She did every night with the two glasses of whiskey she would drink before she settled in with a good book and fell asleep with the light on while reading—every damn night.

"It's just... I've never seen you relaxed. Ever."

Doesn't this elevator go any faster? Laura needed to escape it. Being so exposed in front of *this* woman of all people was too much. She might be pleasant to be around, but that didn't mean she wanted Skylar to pry into her business. Choosing not to answer, Laura held her ground and stared at the crack at the bottom of the elevator doors, which was fast becoming her favorite place when she was stuck inside with Skylar.

When the door dinged their arrival, Skylar took the lead. Laura glanced at her office door as they passed it, wondering how many people had seen her spectacular fumble in the parking lot. Feeling like a lost child, she followed Skylar to the office toward the end of the hall. Skylar unlocked the door and held it open for Laura, locking it again as soon as they were inside.

For the first time, Laura noted Skylar was in yoga pants and a loose T-shirt. Clearly, she had no important meetings that day, although Laura would never stand for someone coming into the office dressed like that. But her shoes did look comfortable.

"It's in here." Skylar set Laura's briefcase on the light blue couch against the far wall.

Laura had wanted a sofa in her office for years but hadn't ever found the right reasons to bring one in. She also didn't want to encourage comfort in her office if she could avoid it—her desire was for personal reasons. Skylar opened a small closet door, which Laura hadn't even noticed when they first walked in. She rummaged through it before pulling out a sapphire blue blouse on a hanger.

"It might be a bit loose on you, since well..." Skylar motioned to herself "...I have more boobs than you do."

Laura tried not to take that personally. She'd been told she wasn't womanly enough several times by Rodney when they had been married. It was, unfortunately, part of why she kept her hair long and down even though she blamed it more on habit than on the reasons behind those habits.

Taking the hanger, Laura stared at the blouse. It was cheaply made compared to what she would normally wear, but she remembered just starting out and having to find good deals on clothes that didn't look awful. Skylar was no doubt in that phase of her life.

"Thank you." Her praise was genuine and heartfelt for the first time.

"Feel free to change in the back if you want. There's another office that I use for storage through that door. If you give me your shirt, I can get it cleaned so it won't stain."

Laura hadn't even thought about that. The coffee was no doubt going to cause issues unless she took it to the dry cleaners. Nodding silently, Laura stepped through the door and into the small office that had boxes stacked along with filing cabinets and bookshelves. Setting her jacket down on top of one of the boxes, she immediately pulled at the buttons on her blouse, ready to see the damage to her bra and her chest.

Sure enough, red puffy skin greeted her as soon as she got her shirt off. All down her chest and onto the top of her belly, including the swells of her breasts where her bra hadn't managed to protect her. She frowned as she ran her fingers along her skin, wincing at the slight pain that echoed. It wasn't awful, at least. And it didn't look like she needed medical attention and time would manage to heal it. She probably wouldn't even notice it by the end of the day.

Sliding the blouse over her head, Laura fluffed out her hair as she smoothed the fabric along her belly and hips. The blue was definitely her color, which she knew would add to the appeal. She wished there was a mirror of some sort so she could check the fit, but even by feel, she knew it was bulky. A few safety pins should fix that, along with her jacket to cover them.

Laura stepped back into the main office area, and Skylar twisted around in her chair, her computer set up in front of her. Her eyes widened as her gaze dropped from Laura's face to her shoes and back up again. She gnawed on her lower lip, her gaze lingering on Laura's breasts a moment too long. Laura shivered at the open appraisal. For some reason it didn't feel forced or judgmental in the way it always had with Rodney when she'd dressed in front of him. This felt heated, as if she was actually desired.

Skylar's gaze locked on hers again, and she had to clear her throat from the moment in order to speak. "Do you have any safety pins by chance?"

"Uh..." Skylar closed her eyes as if she was trying to remember, her cheeks a nice rosy color. "Yeah, I think I do."

"Good."

Skylar pulled out a small container from the drawer next to the desk and rummaged. Laura took a deep breath before she stepped in closer to the desk and Skylar, her stomach in knots. "I'll need you to help."

"Sure." Skylar stood up, a pin in hand and ready.

Laura reached around her front to her back, gathering fabric at the bottom of her shoulder and pulling it tight. "You'll have to do this on both sides."

"Got it."

The tension in the pit of Laura's belly intensified as Skylar pressed against her. The warmth of her breath against Laura's neck as she bent to pin the fabric sent a flutter across her skin, the small hairs standing at attention and waiting for it to happen again. There. Laura closed her eyes against the onslaught of sensations rolling through her.

Skylar's hands were light as she worked. The gentle scent of her shampoo floated through the air. Laura tried her best not to breathe it in, but the closer Skylar was, the more powerful the smell took over her senses. Laura dragged in a deep breath—instantly regretting it—and held her stance firmly. She kept absolutely silent as Skylar pinned the shirt tighter so it would pull more at her chest.

Her heart fluttered, and her palms were clammy. She couldn't move an inch, locked frozen in place while Skylar worked so she didn't get poked by anything sharp. Again that breath along the top of her shoulder and down her front. Her nipples hardened, pulling tightly. Her breathing increased when Skylar's fingers brushed against her sides and then her back, probably to smooth out the material, but Laura was reminded of the kind of touch that for years she had longed for. Tender touch. Loving touch. Sexual touch.

"There. I think I'm done." Skylar didn't step away.

Laura stayed put, not moving as her eyes fluttered open when Skylar's hands moved off her body. She turned her head to look over her shoulder, finding Skylar's lips parted, her cheeks still flushed, and a damning look in her gaze. Skylar stayed put, and Laura realized all too late that it was because she had nowhere to go.

Giving them each space, Laura turned around and glanced down at the shirt. It was tighter against her body, which made it look better, but the V-neck was also wider, exposing more of her skin and the tops of her breasts. She wasn't used to wearing such revealing clothing, but for today, it would have to do.

Skylar hissed, and Laura jerked her head up. "What?"

"You're burned." Skylar's hands curled around the edge of her desk tightly, as if it was her lifeline.

Reaching up unexpectedly, Laura fluttered her fingers over the top of her chest. "It'll be fine by lunch. It's not that bad."

"Coffee must have been hot," Skylar answered, but the words were mostly lost on Laura as she stared into those bright blue eyes, the tentative curl of her hair from the ponytail that rested on her shoulder.

"It was." Laura nearly had to clear her throat in order to speak again, the sound of her own voice nearly foreign to her ears. When had she become so lost in that gaze? Snapping back to attention, Laura shifted her stance. She'd nearly forgotten why she needed the shirt in the first place. "I need to go to work. I have a presentation..."

"Then go." Skylar nodded toward the door, her voice breathy and surreal. "I'm glad I could be helpful today."

Laura took a steadying breath, her gaze dropping from Skylar's eyes and down her body, over her breasts, along the curves of her hips, and back up again. Confusion hit her first because she didn't want to leave, not just yet, and there was no reason she should want that. But she had to leave. Saying nothing, Laura grabbed her briefcase and walked out of the small office.

Once outside, the spell that had been woven broke. She was running late on a day when there was a huge presentation that she couldn't miss. Her heart ran rampant as Greta moved toward her. Laura shook her head. More coffee now would be a disastrous idea—she was already a bundle of nerves in a way she couldn't explain.

"Tea?" Greta asked.

"Yes." Relief washed through Laura. "But after, please. I'm late."

"They're already waiting for you."

"Perfect," Laura mumbled. She brushed past Greta and walked right into the conference room, settling her briefcase onto the table. She nodded at Rodney and Colin, CEO of Earth-Bound Exotica, ready to begin her presentation. They had wanted a more detailed proposal than Rodney could handle, and he'd tossed the ball to her court.

They spent three hours talking about the detailed portfolio and proposal she had put together. By the end of it, they had a contract signed and were ready to begin a project in the next two weeks once the files and information were passed over to them. As they saw their now clients out of the office, Laura relaxed.

Rodney grabbed her shoulders, squeezing tightly and rubbing. His mouth was close to her ear when he said, "You were wonderful this morning."

Laura tried to stiffen, but Rodney hit a particularly annoying knot in her shoulder, and she had to hold back a moan instead.

She wouldn't have managed to do it without Skylar or accepting the helping hand, which only served to conjure up the image of Skylar's hands on her instead of Rodney's.

"I've never seen you that put-together before. What was that all about?"

Shaken from the daydream, Laura stepped out of his grasp and went to the conference room to pick up her papers and the newly minted contract. She would have Greta file that as soon as she brought in her tea. "I knew we needed to land the client."

"And we did that."

"Yes." Laura glanced up at Rodney, a smile blossoming on her lips. "Yes, we did."

"This will carry us through the rest of the year."

"Luckily, because I'm not firing Hannah." Laura made eye contact with him, using the moment to judge if her suspicions before had been correct.

"I know." Rodney ran a hand through his hair guiltily. "That wasn't a good idea of mine."

"Glad you can admit it." She closed up her briefcase with the papers nestled inside. "I've work to get done, if you don't mind."

"We should go out to lunch, celebrate."

"Celebrate a new client?" Laura furrowed her brow, confused. They hadn't done that in quite some time, and she couldn't fathom why he wanted to do it now. Yes, EarthBound Exotica was a much larger client than normal and with the five-year contract, they would be set for a while, but Rodney's shift in mood was unnerving.

"Absolutely. Everything should be celebrated."

Laura held her breath for a second before stepping closer to him. "What is this all about?"

"Nothing."

This wasn't like him, and she knew it better than anyone. Warning bells went off in her head, and she eyed him down. "You can say that, Rodney, but don't forget I know you. What's really going on?"

"I promise you nothing is going on. It's been a while since we sat down to discuss business in a less strict environment." He motioned to the room. "I thought it might be good for us to talk about the business casually."

Laura eyed him carefully, deciding to use this as the unexpected opportunity she had been waiting for. "I'll go to lunch with you to celebrate, if and only if, you listen to me about my plan to update Solace in a way that will attract up-and-coming businesses."

Rodney paused for a brief moment before nodding his agreement.

"Good. Where are we going, then?" Laura grasped her briefcase and held it tightly in her hand.

"Rizzo's?"

He would, of course, pick their preferred date night restaurant. It had been years since Laura had stepped foot in there, too many memories with him to even begin to dine there alone or with someone else. It wasn't worth an argument to pick anywhere else, however, especially if she wanted him to actually listen to her ideas. "Sure. Let me put this in my office."

Laura walked by him, and Rodney stopped her with a light touch to her arm. "By the way, that shirt looks really good on you."

"Oh." Laura's cheeks heated—not because of the compliment, which he had so rarely given her, but because of the situation that had landed her in it, and the woman who had been so warm when she didn't need to be. Butterflies flew in her stomach. Skylar had managed to save the day because Laura had allowed her the chance. "Thank you. Shall we?"

"Yes." Rodney stuffed his hands in his pockets as Laura walked out of the conference room.

The lightness in her step hadn't been there for years. She had landed them the client this time, not Rodney, which meant she could very easily do more than she was. He'd always told her she couldn't deal with the clients directly, but today proved him wrong. Somewhere, deep down, she had known that, but now she had proof in hand. They had worked together like they had in the beginning. Laura smiled at the thought they were finally moving in the right direction, back to the two of them working together instead of against each other.

CHAPTER
Eleven

THE KNOCK WAS SO slight that Skylar almost missed it. When she glanced up, Laura stood at the door, her arms crossed over her chest and a slight smile playing at her lips. Skylar couldn't fathom ever seeing Laura smile, and just the very image of it greeting her was striking.

Grinning back, Skylar spun in her chair and cocked her head in Laura's direction. "I take it your presentation went well?"

"Absolute success." The curl of Laura's lips broadened, her cheeks reddened and her gaze dropped slightly as if she was shy all of a sudden. "Thank you."

Skylar's breath caught in her lungs at the stunning image of this strong woman standing in front of her as if she owned the entire world. It was pure confidence, and Skylar was ready to melt at her feet for just a taste of it.

"Anytime," Skylar's voice was so weak when she spoke that she wasn't sure Laura heard her. Skylar looked Laura over again, from top to bottom, appreciating the gentle curves of her body, the way her shoulders were straight and powerful. She may be small, but she certainly exuded control in every breath she took.

"I came here for my shirt." Laura curled a strand of hair behind her ear, her fingers lingering slightly longer than if it was solely for the purpose of habit. Her gaze still held that intensity Skylar had come to expect, but this time it was a bit softer, as if Laura was truly seeing her.

"Oh! Right." Skylar wrinkled her nose and moved to stand. The sweet pause in the conversation had distracted her, the ease and calm that Laura exuded for the first time since they had met a wonderful feeling. "I cleaned it for you."

"What?" Laura's brows knit together.

Skylar nodded and went into the back room. She'd hung it up to dry after washing it in the bathroom sink. She hadn't expected Laura to come back so soon, but it was a pleasant surprise either way. Her fingers clasped the hanger, and she pulled the shirt off the hook on the back of the door. The fabric was still damp.

"I know you probably dry clean everything, but my ex-girl-friend invented this cleaner."

Laura's lips thinned into a line as she eyed the shirt in question when Skylar stepped back into the main office area. The judgment and suspicion flowed off her in waves. Skylar held the shirt out so Laura could take it.

"But what she invented was perfect for the problem with the shirt. See? It's all cleaned. No stains at all. It just needs a proper wash, which I'd intended to do tonight when I got home and bring it to you tomorrow." Skylar was rambling, and she knew it, but she couldn't make herself stop no matter how hard she tried. "I hope you don't mind."

Laura ran her fingers over the white fabric and said nothing. "Thank you for the shirt today."

"Right." Skylar squared her shoulders, ready to be reamed for something, but she wasn't sure what. Perhaps she would prefer it to this softer side of Laura she had stumbled upon—it was unnerving.

Laura gripped the shirt, pulling it off the hanger and handing it back. Their fingers brushed in the process, but it was back to that cold and firm touch. Skylar shoved her hands into the pockets of her hoodie after dropping the hanger onto the desk.

She stepped away, giving Laura as much room as possible so she could leave, and so they wouldn't land themselves in the same position they had been in that morning.

Without another word, Laura nodded at Skylar and pushed the door open. She walked out of the office and into the hallway, the door shutting behind her as she went. Skylar was left alone, the wake of Laura's joy already dissipated.

Skylar waited until she figured Laura was already in the elevator and gone before walking down the hall to the window at the end of the building. She wrapped her arms around herself as she waited for Laura to leave the building. Surely, she was going home for the day, wasn't she?

Skylar was just about to leave when finally she saw Laura's brown head walk down the stairs, her hands clutching the shirt and her briefcase. Holding her breath, Skylar watched as Laura walked with precision toward her car, the stain from the coffee still all over the asphalt.

What is so interesting about her? Skylar couldn't put her finger on it, no matter how hard she tried. She had thought about almost nothing but Laura the entire day. Even when she was focused on work, she'd been caught up in what Laura was doing and where she was.

As Laura drove off, Skylar went to her office and packed up for the day. She wanted to go home and relax. Brady wasn't working that night, so she could have dinner with him and Callie and relax with a good, stiff drink.

It took her nearly an hour and a half to get to the house in the rush hour traffic. She'd told herself from the start of renting the office space that she wouldn't drive during rush hours, but she'd forgotten all about that promise in her haze.

Pulling up to the house, Skylar parked and grabbed her bag. As soon as she stepped inside, she was greeted with the beautiful scents of dinner. She smiled to herself, instantly knowing that Brady had been the one cooking because it was her childhood favorite. Their mother had made it often when they were growing up.

"Brady?" Skylar called into the house, making her way to the kitchen.

Heat kissed her cheeks as she stepped into the warmth of the home. Callie sat at the counter sipping a glass of wine, and Brady stood over the stove top, stirring something in the pot.

"Did you make potato soup?" Skylar asked, hope in every word.

"I did." Brady turned and grinned at her. "I figured since fall is officially here, it's time for the soups to come out."

"Oh, I knew you were my favorite brother."

Brady snorted. "Pull up a seat. We were just talking about the favors, and I could really use a break from that."

A stab of hurt sliced through Skylar's belly, and she bypassed the counter and went straight for the pantry where they kept all the liquor. She needed a good drink first, that was for certain. She made it efficiently and sat next to Callie, her chest tightening at just the thought that they might go back to talking about the wedding.

"Any adventures today?" Brady asked.

Skylar was about to deny it all when she remembered that morning. "Actually...I got to play the hero today."

"Did you?" he asked.

Callie leaned in. "You the hero? I've got to hear this."

"Nothing like what Brady does," Skylar chuckled lightly. "I was just getting to the office when I saw a woman who works on my floor, Laura Finch. She works at Solace. Anyway, she spilled coffee all down herself this morning."

Brady hissed. "She burned herself?"

"Oh my god!" Callie muttered. "She okay?"

"She's fine. She was mostly surprised, I think. When I saw her before I left, she looked fine, and the redness on her chest was gone."

Brady froze instantly. "Her chest?"

Skylar moved her gaze from Callie to Brady and tried to think over what she'd said and why it would cause so much surprise. He was a trained medic, so she knew he'd want to know about Laura's well-being. But that certainly wasn't what had frozen him and caused so much tension.

"Yeah..." Skylar started, "...from the coffee. It was really hot when she spilled it, and this morning it was all red and swollen."

"You saw her chest?" Brady said, slowly this time.

Finally it clicked in Skylar's slow brain. "Oh! Not like that. I lent her my fancy shirt for meeting with clients on the fly because hers was ruined, and she had this big presentation thing or whatever. Anyway, my shirt was lower cut, so when she came out after changing—"

"Oh, stop lying," Callie chimed in. "You were looking at her boobs."

"I wasn't! I swear!" Skylar's cheeks heated with embarrassment, because she had in fact, looked. "She definitely doesn't feel that way about me, and frankly, I don't feel that way about her. She's cold and aloof, and a bit of bitch, honestly."

"Right." Callie took a long sip of her wine. "That's why you mentioned her chest."

Skylar's cheeks heated even more. "That's not why! I knew Brady would be concerned about burns, so I... oh, for fuck's sake."

Callie laughed in a teasing manner. Brady turned back to the soup in the Dutch oven on the stove and stirred it. He said nothing, and she couldn't for the life of her figure out what he was thinking or not saying. *Would he say something different if Callie weren't in the room with them?* That was going to have to change if they were getting married. She didn't appreciate her filtered brother.

Brady spooned up three bowls of potato soup and set it on the counter in front of each of them before making himself a drink. "Do you like her, Sky?"

Skylar's shoulders tensed, the muscle in the back of her neck pulsing. She shook her head slowly as she stared at him directly in the eye. "No. I don't even know her, and I'm just getting over Trina."

"You two broke up over a year ago."

"I know." Skylar frowned into her soup. Since the run-in with Laura that morning, she had managed not to think about Trina for an entire day, which was a surprise. "I know we did."

"Are you still hung up on her?" Callie set her glass down and snagged her spoon from the bowl.

Skylar swallowed hard, not quite sure how to explain it, and she wasn't sure she wanted to do it with Callie in the room, but getting Brady alone wasn't an easy feat lately. Not to mention, if she was going to hold the standards of keeping their relationship as normal as it used to be despite his engagement, she had to follow the same set of rules.

"Like, I think it was a good thing we broke up. It still hurts like hell some days though." She didn't add that it especially hurt when Callie or Brady brought up the wedding. She and Trina had talked about getting married often enough, planning some of the details, and had been about to sign with a venue. Sighing, Skylar moved her spoon around her bowl. "I think I'm just not ready to dive into another relationship like that again."

"You don't have to date with the mentality that you'll be getting married," Callie said.

"I know," Skylar mumbled before taking her first bite of the soup. What would Laura be like as a wife? Surely different than when they'd first met—perhaps even that soft woman Skylar had seen in her office that evening. "I'm not someone who dates or has sex without strings. I like to know who I'm with and that there's an investment in it."

Callie shrugged slightly. "Just know it's an option."

Skylar chose not to answer her. When she looked up at Brady, he eyed her carefully, and she could tell that he understood more of what she wasn't saying than Callie did. Skylar was still hurting over Trina and being in a business relationship with her to some capacity made that far worse because she couldn't escape the reminders, although she was getting better at dealing with that. Laura was nothing more than a pretty woman to gaze at, because some of the fire that came out of her mouth was just as startling as the hurt Skylar still had from Trina.

But Laura clearly did have a different side to her that Skylar had only just begun to crack open. It would make working with Solace far more pleasant if Skylar could manage to keep that line of connection open between them, and it made the possibility of a contract with them all the more palatable.

Shaking her head, Skylar focused on her soup. It was a passing infatuation, nothing more. No, she would find someone to fall in love with, but it wouldn't be Laura, and it wouldn't be anytime soon. She had enough on her plate with Warehouse Thirty-Three getting off the ground and her other businesses that were giving her the revenue enough to be able to do what she wanted full time. And she needed Laura to be interested in her business and what she could do for Solace, not in her body.

"Sky?" Brady's voice broke through her thoughts. When she looked up at him, he continued, "If you like her—"

"I don't," Skylar interrupted. "It was just nice to help her out today. That's what I'm best at, right? Being there when someone needs help."

Brady grinned at her. "All of us Ross' are, aren't we?"

"Damn right." Skylar laughed lightly.

Callie smiled at each of them before she dug into her bowl. The rest of the conversation that night was pleasant, and somehow, they managed to steer clear of all the wedding talk for one entire evening. It was almost bliss. Except what both Callie and Brady had implied wouldn't leave Skylar's mind. The heat that had settled between her legs that morning wouldn't leave either.

Skylar dismissed the thought of a crush as she settled into her bed with her laptop on her thighs. No, that wasn't it. Laura intrigued her because they were so vastly different and yet both women in business. Skylar needed some sort of connection between them so she could make a pitch to work on their marketing. That's all her interest was in the matter.

But if she managed to get another smile from Laura like the one she had received that evening, she wasn't going to stop it. Skylar stared at her open computer screen until the screen went black. The sudden jarring change shocked her into reality. She had work to do in order to meet the deadlines from her clients. She needed to maintain those relationships because she needed the continued business. What she really needed was a contract with Solace, and now that Laura was playing nice with her, this was the perfect opportunity to seize the moment.

Closing her eyes, Skylar focused her mind. *Work.*

She would finish up the necessities for the day, and then she would finish the proposal for Solace. The first thing she would do in the morning would be to call and set up a meeting with Rodney. She could land herself a job if she played her cards right, and she liked the hand she had just been dealt. The odds were in her favor.

CHAPTER
Twelve

THIS TIME LAURA got to the restaurant right when everyone else arrived. She had exciting news to share and wanted everyone to know it. She sat down as they ordered the wine, waving off the attempts to get her a glass as she ordered a whiskey sour to please her palette.

Joni hadn't managed to make it that evening, which Laura was grateful for because she didn't want anyone to put a damper on her good news. Biting her lip, Laura waited until the drinks were brought over before finding her way through the conversation and the excitement bubbling in her chest.

"We're going to update our company."

Camryn glanced at her, and Anna's gaze narrowed.

"You are?" Lynda pressed. "It's about time."

"I know." Laura grinned broadly. "It's taken me this long to convince Rodney to get it done, but we had a meeting yesterday with a new client, and the client was concerned about the fact we're behind in some things. It was the exact push I needed to make my case, and when Rodney and I were at lunch afterward, he agreed."

Energy nearly vibrated her out of the seat with excitement.

She would get to work on the details of it as soon as morning hit because she was going to need all the extra hours to figure out just what they needed. She couldn't wait to hear what her friends thought of it, that she'd finally gotten what she wanted from Rodney and was doing something new.

"That's exciting," Camryn added.

"It really is." Laura finished her drink with a flourish and ordered another one. "It's going to be for the best."

Camryn looked down into her drink, and Laura knew the conversation was about to shift. She'd wanted more praise, more excitement, but since she so rarely asked for it, they probably didn't even know to give it.

Sighing, Camryn changed topics. "I was talking with Haley last night, and she wants to go to UCLA next fall."

Laura furrowed her brow, thanking the waiter when she received her second drink of the night. As much as she might want to pull the conversation back to herself, she allowed it. She didn't need to ask for more from her friends—she knew they would be happy for her in the end. "I thought she wanted to go to CSU."

"She did." Camryn fiddled with the napkin in her lap. "I mean, that's been the plan for the last year, but last night, she dropped the bomb that she doesn't want to stay in Colorado."

Laura swallowed down the cold liquid, marveling at the flavor. She didn't envy any of her friends with kids and figuring out how to launch them into adulthood.

"Parenting during this stage is so hard," Anna commented.

Laura kept her mouth shut, knowing she didn't have the experience to enter into any kind of parenting conversation. And if she did try in any capacity, Anna would smartly shut her down, bringing up the age old hurt she wanted nothing to do with. She was tired of feeling like she was missing something, as though the one dream she could never attain would leave her out of certain circles forever.

She was the only one who didn't have children. Even Rodney

had a kid now, though Laura maintained that Grayson was one of the most spoiled kids around. She'd only met him a couple times, but from the stories Rodney shared, she was pretty sure he was as spoiled as they came.

"I don't know what to do with Teagan. She got the official notice that all her financial aid is being terminated for the upcoming semester."

"She's on probation?" Lynda chimed in.

Anna nodded. "I told her this was going to happen if she didn't start to get her act together, but she's flunking nearly all of her classes."

"She might just not be ready for college," Laura stated quietly, hoping that it wouldn't seem as an attack but as something that might be true. But Anna clearly didn't take it that way with the look Laura received. Shutting up, Laura finished off her second drink just as their food arrived, and she ordered a third.

"She needs to be ready," Anna argued, her words as sharp as the glare in her eyes. Laura shrank into herself.

"I think Laura is on to something." Lynda leaned over the table to get Anna's attention. "Not every kid is ready for life at this same time, and if Teagan isn't ready, then she'll continue to fail. Forcing her into something she doesn't want to do isn't going to make it any easier."

Delight lit within Laura, knowing that she hadn't been wrong even without experience. Though it was clear Anna wasn't going to listen to her without that. At least Lynda backed her up. She had been right, and she could silently cheer in the back of her mind without lording it over Anna.

Camryn agreed. "You need to let Teagan figure it out for herself. You need to let her fail, and you can't be there to catch her."

Conversations like these, which were the majority of them lately, were the reason her loneliness hit her so hard. She was as disconnected from them as she could be, remaining silent while the rest of them talked and not even one of them seemed to notice.

Laura lifted her third drink to her lips, the buzz from the alcohol making her head feel lighter than it should be. That seemed to be more of her go-to lately. She would get drunk while they bitched about their families.

She loved her friends. They'd been a group since college, since before husbands and children, before divorces and aging parents, and still, she couldn't wait to be out of this phase. When they were younger, they'd all asked her when she was going to have children, and she'd never really answered. Privacy and the need for it had gotten the best of her. Still, it was times like these that she really wished she had shared her struggle.

She would be so alone then, cast into her corner of the table with nothing to say that was worth anything. It felt far too much like she was at work with Rodney, where he dismissed her ideas without truly listening to her, not because they weren't worthy ideas but because of their history.

Laura listened absentmindedly as the conversation continued to stay on kids and husbands and ex-husbands. She ate her dinner, but slowly, ordering one more drink before stopping and having only water. She wanted to revel in her excitement after finally getting Rodney to listen to her, and none of these women would allow that to happen. They all had other distractions.

Skylar wouldn't though.

Laura frowned into her drink at that thought. Skylar didn't have the cumbersome histories that her friends did, she was far too young for them, and she was new in her business, so she would understand the excitement over making a leap of progress.

"Laura, are you done?" Camryn startled her out of her reverie.

Everyone stared at her, their plates empty and the waiter leaving in front of her. She raised her chin up and nodded even though she wasn't finished. She had lost too much time lost in her thoughts. They all walked out together, saying their good-byes in the parking lot.

When she was home, Laura made herself another drink and sat down on her couch, shelves of books along each wall that were her pride and joy. She wanted to get a head start on the rebranding, needing to do something with her hands to distract herself from what had happened at dinner. That empty feeling that settled so deeply in her chest wasn't pleasant, and she didn't want to linger in it any longer than necessary.

She pulled over her laptop and some papers, getting to work right away, but that only lasted for a few seconds. Skylar would be happy for her. Her face would light up, her eyes would crin-kle, and those dimples would shine at the edges of her lips. She would understand completely where Laura was coming from and how much of a feat it had been for her to make any headway with Rodney.

Not to mention this was Skylar's area of expertise, so she would be fully on board with Laura utilizing those resources around her. Laura couldn't stop the smile that lingered on her lips. Her friends, while they were lifelong, weren't what she needed just then. She needed someone far more like Skylar, someone who had gumption and drive to create something that was entirely her own.

Laura relaxed her shoulders and crossed one leg under the other as she leaned back on the couch and stared out the window. The drink in her hand was cold, like the dark night outside, but her mind whirred with images of Skylar, how she would respond if Laura had shared that news with her instead. No matter what she would have said it would have been heartfelt and genuine. Skylar was nothing but authentic. Laura wasn't even sure the girl had a lying, deceptive bone in her body.

That might change if she stayed in business long enough to develop a hard exterior, the cunning that it would require to move her way up and make good income. Laura sipped her drink, closed her eyes, and rested her head back. The scent of

Skylar's shampoo reached her senses again, from the moment they had stood so close together. She shifted, suddenly uncomfortable as heat worked its way through her body.

Humming to herself, Laura squeezed her glass a little harder and shifted again. In an instant, her gaze flung open, her eyes wide, and she uncurled from the position she had been seated in. She put her drink down on the table and bit her lip hard.

"Oh."

Her body was hot, not without cause anyway. The point right between her legs clenched and tingled, and that was something she had so rarely experienced in her life that she could count the number of times on two hands. She'd thought it had just been Rodney, that he hadn't been who she wanted, but maybe it was more than that. Maybe...

Laura let that thought trail off, flicking her gaze back down to the half-consumed drink. What was she supposed to do with that? Skylar couldn't possibly be interested in someone like her. She was old and crotchety, and she'd been anything but kind since they'd met.

Guilty, Laura knocked back the rest of her drink and sauntered her way toward her bedroom. Still, it was an interesting thought. She was more like Skylar than people she had known for years. What did that say about her, that she was able to actually connect with someone close to twenty years her junior? Nothing.

Laura stripped off her clothes from the day and snagged the book she left on the nightstand. With the side lamp still on, she tried to read from where she had left off. After trying to read the same sentence for the third time over, she closed the book and left it next to her on the mattress. She was putting more thought into that one interaction than she should. Skylar wouldn't have felt the same way as they'd been tightly squeezed together against the desk, fingers touching her. Laura shivered. Closing her eyes, she pressed her head back into the pillow. She had to stop thinking about Skylar, and she absolutely had to stop making meaning where there was none.

Laura turned on her side and curled around her favorite pillow. She would get an early start in the morning on the rebranding, and she would quit overthinking once she was sober. Until then, she would let sleep take her.

CHAPTER
Thirteen

FROWNING, Skylar stared at her computer screen as she sat in her quiet office, the music coming from the speaker on the corner of her desk light enough that it wouldn't encroach on her work but loud enough to keep her mind focused—mostly. Because Laura was interfering with Skylar's ability to focus. Again.

They hadn't arrived at the same time that morning. In fact, Laura's car hadn't even been in the parking lot when Skylar had gotten there, which was odd because Laura was always there within fifteen minutes to eight in the morning. Skylar hadn't gotten there until closer to ten. She hoped there wasn't something going on that was serious.

Needing a stretch of her legs, Skylar stood up and stepped out into the hallway. Tea sounded like a pleasant idea. The hibiscus she had the night before had been lovely and warming while she'd finished up her work. Skylar stepped down the hall toward the small common area with a kitchen and started the electric kettle for water. Crossing her arms, she stood at the window as she waited for the water to be ready.

She scanned the parking lot, not willing to admit that she was looking for Laura's brown head to pop out of her vehicle.

Her gaze was drawn to a dark SUV driving down the hill toward the building. Skylar's lips curled as soon as she recognized it as Laura's.

Surprisingly, Laura parked far from where she normally did since the parking lot was full already. She carried her briefcase, her hair pulled back into a bun at the nape of her neck, and her shoulders rigid as ever. Skylar smiled at the sight, all the concern that had been roiling in her belly vanishing in an instant.

The kettle clicked off, and Skylar made up her cup. At the last minute, she took the long way around the hall, circling down past Solace's doors to end up right in front of the elevator. It was a risk and something she needed to time well, but as soon as she stepped into the short hallway connecting one side of the building to the other, the doors to the elevator opened and revealed Laura, dark bags under her eyes, her skin pale and ashen. The worry that had vanished picked right up where it left off.

Skylar stayed still, lifting her chin to look Laura directly in the eye. Now she wasn't sure what she was going to say, every cute intro into a conversation vanishing from the tip of her tongue in an instant.

"Good morning," Skylar said, keeping her tone light and bubbly like she always did.

Laura grunted slightly in Skylar's direction before she brushed her way past and headed straight for Solace's door. Skylar smiled widely as soon as Laura vanished inside the offices, even through the concern that threatened. They were back to normal, something Skylar was learning brought her perverse joy. The harder the nut was to crack, the sweeter the insides would be.

Chuckling softly to herself, Skylar finished her circle and sat back down at her desk. She was another hour into work, her tea cold, when there was a knock on her office door. It snicked open, and she furrowed her brow as she turned to see who was disturbing her peace, secretly hoping it would be Laura.

Instead, Skylar was greeted by Rodney Solace. He looked completely ready for business that morning, his suit jacket buttoned over his stomach and his tie tight around his neck. He raised an eyebrow in her direction and shoved his hands into his pockets as the door closed.

"I looked you up, you know."

"Did you?" Skylar swallowed the lump in her throat. He could have found any number of things on her, including some rather stupid social media posts she had made in college when she was young and ignorant of how those things might follow her.

"I did." Rodney moved into the room, uninvited, before lowering himself onto the couch against the far wall. He crossed an ankle over his knee and looked relaxed, as though he had the upper hand, which Skylar supposed he did, since she still had no idea why he was there.

"Find anything interesting?"

"Graduated from Colorado State University, but you're from the east coast."

"Boston area." Skylar raised an eyebrow at him. So far, any of that information could be pulled from her website. She was curious how deep his background on her had run.

"Right. I'm from Jersey."

"Ah." Resisting the urge to cross her arms, Skylar watched him carefully, trying to judge where this conversation was going.

"I called Johannes Press, and I called someone named Trina Wilmouth."

Skylar tensed. He had done his research then, and she wasn't sure if Trina would give her a decent reference or not. She suspected she wouldn't. Skylar wished she'd been able to control her facial expressions better because she suspected Rodney had intentionally dropped the information this way, wanting to know her reaction.

"Is there a reason you were digging into my work history?"

Skylar reached for her cold mug of tea and then left it alone when she realized it wasn't hot.

"I was thinking of hiring you for a job."

"What?" Skylar's eyebrows nearly disappeared into her hairline as she gaped at him. This was too easy, wasn't it? She'd prepared for this possibility, but to have it handed to her without pitching the idea first was unheard of in her experience. "I haven't even given you a proposal or my portfolio."

"I like to do my research before I meet with someone."

"All right, and what did you find?"

"You're innovative, and you do far more than just marketing."

Skylar's chest tightened. She tried not to let her surprise get to her, but she was also pretty sure that was exactly what he wanted. Giving in to it, she shook her head at him. "What else do I do, Mr. Solace?"

"Rodney, please." He grinned at her. "You don't just rebrand companies and leave, you implement the rebranding with an entire marketing plan, and you also revise and restructure companies and set up new business plans."

"I have done that, yes, though most companies only want rebranding. It's usually a mistake not to take the extra step. They aren't looking at the structural issues in the systems already built when they want to reinvent themselves. They're not very agile when it comes to changing with the times." Skylar wasn't about to launch into her entire spiel, but this was at least a good introduction to what she wanted to offer them.

"Right." Rodney tapped his fingers on his knee. "We're not either, but after much discussion with my partner these last few weeks, I think we need a bit more agility."

Skylar pressed her lips together hard, wondering just what Laura had said to him or why he was there. Had she sent him? Was this how they normally worked? Skylar caught her musings and reined them back in. "It's not just about being agile, Mr. Solace. It's about structuring yourselves to become nimble, which includes being agile, but is so much more than that."

"Which is what, exactly?"

Skylar smiled, feeling as though her random preparations into their business hadn't been just an exercise, though if she did land herself a proper proposal, she could dig into their current structure and find exactly where things needed to transition into something new.

"You need to change the culture of the work environment, so you're all working together, not for each other. Get people on board, and they will want to stay because they feel valued. Companies flourish when employees are giving their all. Engaged staff means being able to shift when the market calls for it, and you'll be able to freely move with the changes in culture, economics, and business. You'll also be creating leaders and not just minions who do your bidding."

Rodney narrowed his gaze at her. "That sounds like a bunch of horseshit, honestly."

Skylar laughed and nodded. "Yeah, a lot of people think so. But being nimble in a basic essence is making sure you have curiosity, clarity, agility, and proximity about every aspect of your Solace. It's not quite as simple as that in practice, but in theory, have all those and Solace will thrive and grow beyond your wildest dreams."

Rodney smiled at her, his eyes lighting up, and she knew she had him. He had drunk her tea and liked it. "Well, Ms. Wilmouth and Mr. Johannes disagree with that."

"They would. I was able to take both from floundering businesses to tripling their income within a year. Trina's business has reached a stale level, but by her own admission, she's not putting effort into it like she was. I can't control what you do, Mr. Solace, but if you go all in on my plans, then Solace, Inc will flourish."

"I suspect so."

Skylar stared at him for a brief moment before the words he said hit her. Her eyes widened with surprise. "Would you like me to draw up a proposal, then?"

"I think Ms. Finch would, but I'd prefer you to begin work."

"Excuse me?" Skylar couldn't believe that Laura would be so on board with hiring her, but if Rodney was there, then she must be. Delight filled her, energizing her. With both of them on board, the job should be well worth it in the end.

"Tomorrow."

"You want me to start on this tomorrow?"

"Yes."

"You don't even know what I charge."

Rodney waved his hand in front of him. "It doesn't matter. I know what you charged Mr. Johannes and Ms. Wilmouth, and I assume it'll be a reasonable increase to have your full package deal."

"Forgive me, but business decisions like this always matter when it comes to cost." Skylar narrowed her eyes at him, cocking her head to the side. Instinctively, she knew Laura would never let that one slide. She would have an eye on detail and would want to know figures ahead of time. Where was her opinion in all of this? And for that matter, shouldn't she be a part of this conversation?

Rodney shook his head slowly and leaned forward, both feet planted on the floor as he looked at her seriously. "In this case, it doesn't. Over the course of the last year, we've had numerous clients choose competitors over us because of our lack of updates, and we've had significant turnover in the last five years. Ms. Finch has been begging to update our company for a while now, and after a discussion this week, I've agreed. Now I'm all in. We need the change, Ms. Ross, and I expect you to deliver."

Skylar wanted to shudder at the command in his voice, but she didn't. "You don't want a specific proposal for Solace before signing a contract?"

"My partner would, but based on my research of you, I know you can handle the job. Starting tomorrow."

"Tomorrow, right," Skylar mumbled. Her stomach dropped as the hint in his words hit her. Laura wasn't in on this, at least not yet. She knew about the idea, but she didn't know about Skylar. At least, Skylar suspected as much. But to land herself this contract would boost her entire business to the next level of income she had planned for, before she had hoped to achieve it. To do an entire restructure on their company would force so many issues and conflicts. She was going to be working late nights just to keep up with her other jobs.

"I expect you in at nine. I'll let Laura in on what's happening, and we can have a meeting to discuss the details of your proposal." Rodney stood up, moving toward the door.

Skylar's heart thrummed wildly. She had been right. Laura didn't know anything about this. "So am I hired or am I working to convince you to hire me?"

"Oh, you're hired." Rodney's stare was cold as he gave it to her. "Let me deal with Laura. I know how she works, and I know how to convince her to take this well."

"She won't take it well." Skylar made it a statement, but really it was a question. Based on what she knew of Laura, which wasn't much, there was going to be some serious resistance to the idea of Skylar coming in and changing everything up. She hadn't wanted to land the job this way. She'd wanted Laura fully on board from the beginning, and she'd been well on her way to making that happen, but then this. "Because, Mr. Solace, this will only work if the leaders in the company are on board."

"She's the one who brought the idea to my attention and has been pushing for it from the start."

"Really?" Somehow Skylar doubted that, but until she was able to corner Laura and ask—not that she would get a straight answer anyway—she was going to have to take his word for it. Though she would make a second plan of action if that wasn't the case, which she strongly suspected it wasn't.

"She is, so I imagine she'll take kindly to my hiring you."

"You haven't told her." Skylar sought out the verbal confirmation to what she strongly suspected.

Rodney looked wary at being called out, but he did nod. "I'll tell her now that you've agreed."

"I haven't signed a contract, Mr. Solace." Skylar stayed put, holding tight to whatever little control she had left in the conversation. Rodney had come in there and laid her flat in minutes. Nothing could have prepared her for this.

"We should do that. Email one to Jana and we'll get it signed."

Skylar still couldn't fathom that he was hiring her without looking over a specific project plan for their company and that he didn't even know how much she was going to charge him. But every time she'd brought it up so far, he had brushed it off as if he knew how much. Perhaps he did, though Trina couldn't have given him that information. Mr. Johannes could, and he was her most recent sign-on as a client, so he would have the most up-to-date information on her inner workings. "I'll see you at nine, then."

"Good." Rodney slapped his thighs and stood up. He held out his hand for her.

Skylar stood and took it, shaking on the job she had not been expecting.

"I'll see you in the morning. Oh, and as much as I like this—" he pointed at her outfit "—Laura will insist on professional attire."

Skylar flushed with embarrassment, hating that was her reaction at the same time. "Duly noted, Mr. Solace, and for the record, I don't dress like this for business meetings and certainly not when consulting."

He winked. "I look forward to seeing you."

Skylar sunk into her chair as soon as the door closed. The possibilities that this gave her, the opportunities it could provide were immense, and it brought a smile to her lips. Yet knowing that Laura was left out the loop didn't settle well with her.

What would happen when she walked in there in the morning to work a contract that Laura hadn't been included on?

She could only imagine all hell was going to break loose. She would have to plan to get no work done in the morning at all. Because she'd be damned if she didn't take the chance to do exactly what she had wanted the moment she'd signed the contract at the co-op. She was going to flourish.

CHAPTER
Fourteen

"WE'RE NOT HIRING anyone for this rebranding," Laura stated firmly. "I'll do it."

"Laura..." Rodney sat on the edge of the conference room table, eyeing her over in a way she hadn't seen him do in decades. He was trying to flirt his way out of this. Wincing, Laura crossed her arms and gave him the best glare she could. She wouldn't be turned by his wiles. "We need someone who has the time to do this. You don't because you're helping me run *our* company."

Laura snorted. She did more than half the work when it came to the business, and Rodney knew that well. That was why he was saying what he was saying—he was too afraid she wouldn't have time for both.

"We can hire someone to design us a new logo, but the rest I can easily do."

Rodney shook his head slowly, that sickening smile pulling at his lips. "I hired someone already."

"You didn't." Cold washed through her at the thought. He was going to talk about this being *their* company and then pull something like this? She wanted to feel appalled, but she lingered in anger since it was easier.

"I did. We have a meeting in ten."

"That's why you wanted me in here?" Laura scoffed and walked toward the window. She was being railroaded, and she hated it. She hated him. "You didn't even give me consideration."

"Actually, it's someone you've been speaking with already. I just did the hiring."

Laura turned around, confused. Her stomach dropped. "Who did you hire?"

"A start up."

Anger surged through her entire body. Rodney knew how much she hated startups, how she knew they would fail without the backing of experience. And she had the sinking feeling she knew exactly who he had hired.

"Before you argue with me, she has experience. I checked references and previous jobs."

Laura narrowed her gaze, not sure why he was making such an argument for it unless he knew she wasn't going to like it. "Who did you hire, Rodney?"

"Warehouse Thirty-Three."

Laura tensed, her entire back rigid, and her chest constricting so it was hard to breathe. She hadn't been able to stop thinking about Skylar, she hadn't had a moment's peace since they'd met in the damn elevator all those weeks ago, and last night was...she refused to put words to that. The more she was around Skylar, the more she couldn't think straight, couldn't focus. That day in her office, every elevator ride, every serendipitous meeting in the parking lot. She couldn't put herself in that situation every day for months. She would lose everything she knew about herself if she did, and she was afraid she wouldn't be able to get it back.

"Absolutely not." She meant to sound firm, but her voice wavered.

"This was all your idea. You should be thrilled we're moving forward."

Putting her hand on the conference table so she didn't fall over, Laura shook her head at him. It was the only thing she could think to do because words failed her. Panic took over every corner of her mind to the point that she couldn't think.

"It's done." Rodney stared at her, that blank stare that meant she couldn't argue with him because he had stopped listening. Laura was about to yell when he put his hand up. "And since this was mainly your idea, I want you to work with her. You understand the inner workings of Solace better than anyone, and if you want to keep Hannah and others, then we'll need to be making money soon. This is on you."

Laura cut her hand across the air. "You're dumping all of this on me."

She couldn't believe him. Aside from the audacity of hiring a contractor for major changes to the company without any prior conversation with her, the fact that she was supposed to take on one hundred percent of the work while he did nothing was out of bounds. She wouldn't survive it.

Skylar would eat her alive for breakfast every day. The fantasy of Skylar working at the table in her office was that much closer to being true, but it had to remain that—only a fantasy. They would be stuck together for hours, forced to work in tight confines. They would get to know each other intimately. Laura balked.

"Ms. Ross is due to arrive here in the next few minutes, and I expect you to behave." Rodney's command wasn't lost on her. She knew she had a temper and that she was right on the edge of leaning into it to defend herself.

Laura hated when he talked to her like that, as if she was so incompetent with people that he was constantly cleaning up her messes—which wasn't true.

"She will need access to information, of course. You can handle that, right?"

"And how do you fit into this transition?" Laura barely kept her temper contained.

Rodney raised an eyebrow at her. "I have that funeral today. I expect I can leave the company in your hands for now."

Laura's stomach dropped. She'd forgotten completely about that in her haste to tick him off. Blowing out a breath, she eyed him and tried to decipher his emotions under the surface of everything he was hiding, but she didn't manage to see anything. She wished she could read him, but she'd never been able to do that well. It was how he got away with cheating for so long.

Laura was close to pouting, so she pulled back. "We can always terminate the contract."

"No. Not an option. You wanted to do this rebranding and restructuring, Laura. Now you have the chance. We need a consultant who understands this far better than we do, and you know I always prefer to hire locally."

She was losing the argument quickly and there weren't many other ways she could turn. She supposed she could work with Skylar for a bit, see if she was up to snuff, and if she wasn't, then they could terminate the contract. That would spare her on two fronts—she would save face in front of him, and it would give her limited time with Skylar. Squaring her shoulders, Laura eyed Rodney purposefully. "Fine."

"Good." He nodded at her. "I'm off to the funeral. Please, play nice."

Sneering, Laura watched him leave the conference room. Her head hurt at the prospect of what was about to happen. Swiftly walking to her office, she grabbed the folder on her desk that held all the work she'd done and went right back to the conference room. She checked her watch probably a dozen times in the next few minutes, waiting for Skylar to show up and begin the torture they would no doubt both experience.

To have Skylar in a small room with her, alone, was going to be agony. Skylar's job was to rip apart Solace and lay it bare under the microscope. Solace was Laura's entire life, everything she had built about herself in the last fifteen years had to do with the company. For Skylar to see every facet of Solace, it meant she would see the same of Laura. Shuddering at the thought, Laura drew what remnants of dignity she had left and held onto them tightly.

When she glanced up and saw Skylar being led down the hall by Greta, Laura's breath caught in her throat. She was stunning. Laura never expected Skylar to be dressed like that—professionally. It was like she was a completely different person, no longer the cutesy kid from next door, but the professional woman who was in control of everything. Laura had always just imagined her in yoga pants and a T-shirt or hoodie, but this was something else entirely. Skylar wore slacks, loose ones that billowed around her legs, and a plain white shirt under a blazer that was buttoned across her belly. Her hair was down around her shoulders, soft waves that Laura had never noticed before. Laura's mouth went dry, and she wished she'd brought water into the meeting.

Skylar opened the door to the conference room and stopped short, her lips parting as she looked around the room, finding no one but Laura. "Is Mr. Solace not joining us?"

"No," Laura answered, sitting ramrod straight in her chair and not giving any more information than necessary. It was the only defense she had left since Skylar had undone the rest of them.

Skylar came around the side of the large table and sat in the chair next to Laura, quite unexpectedly. She'd thought Skylar would sit across from her, which would still give each of them space—which Laura desperately needed right now.

"Shall we get started, then?" Skylar asked, settling into the chair.

Laura looked her over, curious as to how this was going to go. Rodney hadn't told her exactly what he'd hired Skylar to do, but it was more than just rebranding, that much Laura had understood. She would have to pull the contract as soon as she got a chance and look it over. Not to mention that she wanted to know exactly how much money they were sinking into this venture.

"So, I need to look at the current structure you have in place, and we need to figure out where the gaps and breaks are so we can work on them."

Laura bristled. They had set up the business twenty years ago, and they weren't floundering, yet.

Skylar kept on speaking, not seeing Laura's defensive reaction. "I'd like to mostly observe this first week and interview some of your employees about work conditions."

"Conditions are stellar," Laura ground out. She would never admit that they weren't, especially not to *this* woman.

Skylar frowned, her hands folding together on the top of the desk, her shoulders squared, and her face set. She was pure control in a way Laura had never seen before. "All due respect, Ms. Finch, you hired me to help with restructuring and marketing. I can't do that if you don't admit there can be some improvements."

Laura's stomach dropped. Skylar had never spoken to her that firmly, and it sent a thrill through her as she raised her gaze to meet Skylar's head on. The shiver that ran through her body wasn't one of pure respect—it was pleasure. Laura clenched her legs together a little tighter under the table and kept her gaze on Skylar's. She wouldn't back down. "There's always room for improvements."

They eyed each other over the table, Laura's stomach doing things she didn't want to acknowledge. This side of Skylar was utterly attractive. The skill and confidence it would take for Skylar to sit next to her and hold her own was astonishing, and Skylar had it in spades. This was her wheelhouse, and Laura was simply along for the ride, one she had willingly stepped onto at some point.

Laura dropped her gaze, her cheeks heating, and sweat pooling at the small of her back unexpectedly. She had to control her own damn self to get through this. She was nearly fifty years old, damn it, not some schoolgirl after her first romantic interest to come her way.

Clearing her throat, Laura made eye contact again and took back what little control she had. "Shall we begin?"

"Yes." Skylar opened her own folder and laid out papers. "I did this based on the preliminary research I've been able to do so far. I'll need a week of intense research in order to finalize a plan."

Laura reached forward and took the top piece of paper. It was a new logo, eye-catching and memorable. Skylar did have design talent. The mockup was already multitudes better than anything Laura had attempted on her own.

Keeping her look as flat as possible, Laura pulled over the next sheet. It was a plan for the new marketing, where they could go to do some paid advertising, but also a plan for getting the rest of the company on board, when to add the new logo to the letterhead, and when to tell the employees what was happening. It was so detailed that Laura couldn't even comprehend it. She'd attempted to find a method to that madness and had all but given up several times. How had Skylar created something like this so quickly?

Impressed, Laura set the sheet down and picked up the next one. This time there was a list of potential training for the company to go through. It ranged from conflict management and transformation to customer service to writing ad copy. Laura dropped it like it burned her fingers and focused on Skylar. This was going to tear Solace apart, and there was no way they needed all of this. It hurt to see all the ways they needed to improve, to have all the desperation that Laura had felt over the years lumped together onto one piece of paper—she should be thankful it was only one.

Finding her voice, Laura turned on Skylar. "You think we're in that dire of a need that we require a complete overhaul?"

"No." Skylar left the papers where Laura had dropped them. "I think you're a company that has survived the last fifteen years, and that you need to be able to thrive into the next twenty or thirty. I'd like to help you accomplish that."

"I don't need your help," Laura couldn't find the gumption she'd had earlier. Staring at all the problems in front of her, she was forced to admit it was more than just marketing to the next generation that was their problem, and she knew this wasn't even half of it. Skylar was going to find every dust bunny they had swept under the rug, and Laura would have no recourse but to let it happen.

Skylar nodded slowly. "If you think that, then I'm wasting my time."

Laura sat completely still, staring down at the papers again and gave as much of an olive branch as she could muster. "We do need to market our company."

"There's no point in marketing something that can't handle the influx of new clients and taxing workload. Are you prepared for when that happens? Do you have the energy to put into those growing pains and a plan in place when they hit?"

Frowning, Laura refused to look up at Skylar's words because she knew she was right. They didn't have anything planned for that, and they needed to. She pulled herself together inch by inch until she could look Skylar dead in the eye. Her voice was gravelly when she spoke, digging deep for the only hope she had at turning Skylar away one more time. "I don't want to work with you."

"May I ask why? You don't know me or my work yet."

Laura paused, choosing her words carefully. "I don't want to work with a startup or a recent college graduate who doesn't know how to do her job well."

Skylar's face washed with pain, her eyes closing, the color draining from her skin. "Wow. Okay, well, I guess here would be another appropriate use of *okay, boomer*, but I suppose that wouldn't be fair either. You're stuck in a rut, Ms. Finch, and I'm here to help you out of it and work up a plan so it doesn't happen again after we get you out of it. If you don't want to work with me, then I'll gladly work with Mr. Solace."

"No," Laura said quickly and effortlessly. She had a suspicion as to why Rodney had hired Skylar, and she wasn't willing to put that to the test and risk Skylar being put in a position that would harm her in any way. Laura would find out soon enough as it was. Pulling over her own file, Laura laid it out on top of Skylar's. "This is the plan we'll follow."

Skylar raised an eyebrow and looked over the papers. Immediately, she turned to Laura and shook her head. "This is a flawed and partial plan. Nowhere does it involve restructuring for growth."

Laura frowned, questioning all the work she had done. It had seemed like a solid start to a plan the night before, but Rodney might have been right when he said she couldn't do it. Despite that, Laura's defenses kicked in. "I know. I hadn't gotten to that part yet."

"That's my job, so you don't have to do it." Skylar looked at her, pleading.

Holding still, Laura took slow and even breaths. She hadn't planned for any restructuring, and she hadn't planned for growth or how they would deal with it when it started to happen, assuming her marketing worked. There wasn't a damn thing she knew about that. Admitting that was one of the hardest things she had to do since filing for divorce. Laura nodded sharply and closed the file she had brought. "What next?"

"I need to know and understand the structure of how you currently function—the official and unofficial channels of communication. I'll need to observe if the structures and protocols in place are actually working. We can look at the rebranding portion if you have time today."

"I don't," Laura replied swiftly. She couldn't bear the thought of spending that much time in one day with Skylar. "I have time Monday after lunch."

"Fine." Skylar gritted her teeth, causing a pang of guilt to slice through Laura's chest. "Then the current structure?"

Laura dragged a blank piece of paper over and began to draw the basics of how their company functioned, who reported to who, and how work made its way from her and Rodney, down the line and then back up for them to check on it. She managed to add in how they had changed from when they'd first started and it was just Rodney and her working together. Skylar didn't seem all that interested in the past, which irked Laura to no end. The past was what had made them, and without it, they wouldn't have the systems in place today. They were just as important as the present.

"There you have it."

"Interesting," Skylar commented before pulling the paper in front of her. "You're structured like a boomer would do it."

That stab of guilt from earlier hit her again, this time digging deeper and twisting. She had never meant to hurt Skylar in the way she obviously had. She softened her tone slightly as she answered, "You can cut the insults."

Skylar grinned as she looked up into Laura's eyes. "I will if you will."

Laura didn't answer directly as she stood up from the table and leaned over it to pull the papers together. "I have actual work to do today."

"Am I free to roam, then?"

"Do whatever you need." Laura grabbed her stuff and stalked out of the conference room to her office. She'd had enough.

CHAPTER
Fifteen

"WHY IS YOUR OFFICE SO COLD?" A shiver ripped down her spine, and Skylar wished she'd brought a sweater. And maybe mittens. It wasn't the first time she had noticed it. It made Laura inaccessible to her employees.

Sitting down in the free chair on the opposite side of Laura's desk, Skylar waited for a response. She had all weekend to input changes into her plan after her one day of observation and finally having a layout of the structure for Solace.

Laura raised her gaze to Skylar's and dropped it immediately, not answering the question. "We have actual work to do today, Ms. Ross."

"That we do." Skylar crossed her legs, the new pair of pants she had bought that weekend scratching at her skin. She should have washed them first. "It's my understanding that I'll primarily be working with you."

"Yes," Laura stated simply, not looking up from the papers strewn about her desk. "And our office begins work at eight. I expect you here then."

Skylar resisted the urge to smile. "I'm a contractor, Ms. Finch, and the hours I work vary depending on what's going on that day."

Laura glared, and Skylar took sweet satisfaction in it. She wasn't going to back down if Laura was going to try to be a bully, and Skylar knew her well enough by now that she understood that was exactly what Laura was doing. Be stiff and firm to get her way—well, that wouldn't work on Skylar. Not when she was trying to do the job she was hired for.

"This week, I'm observing, so you carry on with work as you will, and I'll sit here and try to not be a nuisance."

Laura snorted slightly. "You already are."

Skylar chuckled. "Then I suppose I'm doing my job, Ms. Finch. You haven't answered my question. Why is it freezing?"

"I like it this temperature." Laura's gaze was locked on Skylar's eyes, and a shiver of an entirely different quality ran through her.

"Your hands are frozen. I can see it from here." Skylar kept her tone soft, placating, with a hint of concern in there. She hoped it would be just what was needed to catch Laura's attention instead of her defenses.

Laura immediately looked down at her fingers, then shook her head and went back to work. Skylar wondered what was going on in that brain of hers, the quiet always worrying her more than the quips that were meant to throw her off-kilter.

"Do you mind if I turn it up a few degrees?"

"Yes," Laura replied. "Are you going to do any work, Ms. Ross, or is your entire goal for the day to bother me as I attempt to work?"

Skylar grinned broadly, unable to hold it back any longer. She had known from the start that Laura was going to be the problem child of the company. Staring Laura down and giving her no reason to argue any further, Skylar shrugged slightly. "You're the one who seems to be bothered, not me."

Laura looked stunned, and Skylar took that as a good sign. If she could keep Laura on her toes, then she would better be able to understand her and how she worked, which would give her great insight into the company.

"Also, if everyone starts work at eight, where's Mr. Solace?"

Laura's back went ramrod straight, and she glanced from Skylar to the door that was closed, as if she could see through it to Rodney's office. "He was likely delayed by his child."

Laura's voice was cold, and Skylar suspected it was meant to come off as aloof, but instead it came off as envy. Skylar furrowed her brow when Laura didn't even use Grayson's name—she was sure Laura knew it, and since she remembered just about everything, she wouldn't forget it accidentally. Taking a risk, Skylar cocked her head to the side. "Do you have something against children and families?"

"No. Whatever would make you think that?" Disdain was evident.

"The way you said that." Skylar pointed at her.

A blush rose to Laura's cheeks, and once again, she glanced at the closed door, as if she could use it to escape the onslaught of questions and Skylar herself.

"I didn't mean it that way," Laura's voice softened unexpectedly.

"Do you always get frustrated when employees are late because of family obligations?"

"No." Laura clenched her jaw, the muscles bulging at the sides of her face.

"Only Mr. Solace then?"

Laura's eyes flashed up to meet Skylar's, her glare deepening. Skylar wanted to probe further into that, but she wasn't sure what it would cost her. And she saw the hurt clearly underneath the portrayed anger. Instead, she pulled back on the questioning.

"I'll leave you be and go ask some of the other employees what they think. You have told them what I'm here for?"

"A memo was sent, yes."

"Good." Skylar brushed her hands over her pants and stood up. She took her notebook and pen with her as she went, shutting the door behind her. Laura really was the queen of the building, closed up and holed off from everyone else, but still doing as much work as any one of them.

Skylar would have to make her more accessible throughout the next few months. Shivering as her arms and hands warmed up from sitting in Laura's office for the last thirty minutes, Skylar made her way past Rodney's doors, still closed because he wasn't in yet. As much as Laura needed to be accessible so did Rodney, which meant he would have to be there to be a support. Two problems that had radically different solutions.

Sighing, Skylar wandered and talked most of the day, asking questions and listening to everyone. She took notes that she could hopefully decipher later. She was finding her suspicions about both bosses accurate. No one felt as though they could go to them for advice or to learn more about their positions. Skylar frowned as she finished her day and packed up her bag, which she had left at the front desk. It was going to be a tough restructuring, but it wasn't impossible, so long as she could get the both of them on board with the changes. That was going to be the hard part.

~

"How was the first official day?" Brady asked as he settled dinner onto the counter.

Skylar shrugged and slid onto the stool next to Callie, all the gumption gone from her. That was what she'd been trying to decide her entire drive home and hadn't come to a conclusion other than she'd at least made some progress in understanding Laura. "Rough."

"What happened?" Callie asked, concerned.

"This is going to be a tough job because I'm not sure how the bosses are buying into it yet. I think they don't want to change.

They want the easy solution, which is to slap some marketing over the problem like a Band-Aid."

The look in Laura's eyes that morning when she'd asked if she didn't like children had been hurt pure and simple. The more she thought about it, the more she recognized it. She wished she had prodded a little further, perhaps found the depth of that pain and been able to comfort her about it. Still, she hadn't been sure how well received that would be.

"I could have guessed this was going to be a hard job from a lot of my interactions with her before signing the contract, and I planned for that."

"Oh right..." Callie snickered. "The red breasts."

"Oh god." Skylar smacked her forehead before rolling her eyes. Embarrassment swelled in her, the image of Laura pressed tightly against her and the desk as she smoothed her fingers across the warm fabric of her shirt. Skylar held back the moan, not sure if it was pleasure or annoyance at Callie. "Can't we be done with that yet?"

"No," Callie teased, giggling. "It's too good to pass up."

"Right." Skylar flushed and dove into her dinner, wanting to end that direction of the conversation as swiftly as she could. Still, the feel of Laura's body under her fingertips, warm and so damn touchable. "There is something going on with Laura that I haven't quite figured out yet. Rodney seems to only pop up when needed, but he's not really around."

"Did they fuck once and regret it?" Brady's offhand comment, while sharp to her ears, caused Skylar to tense.

Skylar wrinkled her nose at the thought. It didn't seem to fit the two of them, though interoffice romances were a thing that happened often, and she usually was the one who discovered it. She shouldn't dismiss the idea outright, but she still couldn't see it happening, especially knowing Laura and seeing the two of them interact several times. The intense look Laura had given her when they were in her office that one morning, when she'd finally given in to asking for help, had been anything but what she'd anticipated. It stole her breath away.

"Do you really think that could have happened?" Callie twisted the spaghetti around her fork.

Brady shrugged. "I don't know. But usually when things get funky sex is involved."

Skylar grabbed her plate and pulled it closer to her. "I'm going to finish up some work and eat upstairs. Thanks for cooking."

She didn't even hear the conversation change, so lost in her thoughts about Laura. She kept flipping from the shirt incident to the office that morning, both vulnerable looks in the end, but both so very different from each other. One had been hurt and pain, and Skylar had been so close to touching on it, and the other Skylar was still confused about. The tension between them had been stronger than she expected.

Laura was a beautiful woman, and Skylar was pretty sure that she wouldn't deny that fact. It was one of the first things she had noticed about her, but the quiet tension had been of an entirely different nature than what she was used to. Her heart sped up just remembering the look, the drop of Laura's gaze to her lips, the way she had lingered there before pulling her gaze back up.

Skylar's stomach fluttered. The more she got to know Laura, the more moments like that they had, when Skylar could swear she could see behind the image Laura wanted to portray.

Reaching her bedroom, Skylar put her plate on her night-stand and changed into much more comfortable clothing. She was going to be up late that night catching up on her other contracts after spending the entire day at Solace, but seeing who Laura was once more had been worth it.

The delicate balance Skylar was going to have to walk was hard, but if she could end the contract with Laura on her side and a good reference to boot, it would all be worth it in the end. She could move on to the next job, knowing she had at the very least tried, and somewhere in the middle had given them one hell of a marketing plan. Laura could at least respect that.

Skylar's lips curled up into a smile as she settled on her bed with her laptop next to her and her plate in her hand. She would work for a few more hours and then try to get a good night's rest before she spent the entirety of her next day in the same place she had spent today—thinking about Laura.

Except no matter how hard she tried to sleep, she couldn't. Her mind kept spinning with thoughts of Laura and those fleeting moments Skylar had witnessed. Finally giving up, Skylar got up and took a shower, heading into her personal office for some work before her day truly began.

CHAPTER
Sixteen

ON HER DRIVE back to the office from lunch, Laura could not get Skylar off her mind. In fact, lately all she could do was think about Skylar and working with her. Everything she did in the office upset their routines, which then left Laura reeling to keep her balance.

Everything they had built was being dissected piece by piece, and Laura hadn't anticipated the pain that would cause. She was still willing to work with Skylar—the marketing plans were excellent and matched some of what she had researched. The rest—Laura wasn't so sure about that.

The deeper Skylar dug into why things were the way they were, the more Laura clamped down to defend everything. Still, she knew Skylar was damn close to unraveling it all, and that intensified fear Laura didn't know how to handle. If Skylar were to learn about their divorce, the entire company would know in an instant, and it would ruin any credibility she had with her employees. What would they think of her?

As she got out of her car, Laura grabbed her purse and slung it over her arm. She walked briskly to the building, up the front stairs, and straight to the elevator. She was just about to push the button when she glanced up to find none other than Skylar, staring at her, with a grin on her lips and a light in her eyes that made Laura all the more jealous. She really was a beautiful young woman, and no one could deny her pleasant personality—even if Laura was envious of it most days.

She dragged in a deep breath, ready to keep her façade in place now that she was back from lunch with her friends. It had been a nice respite to be with them, a place where she didn't have to hide as much. Laura raked her gaze over Skylar's form, her slacks and blouse with a cardigan thrown over her shoulders to keep off the chill. Laura resisted the urge to smile at that, but she enjoyed seeing the many different sides of Skylar.

"Did you have a good lunch?" Skylar asked, her tone so damn happy. Oh to be that free again, that young and careless. She'd been there once, but the years had taken it out of her.

Laura swallowed hard, Skylar standing so close to her as unnerving as on that first full day in her office. She lowered her gaze and pursed her lips, trying to focus on something other than her scent, her body, the calm energy she exuded.

The doors slid open, and they stepped inside, Laura pushing the button for the sixth floor. She was immediately shocked back to the first time they had ridden the elevator together. She had been so unpleasant, but then again, she hadn't wanted to see Skylar again after that. Little had she known the elevator would become a meeting place for the two of them.

"I hope your lunch was pleasant," Skylar tried this time. "I had a good lunch with a potential client. I'm hoping they sign with me for the upcoming year."

Worry etched its way into Laura's belly. If Skylar was looking for another client after just signing with them, was she planning on quitting? They had only begun working together. "How will you manage to do your job for us and them?"

Skylar cocked her head at Laura, their gazes meeting. It was so easy to do that, to linger in these silent *in between*s with her. "Do you only work for one client?"

"No." Laura shook her head and raised an eyebrow. That was

a ridiculous question, but her type of work was far different than what Skylar did. They worked for years on the same accounts.

"Exactly." Skylar looked pleased as piss, which only served to irk Laura even further. She never expected the confidence when it came like this. It was sexy as hell.

Pressing her lips together to keep from saying anything she might regret, Laura stared at the bottom of the elevator doors again, watching the lights move from floor to floor. She would give Skylar the out if she wanted it—that way she could also put some room between them even if it wasn't her fault. It would be the perfect solution for both of them and better yet if it was Skylar's decision. "If you don't have enough time to work on our project, we can always terminate so you can take on other clients."

"What?" Skylar reached forward, her fingers touching Laura's arm lightly before pulling back as if she was stung by something. Their eyes locked in the bright fluorescent lights. Skylar shook her head slowly with wide brown eyes. "I never said I couldn't do this job."

Laura's heart thudded wildly, her breath caught in her lungs. She couldn't tear her gaze away. Something inside her didn't want Skylar to take the chance to leave and it clawed desperately at her insides. "If you're looking for other clients—"

"I'm always looking for other clients. It's a good business practice." Skylar gave her a look as if she should know that. She stepped in closer, her hand once again on Laura's forearm. Laura dropped her gaze to the touch, her heart beating so wildly that it was hard to focus on anything.

Laura nodded, words failing her. She was glad when the elevator opened onto their floor and she could make a quick escape, except Skylar hadn't let go of her yet. Focusing on Skylar's lips, the way they were slightly parted, the tension in them and against her arm, Laura found her voice again. "I'd appreciate it, Ms. Ross, if you didn't try to find other clients while working for us."

"I'm a contractor, not an employee, Ms. Finch." Skylar teased her name, like there was some inside joke that Laura was missing. "You can't tell me what to do when it comes to my business."

All of Laura's defenses went up. No one ever dared to talk to her like this, and the fact that Skylar did put her on the edge. She stepped out of the elevator, determined to go to her office. But as soon as she stepped into the hall, she spun around, that anger flaring into the top of her head.

"I'm in the business industry, deciding whether or not businesses and their products or services will succeed or fail." Laura stopped there, realizing far too late into the argument that she hadn't looked at Skylar's numbers in any capacity, so she couldn't determine whether or not she would fail. Heat flared in her cheeks at the ridiculous mistake she had made. Not only that, but they didn't serve any businesses like Skylar's, meaning she didn't even have a base of comparison to begin with. Doubling down, Laura wasn't about to let Skylar in on that fact and be embarrassed. "It is highly likely you will close based on the statistics."

They stood in the hallway, nearly nose to nose. Laura was being antagonistic, and she knew it. But no matter how much she tried, she wasn't able to stop herself. They were having a pleasant conversation until she had gone and bunged it up. She wanted that back, the soft looks and touches, the connection she was longing for. She wanted to be able to give that to Skylar to make it easy, but she'd never been able to do that.

"Can we discuss this in a place not so public?" Skylar asked, her voice light but with an undertone of fear and frustration. Her face had hardened, her beautiful lips thinning. Laura had done her work, although she was guilty about that. She wished she could be someone else, someone who didn't make everyone want to run the opposite direction when they saw her coming.

Laura clenched her jaw, looking Skylar's body over. She was trying to make herself up as one of them—the way she dressed, the way she acted. She would never be one of them. Surely, she would understand that by now. Skylar couldn't let that freedom she still enjoyed be beaten out of her like Laura had. "Absolutely not."

Laura turned on her toes and headed toward Solace's main door. She was done talking with Skylar, and she was done being party to a plan that would undoubtedly fail. She shut the door to Skylar's surprised look, a sense of satisfaction and sharp guilt washing through her. The former was expected, and the latter was unwelcome. She hated herself all the more for it.

As she stood in the office suite's foyer, Laura eyed each of the secretaries right up front. She was finally back in her sanctuary, the one place she could trust to hold her own and fill the role she was supposed to. She knew what to expect here. Saying nothing to them, she made her way to her personal office and sat down heavily.

With her head in her hands, Laura closed her eyes and fell in on herself. She couldn't believe herself—well, she could, but that didn't mean she wanted to or that she liked how she was acting. Skylar needed to get out of her life because it was just too much.

Laura steadied her breathing. She would push Skylar to quit again as soon as the chance came up. She would need to bulk up her plan in order to put it into competition with Skylar's, that way there would be no question that they didn't need her. However, having access to Skylar's preliminary thoughts would help her immensely when trying to fight against her.

Laura straightened up and put her shields back in place. She would take another minute before she started in on her work for the afternoon. She shuddered, trying her best to push the situation in the elevator out of her mind. She shouldn't regret things that she couldn't change.

Rodney opened the door and stood in the doorway, crossing his arms. "Did you have a good lunch?"

"Yes," Laura answered, not bothering to look up at him. He was the last person she wanted to talk to—well, other than Skylar.

"Good. I want you to work with Skylar on this project, Laura. I'm serious. You have enough on your plate as is, and she's going to need help knowing how we function."

Laura frowned and shifted around the papers on her desk so he wouldn't see what she was working on or her unease at the turn in conversation. Unless Skylar had talked to him in the short time it had taken her to get to her office and straighten herself out, there was no reason he should be bringing this up. "I don't understand why you hired her."

"To give you a break. I know you were ready to take this on yourself, but you simply can't. There aren't enough hours in the day, and her time is dedicated to this project, leaving your time free to keep the business moving as it should."

Laura had rarely seen him be so compassionate about her workload. He had done it before, but not in recent memory. It left her confused, but also strangely warm. This was the side of him that she remembered loving, and it was good to see it again. Laura softened her voice when she spoke, "I'm not unused to working extra hours."

"I know." Rodney stepped into the room, shutting the door behind him. He sat down in the chair, leaning forward with his elbows on his knees. They made eye contact over the desk, and Laura softened into his gaze. "You wanted this. Why are you being so resistant to it now?"

Laura paused before answering, wondering if the world was out to get her. She didn't want to admit it, and she certainly wouldn't to him. She couldn't even put the thoughts and feelings into words yet. All she knew was that it made her incredibly uncomfortable. "I told you *I* wanted to do this."

"You did." Rodney's tone dropped. "And I believe that you can, but not now. Not with this new client coming on board and not with the amount of stress you're already under."

That only served to get her back up even more. Laura clenched her teeth to the point it made her jaw ache. Something had him concerned, but he wasn't going to tell her what it was.

Not only that, but she doubted it had anything to do with her. He was the one who couldn't handle stress and putting his feelings on her was something he always seemed to do when he was losing control. She couldn't even form an argument, so she focused back on her work.

"Laura."

"I heard you, and I respectfully disagree. But I can see you won't give me a choice in the matter."

"No, I won't let you work yourself into an early grave."

Laura flicked her gaze up at him and shook her head slowly. "You can leave now."

Rodney's jaw dropped, but he didn't say anything. After a few awkward moments of staring, he stood up and walked away.

As soon as the door was shut, Laura scoffed and threw her pen down on the desk. She stood up and paced around the room, shaking out her hands before she realized suddenly that it was far warmer than usual. Moving to the thermostat, she saw it was two degrees higher than it should be.

"Skylar," she growled before lowering the temperature back down to her preferred sixty-six degrees.

Anger settled into her chest as she plopped into her chair. She could focus on her work, and then she could concentrate on the revisions she wanted to make. That would have to be enough for the day because the rest wasn't something she had the capacity to think about.

CHAPTER
Seventeen

"WHAT CAN I help you with, Ms. Ross?" Rodney set his bag down and unbuttoned his jacket.

She'd waited around for him to come in that morning, waiting longer than she anticipated, but the hour had given her time to formulate more clearly what she wanted to say. She played the conversation over and over again in her head, changing up her responses and his so she could hit every angle possible. But she needed to get her points across.

Skylar eyed him carefully, reminded suddenly of the cold room across the hall and why she was there in the first place. "I need to know what you hired me for."

Rodney frowned and slowed his movements, looking her over before settling into his chair. Skylar refused to sit down. The energy in her body was about to explode, and she struggled to keep it in check in a way that would be productive instead of a mess of intangible emotions.

"What did she do?"

Skylar tensed, staring directly at him. "What?"

"What did Laura do?"

"I..." Skylar wasn't sure how to respond to that. She hadn't anticipated the conversation going this way. Not one scenario she had played out in her mind had gone like this. "She didn't do anything."

"She certainly did, otherwise you wouldn't be in here ready to quit."

"I'm not ready to quit." Though Skylar had been prepared to do just that if nothing was resolved by the end of their conversation.

"You are. I can see it in your eyes." Rodney sighed heavily and stood up, coming around the desk to lean on the edge of it closer to Skylar. "What did she do?"

"It's more what she didn't do."

"Tell me." His voice was so soft and pleading, and Skylar was compelled to go on with her list of complaints.

"She's not letting me do my job."

"Ah." Rodney slumped, as if he was defeated. "I suspected this might happen."

"You what?"

"Laura is...an acquired taste, as I'm sure you've come to realize. She's not exactly easy to work with."

"She's brilliant," Skylar defended, the words slipping past her lips faster than she could attempt to hold them back. She was right in her assessment though. Laura was smarter than anyone in their building, and she wore her intelligence so quietly that no one knew it. Sometimes it seemed as though Laura didn't know it, either.

"She is, but she lacks people skills that would be useful in our business."

Skylar wrinkled her forehead as she eyed him. "Actually, I think part of the issue is how the two of you don't communicate, how you talk about each other to others, and how you talk to each other. There is so much tension in this office. Can't you feel it?"

Rodney's eyes widened.

"I'm serious. If you want me to do my job and to help you resolve some of your issues so you can move into the future, then you need to treat me as though I know how to do my job. Not just Ms. Finch, but you as well. I'm not here to be your pet."

"All right." Rodney put both his hands up. "I hear you. I threw you to the wolf."

"You did." Skylar glared. "And that wasn't fair to me or to her."

"You're right. I apologize for that."

"Thank you." Skylar's nerves settled in her stomach, making it easier to breathe.

"So, what do you need to continue?"

That was a bigger question that she wasn't sure she had an answer for yet. She knew she needed to confront Laura. It would have been easier if Rodney could do it, but she had to be the one to break down that barrier and to stand up for herself. Laura wouldn't respect her otherwise. Still, it wasn't going to be easy, and Skylar was scared to step into that role.

"I need you to back me up, and I need you to have full confidence in my abilities. If that's not the case, then we can terminate the contract right here and now."

"I fully trust you know what you're doing." Rodney stood up and put both hands on Skylar's arms, holding her still. "I wouldn't have hired you if I thought otherwise."

She tensed from being held. It wasn't intimate, but it certainly was a power move, and she recognized it immediately. Holding her ground, Skylar dropped her voice to a soft tone. "But you also need to be willing to change, otherwise there is very little point in my being here."

"I get it. I haven't been around much."

"It's not just that you're not around, Mr. Solace. You're not here for your staff, and that is far more of an issue than you being here for my job."

"Right. Noted." He nodded and smiled at her. His grip on her lightened, and Skylar knew she had made a dent in his thick skull. He finally seemed to get what she was saying.

"Rodney." Laura's icy tones reached them.

Rodney jumped away from Skylar, removing his grasp from her arms in an instant and strolling to his desk. He seemed almost guilty. Skylar noted that reaction and filed it away as she faced the fury in Laura's gaze. *Ah, so Brady and Callie were right.* She was going to need to remember that one and pry it out somehow.

"I expected you here hours ago." Laura directed the comment at Rodney but slid her gaze to Skylar as if she also was being chastised for not showing up on time. Except, again, she kept her own hours, which Laura knew.

"Jennifer needed some help this morning."

Laura pursed her lips but said nothing else. Instead, she stepped out of the room—leaving the door wide open—and went back to her office. Rodney stepped forward, but Skylar put her hand up to stop him. "Let me handle this one. It's about time anyway."

"Are you sure?"

"Yeah." Though Skylar wasn't positive it was the best idea in the world. "Does she yell?"

"Yes."

"Good to know." Skylar purposely shut the door after she exited. Taking the four steps across the hall, she bolstered herself for the battle to come.

She didn't knock. Skylar confidently moved into Laura's office and shut the door behind her, noting the temperature trick she had tried had already been discovered. She would have to do it at slower increments next time. And there would be a next time.

"What do you want?" Laura spat from her desk, not bothering to look up to even see who it was, though Skylar suspected she knew.

"We need to talk."

"If it ends with our working relationship shattered, I anticipate it'll be a blessing."

Skylar let out a single chuckle. "Do you think you control everything in this room?"

"I know I do."

Skylar couldn't believe that she actually thought that. She might want it to be true, but they both knew it wasn't, especially where she was concerned. And it was the perfect opportunity to prove her point. "Then I must really throw you for a loop, considering the number of times you've tried to shut me down and failed."

That got Laura's attention. She slowly raised her chin, looking directly in Skylar's eyes. "Excuse me?"

"You're unpleasant to be around at best, but this isn't anything you don't already know." Skylar put her hands on her hips, finding her strength to keep going. "You also care and give a damn about your employees. You know how I know that?"

Laura clenched her jaw.

"Because you're the one who pushed this rebranding and restructuring, for quite some time I understand. You want this business to thrive, not just for your own gain, but so that you can keep the people you have employed."

"You know nothing about me." Laura stood up slowly.

Skylar restrained her smile so Laura couldn't see it. She was winning this argument already. "I know far more than you think I do."

"Then tell me." Laura stepped around the desk. "Tell me what you think you know."

"I know that you're hurting. I don't know from what." As soon as the words were out of her mouth, she knew they were true.

Laura took slow steps toward her. Skylar was pleased her plan was working so far. She would get Laura on her side, and she would complete the job that had been handed to her.

Skylar softened her tone. "I know that you don't want to see me fail because you think I might be able to do this—something you can't do. And you know that when it happens, it's going to blow the ceiling off Solace in a way even you can't predict."

"You know nothing." Laura's voice was low, anger in each word, and a warning carried in the phrase. "If you knew anything, you would have never accepted this job, and you would have walked out of this building and gone to find a real job."

Skylar's smile faltered. "I have a real job, Ms. Finch."

"You have a business you're attempting to run, one that *will* fail."

Skylar's heart thudded hard as fear found its way into her heart. That was her biggest fear, but she had to believe in herself. She had to believe in all the work she had done in the past and the goals she was working toward. Skylar squared her shoulders, firm in her understanding. "It won't."

Laura's cheeks reddened, the lines in her face hardening. One sharp intake of breath told Skylar this next accusation was going to be the worst yet. "You come in here, and you try to steal my job from under me."

"What?" Skylar furrowed her brow, genuinely confused. "I'm not trying to take your job, Laura."

Laura raised her voice, her words echoing through the room. "You can't have it!"

"Can't have what?" Skylar pushed her, wanting an answer, because she was pretty sure they weren't talking about the job. She kept everything about her demeanor as calm and gentle as possible. Certainly they weren't talking about the business or her position as an actuary—that was something Skylar could never do.

"You can't take this from me."

"Laura," Skylar said softly, choosing to use her first name again in an attempt to break through to her. "I don't want to take *anything* from you."

Laura's chest rose and fell rapidly as she struggled to take deep breaths. Skylar held the moment in tension, not wanting to let the moment go.

"I don't want to take anything from you. I want to help you."

"You can't help me." Laura raised her chin up, locking their eyes together. Was she still talking about the business? Or something else? It didn't feel like they were having the same conversation that they started.

"Not if you don't let me. Since the first day I met you, you have found something wrong with me. I thought we were making progress on that until I was hired to do a job for Solace, and then suddenly that all changed."

Laura's facial expressions didn't shift, and Skylar had no idea how to read her.

"We went right back to where we started. You have treated me poorly since the very moment we met, and I won't stand for it anymore. Either you accept my role in this company, or I'll leave. I'm good—no, great—at my job. I don't have time or energy to waste on this."

"This is ridiculous," Laura muttered, turning around to go back to her desk.

Skylar stayed put, waiting until Laura stopped and looked up at her again. "You haven't answered me."

"I don't believe you asked a question." Laura snatched up her pen and put it to paper, though she didn't write anything.

"What do you want? Do you want to give up or do you want to fight for Solace to survive?"

Laura dropped her pen. Putting both palms on her desk, she stayed poised, ready to stand at any moment. The room sparked with tension between them, and Laura's features were set. Skylar held her ground for an answer because until she got one, she wouldn't be continuing her work. And she knew from experience that Laura took her time to break down her walls.

"Well?"

"I don't have an answer for you." Fear crossed her face in a flash before she dropped her gaze to the table, raising it again with that same look she had before.

"Then you better come up with one quick." Skylar waited

another minute before walking out of Laura's office and down the hall. Rodney glanced at her as she passed, and she nodded at him. Gathering her bag from the conference room, Skylar packed it up and left.

She needed the break as much as Laura did, that was for sure. They both required space and time to think. Skylar had to figure out if she was going to continue to work for Solace even if Laura did come around. The prospect of walking into an office every day to be treated like that wasn't worth it to her. However, if Laura changed...Skylar snorted as she opened the door to her office—that would be the day.

Sitting heavily in her desk chair, Skylar folded her arms on her desktop and rested her forehead on them. That had been one of the hardest things she had ever done, and still she'd managed to do it. She had put the contract on the line in the hopes that she would be able to see it through in the end. The move was risky, but desperate times called for desperate measures. Solace was her make-it-or-break-it, and she was determined to keep the job.

CHAPTER
Eighteen

LAURA PULLED out the reports she hadn't managed to finish the day before when her door slammed open. Jerking with a start, she stared up to find Rodney glowering at her. "What the hell did you do?"

"I don't know what you're talking about." Laura wiggled in her chair and focused on the papers in front of her.

"Uh-uh. I'm not playing this game. I waited all day for you to fix your mistake, and I'm pretty sure you sat here and pouted."

Laura hadn't been able to stop thinking about Skylar and the argument all day. Her work had suffered for it. Hell, her sleep that night had suffered for it. Still, she was determined not to let it bother her this morning. Walking into her office, she had settled into her desk and prepared for the day.

"I did not," Laura said to her desk and not him.

Rodney came forward, slapping his palm onto the papers and pulling them from her view. Laura scowled as she looked up at him.

"What do you want, Rodney?"

"We hired Skylar to do a job for us, and *you* are preventing her from doing her job."

"*You* hired her. Not me."

"You wanted this. Why are you being so damn resistant to it now? Hmm?" Rodney's lips parted, fury in every word.

Laura had had enough of it all. She knew he was close to letting lose on her—she should know, she'd seen it happen enough times. She slowly stood up and leaned over her desk. "You hired her without my consent, without even consulting me."

"So you're taking it out on her? As if she had something to do with it?"

That was a gut punch. Laura straightened her shoulders and stared at him with wide eyes.

"You want to be mad about that, fine. But she doesn't deserve your wrath for something she had nothing to do with, and we need her, Laura. She's better than either of us at this, and that's exactly why we hired her."

Laura had no idea what to say.

"Fix it. Now." Rodney stepped away from her desk. "I'm serious, Laura. She's exactly what you wanted."

Secluded, Laura had no choice but to admit it. She'd thought at first it was just the age thing, but that wasn't the whole of it. Skylar reminded her so much of herself, all those decades ago, before she'd even married Rodney. Even when she'd been so taken with him.

It hurt to think back to those times, a painful twist of her heart and a sick twist of fate. That woman, who she had been, would have never allowed any of this to happen. She was driven and smart, and willing to take so many risks for nothing because she had nothing to lose. Laura snorted at that thought. Her past self had more to lose than her current self.

Now she really had nothing. She'd allowed herself to become so complacent with the status quo, with just going through the motions of work and ignoring anything in her personal life.

But why Skylar? They weren't all that similar. Skylar was so personable, Laura could never claim to be that, even in her early twenties. She'd always been accused of having a stick up her ass.

Heat rushed to her cheeks and then all down her body. She'd been such a damn fool and such an asshole. Who had she allowed herself to become?

Standing slowly, Laura left her office in silence. For once in his life, Rodney was right. She had to do something about this. The walk down the hall was surreal. She'd only been to Skylar's office one other time, and she'd nearly been groveling then as well. Finding the door, Laura hesitated.

She steadied herself before raising her fist in a light knock. The gentle music coming from under the door stopped, and shuffling echoed before the door clicked open. Skylar stood on the other side of the crack, right in the middle as if she was protecting everything inside from Laura and her temper.

Which, Laura supposed, was accurate and right for her to do. Clenching her jaw, Laura eyed Skylar, back in her tight yoga pants and a T-shirt that bore the words "Great Tits" with two birds above. Amusement flashed through her, but she had to contain it.

"Can we talk?"

"I don't know," Skylar answered. "I'm a bit busy with my other contracts."

Laura nodded slightly, dropping her tone to a level that might be considered pleading. "Please."

Skylar gave her a hard stare, and Laura held her breath, waiting to be permitted inside and hoping that she hadn't broken their relationship beyond repair. Seconds ticked by, elongating into what felt like minutes before Skylar pulled open the door to her office suite and held her hand out to allow Laura inside. Relaxing, Laura stepped inside as Skylar shut the door.

"Take a seat if you're staying," Skylar commanded as she plopped onto the couch and pulled one leg up under the other.

Laura glanced at the other side of the small couch and gave in, lowering herself onto it. She turned slightly to face Skylar, unable to look her fully in the eye just yet. They were bathed in silence, and Laura knew it was her own doing. She was going to have to find a way to break it.

"I'm sorry."

"Are you?" Skylar fired back.

Guilt hit Laura hard, twisting in her stomach like a knife. "I am."

"Sorry about what exactly?"

Nodding slightly, Laura dashed her tongue across her lips to try and gather her thoughts. She probably should have done more of that before she left Solace, figured out exactly what she was going to say to Skylar to get her back on board. "Many things."

"Be specific, Ms. Finch."

The name was harsh when Skylar said it, once again putting that barrier up. Laura had made many mistakes in the past few weeks, and she needed to rectify at least some of them.

"Please," she started, "call me Laura."

Skylar's mouth opened in surprise before she caught it. Laura swallowed hard and carefully crossed one leg over the other as she glanced across the room at the far wall and the painting that hung next to the door. That hadn't been there the last time. Narrowing her gaze at it, Laura focused on the colors as they blended together, losing herself in that instead of in the reason she was there in the first place.

"Laura, I have a lot of work to get done."

"Sorry," Laura interrupted. "I'm apologizing for yesterday."

"Right, but what are you apologizing for?"

"Losing my temper. I can't promise it won't happen again, so I won't, but I was out of line yesterday."

Skylar's lips twitched as if she was resisting a smile, and Laura longed to see it, longed to know that she had put that smile on Skylar's face with only a few simple words. She wasn't sure why she wanted that, so she tamped down the thought and moved forward.

"I'm also sorry for not taking your ideas seriously. Rodney..."

Laura wasn't sure she wanted to throw him under the bus, but Skylar deserved to understand some of what had happened and why she was so resistant to working with her. "Rodney shouldn't haven't done this the way he did."

"Ah." Skylar reached out and touched Laura's arm slightly before letting it go. "At some point, you're going to have to explain your relationship with Mr. Solace to me. It's affecting your business."

Laura whipped her head up at that. "What?"

"You two don't communicate well. Sometimes it's on purpose, like this, but mostly from what I've seen, it's not intentional."

The fact Skylar had been able to pick up on what Laura had known since their first year of marriage was amazing. No one else had been able to figure it out that quickly. Greta and Jana had, and they frequently ran interference when the two of them were attempting to work something out.

"I know," Laura answered, her lips pressed together tightly as she waited for the inevitable next observation that Skylar had. "We've tried to work on it throughout the years, but we've never managed to improve. To be fair, I don't think either of us worked very hard on it."

"I suggest you try again, otherwise this entire process is going to be that much more difficult."

"Right." Laura wasn't sure they would ever learn to communicate, but the idea of it was appealing.

"That is..." Skylar paused, crossing her arms over her chest, protecting herself from whatever was about to happen. "...if you want me to continue working for you."

Had Skylar asked that question the day before, Laura would have told her no, but Rodney was right. Laura didn't have the skills nor the time for the change they so desperately needed.

"Yes," Laura said quietly. "Yes, we still want you to work for us."

"We?" Skylar pushed, and Laura knew exactly what answer she was after.

Her lips pulled tight before she caught the smile. "*I* still want you to work for us. This is a project I have fought years for, and it needs to come to fruition."

Skylar grinned, her entire face lighting up, her eyes brightening, her cheeks flushing. She looked so damn happy, and Laura had never been so jealous in her life. She'd gone into the business because it was a safe way to make money and she was good with numbers, but to have passion behind each day of her work life would certainly change everything, wouldn't it? To enjoy her job —Laura stopped that line of thought.

"Here." Skylar stood up and grabbed her computer from the desk. When she sat back down, she was noticeably closer to Laura, their thighs touching as she held the laptop on the tops of them. "Here's what I think will work from your plan."

Laura had to close her eyes against the touch, tingles floating through her. When she finally managed to focus, Skylar had pulled up Laura's ideas that she had clearly input into the computer. It included a new logo, which they had discussed, but also the best way to implement changing all of the marketing like the website and when to put that into effect.

"What's this?" Laura pointed at the computer screen.

"That's some training I think would be good for your employees as well as for you and Rodney to receive."

"What kind of training?"

"Some of it is basic things like customer service, pitching ideas. If you can train employees to create portfolios and make pitches, then that will lessen the burden on yourself and Mr. Solace."

It made sense, but then what would Laura focus on?

"You need to be a manager, not a micromanager."

Laura dragged in a deep breath. She really didn't want to admit that Skylar was right about that one. Giving up control wasn't something Laura did—ever. To do that would leave her flapping in the wind with nothing to hold tight to. She would have nothing to root her in place. "What else?"

"I can design a course on conflict transformation, which I think everyone should take. It'll help communication between you and Mr. Solace. I was also thinking about a party."

"A party?" Laura furrowed her brow.

"Don't you do any kind of parties or celebrations for your teams?"

"No." Laura hadn't ever thought of it. She'd always wanted to go home from work at the end of the day, and she couldn't imagine wanting to stay on and spend more time with her coworkers. She was there to work, nothing else.

"I think it would be a good idea, and it'd be a great place to do the reveal for the new logo and rebranding, to make the company wide announcement about some of the structural changes that are going to happen, and to reassure people that those structural changes don't involve layoffs during the holiday season."

Laura sighed. She hadn't thought of that. She'd never intended to lay anyone off, but it hadn't occurred to her that changes would make people jittery and worried about whether their jobs were on the line. Staring at the computer screen, Laura gave in. "All right. A party."

"A Christmas party, probably a week or two before the actual holiday so we can avoid other parties and family time."

"Understood." Every time Skylar sat down and explained more of the process, Laura was impressed, and this time was no different. Her ideas and organization of them, how to implement them, were stunningly brilliant.

Skylar stopped abruptly, pulling the lid on her computer closed. She settled it onto the floor beside her and then put her elbow on the top of the couch, turning to face Laura full on. Her shirt pulled tight against her breasts, straining the material. Laura gulped, unable to drag her gaze up quickly enough.

"Are you sure you're on board with all this?"

"Yes," her voice wavered on the answer, so she cleared her throat and repeated it. Laura didn't have another choice. If she didn't agree to work with Skylar, then she knew the outcome for Solace. They could hire another consultant, certainly, but that would take time and money, and if they were the ones to break the contract, they would have to pay half of it out. Skylar had made sure of that when she'd written the contract up for them to sign.

"Laura," Skylar cooed. "I want to make sure you're okay with everything."

Laura finally looked into Skylar's eyes, the essence of worry in the gaze, but also the confidence. That certainly fit Skylar far more than the worry. She'd been confident from the moment they had first met on the elevator. But then Skylar's words hit her. The worry wasn't for Skylar, it was for her. She couldn't remember the last time someone had checked in with her, had spent the time to make sure that she was okay with what was happening.

"Are you okay with it?"

"Yes," Laura answered succinctly, her heart pattering away at the care Skylar surrounded her with. It was genuine. "When will you come back to Solace?"

"We need to work on some of these details. Do you have time tomorrow?"

"I'll make the time."

Skylar flashed a beautiful smile, dimples on each cheek and eyes creased. Laura lost her breath, her mouth suddenly dry, and she barely heard Skylar speak. "Tomorrow morning, then."

Laura nodded, not moving to leave just yet. She couldn't figure out what was holding her to that couch in the small office. It wasn't until Skylar shifted to grab her computer and stand that she realized the conversation was over and that she was relaxed. The sensation was so odd to her. Keeping that to herself, Laura stood up and smoothed her hands down her skirt. "I'll let Rodney know."

"Sure thing," Skylar answered, settling the computer back onto her desk. "I have a lot of work to get done today, so I'll see you at nine?"

Laura nodded sharply and walked out the door and into the hallway, a breath of fresh air that she needed. She took her time going back to Solace, coming into the main offices and looking around at her employees for the first time in a long time. They all had their heads down as they focused on their work—or was that only because they knew she was standing there? Prior to Skylar, she never would have considered that as the reason, but it very well may be.

Nodding at Jana, Laura walked directly up to Greta. "I need you to clear my schedule for tomorrow morning. I'll be in a conference with Ms. Ross all morning."

"Yes, Ms. Finch."

Laura nodded at her and walked back toward her office, one last glance over her shoulder at the office behind her. Skylar was right. It wasn't just about putting a pretty picture on their company anymore, they needed to create an environment where her people could thrive, and she would make it happen.

CHAPTER
Nineteen

LAURA ARRIVED at Skylar's office right on time. Skylar expected nothing less than Laura attempting to be perfect, and she smiled as she let Laura in.

"How was your night?" Skylar asked, pulling over the small side table she kept for times like this so they could set the computer on it in order to work. She couldn't wait to get that back room dealt with and organized so she could really have a front office for company and a back office where her chaos could be kept.

"Fine," Laura answered tersely.

Skylar caught her attention and made eye contact. "Somehow, I sense that it wasn't fine at all."

Laura's lips parted in surprise before she acquiesced. "It was a long night of work and catching up and preparing to be gone this morning."

"Understandable. Did you at least sleep good?"

"Sleep well, you mean," Laura corrected.

Skylar wondered if she was even aware she was doing it before the words were out of her mouth. "Sure. Did you?"

"It was adequate."

"Real talker in the morning, aren't you?"

Laura hummed low and stared at the black computer screen. "Are we going to work?"

"Yes." Skylar reached forward and turned the computer on, pulling up the files she had created. "So I started with the logo since I know that's your main concern. These are just preliminary ideas since we haven't really talked about the details yet, but I wanted to let you see them. These are more finalized versions than what've already seen, and one more option."

Skylar opened each image, pulling them up next to each other so they were all on the screen at once. She had her favorite, and she certainly hoped Laura agreed with her that it was the best one for the job, perhaps with a few tweaks here and there.

"I wanted to capitalize on the name Solace, since I think it lends a lot to what the company is doing, but I wanted to make sure it stood out from other logos as well within similar businesses."

"This one." Laura pointed directly to the one on the right corner, the one that was Skylar's favorite. "I'll run it by Rodney when he gets in, but I'm sure he'll be satisfied as well."

"Good, and I can still make changes to it. In fact, there's a few that I want to make, but this is close to the final draft."

Laura nodded sharply. "I'm beginning to realize the logo and marketing is just the external part of what needs to change."

"Right." Skylar leaned back into the couch, wondering exactly where Laura was going with the conversation.

"The internal parts need to happen in order for us to survive."

"Absolutely." Satisfaction swelled in Skylar, happy that she seemed to have finally managed to get the idea through Laura's stubborn wall. "Once we have a plan of action in place, we can begin to implement some of these processes."

"Which ones?"

"Depends on what we're planning on doing."

The knock startled both of them. Skylar glanced at Laura

before standing and finding Greta on the other side of the door. Skylar let her in and stood still.

"Ms. Finch, I apologize, but we need you to return to the office."

"What for?"

"Um..." Greta seemed anxious, which was not something Skylar had ever seen from her before. "He has to stay home today."

"Why?" Laura's word was sharp and ripped through the small space.

"Grayson is sick, and Jennifer has to work today."

Laura shot up from the couch, her shoulders suddenly tense. "Typical."

Greta turned on her heel to leave. "Sorry, it was easier to come find you instead of calling."

Skylar held the door open for Greta, but as soon as Laura got to it, she reached out and touched her arm lightly for a brief second. "Wait a minute, will you?"

Laura held her gaze before slowly turning to Greta and nodding. "I'll be there in a minute."

As soon as Greta was gone, Skylar shut the door again and dragged in a deep breath. "This is what I'm talking about."

"What?" Anger from Laura was always full force.

"Mr. Solace needing to stay home with his sick kid is no reason for you to be this angry unless there's something else going on. Which, if there is, you don't need to tell me about it, but you need to figure it out because all Greta sees is the two of you arguing and saying nasty things behind each other's back."

Laura's mouth opened to speak, and Skylar held her hand up.

"I advise you to give it a second before you respond because I'm not sure either of us wants to hear what's about to come out of your mouth."

Glowering, Laura pursed her lips. She crossed her arms and shifted her stance. Finally, she released her arms and cocked her head at Skylar. "Rodney takes more time off during the year than I do."

"He has a family, and families are pretty demanding. And it's my understanding—but correct me if I'm wrong—that you don't."

Sadness washed through Laura's gaze, but it was so quickly masked that Skylar wasn't sure she'd even seen it. Then it clicked.

"Laura, come sit down for a minute." Skylar led the way back to the couch, and Laura, luckily, followed her. "Don't take this the wrong way, but are you jealous?"

Laura scoffed. "Why would I be jealous of him?"

"Because you want a family." As soon as the words were out of Skylar's mouth, she knew it was the truth. It explained so much of what was going on, of why Laura would be so mad when it didn't seem as though he was pulling his weight.

Laura tensed her jaw and finally looked down at her hands and spoke. Her shoulders sagged, and the feel of the room deflated. Her tone carried the weight of a hundred disappointments. "I was supposed to have a family."

Skylar's heart broke. This was the most vulnerable she had ever seen Laura be, and it was a gift to witness it. She was honored to witness it and wanted to hold it sacred to make sure that Laura didn't run from this gem of a moment.

"You can still have one." Skylar wanted to reach out and touch her again, hold her hand, but held back, unsure.

"Impossible at this point."

"Laura," Skylar pleaded. "Even if you've given up on that dream, you can't keep taking it out on him for living it."

"That's where you're wrong. I can." Laura shifted from open and vulnerable back to the stoic and closed off person that Skylar had first met. Clearly, Skylar had said something that had set it off, but she had no idea what it was. "Do you know why we named our company Solace instead of Solace and Finch or some iteration of that?"

Skylar shook her head, the tension in the room tightening.

"No one knows this. They haven't been around long enough to have known—no one has."

Skylar let Laura talk, feeling that she had a need to get the weight off her chest, to make the confession to someone who would truly listen because Skylar had a feeling that not many people actually did that for her.

"My last name was Solace." Tears pricked in Laura's eyes, but none broke over the brim and fell down her cheek. "I married Rodney almost right out of college."

The air was sucked from Skylar's lungs. This was so much worse than what Brady and Callie had thought. Everything made sense now.

"You said we don't communicate, and I've known that since the year we married. It's only one of many reasons we divorced—the main reason being Jennifer."

"That's Mr. Solace's current wife, right?"

"And former mistress." Laura tightened, staring at some point on the floor in front of her. Skylar gave in, finally, reaching out and wrapping her fingers around Laura's hand and giving her a gentle squeeze to show comfort and solidarity. "The family he has currently is the family that was supposed to be mine."

"And you wanted it, didn't you?" Skylar prodded gently. "You wanted to be a mother."

Her best guess was that Laura still wanted that. Sorrow screamed inside her for the situation, for the conundrum that Laura had found herself in, unable to leave the job and company she had created from the ground up and forced to work with the man who had cheated on her.

Sighing, Skylar squeezed Laura's hand again and then moved away to give her space she would no doubt crave. "Laura, I can't imagine working with my ex like that. When we broke up, I thought it was the end of our business relationship, and it very nearly was. Even a year later and I still struggle with wanting to work on it. I talk to her only by email, when I absolutely have to, and I'm planning on dropping her as a client in the next six months. But you...you have managed to find a way to persevere through all that and more. I've never met someone as strong as you."

"Hardly," Laura answered. Tension filled the air between them as Laura built her walls right back up. As much as Skylar wanted her to stay in this vulnerable state, it wasn't like Laura to linger in the uncomfortable. "I need to get back."

They stood up together, Skylar finally understanding this woman more than she'd ever imagined she would. All she had seen from Laura from the start was someone who was cold, rude, who didn't seem to care about anyone but herself and her business, but now it was so different. Laura had given her the gift of stepping inside her world for a brief moment.

"Laura, please know I'll always be here to listen."

She seemed taken aback by that comment. Her icy blue eyes were red rimmed from the tears she didn't shed, her pale pink lipstick on thin lips was dry, and Skylar truly noted just how hard and upsetting it was to share that bit of information.

"I understand how hard it is. I promise you."

"You're so young, Skylar. How can you possibly understand?" Without another word, Laura walked out and left her alone.

Shattered, Skylar flopped onto her couch. She had been shown a side of Laura that had been devastating to witness. She wasn't simply envious because Rodney was who she was supposed to be with, but she was envious because he had everything she wanted and thought she couldn't have.

Running a hand through her hair, Skylar stared up at the ceiling in her office and sat with everything flowing through her. She hadn't lied when she'd talked about Tina, and in some ways, she felt she owed Laura more of an explanation on that front. Still, it hadn't been the right time for it. But the accusation at the end had taken her off-guard. They'd had a nice connection together, sharing hopes and shattered dreams for a brief moment, only for Laura to throw it back in her face.

Yes, Skylar was young, but that didn't mean she didn't understand the world or that she couldn't be sympathetic. It didn't mean that she didn't come with her own baggage. However, with that confession from Laura, she now had an idea on how to work on some of the issues at Solace and how to get Rodney and Laura to communicate more. That was going to take some extra effort, and of course, Rodney showing up.

Sitting upright, Skylar pulled her computer over and put it on her lap as she leaned against the arm of the couch. She would get to work on some details for training for the company but also details for how she was going to resolve some of that leftover animosity between Rodney and Laura. Everyone felt it, and now Skylar was the only one entrusted with knowing where it stemmed from. She couldn't be more pleased with the progress that was made. Perhaps she could mend a bit of Laura's broken heart in the process.

CHAPTER

Twenty

LAURA HAD to ask for a tray that morning when she'd made her stop for her coffee treat. With her briefcase in one hand and the tray with two coffees in the other, she punched the button to call for the elevator and waited. She'd needed the night to recover from her conversation with Skylar and had seen no other way than to make up for her having to leave.

Instead of walking toward Solace, Laura went straight for Skylar's door, turning the handle and opening it to peek through. She was surprised to find Skylar on a phone call. She was about to back out, but Skylar put her finger up to indicate it wouldn't be much longer and pointed to the couch. Laura stepped inside but didn't sit down, not quite ready to juggle the coffee and her briefcase more than necessary.

She settled the coffee onto the desk and pulled out Skylar's before snagging her own and holding it in both her hands to warm her fingers. Walking to look at the picture on the wall by the door, Laura considered it far more closely this time. Two hands were wrapped together, fingers intertwined. The colors were blocked but vibrant, a perfect rainbow in how they were settled together in order to make the image clear.

"Right. I'll talk to you later, Jaz. Let me know how it goes, okay? Love you. Bye."

Laura turned around when she suspected the phone call was over and pointed at the drink. "For you."

"You brought me coffee?" Skylar raised an eyebrow at Laura before picking up the cup and reading the side of it to see what kind of coffee it was. "Didn't peg you for drinking something flavored."

"I don't particularly care for the flavor of coffee, but I do quite enjoy the caffeine." Laura stayed put, next to the door, ready to escape, but she had gone in there for a specific reason. "Rodney is home again today."

"Oh." Disappointment filled Skylar's gaze, and Laura's stomach clenched at it.

"I thought we could work from my office. I know there will be more distractions as people will be in and out, but I can't be in two places at once."

Skylar stared blankly, as if she was trying to parse out how logistically it would all work.

"I have a table in my office. You can work from there, so you have a bit more control over who's coming and going."

"Don't want to give me Mr. Solace's desk?" Skylar teased.

A flutter ran through Laura at the thought, but she nixed that idea quickly, knowing it wouldn't end well if she did follow it. It never did. "It'll be easier for us to make progress if you're in my office."

"If you say so," Skylar added before standing. She closed her computer and shoved it into her backpack along with her power cord.

Laura watched with rapt attention as she packed everything up and was ready to move exactly where she was needed—something Laura would never manage to do. She'd been stuck in her ways too long to make changes like that now. When she was ready, Laura held the door open for them to walk out and waited for Skylar to lock up. Together they walked the hall to the other side of the building and Solace's front door.

Skylar settled at the small circular table in her office while Laura went to her desk to set up for the day. She'd already warned Greta that this was her plan, and she wanted to make sure she could get forward movement on the projects that were in her queue as well as the rebranding and restructuring. Sitting down, Laura sipped her coffee, glad it was still hot.

"What do you want me to work on first?"

"Structure," Laura answered. "That will take far more effort than implementing a new logo."

"True." Skylar sat in her chair, scooting it up to the table.

Laura hadn't even noticed that she snagged a blazer and pulled it on until then. Suddenly she noticed just how cold it was in the office, although it was likely at her normal temperature.

Skylar bent over her computer, pulling out the papers she had brought and spreading them out on the desk. Laura made a quick decision, walking out of her office to grab a file from Greta, and as she passed the doorway and thermostat, she bumped it up several degrees before coming back into the office.

No one would have to know.

When she was back at her desk, Laura pulled out the files for their major projects. Skylar hummed lightly from her corner, and Laura stopped working. She eyed Skylar carefully, concentrating on whatever work was in front of her. Laura typically worked in silence, but Skylar likely listened to music. It would make sense. Any time Laura had gone into her office there had been music playing—not obnoxiously but softly. Skylar's voice was lovely.

I wonder if she even realizes she's humming.

Saying nothing so as not to distract herself further, Laura went to work on the files in front of her and let Skylar do what she needed until they had to consult each other. They would readily move on from there and onto the next while they could. This setup, with Skylar in her office, might work to their advantage the best, honestly. Laura would have to consider it for the future.

Greta knocked on the door before stepping in. "I'm sorry to interrupt, Ms. Finch."

She carried over a stack of files and set them on Laura's desk. Skylar glanced in Greta's direction, giving her a full smile before focusing back on her work, but the song she had been humming vanished. Laura focused on the files in front of her.

"This is the Johannes file. We closed that project a year ago." Greta's voice was gently compliant.

Skylar's head moved up at that. Laura noted it but didn't comment.

Greta pointed down to the note on top of it. "Mr. Johannes would like you to call him."

"What about?"

"Well, he requested Mr. Solace, but he's indisposed..."

"What did he call about?" Laura's impatience seeped through her words, though she had tried to hide it. She winced and sent a regretful look to Greta.

"I don't know. He just requested a phone call as soon as possible."

"Okay." Laura pulled the file closer to her, effectively dismissing Greta, who took the hint and left. She read the note stapled onto the front of the file.

Skylar rested her chin on her palm and looked over at Laura. "Do you have electronic files?"

"Of course, we do," Laura mumbled.

"Then why don't you use them?"

Laura snapped her gaze up, locking their eyes together. "It's not my preference."

"It saves trees."

"Millennials," Laura cursed under her breath. "Always about saving the trees and the sea life by cutting up those soda rings."

Laura reached for the phone on her desk before she looked up and found Skylar in a fit of laughter at the table. She almost set the phone back on the hook to ask what on earth Skylar found so funny, but instead she ignored her, and dialed Johannes Press.

It took her nearly an hour to end the call, but shockingly, he wanted to work with them again. When she settled the phone on the receiver, Skylar had a knowing smile on her lips.

Laura called the front desk. "Greta, get a contract ready for Mr. Johannes please. The same terms as before but update the dates and the terms for an entire year."

"Understood."

When she hung up, Skylar was still looking at her. "What?"

"Johannes Press was my client early last year, and he was one of the references Mr. Solace called when checking up on me."

Laura tightened her jaw. That had been why Rodney trusted Skylar so much, especially if Johannes had given her a glowing recommendation.

Going back to the work at hand, Laura didn't answer Skylar. Hyper-focusing on the numbers in front of her, Laura lost herself in her work. It wasn't until Skylar's gentle voice coaxed her out of it that she realized how long it had been.

"Ms. Finch, it's lunch time."

Laura blinked several times before glancing at the clock. Most days she worked right through the lunch hour, but Skylar wouldn't know that, and she certainly wouldn't let Laura do it more than once, would she?

"Go on ahead."

"I thought perhaps..." Skylar paused before changing topics. "I'm going to grab some food with my brother. Did you want me to bring you anything back?"

"No. Thank you for the offer, though."

"Right." Skylar left the room quietly, shutting the door behind her.

The quiet was deafening. Laura should have been used to it. She hated the distraction of other people around, but not having Skylar in there after spending all morning working side-by-side in the same room was a stark difference. It unsettled her.

Grabbing her phone, she called Rodney.

"Hey, Laura."

"Why didn't you tell me one of her references was Johannes?"

"Didn't think it mattered. I told you I vetted her."

Laura frowned, leaning back in her desk. "Johannes called this morning wanting to speak with you."

"What did he want?" Rodney sounded slightly concerned, and she could hear the television playing some kid show in the background.

"He wanted to hire us again. This time for a year."

"Wow."

"Yes, wow." Laura ran her thumb across her finger pads. "I think our hiring Skylar had something to do with it. Not just rebranding in general but hiring her specifically."

"I can always ask him."

"No, don't." Laura pulled back. As much as she may want to know the answer to that question, she didn't want to ask it. There was no point beyond satiating her own curiosity. "Will you be in tomorrow?"

Rodney hissed. "Doubtful."

"Will you be able to work from home? It's piling up, especially if Johannes is back with us this quarter."

Silence echoed through the line. Laura glanced out the window, watching Skylar half jog across the parking lot to her vehicle. It was chilly out that day, and she didn't have a warm enough jacket on for it.

"Rodney?"

"We need to find someone else who can step in when we're not available."

You mean when you're not available. Laura shook her head but didn't tear her gaze away from Skylar's retreating form. "I'll talk to Skylar about it, but we don't currently have that in place."

"We don't. I can't leave the house, Laura. Grayson's got the flu."

He could leave if he wanted, long enough to grab his laptop and work and bring it back home, but this was clearly him saying he didn't want to do that. Laura knew she'd be working into the night to make sure they were prepared for the morning. She hated being chained to the office like that.

"I'll ask Henry and Landon to start on EarthBound Exotica's file, and Ines and Diego and take lead on Johannes Press, then."

"Are you sure they're—"

"I can't do it all, Rodney. I'll see you when you're in next." Laura dropped the phone onto the receiver and watched as Skylar pulled out of the parking lot and up the hill toward the road. She'd never said those words out loud to him before, and while it was freeing, the weight of reality settled deeper into her chest. With all the changes Skylar was going to be making, there was going to be more work than she could handle.

It was the folly of micromanaging, and while she'd known that for years, it finally was catching up to her. Laura swallowed the lump in her throat as she stared at all the work in front of her. She couldn't do it all and make necessary changes— including to herself. And that scared her more than letting Skylar take control of the restructure.

CHAPTER
Twenty-One

SKYLAR PULLED into the parking lot, her belly full from lunch and her brain still spinning circles about her new idea. Her lunch with Brady had sparked off ideas galore in her mind with a simple comment from him about work. She was jittery with excitement to explore it.

With her stuff still in Laura's office, she made her way straight to Solace. When she entered, she noticed no one was back from lunch yet. Skylar checked her watch and noted she was a few minutes early.

Walking straight back to Laura's office, she knocked slightly before entering. Laura nodded at her from the desk, and instead of sitting at the table, Skylar moved to the chair opposite Laura and waited until Laura looked up and a brief smile slipped over her lips. Skylar's stomach did something funny, those butterflies working into her chest again. She knew she took too long to say something, but she was surprised to see any kind of happiness at her return.

Skylar found her voice, finally. "I had an idea at lunch."

"A good one, I hope." Laura's full attention was on her, her lips curled still and her eyes perfectly focused.

Skylar flushed, heat in her cheeks. Laura hadn't immediately shut her down like she'd anticipated would happen. Instead, she seemed genuinely interested in what Skylar had to say. It was amazing. "Right now there's this top-down structure, and while it worked for a time, now the goal is to eliminate some of the work that you and Mr. Solace do that others can, right?"

Laura hummed her agreement, still looking Skylar directly in the eye. It was so damn unnerving, but Skylar was determined to push through it, her entire body heating in a different way. Laura's intensity was never in question, but just how far did that intensity go?

"My brother is a firefighter and an EMT, but they work in teams. Each team has structure, sometimes the structures are a bit different based on who's on the team, what day of the week it is, and the teams change up frequently enough so that everyone gets a chance to work with each other."

"Sounds like a lot of disruption," Laura commented absent-mindedly.

"Structured disruption." Skylar's palms sweated lightly, and she wasn't sure if it was because of the ideas swimming around in her brain or Laura's very presence and energy being so focused on her. "It's planned, so it's expected, but also those with person-alities that conflict aren't stuck with each other forever, and those who need to learn more have the opportunities to do so. It gives more responsibility to the leaders to deal with training but also more buy-in for what the company is up to."

Laura still watched her carefully, her lips tightly drawn, her gaze locked on Skylar's face, but she said absolutely nothing. Skylar was failing to get the point across in a way that Laura could see as useful to Solace. She tried again as desperation clawed its way into her heart. This was the perfect solution to all of Solace's problems—it had to be, and she had to believe that it was.

"If one of the leaders of the groups takes on the charge of an entire project, since that's how the work here functions, then they will be able to see it through from beginning to end. Or we can structure it so that they only have one small portion of the process before working with another team to hand it off. That means the different teams also have to work together. This is all before any information gets to you or Mr. Solace, so that when you're checking the work and finalizing, it's pretty much all done instead of trying to fill the gaps where things were missed."

Laura dragged in a deep breath, leaning back in her chair and canting her head to the side with her fingers steepled in front of her. "You had all those thoughts over lunch?"

"Yes?" Skylar hesitated, the question in her voice unexpected. It was a good idea, and she would defend it no matter what Laura said.

Laura raised an eyebrow, her lips playing at a smile again though not fully blossoming into one. "I suppose I should take lunch more often."

Skylar laughed, her eyes crinkling in the corners. "You probably should but for entirely different reasons."

Laura seemed to agree, though that was only because Skylar had to read into the look she received. "I suppose this could work. It would certainly ease up my hours and workload."

"Yes, but what would you do with all that extra time?" Skylar teased. "Find more work to fill the void?"

Laura's lips parted before she snapped them shut, something flashing across her gaze that Skylar couldn't quite read. But she wanted to know what it was, what exactly Laura had been thinking. Taking the energy of the conversation down several notches, Skylar softened her tone.

"What were you thinking just now?"

"It's nothing," Laura answered, her gaze immediately dropping to the top of the desk as shame filled her features.

"Thoughts are never nothing. If you don't want to share, that's okay, but thoughts are never nothing."

Laura took a second before she eyed Skylar carefully. "Who would I go to lunch with? I have a few friends, yes, but they have families and work. I didn't realize how insular my life had become."

Skylar looked at her in wonder. They had gone from brief windows and moments of opening up to Laura going full force into it willingly. She wasn't quite sure which way to go with the conversation, instead choosing to remain quiet and see what else Laura might come up with.

"My friends were asking the other night when I'm going to date again." Laura scoffed. "I haven't dated in fifteen years. Not since..." she trailed off and looked at the closed door, no doubt seeing through it to Rodney's office in her mind's eye. Skylar wondered if Laura realized how often she did that. "I don't want to."

"Then don't," Skylar answered. "I don't know why you think you have to."

"Isn't that what people do? Get married, have a family?"

"Some do." Skylar chose her words carefully. "You don't need a man in your life, or anyone in your life, in order to be happy. But I guess that brings us to the question, are you really happy or have you just accepted that this is the way it is?"

Laura's face pinched, but she seemed to consider Skylar's words. The silence stretched longer and longer, and Skylar feared she had lost control of the conversation by pushing too hard too fast. When Laura spoke, Skylar knew she was right.

"Draw up the plans for the teams and show me how they'll work."

"Right." Disappointment filtered through Skylar, but she should have expected as much. She'd asked a super personal question in the middle of Laura's office. Laura stared at her directly until Skylar shifted to get up, but she did note that Laura wasn't as hardened as she was before. The echo of softness she had seen remained.

Greta opened the door, noise bustling from outside as everyone returned from their lunch break. She set down a few notes for Laura and walked out without saying a word. Skylar went to her seat at the table and turned her computer back on. She really wanted to know the answer, and perhaps more than that, she wanted to know the solution.

They worked separately for the rest of the day. Skylar would have the preliminary setup for the teams idea done by the next day, and she would need to work on some of the marketing promotions when she got home, but she didn't want to stay in Laura's office longer than necessary and bother her more than she had to. She could very easily have worked from her office that day, but the simple request from Laura with a peace offering of coffee had been too much to resist.

She left as soon as five hit, and instead of going to her vehicle and driving home, Skylar went back to her office and set up for more work. Laura had told her not to look for alternative clients, and she would be hard pressed to even find the time to do that with the immense amount of work and time this project was taking. It was as much as she had anticipated, but that still didn't make it easy.

Skylar turned her music on, missing the gentle beats of Bonnie Raitt and The Chicks on her radio while she'd been working all day. Refocused, she grabbed the small bag of snacks stashed in her desk and added to her normal routine since she was back in the comfort of her own office. It was exactly what she had needed. She knew she would have to pitch the restructure plan to Rodney, but at least if she had Laura on her side then he would more likely accept it, wouldn't he?

That was how it should work in a normal company, but if there was anything she had learned, it was that Solace wasn't a normal company. They came with complications that weren't average, including a divorce that was still painful for at least one party, though whether Laura would admit that or not was another question.

Laura had some sort of block. Skylar mulled over that thought. Sharing and being open weren't things that came easily to her. Skylar could recognize that, but in order to be a better manager, supervisor, and business owner, Laura was going to have to find a workaround to that—at least to an extent. That could be something Skylar worked on each day a little at a time.

"You should have left hours ago," Laura's firm voice startled her.

Skylar had been so lost in thought that she hadn't even heard her door open. Spinning around, she stared at Laura, wrapped up in her winter jacket with her briefcase in her hand at her side.

"I did leave hours ago."

"You're still working."

"So were you," Skylar pointed out.

"It's time to go home, Skylar." Laura sounded exhausted, the way she said Skylar's name in that husky voice as if the weight of the world was on her shoulders sent an entirely different kind of shiver through her, one that landed straight in her gut and between her legs. That same intensity Laura had after lunch came rushing back to her, and Skylar recognized it immediately. Except she didn't want to be attracted to Laura, not in that way. It would only end in heartache and a repeat of her problems with Trina.

"Sure. Just uh...let me pack up."

"No. It can stay here for the night."

Skylar cocked her head at Laura, confused as to where this commanding woman had come from, someone who wasn't demanding work but rest. It was such a contradiction to everything Skylar knew about her. Listening, because she didn't want to argue with that soft and weary look, Skylar unfolded her legs from her chair and grabbed her jacket and scarf.

She locked the door, then they walked in silence toward the elevator. Something in the way Laura held herself was different tonight, and Skylar was at a complete loss for what it was. They stood side by side in the elevator as it took them down to the lobby and walked in step toward their vehicles. They reached Laura's car first, and Skylar paused, not quite sure what to say or do.

Laura nodded at her simply as she slid her briefcase into the backseat. "Goodnight, Skylar."

"Night, Laura."

Skylar moved to her car, starting the engine as Laura drove off. Except she couldn't step on the gas, not yet. She stayed in place, watching Laura's taillights vanish into the night, absolutely confused by what had just happened.

CHAPTER
Twenty-Two

"I NEED you to prepare another portfolio and proposal."

Laura tensed. Rodney had been out of the office the entire previous week, and now, supposedly, he had gotten whatever virus Grayson had and was stuck home for the week. "For whom, exactly?"

"Grandeur Associates."

Laura frowned. She didn't remember that name in any conversation they had about potential new clients and work, and they certainly weren't a past client. Laura paused, taking her time before asking another question because she worried what her response would be. "A proposal for what?"

"Their company." Rodney seemed annoyed.

He shouldn't be. She was the one who had dealt with all the drama at the office for the last week, the one who had to run the entire business by herself since he was refusing to work from home, and now he was likely out for another week. *What good is he anyway?*

"I need more information than just their company in order to create a proposal. What exactly are they looking for?"

"I don't know yet."

"Rodney, I can't make a proposal without more details."

"Fine, put together a portfolio. Have Jana do some research on them. I've got to go." He hung up sharply.

Laura growled as she slammed her phone on the receiver harder than necessary, but at least it felt good. Jana was already overwhelmed trying to cover his ass for being gone, and Laura really didn't feel as though she could put any more on her. Which meant once again, Laura was going to be doing his job and working longer hours because of it.

The number of potential clients Rodney had come up with lately was also astounding. She wasn't used to giving out that many proposals in such a short span of time. If they landed all the jobs, they would be in dire straits. Skylar would be right in the end—they weren't prepared for the influx of clients. If they had teams, then she could also train them how to make proposals and follow them up from beginning to end. That idea sounded all the more appealing each second.

Laura ignored Rodney's request all night. She'd have to deal with it another day while she attempted to catch up on everything else. It was nearing nine when she finally couldn't keep her eyes focused on numbers any longer. She packed her briefcase and closed up her office.

As she got to the elevator, she was greeted with Skylar's bubbly smile. Warmth spread through her, a calm and ease she hadn't felt all day. Shifting her briefcase from one hand to the next, Laura nodded in Skylar's direction.

"Ms. Ross."

"Ms. Finch," Skylar answered with a tease in her voice.

"You're leaving late, don't you think?" Laura asked as the elevator doors opened.

Skylar chuckled lightly, stepping inside and hitting the button to take them to the lobby. Laura followed her in. "Hardly later than you."

"Well, I'm old and single. It's my prerogative to work late."

Skylar's eyes glittered with amusement. "I'm not sure I'd call you old, but it is your prerogative. I was actually finalizing some things for Solace for our meeting tomorrow."

Laura's lips parted in surprise. She'd completely forgotten. "Rodney's out sick this week. We'll have to reschedule."

"Still?" Skylar looked concerned. "Is he okay? He must have gotten hit hard with it."

Laura resisted the urge to shrug and ignored the comment. She had her own suspicions as to why he was out for so long. She knew he was sick, but she also knew he didn't handle being sick well. "So far it's him and Grayson who have had it."

"Poor guys."

Poor me, Laura inwardly sighed. She held her hand in front of the elevator door when they parted to allow Skylar to exit first. She then followed her out, walking side by side as they left the building. "It's been a long day."

Skylar raised her eyebrows at the comment. "Has it?"

"Yes." Laura sighed, her hands fisting tightly as the cold air surrounded them. She hit the button to unlock her car and shove her briefcase into the back seat. When she shut the door, she was unnerved to find Skylar still standing right next to her. "Did you need something?"

"Do you want to get a drink?"

"I..." Laura trailed off, her mind thinking overtime as to whether or not she should take advantage of the offer. She'd never done that with an employee before, but Skylar's offer seemed so genuine. And Skylar was a contractor, not an employee. "What for?"

"I get the sense you could use it." Skylar smiled again, her damnable lips curling upward like they always seemed to do. "And honestly, I could, too."

"Could you?"

"And there's this place just up the road from here."

"Bistroporium?" Laura had been there many times over the years, but it'd been a couple since she'd been back.

"Yeah." Skylar hiked her backpack higher on her shoulder. "So...do you want to grab a drink?"

Laura clenched her jaw, the answer on the tip of her tongue. She was holding herself back, unable to reconcile the fact that she thought of Skylar as more than just a contractor. This young woman was far more gregarious than Laura had expected, and she was so intrigued by the subtleties that she had to know more. Raising her gaze as the cold bit at her nose when she breathed in, Laura nodded.

"Meet you there," Skylar said before skittering off to her car.

Laura couldn't even tell her no or change her mind now. She had to go. Hesitating as Skylar got into her car, Laura got behind the wheel and started the engine. It was too cold for the heat to start working by the time they got to the restaurant.

Pulling into the parking lot first, Laura grabbed her keys and her purse. Her stomach was full of knots as she stepped out into the dark and waited for Skylar to pull in next to her. Guilt tugged at her as they went inside, as if she shouldn't be there doing this, but no matter how many times Laura thought it through, she couldn't find a reason why not. They were adults who worked together, and it wasn't like anything was going to happen.

Skylar held the door open for her to walk inside. Immediately, Laura unbuttoned her wool jacket.

"Let's sit in the bar," Skylar said. "We can get food there, too, if we want."

Laura followed Skylar's lead, and they moved to the narrow tables along the windowed wall across from the bar. Skylar sat at one of them, as if she had been there several times already and knew exactly where she was going, which perhaps she had. Laura was so out of touch with life outside of work and her tight circle of friends, that it wouldn't surprise her if Skylar had been there on a date or something.

They ordered drinks, and Skylar ordered an appetizer. Laura declined the offer, not wanting food but a stiff drink. She rested against the metal back of the chair, the rush of what Rodney had pulled on her flooding back into her mind despite her great desire to forget it. She scowled.

"What's wrong?" Skylar asked.

"Nothing important," Laura replied, keeping that information to herself. With as much as she had shared about Rodney and her troubles already, she really didn't want to add more to it than was already there. Skylar eyed her warily but didn't push. "You said you worked on something for us today?"

"I'm not here to talk shop, Laura."

The use of her first name was intentional to set the tone, Laura knew, but still, it sounded odd in the moment. "All right, then what will we talk about?"

Skylar shrugged. "Where did you go to school?"

"I majored in statistics and mathematics at CSU." Laura grabbed her drink as soon as it was set on the table, consuming nearly half of it. It burned down her throat, pooling in her belly and warming it.

"I went to CSU, too."

"It's a good school," Laura answered. "My sister went there as well."

"You have a sister?" Skylar raised an eyebrow.

Laura pursed her lips. "I do. We don't talk much anymore. She got married and moved to Alabama. I did get two nieces out of the deal, though."

"My sister is trying to have a baby." Skylar didn't quite look as happy as she should saying that, but Laura wasn't about to pry any deeper. "I live with my brother since rentals are so expensive."

"I'll drink to that." Laura held her glass up before downing the rest of it. She flagged down the waiter for another. "Rodney and I lived with his mother when we first started Solace. Never again."

"I don't envy you that one."

"She's a pleasant woman, for the most part. But living with a family that isn't yours…" Laura shook her head, leaving the comment there. "In the end, I suppose it was worth it. Gave us the advantage we needed to get the company going."

"And it's still around, so it must have been worth the sacrifice."

"That it was." The alcohol burned its way down Laura's throat.

The more Laura drank, the easier the conversation became. She stopped worrying about being proper and instead focused on sitting with someone who was so willing to listen. It was exactly what she needed that night, even if she withheld how upset she had been all day with Rodney and the amount of stress she had on her shoulders to keep the business running.

When she was on her third or fourth drink, Skylar tried to get her to eat something, even offering some of her appetizer. *It does look good.* But Laura declined. She smiled broadly when she glanced outside, the snow falling in large flakes.

"Skylar, look."

Skylar's cute little gasp as she saw it too was exactly what Laura had hoped for. She loved the first snowfall of the year, and it was amazing that she was still out and able to see it. She found herself grinning as she faced Skylar again. "As much as I hate the cold, winter is my favorite season of the year."

"You hate the cold? I don't believe that."

"Why not?" Laura fired back, leaning forward. "It makes my old bones ache."

Laughing, Skylar pointed a finger at her. "Because you keep your office like a freezer."

"Oh. That." Laura chuckled lightly. "That's to keep people out."

She wrinkled her nose at the fact she let that little tidbit of information spill out into the open. She'd never told anyone that before. She swirled the ice in her glass slowly in front of her, licking her lips. On impulse she ordered another one. If Rodney could be out all week, then she could enjoy herself for one night at least.

"Why would you want to keep people out?" Skylar looked so concerned. *It's adorable.*

"I always want to keep people out, Ms. Ross."

"Don't you have friends?"

"Yes." Laura nodded, though she hadn't had fun with them like this in nearly a decade. Their lives had added such an uncomfortable wedge between them. "There are several women I still get together regularly with from school. We kind of grew up together, you could say."

Skylar flushed, her face taking on a wistful look. "I wish I had friends like that. Most of mine from college moved away after graduation or went on to grad school and made different friends. The rest I lost when my ex and I split."

Laura laid her palm flat on the table, appalled by Skylar's confession. "Sometimes I don't like my friends, so it's not always pleasant business."

"How can you not like your friends?"

Sighing heavily, Laura stared into her empty glass and wished the next one would be there already. "Only sometimes. Anna particularly annoys me. She has everything she could ever want —has had, I should say, because she gets rid of it so frequently."

"And what does she want?"

"Someone to love her," Laura muttered. "Ah!"

Her new drink appeared in front of her, and glee settled into her chest. The liquid was cold against her hot tongue, cooling down her cheeks, but it didn't taste nearly as strong as the last couple she had ordered. She nearly complained but thought better of it, since Skylar was right there.

"Camryn, on the other hand, is a saint. She deserves it, truly. I've never seen a woman put up with so much and remain as rooted in her marriage." Laura took another sip. The snow fell heavier now, and she knew if she didn't get home soon, that it was going to be a long and slow drive. "We should probably head out soon."

"They're closing in fifteen minutes."

"What?" Laura shook her head and stared into Skylar's eyes, trying to read the truth in them. She glanced down at her watch on her wrist, noting it was nearly midnight. *When did that happen?* "So they are."

Laura knocked back her drink and waved the waiter over to pay the entire bill for the night. Skylar had entertained her intoxicated brain long enough. When she looked at what Skylar had in front of her, she noted the soda and empty plate of food, and she had a sinking feeling of where the conversation was going to go next.

"I can call a ride."

"I can just as easily drive you," Skylar countered. "I really don't mind. You can call a ride in the morning to come get your car."

Laura looked out the window again. The snow accumulating on the ground looked like a perfect fluffy pillow. She wished it was. She was so tired. Not just physically but from everything that had been going on lately. She'd needed to let loose, and Skylar had given her the golden opportunity. She should be worried about how relaxed she was, but she'd gotten so used to it when Skylar was around that she couldn't be bothered.

"All right," Laura murmured, unsure why she was agreeing to it. Calling a ride would definitely be better for her sanity in the long run, but Skylar's look was so inviting. Besides, it was just a ride, right?

As they left, Skylar held onto Laura's arm. Heels were not made for snow, and the cold flakes fell into her shoes and melted as soon as they touched her skin. It didn't help that the world was spinning. She held Skylar's hand tightly to make sure she didn't fall down. The cold air was the perfect wake up call, telling her exactly how intoxicated she was, and Skylar was right—she shouldn't be driving home that night.

Laura stared longingly at her car from inside Skylar's. She would have to trust it would be fine there overnight. Cringing, she closed her eyes as they pulled out of the parking lot. She gave directions while Skylar drove, the roads already covered in a blanket of snow. She wished she was young again, able to get out and stand in the center of the road to try and catch snowflakes on her tongue.

Smiling at the thought, Laura turned to Skylar and made brief eye contact before she looked back out the front windshield. She was so unsettled by that look. She could imagine Skylar standing outside with her, hands clasped as they laughed like idiots. But worse yet, Laura wanted that. She wanted the freedom back, the dreams that Skylar had. Heat poured through her body, settling between her legs, the same way it had all those weeks ago, and her nipples hardened as she closed her eyes, Skylar's bright smile coming to mind. Shock ripped through her as soon as the feeling settled, and she refused to relax like that again.

"Thank you." The words still felt foreign in her mouth, though she'd been saying it more often as of late.

"It's no big deal to give you a ride."

"Thank you for listening," Laura corrected.

Skylar's lips formed into a circle, her cheeks bright red with a blush. "Oh, well, you're welcome."

Laura finished giving directions to her condo. Skylar parked outside the front doors to the building. Stepping out of the vehicle, snowflakes kissed her cheeks and eyelashes as Laura gave Skylar one last look. "Talk to Greta in the morning to reschedule that meeting."

"Right," Skylar answered.

Shutting the door, Laura hurried inside more confused than ever about what was happening.

CHAPTER
Twenty-Three

SOLACE WAS BUSY. People moved in and out of their cubicles. They had all stopped eyeing her so warily, as if she was the one who was going to determine whether or not they would be fired. Walking right up to the front desk, Skylar caught Greta's attention. "I'm here for my meeting with Ms. Finch."

"Go right on in."

"Right." Skylar strode past the desk, shoving her hands into her pockets. She'd dressed up that day, even though she technically didn't have to. She knew her way by heart at that point. Rodney's door was still shut and the lights off, but Laura's lights were on. Skylar readied herself for the conversation, knowing Laura might be slightly perturbed by the fact that she hadn't canceled the meeting and was about to waste some of her precious time.

"Ms. Finch?" Skylar knocked as she entered. Her entire purpose that morning was to make sure whatever had been bothering Laura last night was at least somewhat resolved, and she needed sober-Laura for that conversation.

Laura's head shot up, but she looked far paler than she should. Clearly, the alcohol had done a number on her, and she was still recovering, although she was upright. Skylar was glad to see that. Then again, she probably didn't have a choice about calling in sick that day either. Skylar paused at that thought, understanding what pressure Laura must be under and the expectations she put on herself. "What are you doing here?"

"I wanted to check in on you."

Laura wrinkled her nose, something that Skylar had seen her do several times throughout the past few months, and she was glad to see it now. It was a tell that she didn't have all of her defenses up.

"I'm fine. As you can see." Laura raised an eyebrow quickly before tilting her head down to whatever was on her desk.

Skylar sat in the chair across the desk and waited her out. One thing she had learned in their short time together was that Laura took a while to warm up—every time. It was almost like starting from scratch each time they saw each other, but especially after Laura had to show some depth to her humanity.

"I was glad to see you made it in safely this morning. Did you manage to get your car yet?"

Laura eyed her, her gaze flicking to the closed door before back to Skylar. "Not yet. No."

"I can go with you to get it at lunch or after work if you want."

"That *won't* be necessary," Laura stated firmly.

Skylar had suspected as much. The night before, she'd managed to catch Laura in a rare form—vulnerable. It was likely the only reason Laura had agreed to go for drinks.

"Thanksgiving is coming up soon."

"Are you planning another building-wide event for that?"

Skylar smiled. "No, not at all. Though that's not a bad idea. Maybe next year we can do a Thanksgiving feast down in the lobby during lunch one day."

Laura didn't respond, and Skylar hadn't expected her to. Skylar stayed put in the chair across from Laura. She wanted to make one more connection with her, push past these walls she was throwing up far more easily than any other time she'd done it before.

"How are you feeling, really? Because you look like shit."

Laura's lips parted as though she was going to yell at Skylar for being inappropriate, but she stopped herself. Skylar found that interesting, but she wasn't about to comment on it either.

"I feel like shit, thank you." Laura finally answered, her voice low and quiet. "Clearly, too much to drink."

Skylar couldn't stop the satisfaction. She had called that one right. "Do you want me to get you coffee?"

Laura shook her head. "I think consuming anything would be a good idea today."

That was honestly probably what had gotten Laura in so much trouble the night before. "If you want something, let me know and I can get it. That way your minions won't know a thing."

Laura's lips twitched, and Skylar could have sworn she was about to smile.

"Do you want to get dinner tonight?" Skylar asked, not even sure why, but she was desperate to spend more time with Laura and get to know her better and in a more meaningful way.

"No," Laura answered firmly. There was no arguing with it, which Skylar appreciated on one hand, and on the other, she wanted to. She wanted to say there was absolutely every reason to spend more time together. The chance to just be with Laura was addicting, and Skylar was willing to lean into that every opening she got.

"Right," Skylar murmured, not sure where to go with the conversation. "Well, my family is having a big Thanksgiving thing, and you're welcome to come if you want. It'll mostly be me and my brother, Brady, and his fiancée, Callie. My parents are going down to be with my sister Jaz because of..." Skylar trailed off, catching herself. "They're going to Jaz's, so it's just us in town."

"Thank you for the offer, Skylar, but I'll have to decline."

Skylar pulled her lips tightly together in a forced smile. She hadn't known what to expect, but she had wanted Laura to accept the offer. Hurt poured through her, devastation that once again she was being pushed away when all she wanted was—Skylar froze. *Fuck. Shit.* Skylar held in her groan but barely. She looked around Laura's office wildly, needing to escape as fast as possible.

"All right. Well, I mainly just wanted to check in on you and see that you were alive and mostly functioning after last night."

"Rest assured, I am alive and *mostly functioning*." A twinkle lit up Laura's eyes until she focused fully on Skylar.

Being in the full gaze of this woman did something to her insides. Skylar held the look, smiling into Laura's pale face, her hooded eyes, her tired expression. Even being hungover, she was beautiful. Skylar faltered for a moment before she pulled herself together.

"Good." She stood up, her hands trembling. "I'll uh... reschedule the meeting with you and Mr. Solace on my way out."

"See that you do."

~

"Brady!" Skylar called through the house as soon as she burst through the door. She needed to talk to him. Immediately. "Brady!"

"He's at work!" Callie's voice echoed down the hall from the living room.

"Fuck," Skylar mumbled. She toed off her shoes and settled her backpack next to the front door. She hesitated before walking down the hall and finding Callie curled up on the couch. She had to talk to someone, and she couldn't wait for Brady to come home. Even if it was Callie, Skylar needed her.

Sighing, Skylar sat carefully on the edge of the couch cushion and eyed Callie over as she surfed social media on her phone. Callie was so comfortable in the house, as she should be, but over the intervening months Skylar had learned to be more comfortable with her as well. This was her future sister-in-law, someone to be added into the folds of her family and friendships. Skylar took another minute before she dared to interrupt her thoughts. "Got a minute?"

"Sure." Callie put her phone down, pulling the blanket wrapped around her legs a little tighter. "What's up?"

"I uh..." Skylar panicked. How was she supposed to say it out loud and how was she supposed to say it to someone she wasn't sure she fully trusted? "I think I like Laura."

"Oh fuck," Callie whispered. She looked around the living room, like she was going to find someone else there, like she was going to find Brady to save her from this conversation. "We need booze for this."

Immediately, Callie got up and walked to the kitchen. Skylar stayed settled on the couch, startled by how easy that confession had been, by how readily she fell into Callie's safety. It was probably easier than saying it to Brady, who would go into big brother mode and shut her down. Callie came back with two mixed drinks, and Skylar didn't even ask what it was as she sipped.

Callie's lips parted as if she was going to speak and then stopped. Skylar hadn't realized she would be so wary to do this either, but neither had put themselves on the line before now. Callie tried again, finding her voice. "Tell me everything."

"I don't know what there is to tell. I just figured it out today, and I...normally I would talk to Brady—"

"But he's at work." Callie nodded, her face reflecting complete understanding. "I hate when he works such long hours sometimes. How did you figure it out?"

"We went out for drinks last night. It's the first time we've spent any time together outside of her offices, but I don't know. It hit me this morning. I went over there to check on her because she was pretty drunk last night, and it hit me that the only reason I was doing that instead of calling or texting was because I want more between us."

"Really?" Callie looked so excited.

"Yeah. It's the first time I've felt this way since Trina." It scared her because the situation was so similar in some ways. She and Laura worked together, and this was, yet again, another contract she couldn't afford to lose.

Callie frowned into her drink, spinning it between her fingers before she finally said something. "Is Trina the reason you suddenly started hating me?"

"What?" Shock didn't even cover what she felt in that moment. "I don't hate you."

"Sure you do. You barely look at me or talk to me."

Guilt wracked through her. She hadn't known it was that obvious, or that the reason why could be so distorted. "All you do is talk about the wedding, and yeah, Trina has something to do with that part, but I don't hate you."

"We used to be friends."

Skylar's lips parted before she smartly shut them. They had hung out a few times, but she wouldn't have considered Callie one of her close friends by any means. She had always been her brother's girlfriend, most recently fiancée, and that meant that they had a certain kind of relationship. Did she want more than that?

"I mean, we used to hang out and stuff and talk, and well... that stopped."

Skylar ran her fingers through her hair, running through the conversation very quickly in her head before she said the words out loud. "We used to talk, but then everything became about the wedding. Trina and I had talked—at length—about getting married, and it just... It hurts to talk to you and Brady about it. It hurts a lot. I can't help thinking about what might've been, I guess."

"Skylar, I'm so sorry. I didn't realize." Callie's eyes softened, her face easing from the tension that had taken root there.

Skylar shook her head, tears stinging her eyes. She hadn't wanted to talk about this. She'd only wanted some advice on what to do with her crush on Laura, and instead they were finally breaking down the wall that had been between them for the better part of the last six months.

"You should have told me."

"I should have. I'm sorry."

They fell into a comfortable silence, one they hadn't found for several months, and it felt so good. Skylar sipped her drink until it was nearly empty, already knowing that she wouldn't refill it.

"You should take her on a date."

Skylar snorted loudly, nearly choking on the last sip of alcohol. "Excuse me?"

"Take her on a date—woo her if she's someone you want to be with."

"We're so different from each other. There's got to be at least twelve years between us. She's all business and I'm all comfort."

"Sky," Callie interrupted. "*Opposites attract* is a thing for a reason. You know that."

Frowning, Skylar buried her feet under the edge of Callie's blanket. "I guess."

"Do you want to date her?"

"I don't know. I did ask her to dinner earlier today, and she told me no."

"Did you ask her to dinner or on a date?"

Skylar shook her head. "Dinner. I don't even know if she likes me. I mean...she was married to a man, so that may mean she isn't into women. This could just be a crush that will be unrequited for the rest of the ages."

Callie laughed lightly. "What are you going to do to find that out?"

Groaning, Skylar sank into the couch. Having the realization surely was enough for one day without navigating all of the complications, wasn't it? And she would figure them out, because if there was any chance, Skylar wasn't going to let it go to waste. "Do I have to?"

"If you want something to be different than it currently is, you do."

"Maybe tomorrow." Though she knew she would be thinking about it all night. Her crush on Laura wasn't simple, and it was something she was compelled to explore, even if it only got Laura to open up a little more in the process. She had a few weeks left until the end of her contract, and by Christmas, she should know whether or not there was more between them and enough to pursue.

CHAPTER
Twenty-Four

LAURA FOUND herself at home with her favorite drink in her hand and the TV news on in the background. She'd sworn herself off work that day, and since no one was in the office, she might actually stand a chance at accomplishing that.

The first text that came through was from Rodney. Frowning, she read the message and couldn't stop from laughing out loud. Rodney's mother, while not someone she ever wanted to live with again, was also someone she admired. She pulled no punches when it came to her son and his choices in life, and she had been one of the few people who had told him he was in the wrong when Laura had found him cheating.

Today, however, she was apparently putting on her best show of the year, making snarky comments about Jennifer's cooking. Laura answered, even though she knew she'd regret it later. She could blame it on alcohol and loneliness when she thought about it tomorrow.

The entire day went that way, back-and-forth texts between her and her ex-husband about his personal life—something he rarely let anyone in on. Laura was just about to shoot another text back about the dry turkey when the intercom buzzed.

Confused, she stood up and walked to the door, pressing the button.

"Hello?"

"Hi, Ms. Finch, it's Skylar. Will you let me up?"

Laura's stomach fluttered, and before she knew what she was doing, she hit the button to buzz Skylar into the building. She stepped away from the door before looking around her small condo, wondering what the hell Skylar would be doing there without any warning.

Opening the door, she stood and waited for Skylar to round the corner from the elevator. It had been a week since they had seen each other last. Rodney was back in the office, but they didn't have any spare time to meet with her until the following week, and Laura had been so caught up in the new proposal that she hadn't had time to stop by and find Skylar either.

The elevator dinged, and Laura's heart quickened at the thought that it wouldn't be long until she saw Skylar again, until that bubbly and contagious smile was in her presence. She straightened her back but kept resting against the frame of the door with her drink in her hand, poised perfectly. She hoped it would be an image that would make Skylar stutter.

Sure enough, Skylar stumbled in her step as she came around the corner, a large tote bag in one hand. Laura cocked her head to the side, still not moving as she waited for Skylar to get closer. She knew when Skylar raked her gaze down and up her body that it was more than a simple glance. She'd seen many men do it throughout her life, but this time, she took great satisfaction in it happening. She and Skylar locked gazes, and Skylar blushed furiously.

"What are you doing here?" Laura asked, curiosity getting the best of her.

"I brought leftovers." Skylar lifted the tote bag. "My brother cooked, so it's all edible. I promise. He even made deviled eggs."

"Oh, do share." Laura straightened and stepped out of the doorway so Skylar could come inside.

Skylar put the bag onto the small dining table that Laura had bought on a whim. She started pulling out containers of food and stacking them. Laura touched her arm lightly.

"Want a drink?"

"Sure. Anything but wine."

Laura wrinkled her nose. "I despise wine, so I don't have any."

"I don't like it either," Skylar added, humor in her eyes. "Never thought I'd find someone else who didn't care for it as much as I don't."

Laura had thought the same thing many times throughout her life and was surprised to find that in Skylar. It was comforting to know she wasn't the only one. Humming, Laura padded barefoot to her kitchen and mixed up a simple drink. Bringing it back, she stared at all the containers on the table. "Did you bring the entire meal?"

"A little bit of everything. We weren't eating it anymore. Plates?"

Laura left her drink and fetched plates and silverware. Together, they filled plates with food and went to sit at the couch, the television still playing the news station on the far wall. The food was delicious, and Laura had to hand it to Skylar's brother for the meal. She would eat anything he made in the future.

"You could have come over and eaten with us if you wanted."

"I didn't," Laura replied, biting into a deviled egg. They were one of her favorite treats at family dinners growing up, but she'd never shared that with Skylar. She wondered exactly what traditions Skylar had compared the ones Laura used to hold to. "You've rescheduled your meeting with us, right?"

"No work talk today. It's a holiday." Skylar filled her mouth with a bite of stuffing and cranberry sauce.

Laura wasn't quite sure what to say to that, not sure how to have a conversation without work involved when it came to Skylar. She breathed easy knowing the expectation of deep conversation wasn't there. Never had Skylar pushed for more than Laura was willing to give, something she appreciated immensely.

"Did you watch the parade this morning?" Laura asked out of nowhere.

"I used to when I was a kid. We don't have television other than streaming now, so no, I didn't watch it this morning. Instead, Brady made me help him slice potatoes for that dish." Skylar pointed with her fork to the scalloped potatoes on Laura's plate.

"Well, they're delicious." To prove her point, she stabbed some more and took another bite. Everything really was excellent and reminded her of the large meals they'd had when she was growing up. She'd always wanted that with her own family, the comfort and warmth that these kinds of meals would bring along with the chaos.

"Did you watch it?"

"Yes," Laura whispered as if it was a secret. "Then I called my sister and mom to wish them a Happy Thanksgiving. Apparently, the girls don't watch the parade anymore either. Must be a generational thing."

"Probably is," Skylar commented, eyeing Laura. "You didn't want to go home for the holiday?"

"I wasn't invited." Laura moved her food around her plate suddenly, her stomach twisting at the thought. She probably would have been, except they would have known she'd decline the offer, so they hadn't even bothered. Their mother went to her sister's for the holidays since she was the one with kids and that was certainly more exciting than a woman about to turn fifty. "It's fine, really. I understand."

"How could you?" Skylar prodded. "They're your family."

"You said your parents went to your sister's."

"Yeah, but Jaz..." Skylar trailed off as if she was debating whether to continue or not. "Jaz had a miscarriage a few weeks ago. She's been struggling to get pregnant for years, and this is her last in a series of miscarriages. They went to be with her because she needed their support."

"Oh. I'm so sorry." Laura reached out for Skylar's hand and gave her fingers a squeeze. The touch sent a heat wave through Laura's body.

Skylar shrugged, no doubt trying to ease the emotion off her shoulders, but Laura didn't want to let her get away with it that easily. She was about to say something when her phone chimed loudly. Sending Skylar an apologetic glance, she grabbed it, seeing Rodney's name light up the screen. She almost read it but decided against it and set the phone down again.

"It's just Rodney."

"If you need to answer it, that's fine."

Laura shook her head and flashed a conspiratorial smile. "He's complaining about his mom."

"Really?"

"He isn't her favorite child, and let's just say after she found out that he was cheating on me, she made him miserable for a while."

Skylar laughed, the sound billowing out of her pleasantly. Laura loved how genuine it was. "Sounds like you had more of a friend in her than you thought."

"You're probably right about that."

"Would you consider going to your sister's for Christmas?"

Laura sighed heavily, setting her mostly empty plate onto the coffee table in front of them. It was a tempting thought, but it wasn't the family she wanted to be around. "Likely no, not this year."

"Why not?" Skylar set her plate down but kept her drink in her hand. "It sounds like you'd be welcome."

"I would be. I just..." Laura stopped, not quite sure how to answer that question and put into words what she hadn't ever before. "I just never thought about going is all."

"What will you do for Christmas then?"

"Christmas is for families." Laura grabbed the plates and

214 ADRIAN J. SMITH

moved to the kitchen, ready to rinse them and put them in the dishwasher. Skylar following wasn't part of that plan. When she turned the water off, she was surprised to find Skylar leaning against the wall.

"I'm pretty sure you have a family."

"Not that kind of family," Laura muttered, closing up the dishwasher and putting her hands on her hips. She needed another drink. They both knew what kind of family she was talking about—Christmas was for kids. She didn't have any kids, so that meant Christmas wasn't going to be a priority for her and she wasn't going to be a priority in anyone else's life.

"Laura, Christmas is for all kinds of families."

Just the thought made Laura uncomfortable. Skylar didn't understand, and she wasn't explaining it well, mostly because she didn't want to bare that part of her soul yet. Laura stepped around her to retrieve her empty drink glass. When she returned, she nodded at Skylar's. "Want another?"

"One more would be good."

When she handed the new drink over, their fingers brushed. Skylar's were so warm compared to hers, and Laura held the tension until she had to break it. "Will you be in the office tomorrow?"

"No," Skylar replied. "You?"

Laura shook her head. "We give everyone the full four days off, if it's possible."

"Do you take the full four days?"

Oh, she's getting smart. Laura leaned against the counter in her kitchen, eyeing Skylar over. She was back to her regular outfit of yoga pants and a T-shirt. These pants had a blue stripe down the side from her hip to ankle, and the shirt read "Be Kind. Be Grateful. Be Thankful. Be Yourself."

Laura slowly moved her gaze from Skylar's chest to her face, the rounded curves of her cheeks, the depths in her eyes, and her brown hair tousled around her shoulders. She was the quintessential millennial, there was no denying it, and the blush that reached Skylar's cheeks was the reaction Laura had expected and wanted. She was willing to bet that Skylar liked her, and while that made her feel powerful, it wasn't something she was going to play with either.

Skylar might have a crush, but Laura didn't. And the more Laura got to know her, the more she liked Skylar exactly as she was—young, brave, candid, and brilliant. She had a head for business that rivaled Laura's own, but they put those brains to use in very different ways.

She took a sip of her drink, keeping her gaze locked onto Skylar's face, wondering just how long Skylar would hold the look. She was fine with taking her time and holding the tension —in fact, it was something Laura enjoyed doing in many different environments.

"Laura?"

"Hmm?"

"You didn't answer my question."

"Which question?" Laura took another sip, trying to play it off as sophisticated that she'd completely forgotten what Skylar had asked in her own distraction.

"Do you take the full four days off?"

"Ah." Laura set her drink on the counter. "No."

"Why does that *not* surprise me?" Skylar chuckled lightly.

"Because you know me better than you think you should." Laura couldn't stop looking at her. No matter how hard she tried to look away, her eyes were riveted to Skylar. "Where will you go for Christmas?"

"I think we're all going to Jaz's, but I'm not sure. We might all end up here if Brady has to work."

"Your sister?"

Skylar nodded.

"Where does she live?"

"The Springs. They've got a good fertility clinic there, so Bryant and she moved there when they started IVF."

Laura's heart raced, cold washing through her. She knew

those halls intimately well. Laura tightened her fingers around her drink and stood up straight, making her way back to the living area. She spoke as she passed Skylar, "I know it well. It's where Rodney and Jennifer met."

"What?" Skylar raced to catch up. "Why was he there?"

"*We* were there for some testing." Laura sat back on the couch, folding her legs under her body and keeping her drink in her hand. "So was Jennifer. Though at the time she was looking into surrogacy for her sister, I believe."

Laura played with the edge of the Afghan that hung over the back of the couch, the soft fibers from the fringe against her fingers distracting her from what she was really feeling and what she didn't want to share.

"I'm so sorry, Laura." Skylar's voice was gentle. "I know how hard it is to go through that process."

Laura nodded, compelled to share even more by the tenderness and care Skylar offered. "I have unexplained infertility—although now it's probably explained. I'm turning fifty in a few weeks."

"Your birthday is in a few weeks?"

Laura nodded. "The thirteenth."

"Almost a Christmas baby."

"Almost, but not quite." Laura finished her drink and put it on the table. She wasn't driving anywhere that night, but she didn't want to risk being drunk in front of Skylar again. "Now I'm just too old to have babies, so I gave up on that dream."

Admitting that was the hardest thing Laura had ever done. She'd never said those words out loud, not even to herself. Her heart shattered around them, tears prickling her eyes, but she was able to hold it all in. She stared at the floor between them, unable to drag her herself out of the pit she found herself in.

Skylar stayed silent, thankfully.

"I'm sure you have to be getting back soon," Laura's voice was so quiet after the loud silence between them.

"Sure." Skylar set her drink down, recognizing the dismissal for what it was. "I'm glad you liked dinner. I'll let Brady know."

"Please do. It was excellent, especially the scalloped potatoes."

Skylar hesitated at the door after gathering everything she had brought. Laura sucked in a breath and looked her in the eye, unsure of what to expect. Skylar snagged her hand, lacing their fingers together. She tugged Laura a little closer and whispered, "Thank you for being willing to share that with me."

Laura shuddered. She stepped away, unsure of what to say or do. Skylar let go of her hand after a gentle squeeze and left her condo. Laura was cast into the shadow of being alone, but unlike hours ago, she didn't feel lonely. It was the first time in years she had celebrated a holiday in any capacity, even with friends. She stared after the door, lost in thought.

What Skylar had given her was beautiful, a moment where someone had considered her wellbeing over and above their own. To be given that kind of connection in the wake of deep-rooted memories of all that she had lost was beyond what she could have ever asked for. She was unraveled. Turning away from the door, Laura snagged her phone and stared at the text notification from Rodney. Without the echoing ache of loneliness in her chest, Laura had to hope she wouldn't regret letting Skylar in.

CHAPTER
Twenty-Five

SKYLAR HAD PUT on her favorite blazer that morning before she left the house, ready to tackle the meeting with Rodney and Laura head on. Laura had already seen the preliminary logo, but Skylar had fixed it up and added some flair to the other ones as well just in case.

Rolling her shoulders, she set up in the conference room while she waited for Laura and Rodney to arrive. She heard them through the open doorway first and seeing the lighthearted conversation and the smile on Laura's lips warmed her. They must have figured out whatever issue was between them for now.

Skylar pulled her computer from her backpack and opened the lid. She stayed standing as they entered, Rodney turning his smooth smile on her, and Laura stopping hers completely, morphing into the hard woman everyone saw around them. But Skylar knew different. The previous week she had gotten quite a good glimpse underneath the armor that Laura wore, and she wasn't bound to forget it any time soon.

"Morning," Skylar greeted.

"Good morning," Rodney answered as he sat at the head of the table.

Laura said nothing as she slid into the seat opposite Skylar, effectively putting her between the two of them. It made sense for having to stare at the same small computer screen, but it made Skylar uneasy to be positioned between the two heads of the company who normally were contentious with each other.

"I hope you're feeling better," Skylar commented to Rodney as she sat down herself.

"Much better, thank you."

She nodded, noting he didn't exactly give much personal information either. That was something he and Laura had in common. Rolling her shoulders, Skylar pulled up her computer and the logos, putting all three of them on the screen at the same time.

"I have some logo samples for you. We need to pick one so we can start the second phase of implementing if we want to get this done by the end of the year."

Neither said anything. Skylar swallowed hard and let Rodney look first since he hadn't seen them and Laura had. He stared at the screen in silence before sliding it over so Laura could look. Laura pointed at the one she preferred before.

"I still think this one is the best representation of who we are."

Skylar hit a high at the understated compliment. She had made one of the hardest people to satisfy at least a little bit happy.

Rodney furrowed his brow. "I don't like any of them."

The breath was knocked out of her. She had figured Rodney would at least find something good to say instead of just dismissing all of them. Something he liked about at least one of them. This cold reflexive reaction was not what she had been expecting, especially from him. It was far more like Laura had been in those first few weeks.

"Is there anything you like about any of them? Design can always be redone, but I'd like to remind you that my contract expires at the end of the year and with the delay of the last couple weeks, this will put a real crunch on the timeline."

"No," Rodney answered.

Laura leaned over the table to catch Rodney's attention. "It's one of these three, so pick one."

"I don't like any of them, and if we're paying her for a job, then we should be able to get what we want."

"She's done her job, and she's done it very well."

Skylar's chest swelled with pride at that statement. Laura wasn't someone who threw out compliments readily, so to receive one meant she had done something right.

"You need to give up the dream of the logo we had and move forward with a new one. This is the dressing on much bigger issues, and that's where we should be spending more time, not arguing needlessly."

Skylar couldn't have said it better, and since it wasn't coming from her, it was likely—she hoped anyway—that Rodney would actually listen. She guessed it would depend on how mad he was at her still.

When he didn't say anything, Skylar switched topics. "Right, well, putting the logo debate to the side for right now. I was thinking a Christmas party would be a great place to implement these changes and to let everyone know exactly what's going on and how the restructure will begin in the new year."

Rodney didn't look pleased. In fact, he looked like he wanted to walk out of the room and never have to deal with her again. What in the world had changed with him? He had been the one to hire her, but it was as though he and Laura had flipped roles completely. What had she done wrong? Or worse yet, what had she missed?

"We could do the party the week before Christmas, so no one has to miss the holidays with family."

"It's a really busy time of year for me," Rodney fired back.

Skylar was more defeated by the minute when it came to him. He was being so antagonistic in a way she had never seen before. She'd thought Laura was going to be her only hurdle but adding him into the mix made the job seem impossible.

"It's the best time to do it unless you want to extend my contract."

"It might be best to do that anyway," Laura added, and Rodney shot her a murderous look. "We'll need her help implementing the structural changes. I've had a chance to look over the first round of plans for it, and it's going to be quite a bit of work."

"You can handle it," Rodney answered.

Laura clenched her jaw tightly. Skylar wanted to reach under the table and touch her thigh, comfort her because of what was happening, but she knew that wouldn't be acceptable, so she kept her hands on the tabletop, attempting not to fist them in her own anger and frustration.

"I can set everything up so all you have to do is hit the milestones in order to implement the next set of changes."

"See?" Rodney pointed at Skylar. "Easy." He stood up and pushed back from his chair. "I have work to catch up on."

Without another word, he left the room, anger in his wake. She wasn't sure what to do. This had gone in a way she hadn't anticipated at all, and usually she was very good at figuring out exactly which direction the conversation was going to take. This time, however, she'd been blindsided. Then again, she had mainly been working with Laura, who at the beginning had been her biggest adversary in all of this.

"He'll come around," Laura commented, shuffling the papers Skylar had put on the table that they hadn't even gotten to. "Let's go with the logo that I like and start to process everything for it. If you send it to Greta, she can get orders for the things we'll need."

Skylar wasn't completely comfortable with that idea, but she was still in such shock from the turn of events that she didn't comment on it. "I know someone who can do a website redesign."

"We'll need that too," Laura added. "Feel free to give Greta that information as well."

"Right." Skylar sat still, not quite sure what else to do when it came to the meeting that still had forty-five minutes left. "Do you want to continue the discussion or reset a time?"

"Let's continue." Laura looked out the glass walls toward Rodney's office. "He's been in a mood since he came back. Remember, he was the one most resistant to these changes to begin with. I was simply resistant to you."

Laura covered Skylar's hand and gave a gentle squeeze. The look in her eyes was soft, which was contrary to what Skylar would expect. Everything about this day was working in opposites, and it left her completely confused.

"Right." Skylar had forgotten that. In all his smooth talking, she had completely forgotten that he had been the holdout for years on doing something like this. She rolled her shoulders and pulled up the map of the company on her computer. "Here's the current structure, which is functioning, but it's not allowing everyone to shine and it's not allowing efficient productivity."

Laura said nothing as she leaned forward. Skylar caught a hint of her perfume, though subtle, and she had to double down on her focus to keep from thinking about it.

"Here we'll have teams. We'll start with teams at the bottom levels and work our way up when implementing the changes. Eventually there will be two streams, one that reports to you and one that reports to Mr. Solace."

Her lips pursed, and Skylar took that as not a good sign. She waited a second before continuing, wondering if there was something Laura had seen in the structure that would be a hindrance instead. Finally, Laura spoke up.

"I would rather keep the two of us as head, all upper teams reporting to us than divide us."

"Friendly competition can foster advancement."

"I understand," Laura stated firmly but softly, coming to terms with something. "But Rodney and I are already seen as not communicating well. This can only add to that if we also make it a competition."

"We can certainly change that," Skylar mumbled, staring at the structure on her screen. It wouldn't be too hard to fix, and in the end, it would be one less step that they had to implement. Or they could put that off for years until she and Rodney figured their lives out and were able to work out some of their problems.

"Thank you." Laura leaned back in her chair. "I think the Christmas party is an excellent idea, although I know Rodney will be opposed to it until it happens. We can open it up for families. Jana can help you organize it. She has a flair for those kinds of things that Greta doesn't."

Skylar realized belatedly that she would be planning the entire thing without Laura's help. For some reason, she'd thought that the planning would be done by the two of them, but it was just a stupid fantasy. Probably spurred on by the crush and wanting to spend more time with Laura rather than less.

"Sure. Do you have any particular date in mind?"

"They can help with the calendar more than I can."

Skylar nodded, concerned that she wasn't getting as much help from Laura as she originally thought. "And Mr. Solace...?"

"I'll make sure he's there. He won't be happy about it, but if I can get Jennifer on board, then he will be." Laura leaned back and crossed her legs as she sat at the table. "I really do like that one logo. I like the reflection that you added to it."

"Thanks. I enjoy doing design work most days."

"I can see that," Laura commented. "My other concern with the structure changes is the turnover that they'll create."

"I think if we explain it well enough there should be limited turnover on that front."

"I already know of several who are interviewing at different companies. We're at the point where our pay can't be competitive." Laura's voice wavered, and Skylar could tell that she was worried under the front she put up.

Skylar sat there in thought for a moment. "You can always offer incentives to stay through the first three, six, or twelve months. But I really don't think there's going to be a problem with it. Most people aren't having a change to their title or pay, and since the leadership will rotate on the teams, it gives everyone a chance to prove their worthiness in order to move up in the company itself."

"I suppose. But with each major change like this, someone always jumps ship."

"So let them." Skylar looked Laura directly in the eye. "Let them jump. If they don't want to stay around to be innovative, do you really want them working for you?"

Laura hesitated in her answer. She went from thinking to smiling, a light laugh. "You do always look on the bright side, don't you?"

"Most of the time," Skylar answered.

Sighing heavily, Laura sat up a little straighter. "I've got another meeting to get to, Ms. Ross. Do let me know how the party planning is coming along, and what else I can do to help."

"Get Mr. Solace on board with everything."

Laura flicked her gaze back toward Rodney's office. "I'll work on that as best as I can."

"You two seemed chummy this morning."

"We usually are after he spends time with his mother. He doesn't like her and sees me as an ally in that."

"Little does he know," Skylar commented under her breath.

"Right," Laura agreed, but she looked upset by something Skylar had said. Skylar couldn't put her finger on it, but she didn't like the fact that she could so easily read Laura, but at the same time she had no idea what the reason behind the look was.

"Do you mind if I work from here today?" Skylar asked.

"It'd be better if you didn't."

"Okay." Skylar's stomach dropped, the fear that it would be a week again until they saw each other ringing loudly in her ears. She wasn't sure what to do with everything. She knew she was pushing the boundaries because of her crush, and that Laura likely didn't feel the same way, but she couldn't stop herself. She wanted Laura as happy as she could make her by the time this all ended, and that was now as important as snagging herself the contract in the beginning.

Gathering up her things, Skylar shoved them into her backpack in silence. Laura stayed in the room until she was ready to leave, and then walked her to the front desk, still in silence. They were going to have to find some way to talk in the upcoming weeks. Skylar only had a month left on her contract, and she wasn't planning on wasting it without doing any work and waiting for Rodney to catch up with the rest of them.

Once she was back in her office, Skylar collapsed onto the couch and toed off her shoes, curling her legs underneath her. She was going to have to figure out another plan to work on Rodney in order to get him involved and interested in the work that she was doing. He needed to be on board, otherwise the rest of it was going to fail.

CHAPTER
Twenty-Six

THE MEETING with Skylar had been less than stellar, and Laura had seen the disappointment riding in Skylar's shoulders as she'd packed up and left. Laura hadn't wanted to leave her alone in the office again, not without some kind of protection.

Walking past the front desk, she made her way to Rodney's office, shutting the door with a sound click and putting her hands on her hips. She eyed him. "Well, that was rude."

"What was rude?" he mumbled, not even bothering to make eye contact.

He knew exactly what she was talking about, that's what ticked her off. Rodney wasn't an idiot. Laura glared at him, stalking forward.

"You were rude," she stated again, making eye contact so he understood just how enraged she was. "We hired her to do a job, and she is doing that job. The least you can do is put in the time and energy it takes to look over the work she's done."

"I don't like the logo."

"Well, live with it!" Laura's voice rose. He was being so obstinate in a way she rarely saw from him. "What's your problem with her? You're the one who hired her."

"Because *you* insisted." Rodney's petulant attitude irked her.

Flinging her hand out to the side, Laura shook her head. "No, you're not going to blame this one on me. I was fine with doing the work on my own. You're the one who insisted we hire someone from the outside."

"I don't like the logo."

Hitting her limit, Laura snapped. Her chest tightened, her shoulders were rock hard, and fury took over her. "I don't care about the logo! What I care about is the reputation of this company, and you're single handedly taking us down."

"That's rich coming from you." Rodney sat calmly in his chair, watching every reaction from her.

She knew it was one of his tactics to annoy her. Unfortunately, it was working. She was exhausted from trying to fight this battle against him, and just when she thought she was making some progress—she stopped. Betrayal slammed her hard like a bucket of ice water tossed on her head. She would protect Skylar with everything she had because she didn't deserve to be thrust in between them. "Did you hire her to set this up to fail? Rodney...you wouldn't..."

He looked surprised... just before he looked guilty. "No. You were right, we do need to update some things around here, but I don't like the logo."

"It doesn't matter if you like it. It matters if it's marketable." That had been a hard lesson for her to learn twenty-five years ago when they had started Solace, but it was a lesson she carried with her still.

Rodney glowered, his face drawing in, and he tried to make himself larger, taking up more space. It was a stupid male intimidation routine that he did, and she hated it. Laura held her ground.

"You don't have to like it, Rodney. You need to approve it so we can move forward with the plans for the future."

"Let's talk about the future."

Laura's heart thudded hard. Anytime he had that tone of voice, it never boded well for the conversation, and she couldn't bring herself to stand there and take it. She wasn't going to let him slip the chastisement in favor of something else. "No. I'm not doing this now. We're talking about how rude you were to our contractor this morning. If you would like to make a formal apology to her, as you have made me do in the past, then I suggest you do it sooner rather than later. And actually... it's not a suggestion. Do it."

Rodney seemed to give in to her demands. "Fine. I'll apologize. But I still don't like the logo."

"Because your logo has been it for the last twenty years, and you can't have it anymore. You're pouting."

"Hardly," Rodney tossed back in her direction.

"Right. I told her to go ahead with the logo I chose. We'll be purchasing new letterhead and everything in the next few weeks. Greta is working on that project." Laura caught the flicker of annoyance, and she knew he was going to object to her giving the go-ahead without him, no doubt making the same argument she had weeks ago about hiring Skylar. Not giving him the chance, she moved on. "Now, about the party."

Rodney groaned, sounding absolutely childish. "I don't want a party."

"Skylar had a point when explaining it—which you would know if you'd stayed in the room long enough to hear it."

"What is the plan?" He sighed.

"We'll throw a Christmas party for all employees and their families where we'll hard announce the restructure. We'll soft announce it prior to that. But the goal is retention, no matter what. Skylar will leave us with a detailed plan for implementing the restructure."

"She better with as much as we're paying her."

Laura ignored his comment. He had been the one to work out the details of the contract, not her. He would know exactly how much they were paying Skylar for the work and the exact details of the timeline—if he remembered them.

"The idea is to split the employees into teams that rotate

every six to twelve months. Different people get different leadership opportunities so they can get the experience, but we can see who is doing well and who needs some extra assistance. It'll also increase their ability to work together and rely on each other."

"Sounds like you've drunk the water."

Laura sighed heavily, sliding into a seat. This was going to take time, and she was annoyed that she was the one having the conversation because he refused to sit in the meetings with Skylar to begin with. "You asked me to deal with this, so I am. Now I need you on board. All teams will report to us, and we will go from there with the work. But I also want to start giving them more responsibility to try and take some of the pressure off me."

"Off you?" Rodney raised a bushy eyebrow, looking surprised. Laura wasn't sure if it was because she admitted it or because he actually decided to give a crap that day. "Are you working too much?"

Laura had to work hard to bite back her anger at his sudden concern when he'd thrown more work her way in the past month than she could handle, and she'd even told him as much and been ignored. "Yes. I've got too much on my plate. I would like to let the teams start to do proposals—with supervision of course."

Laura waited for him to answer, to give some sign that he had actually heard her this time. She needed to know that they could still care about each other, even after everything they had been through over the years.

"I'll have to check with Jennifer about the dates for a party."

"I'm telling you this isn't an option, Rodney. Check with her all you want, but we need to be here for it and make it happen."

"Fine," he grumbled.

Laura was pleased to have gotten her way for once, without a great amount of arguing. She rolled her shoulders, relaxing a bit. "It'll be good for us to show our employees that we care about them. There's been too much arguing between the two of us, and while they don't know the cause, they can feel the tension."

"You might be right about that." Rodney sighed. "Mom said something to that effect while she was here for Thanksgiving."

Laura wanted to know. She really did, but at the same time, spending Thanksgiving with Skylar—and the drama of that day —had shown her one thing. They needed some better-defined boundaries, and they needed to figure out how to talk to each other.

"She said that you might as well come to dinner if I was going to text you throughout it."

Laura had the same thought at one point that day, but she didn't dare tell anyone that.

"You really shouldn't text me so much while with your mother and at a family holiday. In fact," Laura took a deep breath, making sure this was what she wanted to say before she loosed the words, "you probably shouldn't text me very much unless it involves work things. I may be your ex-wife, but that's it. We're not in a relationship any longer."

Rodney was thoroughly scolded, his eyes wide, his lips ajar, and his face pale.

"We need to set some boundaries, something we should have done fifteen years ago when we filed for divorce."

"Laura..." he tried to interject.

She held up her hand to stop him. "We never tried counseling and maybe the benefit would have been to learn how to talk with each other. I don't want you to text me about your mother anymore. I want you to support your wife as she deals with your mother, since we both know Jennifer isn't her favorite person."

"I don't understand why. Jennifer gave her a grandson."

Laura nodded slowly, pain stabbing at her heart as she had to explain this one very simple thing he could never understand. He'd never tried to. "She's the other woman. It's as simple as that, and to your mother, she's the homewrecker, not the one who created a family."

Pain stabbed her heart, and tears stung her eyes. One rolled down her cheek and she brushed it away haphazardly. She never wanted to let him see her cry again, but she just couldn't keep herself together this time. He had wounded her, deeply, and she wasn't sure she could ever fully forgive him for that.

"I tried to stay with you, Laura. I really did." His tone was so soft, and she knew he was telling the truth.

Putting her hand up swiftly to stop the conversation, Laura shook her head. "This isn't the time nor the place. And I'm over it. I don't want to hear excuses any longer."

"For what it's worth, I'm sorry."

Wind rushed from her lungs, another hot tear streaming down her cheek. It was the first time he had ever said that to her. Laura stared down at him and said the only thing she could think of because he actually sounded like he meant it. "I know you are."

She left his office, lighter in step than she had been for years but weighed down from the exhaustion of feeling so many emotions in one go. She'd never thought to take that stance with him, to defend herself in quite that way before. But it was so worth it.

Laura went back to her office, and as soon as she entered, she was reminded of Skylar. It was warm inside. She smiled at the thought before she went to her desk and sat down, ready to get some work done. Perhaps not all of the gumption she'd had as a young woman was gone. If only Skylar could see her now.

CHAPTER
Twenty-Seven

SKYLAR SPENT the next week going back and forth with Jana to figure out the details for the party. Planning the party at the same time as trying to finalize the very specific steps and movements for restructuring was taking all of her time and focus. She hadn't wanted to do both at the same time, but with the delay in finalizing the logo and agreeing to the party, there hadn't been much of a choice. She'd had to rework her schedule to fit everything in.

Staring at her computer for so many hours, however, killed her eyes and her back. Skylar took a break and walked to the small common kitchenette. She made herself some tea, staring outside at the chilly winter day. Denver was known for being cold, but she just wished it would snow already.

It would be wonderful, like that night when she'd been out with Laura at Bistroporium. Skylar smiled to herself at the memory—that was Laura unhinged. It had been beautiful to see but also a little unnerving. The woman could let loose, which was nice to know, but she also did it without even knowing that's what she was doing.

Raising her mug to her lips, Skylar glanced to the sky and

begged the snow to let loose. She'd felt it in the air that morning, and she didn't want it to hold back.

"I was just coming to find you."

Skylar turned around, finding Jana standing rather awkwardly at the entrance to the hallway. "Sure, what's up?"

She sighed heavily. "I'm not sure we can do exactly what you want. She'll find out."

Skylar's eyes wrinkled as she gave a wry smile. "Come to my office."

They walked to the small room that was coming to feel like home. Skylar settled into her desk and at her computer while Jana remained standing, clearly agitated. They had spoken at length about the details, mostly in confidence since Skylar wanted part of it to be a surprise. She wondered if Laura had even caught the date, but she hadn't commented on it. Not that Skylar expected her to, but the date had been approved, so that was when they were having the party.

"What's wrong?"

"She's going to know."

"Not if you don't tell anyone," Skylar replied. "You're the only other one in that office who knows. Mr. Solace knows the date, but I have a feeling he'll have forgotten it. He doesn't strike me as someone who remembers the birthdays of those around him."

Skylar had almost said of his ex-wife, but she'd caught herself at the last minute.

"She's going to find out," Jana reiterated. "And I don't want to be on the receiving end when she does."

"Now that I can understand." Skylar crossed her arms and leaned back in her chair. Skylar worked through all the possibilities and Laura's reaction, and she really only saw this going well one or two ways. "All right, here's the deal, we'll scratch the birthday idea, even though it would do exactly what I need it to do. I'll find some other way."

"You sure?"

"Yes. The focus will be on Christmas and the plans for

restructuring."

"She sent out a memo this morning about it. There's a lot of questions running around."

Skylar pressed her lips together hard. She knew it was going to happen, but she hadn't expected it so soon for some reason, though logically it made sense. The rumors would be starting with the party anyway, and they had talked about minimizing the fallout. "I assume you're sending those questions Ms. Finch's way?"

Jana looked guilty.

Skylar sighed. "Please send them her way so she can deal with them as they come in. Don't try to protect her from the office drama, especially where it concerns this. She needs to know what's going on and what people are thinking."

"Okay," Jana answered, finally sitting on the couch. "The other problem is the caterer."

"What's the problem?"

"They overbooked, and so they won't be able to have servers here. We can have the food here early enough, but no one to serve it."

"Great," Skylar mumbled. She trusted that caterer for years, but this was a failure on both their parts. Skylar should have booked it sooner, but she hadn't had permission to do it until recently. Add in that this was the busiest time of the year for something like this and she wasn't surprised they were double-booked. "I have a favor I can call in to try and get some servers, at least a couple."

"Are you sure?"

"Yeah." Skylar was already flicking through her phone to send an SOS text message. At the very least, she could make her brother and Callie do it if they weren't working or didn't have anything else going on that night. "We've got two weeks to this party, and we need to make sure that the focus is on the announcements, not on what's going wrong at the party."

"Right," Jana agreed.

Jana stared at her in silence for a while before Skylar figured out what the other underlying issue was. Skylar shifted in her chair. "Do you want me to update her?"

"Yes."

Standing up, Skylar eyed Jana carefully. "You know, celebrating her birthday will do exactly what you don't want it to do."

"What's that?"

"It'll humanize her, so you're not so scared of asking her questions or giving her updates."

"I don't know how Greta does it."

Skylar furrowed her brow in confusion. "She can't be that bad as a boss, can she?"

"She's quite...abrupt."

Giggling, Skylar held open the door as they walked out of her office. "That she can be. Definitely takes a bit of getting used to, doesn't it?"

"I've heard her yell at Mr. Solace so many times. I never want to be on the receiving end of that."

"Have you been?" Skylar was genuinely curious about that one. She hadn't ever seen Laura lose her temper with an employee, only with Rodney and herself.

Jana shook her head. They rounded the corner toward the main office door to Solace. "She hasn't."

"Then I don't think you have much to worry about. She and Mr. Solace have a long history together. Bear that in mind when you hear them argue. It likely has nothing to do with what she's yelling."

Jana was confused, clearly, but Skylar wasn't about to elaborate. Jana stopped at the front desk while Skylar walked straight to the back and Laura's office. She knocked twice before opening the door on command, noting that it was still warmer in there than it had been the couple months prior when they had originally met.

Laura was startled when she came in, and Skylar's stomach

settled at the sight of her at her large desk, buried in work. Skylar struggled to focus lately when she shared a room with Laura, but all she wanted was to be with her. Now that she'd admitted her crush, she wanted to do nothing but pull Laura out of her hidey-hole and make her smile.

"Plans for the party are coming along nicely." She sat in the chair that she'd declared as her favorite.

Laura eyed her down and up before settling back into writing. "I'm glad Jana could be of help."

"She's been most helpful." Skylar sipped the tea she'd brought with her, the heat from the water warming her entire body even more. "She's a bit concerned about some things, but I get the sense that she's a worrier in general."

"She is," Laura commented, not bothering to look up from the papers on her desk.

She really was the queen to this hive, wasn't she? Skylar could easily sit there and watch all the workers move around her, bringing her exactly what she needed and searching for her approval. It wasn't the same with Rodney. Skylar had been in his office enough times to know they all treated him far more like a friend than a boss they couldn't touch.

"You know part of the goal of this party is to make you more accessible to everyone who works here, right?"

"I understand that." Though it didn't sound like she wanted to admit it or let it happen either.

Skylar took another slow sip from her drink. "Would you mind looking at me when I say this?"

"Why would you want that?" Laura jerked her chin up.

"So I can see your reaction."

Laura glowered.

Skylar grinned and raised her eyebrows in a tease. "You should leave your door open."

"What?" Laura's brow pulled tightly toward the center, clearly confused by Skylar's statement.

"Leave it open. See if people start to come in here and ask

questions and voice concerns. You know there's a lot of talk going on now that you've sent out the memo, which means there's a lot of worry and speculation."

"I doubt that." Laura turned her chin down, but Skylar wouldn't have it. She wanted to see those ice blue eyes and every reaction she found find in them.

"Ms. Finch," Skylar started again, keeping her tone light if only just to irk Laura. "Who do you want answering those concerns? Greta and Jana who don't know the plan? Or Mr. Solace...?"

She left it there, letting Laura come to her own conclusion about what Rodney might say concerning the restructure.

"No one will ask questions."

"They *are* asking." Skylar sipped her tea, pretending as though she had all the answers in the world and all the power in the room. She knew neither was true, but it felt good to be in control for a single moment.

"They aren't."

"Laura," Skylar chose to use her proper name, hoping that it would catch her attention sharply. When Laura looked at her, she knew she'd accomplished that at least. "They *are* asking questions."

Laura rubbed her lips together, flicking her gaze toward the door. Skylar couldn't ever figure out what she was looking at when she did that. At first, she'd thought it was Rodney's office, but on second thought it might just be a tactic to give her some time to answer.

"What questions? I can draft another letter."

"These are questions that need to be answered and smoothed over in person. You need to be able to reassure them that they won't be laid off."

Laura clenched her jaw, the muscles in the side of her face and neck so tight that Skylar feared she had said the wrong thing. She would love to smooth her thumb across those muscles.

"Fine. Open the door."

Skylar grinned broadly. Standing up, with extra energy and lightness to her step, she opened the door and propped it. The entire feel of the office changed in that one instant. Skylar stood by the door, grinning again as she stared Laura down. "See? It's not so scary."

Laura snorted lightly. "If I deal with so many interruptions that I can't manage to get my work done, that door will end up shut again."

"Aww, I bet no one will even come in today other than Greta and maybe Mr. Solace."

"You interrupted me."

Skylar's smile faltered for a moment, her stomach flipping at that intense stare she received. "You're right. I did. My apologies."

But she didn't feel as though that was what Laura was really fishing for.

"It's an acceptable interruption, I suppose."

"You suppose?" Skylar nearly bust out laughing, but she managed to hold it in. Staying by the door, they looked at each other from across the room.

"I appreciate your interruptions."

Skylar did laugh at that one, her heart warming and her body doing that damn thing she told it not to. "You're hilarious. I'll see you around, Ms. Finch."

Walking out of the office, Skylar grinned at Jana as she walked by and caught her attention. "All taken care of."

"Thank you, Ms. Ross."

Her walk back to her office was too short for her to figure out exactly what Laura had meant by appreciating her interruptions, but there had been no animosity in her voice. Skylar opened her door with a smile still on her face. If Laura liked them, she would have to find time to make a few more unexpected interruptions. Perhaps then she could figure out what Laura meant by that.

CHAPTER
Twenty-Eight

LAURA JUGGLED two cups of coffee as she stepped out of the elevation. She hadn't thought she'd grab a second coffee after her lunch with Camryn, but she couldn't get Skylar off her mind on the drive back, and she'd ended up with two.

"Skylar?" Laura asked through the door, hoping she was inside so that she could open it up, her hands too busy holding the hot coffees.

Thankfully, there she was, all her bubbly smiles and easy personality. Laura held out the coffee for Skylar to take.

"I thought you might like something to keep you warm after lunch."

"Oh, thank you." Skylar held the door open wider for Laura to step inside.

She immediately sat on the couch, crossing her legs, and quite enjoying the way Skylar's gaze roved up the length of them to the edge of the hemline on her skirt. It had been years since someone had looked at her that openly.

"How are the party plans coming along?" Laura asked, not quite sure what else to say to break the silence.

Skylar plopped onto the couch next to her, curling her feet under her as she often did when they sat together like this. Laura had been doing it more often. Ever since Skylar had convinced her to open the door to her office, she had used Skylar's office as an escape from the interruptions. She'd been right, however. The questions about the restructure were abundant, and there was a general sense of worry and fear among her employees. She should probably tell Skylar that at some point, but it hadn't come up in the last week and a half.

"It's good. We're ready to go any time, really. Just have to pick up supplies."

"That's it?"

"That's it," Skylar answered with a smile. "Jana is highly organized, and she knows how to plan a party. I honestly suggest you utilize those skills far more frequently. I think she'd appreciate it too."

"I'll have to think about it," Laura replied, sipping her extremely hot coffee and burning her tongue. She swallowed down the pain, trying to maintain her composure. "What are you doing for Christmas? Going home to your family?"

"Oh, I think we're all going to stay here for Christmas Eve. Brady volunteered to work Christmas Day to give some of the other guys a break."

"No one else for you to be with during Christmas?" Laura couldn't stop the question from leaving her lips. She'd wanted to know, honestly, for weeks now, but she hadn't found a good way to ask. Skylar had been flirting more with her as the days wore on, but that also just seemed like her personality. Flirt and be kind to everyone and that would eventually lead to connections and networking. She was very personable.

"As in a girlfriend?" Skylar asked, looking confused.

"Yes," Laura answered simply, taking another sip of her steaming hot coffee.

Skylar shook her head. "No, just my family this year."

"Ah." Awkward silence fell between them. Laura stared down at the coffee in her hand. "Someone young like you should have someone else to spend the holiday with."

"I don't think age has anything to do with that," Skylar responded, holding her cup with both hands and not drinking it.

Laura didn't miss the tension in the room skyrocketing, and she hated that she was the cause of it. She hadn't meant to put Skylar's defenses up or to put her on edge. Pressing her lips together hard, she tried to find another way to step out of this field of landmines she found herself in.

"You should have someone to spend it with."

"I do. My family."

"Don't you have any friends?"

Skylar cocked her head to the side. "My brother is my best friend. He always has been."

"You're the youngest, right?" Perhaps going this direction would ease up the conversation slightly.

"Yes," Skylar answered, eyeing Laura suspiciously. "Why the sudden interest in my family?"

Laura hedged. She didn't have an answer to that. "You talk about them often."

"I live with my brother, and I spend a lot of time with them." Skylar shifted into a more comfortable position, but it brought her knee against Laura's thigh. Laura had to hold in a gasp, her chest tightening as tingles filled it. "Why are you so curious about them?"

Laura wanted to know more about Skylar, and if the way to learn more about Skylar was to learn about her family, then she would. Still, she couldn't put her finger on why. She hadn't been so taken with figuring someone out in years.

"Laura," Skylar's voice was gentle, soft, pleading almost.

Laura tensed in reaction to it, still not sure how she would get around that one without giving an answer. "What about exes? You know about mine, and I believe you alluded to working with yours still."

Skylar didn't seem as though she missed the topic change, but she also didn't push back, which Laura appreciated. She wasn't ready for that depth of conversation.

"I work with Trina still, yes. I run all of her marketing. We created a product together, mostly her, but I was the one who got it into the right hands. It's what I used on your shirt, actually. Remember, the day you spilled coffee—"

"Yes, I remember." That was the day she'd managed to score their largest client to date. "You two have found a way to work together then?"

"Yeah, for the most part. Some days I can't wait to drop her as a client, but the income from that little invention is what keeps me going half the time financially."

Laura nodded in surprise. "I'm surprised I'd never heard of it before."

"You probably have and just didn't pay attention, but you also don't strike me as someone who pays attention to marketing quite like the average person."

"What makes you say that?" Laura spun her coffee cup in a circle on her knee, the heat from the cup burning her fingertips even more, but it was such a pleasant burn at the moment.

"Do you watch television?"

"The news."

"Do you read books or listen to the radio?"

"I read frequently, and no, I listen to audiobooks."

"So my point is, when do you receive marketing? Not in the usual ways American households do." Skylar shrugged slightly. "And I suspect most of your clothes are dry-cleaned."

Laura shook her head, humor lighting in her eyes. "No, actually."

"Really?" Skylar tilted her coffee cup toward Laura in a silent salute. "I stand corrected."

"You shouldn't judge and make so many assumptions."

Skylar laughed, the trill of her voice echoing through the small office in a way that warmed Laura. "You're right. I shouldn't. And neither should you, Ms. 'I hate millennials.' If you want to ask me a question, Laura, ask it. Don't beat around the bush."

Laura swallowed, her grip tightening on the cup. She raised her gaze, their eyes locking. Skylar's look was intense but so open and readable in that moment. Laura envied her ability to not hide away her feelings. Listing forward, Laura dropped her gaze to Skylar's bare lips. They were slightly parted, the lower one fuller than the top one, but a shape that was made for smiling.

Her breath came in quick rasps, and she didn't want to look away. Laura stayed where she was, holding the moment as every possibility of what could happen raced through her mind. Straightening her back and leaning away, Laura couldn't stop looking at Skylar's mouth. She wanted to, which surprised her—the thought of what it would feel like to press their mouths together a tantalizing prospect.

"How shall I dress for this party you're planning?" She distracted herself with something she knew would put them back on even footing.

"All right, don't ask your actual question." Skylar unfolded her legs and moved to her desk, setting her coffee next to her computer. "It's semi-formal, so whatever you have that works. Maybe a little black dress or something."

"Little black dress?" Amusement etched through each word. "What makes you think I own something like that?"

"Come on." Skylar rolled her eyes. "Just look at what you wear every day. I'm pretty sure you can find something suitable."

"I'm sure I can." Laura stayed still, watching the blush rise to Skylar's cheeks. She wanted to know exactly what was running through her mind, what dirty little things she was imagining Laura dressed up in.

What? Laura swallowed the sudden lump in her throat. She had no idea where that thought had come from.

"What would you like to see me in? Since this is your party."

"It's hardly my party," Skylar answered, turning away from her computer to look Laura over. "The party is for Solace, and trust me when I say, you are Solace far more than you probably care to admit."

"Rodney is the one who started the company."

"It may have been his idea at one point, but it was your dream, too. And, Laura, you're the one who keeps the company running. People come to you with actual problems, not him. He couldn't come in for two weeks and you still managed new proposals on top of the old work. I wonder if Solace would run just as smoothly if you couldn't come in for two weeks."

Laura found she couldn't agree with the assessment. After all, she wasn't that important. But she didn't want to argue either. They'd been having such a pleasant conversation. "I appreciate your enthusiasm where it comes to my work, but Rodney is the heart of Solace."

"If you say so." Skylar's sing-song answer didn't boast of her agreement.

Laura flinched when her phone buzzed in her purse. Sighing, she set her coffee on the small side table and dug around for the obnoxious device. Her office number lit the screen, and intuitively, she knew they were looking for her. She'd taken an extended lunch that day without warning them about it, and the last thirty minutes spent with Skylar had been well worth it.

"Yes?" Laura answered, sending Skylar an apologetic glance.

"Ms. Finch, oh good, you answered. Mr. Solace is looking for you, and he wants to speak with you immediately."

He could have just called her instead of making poor Greta be the messenger. She also suspected with the tone of voice Greta was using that Rodney wasn't in a mood to be trifled with. Laura checked her watch to see how late she actually was. She didn't have any scheduled meetings that afternoon, and her thought had been if she had to stay an hour late to spend some time with Skylar, then she would do it.

"I'll be there in a few minutes." Laura hung up without waiting for an answer. She wasn't going to come when beckoned where it concerned Rodney, not anymore. "Seems I have to go back into the fray."

"Charge!" Skylar said with a giggle. "Sorry, that was a bad joke. Is everything okay?"

"I'm sure it's fine." Laura planted both her feet on the floor, her purse in one hand and her coffee in the other. "When will you be by again?"

"I don't know. Jana is handling a lot of the details, which is giving me the time to work on the structural changes. I'll need to explain everything to you and Mr. Solace before I officially hand off the baton."

"Schedule it with Greta, will you?"

"Absolutely." Skylar didn't get up as Laura moved toward the door.

Laura held her hand on the doorknob, not wanting to leave just yet. She wanted to stay in this little oasis that Skylar had created, where she could be free to relax and talk about the mundane. Their eyes locked. Laura's stomach tightened, and she held the moment for as long as she possibly could.

"I'll see you around, Skylar."

"You too, Laura."

The way she said her name sent a shiver through Laura. It was absolutely perfect. It was gentle and confident at the same time. Laura still couldn't force her feet to move. She couldn't.

"Is everything okay?" Skylar's words broke through her thoughts.

"Yes." With her trance shattered, Laura left.

She walked slowly back to Solace, taking her time as she went. Greta and Jana greeted her when she entered, and she went straight to her office. Rodney would find her, she was sure, because Greta would tell him she was back. Closing her purse in the bottom drawer of her desk, Laura sat down heavily, her mind spinning with everything that had just happened.

CHAPTER
Twenty-Nine

"I THOUGHT she was going to kiss me."

"What?" The pot clanged against the kitchen sink.

"You heard me," Skylar fired back, not wanting to have to repeat herself. Callie, thankfully, was nowhere in the house, which meant she had Brady all to herself for at least an hour.

Brady looked over his shoulder at her as he drained the potatoes. "What happened?"

"I have no idea. She came into my office to talk yesterday afternoon, and she clearly didn't want to leave, and we were talking, and it just... I swear she was going to do it, Brady. I had to get up to move to my desk just to put some space between us."

"Are you sure it's not all in your head?" He put the pot back on the stove, adding milk and butter and seasoning before taking the masher to it. His shoulders moved with the motions, and Skylar stared at him, as if she could find the answers to all the unasked questions spinning in her brain for the last twenty-four hours. "Sky?"

"Huh? What?"

"Are you sure it's not all in your head? You know how you get when you have crushes."

Skylar frowned. He wasn't wrong, per se, but that also didn't mean she made things up when they didn't exist. Laura had been prying into her personal life more and more. Skylar had willingly divulged a lot of the information, but she'd been careful to only answer what she was willing to share, even though it was clear Laura wanted to know more.

Likewise, however, it was also clear that Laura wasn't quite willing to answer everything either, which made Skylar lock down her walls as best as she could. Putting her arms on the counter, she rested her forehead on them and groaned. What was she supposed to do?

Her heart raced, and she was so uncomfortable with the entire situation. Finally, she answered Brady. "It's not in my head, I don't think anyway. But she's not exactly someone who's easy to read."

"What do you mean?"

"Laura plays everything very close to her chest. Like, I don't even think her admin assistant who has worked for her for five years knows what she's thinking ninety percent of the time."

"Really?" Brady frowned as he glanced over his shoulder at her. "How does anyone live like that?"

"I don't know, but she does."

Brady sighed heavily and put the potato masher down, turning on her. "What do you want from her?"

"Nothing, really. I want to finish the job I was hired to do and find the next one. I'm not looking for anything."

"But you like her."

Cold washed through Skylar. "I have a crush on her, and I'm intrigued by who she is and how she got to where she's at. Beyond that, I don't know anything, and it's not something I'm willing to pursue."

"Are you sure about that?"

Skylar paused, thinking deeply. If she wanted a relationship, Laura wouldn't be the first person she would go for. Yes, she was attractive, and certainly Skylar's type when it came to looks, but personality wise, Laura left a whole lot to be desired.

The least of which was the communication barriers they seemed to have.

"I don't even know if she's a lesbian."

"She could be bisexual or pansexual."

Skylar frowned. "You know what I mean. I'm pretty sure she's straight."

"What makes you think that? You just told me five seconds ago that you thought she was going to kiss you."

"Maybe that was all in my head." Laura hadn't made any outward signs of wanting more, but Skylar hadn't been able to get her mind off the almost kiss since Laura had come into the office that day.

"Dang, you got it bad, don't you?" Brady leaned over the counter and waggled his eyebrows at her. "What are you going to do about it?"

"Absolutely nothing, and you, dearest brother, should stop trying to encourage me." Skylar's cheeks heated with embarrassment.

"I am always going to encourage you to do something fun, baby sister!" Brady touched her hand briefly. "Besides, you've been wallowing in that Trina pit far too long."

Groaning again, Skylar buried her face in her arms as he turned around to finish making their Shepherd's pie for dinner. She couldn't believe he was pushing her on it. She shuddered at the thought. No, it would be best for her to keep her hands and lips to herself for the time being. Doing anything else would only get her hopes up and make moments like the day before way worse.

"Ultimately, Sky, here's my advice." Brady spun around on her after putting the dish in the oven to finish baking. "Go with the flow. If you two end up having some fun, go with it. And if you don't, then you don't. I want you to just pay attention to what you're feeling, what she's feeling, and if the two happen to be the same, then go from there. All right?"

"Fine." Skylar pouted. She wasn't sure she wanted that advice from him, but it was better than nothing, she supposed. "How much longer until dinner?"

"Twenty minutes."

"I'm going to take a shower."

"You do that! I hear shower heads are fun!" He called after her. If she had something to throw at him, she would have. With her face beet red, Skylar walked to the bathroom and shut and locked the door behind her.

~

Skylar had managed to sleep that night, though her dreams had been wrought with images of Laura pinning her with a saucy, flirtatious look. When she woke, she knew it was all in her head and that going their separate ways in a week would be good for her heart. Brady was right, she needed to get her head under control so she could focus on what had to be done.

Her office was warm as she stepped inside and dropped her backpack onto her chair. She was in the middle of pulling out her computer and notebooks when the door opened. Laura stood there, just inside the door, a tray with two coffees in one hand and her briefcase in the other with her purse slung over her shoulder.

"Morning?" Skylar asked, confused. "We didn't have a meeting scheduled, did we?"

"No," Laura answered, stepping farther into the room to set the tray with coffee on the desk. She said nothing as she pulled the two cups out and handed one to Skylar and kept the other herself.

Skylar glanced at her calendar, noting it was empty that morning, and then looked back at Laura. "Did you need something?"

"No." Laura sat down on the couch, crossing one smooth leg

over the other, her skirt riding above her knee and her calf straining from the angle of her stiletto.

Skylar's entire body was tuned into Laura's. Every move she made, Skylar felt as though she were right there with her. She tried to keep her gaze on Laura's face, not wanting to give away where her thoughts had strayed, not just that morning but the night before.

Standing still, Skylar watched Laura carefully, that long stare, the confident pose on the couch, the silence that emanated from her. She couldn't tell for a brief moment if she was thrown back in her dream or not, but since Laura continued in silence, Skylar was pretty sure this was reality.

"I thought you might like a treat." Laura indicated the coffee.

Skylar looked at it, holding it between both her hands. "Uh...thanks."

She'd never thought of a coffee as a treat. But Laura got one every single day, sometimes twice a day. Giving in to temptation, Skylar sat on the couch next to her and sipped the coffee.

"Did you have a good night?"

"I did," Laura answered, not giving more than she had to no matter how many questions Skylar asked. That was likely the most annoying thing about her to date, and really put the thought in her mind that any type of relationship beyond business wasn't a good idea.

"Good. Brady made Shepherd's Pie last night. It's one of my favorites."

"I've never had it," Laura replied before they fell into another awkward silence.

Laura's phone buzzed, but she didn't pull it out of her purse this time like she had before, and she didn't answer it. Skylar was about to comment about it when Laura held out her hand to stop her.

"Is everything ready for tomorrow?"

"You know it is," Skylar answered. They had gone through everything the day before when they'd met with Rodney, and

Skylar had officially handed them the plans for the restructure. All she had left to do was the party and her contract was complete.

"Jana is pleased with the work you've done on it."

"Well, that's high praise coming from her." Skylar knew what she said could be taken as an insult, but she hadn't meant it that way. Jana saying something about her skills in party planning was a rare compliment from what she could tell. "Are we going to talk shop or are you here for a different reason?"

"Rodney is pleased with the plans you left us. He wants to implement them immediately."

"Shop talk it is." Skylar nodded and sank deeper into the couch as Laura's phone started buzzing again. "Are you going to get that?"

"No."

"Fine. Please don't start the process yet. There's time and milestones to reach before each step is implemented for a reason."

"I know," Laura answered. "I'll keep him in line, I promise."

Her phone—again.

"Ms. Finch, you really should answer that."

Frowning deeply, Laura reached into her purse and looked at her phone. Skylar caught sight of Rodney's name on the screen before she silenced the call and plopped it back into her purse, putting it on the floor next to her.

"Is there something going on?" Her stomach dropped. Now she was concerned. Laura wasn't someone who readily skipped calls like that, but it was the third one she had ignored that morning already. "Is everything okay?"

"Everything is fine, Skylar. Relax a minute." Laura's voice was like smooth whiskey, smokey and perfect. This, from the woman who'd taken almost an entire season to do that around Skylar.

Skylar couldn't help but be soothed by it. Yet, as Laura's phone rang again, Skylar's worry built back up. "Aren't you late?"

"Not today," Laura responded. "Do you like your coffee?"

"Uh...yes." Skylar was so confused by what was happening, unable to come to terms with the lack of conversation or explanation as to why Laura was there to begin with. "Laura, you're going to have to tell me what's going on."

"Sometimes us old folk just need a break from life and a treat to go with it." Laura held up her coffee in a half-salute.

Skylar grinned broadly, her eyes crinkling at the corners as she looked Laura directly in the eye. "Okay, boomer."

"I think I'll take that as a compliment today."

"You do that," Skylar answered. "It's always been one."

"Sure, it has." Laura chuckled lightly, and Skylar was glad they seemed to have found some sort of rhythm to the conversation now, even though Laura still wasn't answering any of the questions Skylar had posited.

"Well, the last few times it was a compliment."

Laura eyed her dubiously.

"Fine, this time it was a compliment."

Laura's lips twitched up in the corners just as her phone went off again. She reached into her purse and pulled out the phone, silencing it. "Christ. They really can't function without me for one damn hour, can they?"

"I told you that you were the backbone of Solace."

Laura sat on the edge of the couch, her briefcase and purse in one hand and the coffee in the other. "Thank you, Skylar. For everything you've done."

"I haven't done much."

"You've done more than you know." Laura stood up, making her way to the door. "And thank you for the coffee talk this morning."

Skylar was more confused than ever as Laura left her office. They hadn't actually talked about anything, but Laura had at least come away satisfied with whatever had happened—at least, Skylar was pretty sure she had. Shaking her head, she set her drink on her desk and pulled out her computer and notebooks, putting everything in place so she could get to work that day.

All she had to do was set up the next day for the party, stay for the party and the announcement, and her time working at Solace would be up. As eventful as it had been, it was actually rather uneventful. Skylar was glad for that, but the sting of not seeing Laura on such a regular basis saddened her. Maybe that had been the entire purpose of the coffee conversation, a distant and awkward goodbye just between the two of them. No, that was Skylar's crush talking again. She had to stop that—it wouldn't be good for anyone.

CHAPTER
Thirty

THE BUZZ in the air was intoxicating, and Laura knew they had made the right decision to hire Skylar and move forward with a restructure. There were concerns still, but that was expected with anything new. However, staring Jennifer down across the room wasn't what Laura had wanted to do the majority of the night, especially on her birthday, which Rodney hadn't even remembered.

Rodney put his hand against Jennifer's back and guided her around, introducing her to people and making small talk. Laura tried to distract herself by talking to anyone who would let her, but she wasn't the personable boss. She wasn't the one they wanted to talk to when there wasn't a problem. She wasn't the one they flocked to.

"How's it going?" Skylar's sweet bubbly voice startled her out of her thoughts.

"I think it's going well, don't you?"

Skylar's eyes lit up as she turned to face the room. "I think it's going perfectly. You did a great job with your speech, by the way."

"Thank you," Laura said, bringing her drink to her lips for a sip. She wasn't sure how many she'd had already, but as soon as she was done talking, she'd taken to drinking and skulking. She would much rather be spending the night with only Skylar, perhaps even celebrating her birthday. Her gaze fell on Jennifer again. She was, younger than Laura by ten years. At the time when Rodney had cheated that had been an insult, but now it didn't matter so much.

Chuckling, Skylar reached over and touched Laura's arm gently with her fingers. "You're glaring at her."

Damn it. Laura tore her gaze away and looked at Skylar, focusing on her soft hair and big eyes. She looked damn near perfect in the outfit she'd chosen for the night. It was a simple A-line dress that flowed down just below her knees. The deep emerald green color brought out highlights in her eyes that Laura hadn't noticed before, and the high neckline was modest but left no room for debate as to how well-endowed Skylar truly was—not like the T-shirts she wore daily.

"All right, now you're glaring at me."

"Hardly." Laura lifted the glass to her lips and took another cooling sip, this time absolutely pleased with her view. She needed it. Her cheeks were on fire, and her body was overheated at best. Too many people in the room, and the music and conversation and noise were all more than she could handle. Instead, she focused on Skylar, the beautiful woman who stood next to her.

"Laura, what a wonderful party."

Laura stiffened. She hadn't expected to be interrupted in her gazing of Skylar and certainly hadn't expected the culprit to be Jennifer of all people. "Ms. Ross is responsible for most of it."

She was going to drag Skylar into this conversation come hell or high water because she knew without a doubt Skylar would save her. She had managed to find a balance with Jennifer in the last few years, but that didn't mean she liked her or wanted to talk to her outside of what was necessary.

"Hi, I'm Jennifer Solace."

"Skylar Ross. It's good to meet you." They exchanged handshakes. "I'm glad you're enjoying the party."

"I am. Rodney wasn't sure about all this, but I think he's coming around."

Laura wisely kept quiet, using the drink to distract herself again. Her mother had told her for years that if she couldn't say anything kind, not to speak at all, and while she failed that lesson most days, this wasn't going to be one of them.

"I think he's warming up to the ideas." Skylar shot Laura a confused look, probably wondering why she wasn't saying anything, but Laura only returned a hard stare. "I'll be interested to follow along as soon as the restructuring starts and see how effective it is."

"Yes, that will be most interesting." Jennifer crossed her arms over her chest, her gaze falling on Laura.

Laura knew she wanted to say something and that she didn't want Skylar to hear it. But she couldn't be trusted to be alone with Jennifer, not with this much alcohol running through her system. Knocking back her drink, she turned around to the tip bar they were standing by and ordered another one.

As soon as the cool drink was in her hands, she sighed heavily. Skylar and Jennifer were talking about something, and her cold heart hadn't been burned to the ground yet. Laura finished that drink swiftly and ordered another one. This would be her last, but even at this rate she'd be ordering herself a ride.

She walked toward her office to escape, but Jennifer caught up with her again. "Laura!"

Pursing her lips, Laura stopped and faced the mistress she couldn't ever get rid of. "Was there something else?"

"I wanted to thank you for letting Rodney have extra time with me this fall."

Laura furrowed her brow, not understanding a lick of what Jennifer was saying.

"We went down to the Springs for some fertility treatments. I'm expecting again."

"Ah." There was that cold pit of hell she knew she was going to find tonight. She had wrongly assumed it would be because of the milestone birthday, and instead she'd been thrown this. Laura clenched her molars together, congratulations and anger on the tip of her tongue, and she had no idea which one was going to show face in that moment.

"That's amazing news," Skylar interrupted, reaching down and wrapping her fingers around Laura's hand and giving a firm squeeze. Laura sucked in a sharp breath, coming to her senses instantly.

"Yes," Laura added. "Congratulations. If you'll excuse me."

She stalked to her office, Skylar hot on her heels. With the door shut, Skylar gave her space, eyeing her as if she was going to crumble. Laura couldn't stand it. Tears stung and her chest tightened, making it hard to breathe. She couldn't let it loose, not here, and certainly not with the entire world out in the other room.

"Take deep breaths," Skylar cooed. "What do you need?"

"Another drink."

"One more." Skylar pointed at her, and at Laura's nod, she exited the room.

Cast in the silence, the muted noises from outside her office echoing under the door, Laura collapsed. She leaned against her desk and wrapped her arms around herself, wiping the few tears that managed to fall off her cheeks, each with a different curse. It had been fifteen years—she shouldn't still be feeling this way.

Skylar returned with the drink, concern etching every line in her face. Guilt pelted Laura. "I'm fine. I swear."

"Sure you are." Skylar handed the drink over. "Stay in here a bit, order a ride, and be done for the night if you want. They're winding down anyway."

Laura wanted to protest, but at the same time the prospect of going home and escaping Jennifer and her announcement was so tempting. She nodded, keeping silent as she finished one drink and started on her last one of the evening. Skylar left her alone again, the blissful quiet taking over. Skylar had rescued her from saying something she knew she would regret and have to spend years make amends for.

"Well, that's a bonus," Laura said to no one but herself. But it wasn't just that. Skylar had been on her mind every spare moment she had and some in between. That almost kiss in her office had fostered more than one dream, and seeing her in that dress tonight—Laura groaned. She couldn't think straight.

She did exactly as Skylar had told her, getting on her phone and requesting a car to come and get her. She could come back on Monday without the weight of the night on her and deal with Rodney head on.

Grabbing her purse and jacket, Laura got ready to leave as soon as the car said it was five minutes out. She could wait the rest of the time in the lobby. With the empty glasses in her hand, she left her office with her shoulders straight and all the confidence in the world. She would put on a show for Jennifer if it was the last thing she did.

She dropped the glasses by the bartender and started for the main door. Skylar caught her eye and came over. They walked in silence out into the hallway and down to the elevator. Laura pressed the call button, shoving her hands into the pockets of her wool jacket to keep herself from grabbing Skylar's hand.

"Thank you for the save."

"Anytime," Skylar murmured.

They stepped into the elevator, and Laura dragged in a deep breath. "You don't have to see me out."

"I want to." Skylar winked as she pressed the button for the main level.

Laura's stomach was a mess of nerves. This was the exact situation she hadn't wanted to end up in tonight because she knew she would do something stupid. Skylar stood so quietly next to her. Swallowing hard, Laura twisted on her toes and faced Skylar full on. "The party was lovely."

"I'm glad you enjoyed it."

Laura took a step forward, and Skylar stayed put, cocking her head to the side. Laura's heart thudded hard, her breathing coming in rapidly. She'd made her decision—even if she might regret it later, Laura wanted to know what would happen. If she was going to do one thing now that she was fifty, it was going to be this.

She lowered her voice, nearly whispering, "You look beautiful tonight."

Skylar's cheeks reddened, the color highlighting her humility, and Laura smiled fully. She knew she wasn't the only one who had thought about this. Skylar was so obvious. Laura had ignored it for weeks now, but after tonight, it was impossible. Stepping forward, Laura reached out and snagged Skylar's hand with her own. Her lips tingled, butterflies flying in her stomach.

"Laura?" Skylar's voice wavered in uncertainty.

"Hmm?" Laura dropped her gaze from those expressive eyes to Skylar's lips, the slight fullness of them, the pink gloss she'd put on them for the party that wasn't her norm. *What does it taste like?*

"What are you doing?" Skylar's voice dropped to a whisper, as though someone might catch them, but for the first time all night, they were alone, and Laura had no fear of being interrupted.

"Kissing you." Her voice was low, husky. Laura inched forward, their chests brushing in the height of anticipation. When their mouths pressed together, just the slightest of touches, heat flared. Laura hummed at the heavenly moment, listing her entire body into Skylar's and pushing in even more.

Skylar's lips were wet from the gloss, her breath hot as she breathed out. Laura dropped Skylar's hand and reached up, sliding her fingers behind Skylar's neck. She held their mouths together as she teased her tongue against those perfect lips. Skylar dragged in a ragged breath, her hands against Laura's back as she held on. Laura smiled and did the only thing she could think of—she felt everything.

Skylar's body against hers. The heat of the wool against her skin in the warm elevator. Her nerves giddy with excitement. Warmth pooling between her legs, racing as if they had to beat her there. Her hands shaking as she touched. The pads of her fingers warm against searing skin.

Laura couldn't stop. Leaning in even more, she pressed herself against Skylar, their lips moving, their tongues teasing. Her entire body and mind were focused on nothing other than Skylar in her arms, on making Skylar feel exactly what she was experiencing.

Laura nipped at her lip, grinning as she pushed back in for another long kiss and raising the urgency. Skylar groaned, hands on Laura's hips, her waist, up over her breast through the thick material of her coat. *God, I just want her against me.*

Reaching between them, Laura pulled at the buttons on her jacket. She needed Skylar's hands against her, closer to her. Everything in this moment was perfect. Laura skimmed her fingers from the back of Skylar's neck across the top of her chest, feeling her deep breaths through the thin material of her dress, brushing her breast so slightly that it could be mistaken as an accident.

The elevator dinged—its movement halted. Laura stayed put, clinging to Skylar as she kept the embrace heated, full of passion she didn't know she possessed. Skylar stumbled a step forward and pushed Laura back, spinning her into the wall of the elevator. Laura arched her back, dragging her fingers back up Skylar's chest to wrap her hands around the back of her neck and keep them locked together.

This could end—whatever this was that she had found, she needed Skylar to keep it unlocked. Moaning softly, Laura held Skylar to her. She wanted Skylar to touch her everywhere, use those fingers on her, this mouth that was suddenly wicked. Laura's eyes fluttered shut at the thought, a burst of wetness pooling between her legs.

Laura broke the kiss sharply. Her breaths came in short rasps as she raised her eyes to Skylar's. Sliding from her grasp, thoughts clouded her. Too many thoughts at once, confusing everything they had done. Backing away, she pressed the button to open the elevator doors, not taking her gaze off Skylar's swollen lips, her surprised look, and her mussed hair. Warmth spread through her chest, and she curled her lips in a smile. Skylar was stunning.

"I should have started earlier, so I had all six floors to kiss you."

"Laura," Skylar's voice broke.

Laura shook her head slowly, stepping out of the elevator. "We'll talk soon, when I'm sober and not a mess."

And when I have some time to figure this all out. It was painful to walk away, to watch the doors close on Skylar silent in the elevator, to know that she had to go home, sober up, and try this again.

Laura buttoned her jacket and hitched her purse up on her shoulder again. She fluttered her fingers over her lips, a smile greeting her in response. She couldn't have asked for a better kiss, from someone so passionate and energetic and who wasn't afraid to back down.

The car she'd requested pulled up outside, the headlights shining through the falling snowflakes. Not waiting another minute, Laura walked out the lobby doors and down the stairs. She needed the weekend, and then they would try this again.

CHAPTER
Thirty-One

THAT KISS. Skylar had been thinking about it all weekend, but her phone had remained silent. She'd gotten no calls and no texts from Laura, and by the time Sunday afternoon rolled around, Skylar had decided it was a drunken experiment since Laura knew she dated women. Not that Laura seemed like someone who would experiment or toy with emotions, but any text or call Skylar had attempted had gone unanswered.

She sat in her office late in the afternoon on Monday catching up on all the work she had skipped out on while she'd been cramming for everything Solace had wanted. That was the shortest deadline she'd ever had for a project that size, and it had been insane to try and fulfill it, but so worth it.

Stepping out into the hall to make herself some more tea, Skylar dragged her feet. She wished Laura would at least answer with some sort of text or phone call. It had been all weekend with nothing, and since they weren't working together anymore, she had very little excuse to go find her in her office.

She stood at the small kitchenette and waited for the water to boil, picking her tea flavor based on her mood. She needed something light and fruity, something that would warm her up from the cold tundra she found herself on. Skylar grabbed her mug and walked back to her office, stopping short at the sight of Laura, standing at her door.

"Uh...hi?" Skylar said, cursing inwardly at her own indecision. She should know better than that by now, and she'd wanted to talk to her all weekend.

"Got a minute?"

"Sure." Skylar pushed open the office door and held it for Laura to join her.

Laura set her briefcase and purse on the floor next to the couch, sliding onto the cushion as she raised an eyebrow in Skylar's direction, as if expecting her to follow suit. *Right,* Skylar thought as she set her steaming mug on the desk and moved in to sit next to Laura.

"I want you to know that I left my phone in the office all weekend, accidentally. I wasn't..." Laura blew out a breath. "I wasn't exactly in a good state of mind when I left on Friday."

"Yeah, okay." Skylar had known that. It had been how she'd tried to convince herself that there was nothing to the kiss. No matter how much she wished differently.

"What I'm saying is, I didn't get your calls or your texts until I got to the office this morning." Laura's hand was on top of hers, their fingers folding together with a gentle squeeze.

When Skylar expected Laura to release, she didn't. She held on, her thumb playing against the side of Skylar's hand tenderly. The move only added to Skylar's confusion about the situation. What was happening?

Laura sighed slightly, the sound echoing loudly through the room. Skylar broke Laura's hold on her, shoving her hand back into her lap as soon as it was free. She would sit there and take the quiet letdown, but she should make it easier for Laura. They didn't need to have this conversation.

"Rodney used to tell me no one would want me, that I was cold and lifeless—sexless."

"What?" Skylar's eyes bugged, and instantly she was reaching out for Laura's hand again. "What a cruel thing to say."

"Hmm." Laura glanced down at their hands, then lifted her chin and faced Skylar. Her features were set, determined in a way Skylar had never seen before. She wasn't masked in this moment, and everything she felt flitted through her eyes. "I used to agree with him, but Friday was so different."

"What do you mean?"

Laura reached up with her free hand, cupping Skylar's cheek. "I wonder if perhaps I wasn't looking in the right direction the entire time. And it wasn't until the party that I realized I needed to do something different."

Skylar shook her head, confused by the direction the conversation was taking. "Laura?"

Laura smiled, the lines creasing around her lips and her eyes, and when she dropped her gaze to their joined hands and looked back up, the glance was coy. She was shy. The confusion vanished in an instant and was replaced with complete understanding and awe. Skylar couldn't help the responding smile.

"Go out with me."

"What?" Skylar shook her head. "You want to go out?"

"Yes. Come to dinner with me."

"Just to be clear, Laura, are you asking me on a date or as a friend?"

Pink rushed to Laura's cheeks, the flush in them adorable and something Skylar had never seen before. This Laura was someone completely different from the one she'd met in the elevator all those months ago.

"A date," Laura finally answered, her lips pressed together firmly. "Go out on a date with me."

"I..." Skylar paused, not sure how to answer that particular question. Did she want to go on a date? Absolutely. Yet, something held her back. Brady had told her to go with the flow, but it wasn't all in her head still, was it? "I want to."

"It sounds as if there's an objection in that."

Skylar frowned. "Why did you kiss me the other night? Was it just for experimenting?"

"No." Laura reached up and cupped her cheek again, pulling Skylar's face toward hers. "No, that's something I've thought about doing for weeks now."

"Then why Friday?"

Sighing, Laura closed her eyes in embarrassment. "I was upset and drunk. I wasn't thinking properly, otherwise I likely wouldn't have. But that doesn't mean I didn't want to."

"Are you sure? Because I don't want you think—"

"Skylar," Laura chastised. "Look at me and then decide whether you think I'm telling the truth or not."

Finally, Skylar looked into Laura's ice-blue eyes. They were so close to touching again—Laura's warm hand on her cheek, her thumb on her mouth. Skylar's heart raced, and she did the only thing she could think of. She dashed her tongue against Laura's thumb, glad to see the echoing smile from Laura. She did it again just as Laura slid forward, pressing their mouths together in a chaste but warm kiss.

This kiss didn't carry the heat the one in the elevator had, but at the same time, it was just as perfect. They were together in this moment, no inhibitions, no questions, no alcohol or drama surrounding them. Skylar pressed in closer, dashing her tongue out to taste just as Laura curled her hand through the hair at the back of her neck. Skylar sighed into the embrace, holding on and clenching her eyes shut, going with her instinct in every moment.

When she pulled away, she pressed her forehead against Laura's and closed her eyes. "Yes."

"Tomorrow."

"Yes," Skylar answered with a giggle in her words. "Tomorrow night."

"Good." Laura surged in, their lips melding together again.

Skylar could stay there all day and lose herself in Laura's mouth and her soft touches. She just wanted to melt into her. Finally Laura broke the kiss, a smile lingering, one that reached all the way to her eyes. Skylar loved seeing that.

"I have to go. I need one more night to recover from this weekend. I'm not as young as I used to be."

Skylar wrinkled her nose and leaned in to steal one last kiss. When Laura left her office, she was enamored and lost to everything that had just happened. She had to talk to Brady. Finishing up her work as quickly as possible, Skylar packed up her backpack and left.

When she arrived at the house, dinner was ready and set for three of them. Skylar grabbed a plate and made up her own before sliding to the kitchen counter and staring intently at Brady. She wanted him to know what she was thinking, what had happened.

"What?" Brady asked, pointing his fork at her. "You look like you're going to burst, so you better spill."

"I have a date." Skylar's voice was so quiet that she wasn't sure Brady even heard her. Callie, however, had. She dropped her fork loudly against her plate, the clang echoing in Skylar's ears.

"With who?" Brady asked.

Skylar raised an eyebrow at him, daring him to figure it out on his own.

"With Laura, you idiot." Callie hit Brady lightly on the arm.

Skylar couldn't stop the grin. She nodded vigorously. "Yeah, with Laura. Tomorrow. We're going on a date."

Brady sat stunned for a moment, no doubt unsure what to make of it all. Skylar bounced on her stool, no longer able to contain the energy as it was trying to burst from her.

"I can't believe it," she whispered. She had agreed to it. She'd been there for the quick make out session in her office, and yet she still struggled to fully believe that was what was happening. Laura had barely shown any signs of interest in her until the party on Friday, and Skylar could have sworn it was all in her head.

"Believe it," Callie said, grinning from ear to ear, her eyes twinkling with enthusiasm. "Where are you going?"

"No idea," Skylar answered. "I guess I should text her and ask so I know whether to dress fancy or casual, but we didn't get that far in detail planning."

"Are you sure she asked you out?" Brady asked.

Skylar rolled her eyes. "She made it super obvious. There's no mistaking it this time."

"This time?" Callie pushed.

Brady waved her off. "Are you sure this is what you want to do?"

"I thought you said I deserved this!"

"Good." Brady straightened his back, awkwardly eating his food. Skylar couldn't figure out what the shift in his mood was. When she'd dated Trina, he had been distant too. Perhaps it was just the same situation she found herself in with Callie, not quite sure where they stood with each other. She'd expected him to be happy for her, excited even, but the stark contrast put her back up.

Skylar watched him carefully, trying to decipher what exactly was running through his mind, but she couldn't read him. Callie got her attention. "So tell me about her."

"Oh, um...I think she hides a lot of what she's thinking and feeling because she's unsure of herself. But she's ridiculously strong. She works with her ex-husband, and for anyone to remain in a business relationship with their divorced spouse they have to be either strong or insane."

"Or both," Callie added.

"True." Skylar moved her food around her plate, her appetite waning. "But she loves her job, and she's brilliant. The little that we did work together on details was amazing. She picks things up so quickly, and she knows so much."

"Sounds like the two of you will get along on that front."

"Yeah, maybe." Skylar never thought of herself as particularly smart. Still she had managed to keep up through most of the conversations they'd had. "I think she's worried about our age difference."

"What?" Brady interjected. "How much of a difference is there?"

"Fifteen years." She wasn't about to add that it was technically sixteen until her next birthday since Laura just turned fifty. She wasn't sure she wanted to see Brady's reaction to that one. He had to have known Laura was older than her, though, didn't he?

"Fifteen..." he trailed off, his eyes wide with shock. "Mom's going to kill you."

"I don't really care about that right now. I'd like to maybe make it beyond the first date before we start talking about the future. Don't you think that'd be a grand idea?" Her defenses were out, no matter how much she tried to tame them. Skylar swallowed hard, her appetite now completely gone. He had been so encouraging the other night, what difference did it make now other than it wasn't mere speculation?

"Fifteen years is no small potato."

"It's not, but that doesn't mean we shouldn't at least give it a chance."

"I'm with Skylar on this one." Callie gave Skylar a comforting look. "If they want to try it, then they should try it. And I think, in some ways, it's different when it comes to gay relationships."

"It's not!" Brady tightened his jaw.

"It is," Callie argued. Turning to Skylar, she asked, "Has she ever dated another woman?"

Skylar shook her head. "I don't think so, not from what she's told me, anyway."

"There. She's learning just as much as Skylar is. And you know what, Brady, you're just going to have to get over it. This is Skylar's life, not yours. And just like she supports us, you have to support her."

Brady blew out a breath. "I don't like it."

"I don't think she cares if you like it. And I don't either." Callie crossed her arms, putting her foot down on the entire conversation.

Skylar was impressed. She'd never seen Callie go to bat for her like that before. They'd always tiptoed around each other for the most part, so to watch her take Brady on like this was amazing to see. She'd heard their arguments before, but it had never been about Callie protecting Skylar. Knocking her shoulder into Callie's, Skylar whispered, "Thanks."

"Anytime. You're my sister now, and he's going to have to get used to that."

Skylar had to get used to it too, but they were definitely making progress in that area, though she was still left bewildered by this change in Brady. Her excitement returned about her date the next night, and Skylar happily ate her dinner, the awkward silence dissipating as soon as they started toward a safer topic of discussion.

CHAPTER
Thirty-Two

IT WAS ALMOST time for her date with Skylar, and Laura kept her eyes glued to the clock as the final minutes ticked by. Grabbing her purse from her desk drawer, Laura went to stand just as her office door opened loudly. Rodney stood in the doorway, a shadow in his eyes and a grimace on his face. Her curiosity ratcheted up, but she refused to be distracted. It was five, and for the first time in months, she was going to clock out exactly when she was supposed to.

"Do you have a general portfolio I can have?"

Laura pursed her lips, sitting heavily back in her chair. "What for?"

"I'm meeting with a potential new client tomorrow, and I want to bring it with me."

"Why don't you bring the one that you sent EarthBound Exotica the last time?" Laura dropped her purse by her feet, not sure how long this was going to take but not wanting it to take longer than necessary.

"It's not suited for this company."

"And what is *this* company?" Annoyance edged its way through her tone, and Laura didn't even bother to hold it back.

"Markam Investments."

Laura pressed her lips together hard. "And you're meeting them tonight?"

"Tomorrow."

"Then it can wait." She grabbed the strap on her purse and pulled it up, flopping it heavily onto her desk. She hoped it would indicate to Rodney that she was done for the day and ready to leave.

"Now, Laura."

"Not happening, Rodney," she fired back, standing. "I have someplace to be."

"Where are you going?" He sounded so indignant, as if she was the cause of his entire upset that day. She knew she wasn't, but she also knew Rodney, and if she could be the cause of it, then he would make her the cause.

"I'm going on a date, if you must know, and our reservations are for five-thirty."

Rodney paled, his bravado gone. "You have a date?"

"Yes." Laura put her purse high up on her shoulder, coming around the desk to grab her jacket.

"Who are you going out with?"

"It's none of your business."

"Laura, I know everyone in the industry. Who is it?"

"It's no one in the industry." She grabbed her jacket and was about to swing it onto her shoulders when Rodney put a hand on her arm, catching her attention.

"Who are you going out with?"

"It's none of your business," Laura tersely replied. He took her jacket, as if he was going to help her get into it, but instead, he dropped it on the chair to the table in office. Laura glared at it and then him. "What do you think you're doing?"

"You can't go out with some random man."

"I'm not." Laura wasn't about to tell him who she was going on a date with and certainly not that it wasn't even with a man. He would have a heart attack if he knew that.

"Laura... Laura..." He softened his tone, as if that would work on her. Sometimes it did, she had to admit, but not today. Today she was determined to get the hell out of the office and go on her date with Skylar. "Are you sure this is the best decision to make at a time like this?"

"What do you mean *a time like this?*" Confused, Laura stared at him with wide eyes.

"You just had a big milestone birthday. It's not right for you to be throwing yourself at random people just to get laid."

"Oh my god." Laura's cheeks heated. The audacity of this man—she wasn't sure what she ever found attractive in him. "We're not having this discussion."

Laura tried to reach around him to grab her jacket, but Rodney blocked her attempt. "You don't need a man in order to tell you that you're worth something."

Her heart clenched sharply. He had been the one to tell her for years she wasn't worth anything when it came to being a wife, that she failed every check mark it would take to complete that role. Why the hell would he start this now?

"I'm well aware of that, Rodney. Why do you think I divorced you?" She knew she was the one bringing the conversation that direction, but she was backed into a corner, and she didn't like it.

"That's not why we got divorced."

"Oh, really?" Laura dropped her purse onto the table. "Then share with the class."

"We got divorced because you're cold as a fish, unable to do anything for me. No one would want you like that."

Laura nodded slowly, attempting to choose her words wisely. The problem was that she had believed him for so long that she hadn't even bothered to seek out another relationship. She'd always just assumed that she wasn't built for them, that her inability to perform during sex was the reason she was destined to be alone, and she liked it that way. She'd convinced herself she liked it. But being with Skylar held an entirely different meaning.

Skylar liked her, not because of who she couldn't be but

because of who she was. Skylar had agreed to go on a date, one that Laura desperately wanted to get out of the office to go on, because they felt similarly about each other. Laura wasn't dead inside—she just hadn't found the spark to bring her to life yet.

"You can believe that all you want," Laura stated, her voice firm and brokering no room for argument. "But that isn't why we got divorced."

"Who are you going out with?"

That's really what the entire argument was about, wasn't it? He was upset that he didn't know something about her and that she hadn't told him who it was. Maybe it would get her out of there faster if she gave in. "Skylar."

"You're... What?" He couldn't believe her. His face paled from its angry red and his jaw was nearly to the floor. "You're going out with Skylar Ross? The *girl* we hired for a logo?"

"We hired her to do more than our logo, and she delivered on everything she promised us she would."

Rodney put his hand up, stopping her dead in her tracks from talking. "Is this why you two were so insistent that I accept the proposal? Damn it, Laura, I never expected this kind of manipulation from *you*."

"Hardly." Laura dismissed the idea out of hand. "She and I haven't even begun a potential relationship yet."

"How inappropriate were you with her?" Rodney stepped closer, getting in her face.

Laura wanted to smack him, wanted to give him a piece of her mind that she had never done before. "I wasn't inappropriate. Like I said, we're just now beginning a potential relationship."

Rodney shook his head sharply from side to side. "She must be a gold digger then. She knows how much you make and wants in on some of that so she can keep her business afloat."

"Rodney." Laura was at a loss. Nothing in any of her conversations with Skylar had indicated anything like that. It wasn't even a thought that crossed her mind.

"Were you screwing her when she worked for us?"

"No." Laura straightened her shoulders as she stared him down. "This conversation is inappropriate."

"Hardly, considering you have now tainted working relationships."

"You know what? I wasn't going to do this. You're the one who is inappropriate. You want to talk about making mistakes, let's talk about Jennifer and the fact that you cheated on me with her for years—*years, Rodney*—before you had the damn courage to bring up divorce."

"That was different."

"You're right. It is different." Laura put her hands on her hips, not willing to back down for more than a second. "It's different because I'm not cheating and both of us are willing to be in this relationship. There are no power issues because I'm not her boss anymore."

"A young girl like that?" Rodney scoffed. "You're manipulating her."

"I'm doing no such thing," Laura's voice was low, dangerously so. She was ready for war. "You want to know what's inappropriate? Fucking Hannah from accounts receivable, and then trying to fire her."

Rodney blanched.

"Don't think I don't know about your next in line for cheating. You have always cheated. If it wasn't on me, then it was on tests in school—it was on certifications. You have skated through life with nothing more than a pat on your back for a good job."

Rodney's face turned beet red. Laura shook her head and put up her hand to stop him from saying anything.

"You tried to have me fire her because you knew you couldn't do it. You knew you couldn't do it and not get hacked for your inappropriate behavior, for using your position in order to get into her pants. And that isn't her fault, Rodney. It's yours. You're the one who has to take some damn responsibility for the situation you've found yourself in."

"This conversation is done."

Laura scoffed. Now he wanted the conversation to be done? Now that he was the subject of the embarrassment and degradation instead of her? Typical Rodney. Well, tough luck.

"No, it's not." Laura wasn't going to let him off that easy. He'd started it, and now she was going to finish it. She'd been waiting years for this confrontation, and she wasn't going to back down now. "You need to grow up. I'm not the enemy. I'm not the one who cheated, and I'm not the reason you're a mess."

Rodney laughed. "This is perfect, coming from the woman who was like fucking a corpse."

"Throw insults all you want, but we both know that it takes two to make a marriage work. I'm not perfect."

"You like to tell everyone that you are."

Laura clenched her jaw. "Shut up and listen for once in your damn life."

Rodney's eyes narrowed.

"You want to make sure that baby you just spent hundreds of thousands making has a family to come home to, then worry about yourself. Stop worrying about me and my personal relationships that have nothing to do with you. I've done nothing wrong with Skylar, and she will attest to that. Can you say the same about Hannah?"

"I haven't done anything with *Hannah*."

"Sure you have. Just like you did nothing with Jennifer." Laura snagged her purse and her jacket. "This conversation is over. Feel free to talk to me when you find your damn brain."

She stalked toward her office door.

"Oh, and Rodney, make your own fucking portfolio."

Laura left the office with a huff. She was just stepping past the front desk when Greta flagged her down. "Ms. Ross was here for you."

Damn it. Laura put her hand on the top of the desk. "Did she say what she wanted?"

"No, she didn't."

"Thank you." Laura left immediately, turning down the hallway to take her to Skylar's offices rather than the elevator. When she got there, the lights were off inside, the door was locked, and there was no answer. Her heart sank.

Laura snagged her phone out of her pocket and texted, hoping that Skylar would answer. In the meantime, she made her way down to the lobby to see if she could catch Skylar in the parking lot before their planned date was a complete wash. When she reached the lobby, she knew the date was already a loss. Skylar was nowhere down there, and she hadn't answered her text yet.

Lifting her phone to her ear, Laura called her. Her hands shook, not just with anxiety but anger at Rodney. Perhaps a phone call would get a response instead of just texting, because desperation clung to her heavily. She needed to right this. Laura got to her car and slid behind the wheel as the call went through. Eventually it moved into voicemail.

"Skylar, I think I know what's going on. Give me a call, please." Had her voice wavered?

Hanging up, Laura looked around the parking lot for Skylar's car and didn't find it. She nearly screamed out in frustration. She'd wanted one thing—one thing—that Rodney couldn't screw up in her life, and he'd managed to do it anyway. She had fallen into that trap with eyes wide open.

She drove by the Bistroporium where she'd made their reservations and still didn't find any sign of Skylar. Parking, she called and canceled the reservation and tried Skylar's cell phone again, coming up empty as she waited for an answer. Nerves ran through her, vibrating through her hands and feet as desperation clawed at her throat.

Skylar no doubt heard at least part of the argument. Laura knew she was already insecure about dating, and this must have pushed her over the edge. Rodney would get what he wanted in the end. Never before had Laura wanted to explain, to make sure that Skylar knew where she was coming from, but that was impossible if she wasn't going to answer. At least not until the next day when Laura would know where to find her.

Still, she wouldn't give up, not just yet. Skylar deserved an explanation.

CHAPTER
Thirty-Three

SKYLAR'S PHONE rang several times, and she didn't answer until she was home and safely parked on the street with her car still running. Taking a deep breath, Skylar put the phone to her ear and tried to sound as together as possible even though her heart ached.

"Hey." Her voice dropped at the end, becoming a whisper that she was sure Laura couldn't hear.

"Hey," Laura stated, her voice strong though she sounded down. "Want to talk?"

Skylar's heart sank as dread settled into her. "Not really, but I know we need to."

"Will you come to my condo? Or do you want to meet somewhere that's more neutral?"

Skylar looked around her street, the dark already settling in. Laura's condo was a good forty-minute drive from her house, but she didn't exactly want Laura at her house either—not with Callie and Brady home. "I'll come to you."

"All right, when?"

"Now." Skylar glanced at the clock on her dash before staring down at the gift on the front seat of her car. "It'll be forty minutes before I can get there, assuming traffic isn't awful."

"Want me to order something in?"

Skylar's stomach clenched hard. She had no idea how to answer that. If the conversation went well enough, then yes, she would want to eat something, but if it didn't, she didn't want to be stuck there longer than necessary.

"I'll order something. We can eat or not eat."

"Okay," Skylar murmured.

"I'll see you soon," Laura's voice was firm in her ear.

Skylar hung up and took a steadying breath. Her knuckles were white where she gripped the steering wheel. They were going to have to talk, and honestly, sooner would be better than later, but that didn't mean she was ready for this kind of conversation either. It seemed as though every time Skylar figured out where she stood with Laura, something upset it—the kiss in the elevator, her past history with relationships, Laura's struggles with Rodney.

It took the promised forty minutes for her to arrive. Skylar parked in the guest spots out front and buzzed the door, waiting for Laura to let her into the building. Her hands shook as she pressed the button to call for the elevator. Skylar stretched her fingers, trying to get herself under control. Everything about this visit felt so different compared to her last.

Now there were different boundaries in place. Her lips tingled at the memory of Laura against them, the desire to take everything further physically. But it all came to a stop at the memory of those words flying between Rodney and Laura, the pain and anguish she'd heard, the desire to hurt each other. She wasn't sure she could handle another breakup like the one she had with Trina, not when she knew it would take everything she had left from her and leave her empty.

Just like last time, Skylar didn't have to knock on the door because Laura stood in the doorway, waiting for her. Skylar's heart skipped a beat as soon as they made eye contact. Laura wore loose pants that billowed around her legs, and a tight shirt that definitely wasn't made of cotton. Skylar's mouth went dry, not quite sure how they were going to greet each other, not after witnessing the cruelty both she and Rodney had inflicted, the lengths they had gone to in order to tear each other down.

Laura gave her a small smile and shut the door as soon as they were inside, locking it. "The food is already here if you're hungry."

"I...don't think I can eat right now."

"All right." Laura made her way, barefoot, to the sofa in the center of the living room. She sat down and eyed Skylar, telling her silently to come and sit with her.

Giving in, Skylar made her way to the sofa and gently lowered herself down. She hadn't even taken off her winter jacket, not sure how long she would end up staying.

"Greta told me you stopped by the office."

Skylar pressed her lips together hard, staring at her hands folded in her lap. She still wasn't sure what to say or how to broach what was going through her mind.

"I don't know what you heard—"

"Has he always been that cruel to you?"

Laura clenched her jaw tightly. Skylar looked directly in her eyes, wanting her to know how serious she was and that she expected a response. Her heart raced while she waited. Laura glanced to the ceiling, and Skylar wondered if she was trying to avoid crying or if she was simply thinking deeply.

"What did you hear?" Laura finally asked.

"It doesn't matter." Skylar furrowed her brow. "What he said—"

"Is nothing he hasn't said before." Laura was so tight, every muscle in her body ready to move at a moment's notice.

Reaching forward, Skylar settled her hand on Laura's arm, and she flinched. "I'm not going to hurt you."

Laura didn't answer. She stared at Skylar's intruding hand. What Skylar would give to be able to have a window of insight into what Laura was thinking and feeling in the moment. Anything that would help ease their way into the conversation.

"Laura, what he said to you isn't okay."

"I know that," Laura ground out. "What did you hear?"

"It doesn't matter what I heard. I heard how he talked to you, and I've never heard that from him before. I thought..." Skylar trailed off, her heart racing as she tried to figure out the best way to say it. "I thought you two had figured out how to work together."

"Hardly," Laura murmured, tilting her head down. "We work around each other for the most part. I'm sorry for what you heard."

"I'm not." Anger grew in the pit of her belly. Where had that been hours ago? She wanted it then, not now. She'd wanted to be able to do and say something, but she'd been so shocked by the argument that she'd run.

"He was appalling. Monstrous." Skylar swallowed hard.

Laura's face was downcast, her cheeks red and her eyes closed as embarrassment consumed her. Skylar's heart pattered steadily, everything in her body telling her to move forward and hold Laura through all of this. Laura hated it, clearly, hated being made to feel that way but also that Skylar had witnessed it all. Compassion choked her, and she dared to keep the conversation going. She needed some kind of resolution to this.

"How can you keep working with him?"

"I can't afford to buy him out, and he wouldn't sell to me anyway. I don't want to start over. Ten years of marriage and business together was tough to give up, and now after twenty-four years of business? I don't want to do it."

"But he was so cruel." Skylar stared at the floor and Laura's toes as they peeked out from under her pants. She couldn't wrap her head around it at all. Laura was one of the strongest women she had met, but she continued to put herself in a situation where he would be allowed to do that.

Laura nodded slightly. "Some days he can be. He was upset and pulled out everything in his arsenal to fire at me."

Skylar rolled her eyes, Laura's comment coming off as acceptance and compliance when there should absolutely be none. She wouldn't stand for allowing any kind of abuse to happen. "It's fucked up."

"I know it is," Laura whispered. "He was angry."

"Stop defending him!" There was that fury again, and Skylar leaned into it. "Seriously. I walked out of there because I couldn't handle what I saw, but this is worse than that. This is you giving up, and if there's anything I know about you, Laura, is that you don't give up. You're too smart for this shit."

Laura wouldn't look at her. She stared out the window of her condo. Skylar let the silence linger, knowing Laura likely needed it to gather herself. She'd been through an insanely rough day with that argument, only to end up in another one with Skylar. Even if Skylar wasn't beating her down like Rodney had, it was still emotional whiplash.

Skylar leaned into the couch, pressing her hand over Laura's to give her whatever comfort she could for the moment. She had no idea where they were going from here, but she would stay until Laura was more on her feet.

"I'm not defending him. I'm explaining. And I can handle my own when it comes to him. You would have known that had you stayed for the entirety of the conversation."

"There's no need to stay and listen to abuse."

"You don't understand." It was an accusation, one that stung deep in Skylar's chest. She prided herself on reading people and understanding where they were coming from, to know what they needed at any given moment, and to have it tossed in her face hurt.

"What don't I understand?" She wanted nothing more than to know what was going on behind those eyes, but Laura was so closed off, so damn hard to read.

"You don't understand what it's like to end a marriage."

Skylar clenched her jaw at the ridiculous juxtaposition. "You're right. I don't. Because I've never been married, and I've never had to do that, but I have ended relationships. I do have experience with nasty breakups, unhealthy relationships, and continuing to work with my ex after the breakup. What you put up with from him is out of line."

"It is. Today was." Laura turned on her. "But it's not like that every day."

"You think I don't see the way he hurts you when it's not in your face? Laura, you nearly broke down in tears at the Christmas party because Jennifer announced she was pregnant."

"That's different." Laura stood up sharply, walking to the window and back. "That's... It's not just her that I have that reaction to, all right? Yes, it particularly stings with her because I know that's partly why we divorced, not just the cheating but because the likelihood I could have children was slim, but I can't —" Laura's voice broke, tears in her eyes as she stood stoically with the window at her back. "I can't stand when anyone tells me that. It's not a hurt I've ever managed to get over."

"You don't get over shattered dreams," Skylar whispered, standing and moving right up to Laura. She took both her hands, lacing their fingers together as they stood face-to-face. "Broken dreams are the hardest grief to work through."

Laura's shoulders shook, her face falling again, and her chin dipping down. Skylar's heart broke for the second time that night witnessing the strength Laura used every day just so she could walk through life like she was unaffected by it.

"Come here," Skylar murmured, wrapping her arms around Laura's shoulders and dragging her in for a hug. She ran her fingers up and down Laura's back, against the silky-smooth material of her shirt. She didn't want to let go. Laura's warm body against her was perfect, even with all the upset from the last few hours.

Laura shuddered against her, and Skylar knew she was trying to hold back more tears. Pressing a kiss into the side of Laura's head, Skylar closed her eyes. Laura was as broken as she was— she just had more walls built up around her, more defenses in place. Skylar never was one for making things more difficult than they had to be.

"This isn't how I thought tonight would go," Laura mumbled into Skylar's chest.

"Well, it seems we don't ever have regular conversations like we're supposed to." Skylar dropped another kiss to the side of Laura's head and pushed her hair over her shoulder. "Come on, I realized on my drive over here that I never actually gave you your birthday present."

Laura's head popped up, her eyes red and swollen, but Skylar wasn't going to comment on it. She cupped Laura's cheek, tilting her chin up to land a tender kiss on Laura's lips. She hadn't thought they would end up here, not with the way she'd felt driving over there, but for now they had found a balancing point. Laura tried to deepen the kiss, and Skylar pulled away.

"This isn't your gift."

"Well, I'll take it." Laura tugged Skylar back, dragging in a deep breath as their lips connected again.

Skylar lost herself in the moment for a brief time before she broke the kiss again, needing to keep it short and distanced. After what she'd witnessed, she wasn't ready to leave just yet. "Buzz me in. I'll be right back."

She took off before Laura could catch her and raced down to her car. She'd left it in there on purpose, not sure if she should bring it up for whatever conversation they were going to have. Skylar grabbed the small gift and tucked it under her arm, trudging through the snow and back into the building.

By the time she made it to Laura's condo, the cold air had chilled her. This time she took her jacket off and hung it up next to the door. Laura had pulled out the food she ordered, setting

288 ADRIAN J. SMITH

places for them at the table, and Skylar's stomach rumbled loudly at the mere thought of eating it.

"That looks amazing."

"It's one of my favorite places to order from," Laura answered as she set the last container in the center of the table. "Are we still going to do this?"

"Do what?" Skylar moved in closer.

"Date."

Skylar hesitated. She had to think about that one, whether or not her heart could handle everything that came with Laura, whether or not this was what she really wanted. Nothing with Laura would be a fling, that much she knew, not that she was that kind of person either, but she didn't want to shatter Laura like she had been in the past either.

"I don't know," Skylar finally answered honestly.

Laura blew out a breath and pulled out a chair to sit down. Skylar moved to the seat next to her, handing over the small package that was wrapped in colorful paper.

"You were too drunk and upset the other night for me to give this to you. I thought about leaving it on your desk, but I wanted to see you open it."

Laura furrowed her brow in confusion. "You didn't have to get me a gift."

"I wanted to. Open it."

Laura took her time, finding the tape and sliding her finger underneath it. "You do always think of everything, don't you?"

"I try to." Skylar grinned as the paper popped up.

Laura gasped when she flipped it over, finding a hardcover book of *Imperfect* by Brené Brown. "How did you know?"

"You have a wall of bookshelves. It's hard to miss, and she is one of my favorite authors. I noticed you didn't have it when I was here for Thanksgiving."

"You're so sneaky. Thank you." Laura looked as though she was going to lean in and kiss Skylar, but she stopped herself, no doubt unsure of where they stood now.

Skylar moved in and pressed their mouths together, pleased that they seemed to find themselves on steady ground again, and that Laura had been pleased with the gift. Her stomach rumbled loudly again, and she giggled when she pulled back. "I was really looking forward to tonight, for the record."

"Me too," Laura answered, her tone soft. "So let's enjoy it."

CHAPTER
Thirty~Four

CURIOUS, Laura stepped into her office and sat in her chair, more at ease with herself than she could ever remember being. She put her purse into the desk drawer and closed it up before pulling out her paper calendar and her electronic one, checking to make sure all the dates matched. She felt far lighter than she had in years, her shoulders not as locked together, and ready to tackle her workday, knowing she had something to end the night with.

Rodney would be in soon, and she wasn't looking forward to that conversation. While everything Skylar had said was from her heart, Rodney rarely did that when it involved her. They were two stark contrasts, and yesterday had proven that readily.

Even though she and Skylar hadn't come to any conclusion about their relationship, Laura felt more on even ground with Skylar than she ever had with anyone else—even Rodney for that matter, and what had happened the night before was appalling. Seeing that reflected in Skylar's pure face was a beacon to how bad it had become between them. Rolling her shoulders, she set to work, wanting to get at least something done before Rodney came in to grovel.

As if on cue, he stepped into her office with a large bouquet of tiger lilies. He settled them onto the corner of her desk where she normally kept flowers. Laura remained silent as he stood awkwardly with his hands in his pockets in front of her, a schoolboy about to get scolded.

"I shouldn't have," he started.

"Damn straight you shouldn't have." Laura eyed him hard. She wanted him to know that she had him by the balls and she wasn't about to let go.

Rodney blushed and looked guilty. Laura would call that a win any day.

"Do you realize how much work I've been doing? How much more work than you? If we're partners in this company, fifty-fifty, then why am I covering your ass so often?"

"I know," he muttered. "You're just so good at it."

Laura shook her head. "We're not even talking about how inappropriate the conversation was yesterday. I'm sorry...argument. You're not my husband, Rodney. You have made that very clear to me throughout the last fifteen years."

"I said I'm sorry."

"You didn't actually say that yet." Laura pointed a finger at him. "I'm free to date whomever I want so long as it's appropriate. I'm not dating an employee, and I'm not married, so it doesn't matter who I go out with. You, on the other hand—"

"I didn't sleep with Hannah." Rodney eyed her directly. "I swear to you, I didn't do it."

"Then why would you want me to fire her?"

"Temptation?"

Laura fumed at his immaturity, at him thinking all women should bow to his idiocy because he couldn't be trusted to make good choices. "You need to learn how to keep it in your pants. I'm not covering for you if you can't do it."

"Okay. I hear you."

"Good." Laura shifted her calendar back into the top drawer on her desk. "And you'll have to grovel more than just with flowers."

"They're your favorite."

Laura's lips thinned as they pulled tight. Tiger lilies weren't her favorite flower. They were beautiful, for sure, and she'd had them in her wedding bouquet, which was why he thought they were her favorite, but she much preferred a simpler flower like tulips. "Fix the issue, Rodney. I'm not going to stand for another argument like yesterday. I deserve better than that."

The tension in the room eased. Rodney winced and stared down at his toes, his hands in his pockets as he rocked forward on his feet. There was a beat too long before he asked. "How did your date with Skylar go?"

This she wasn't prepared for. Talking with her ex-husband about current dates was too far over the line, not to mention they didn't really have a date because of his obnoxious behavior. "It was perfect."

He looked as though he was going to ask something else, but he stopped himself. Rodney rubbed his lips together and nodded slowly as he rocked on his heels. "Right. Good. I guess I'll get to work."

"You do that. It's about time you started holding up your end of the business." Laura watched him leave, making sure that he wasn't coming back into her office any time soon.

When the lunch hour hit, she put everything away on her desk and left her purse in her drawer. She had business to discuss, and she wanted to make sure that she caught up with Skylar before she ran off to go do something else or meet someone for lunch.

Laura rushed into Skylar's office, shutting the door and leaning against it. Skylar eyed her, surprised, and confused. "Can I help you?"

"We need to talk."

"What about?" Skylar furrowed her brow.

"I need to explain something to you." Laura stayed right where she was against the door, eyeing every part of Skylar that she could see. The yoga pants and T-shirt were becoming on her, and Laura preferred it to the nicer clothes she wore some-times. Today the T-shirt read "love is love is love" in a heart shape.

"Okay..." Skylar trailed off. "I have a meeting in thirty minutes."

"This won't take long." Laura had to drag her gaze away from Skylar's breasts. "Rodney apologized with flowers he thinks are my favorite, but he can't even remember my birthday so that doesn't surprise me. He did apologize."

"A true apology?" Skylar checked.

Laura nodded—the apology may not have felt real at first, but they did make a breakthrough somewhere during that conversation. "Yes. Everything is fine for now."

She still had her back to the door, unable to force herself to move and take a step. She was so used to being in control of everything, but when it came to Skylar, she found that she broke her rules more often than not. She wanted to.

"Is that what you wanted to tell me?"

"No." Laura had to find the words. She hadn't prepared for it. But everything was so different this time around, and she wanted to keep it that way. She didn't want to be the cold-hearted woman Rodney thought she was.

"Then what is it?" Skylar stayed seated, almost perfectly still as she waited for Laura to say something that made a lick of sense.

"We never finished our conversation last night."

"Oh?" Now Skylar looked even more confused than before.

Laura was awful at this. Anything that required her to express her feelings and desires she made a mess of. "I think we started but never finished."

Skylar furrowed her brow. "You've lost me."

Sighing, Laura wrung her hands together as she stood by the door. If she went to the couch, she wasn't sure she wanted Skylar to follow. Close proximity would make this harder, especially when all she wanted was to kiss her again. She knew that wouldn't be happening until they had this discussion. Laura pointed at the couch. "May I?"

"Since when have you ever asked?"

Never, but I haven't been this nervous, either. Laura said nothing as she folded her hands under her butt to smooth down her skirt as she sat. "We have thirty minutes to discuss this, so please bear with me."

"Twenty-six."

Laura gave Skylar a hard look.

Skylar threw her hands up in the air and laughed lightly. "Fine, thirty minutes starting now."

Again, Laura was thrown into the chaos of what was in her mind, and not being able to form words for it. Staring at her folded hands, she spun through thought after thought, unable to settle on one thing to say. Skylar moved swiftly, getting down on her knees right in front of Laura and holding her hands.

"Don't do that," Laura whispered.

"What's going on? You look so torn."

The debate raged as to whether or not she would break Skylar's grasp, but the skin on skin was more than she could handle and yet not enough at the exact same moment. "I don't do this well."

"Do what well?"

"Share," Laura answered simply.

"I've kind of noticed that."

Laura sighed heavily, her gaze locked on their hands again. Skylar was far too gentle and sweet for her own good. Laura would topple her in seconds, although she hadn't managed to do it yet, and Skylar had shown quite a backbone in the past. "When you look at me like that, all I want to do is kiss you."

Skylar's lips curled up, and Laura sent her a chastising look.

"Stop that. I won't do it, not until we have this talk."

"What talk? You haven't said anything."

"I've said more than I ever have before." Again she was whispering, as if Skylar had stolen her voice. She still wanted to kiss her, to feel that heat and warmth and comfort. It had become addicting in the last week, something Laura wasn't sure she wanted to give up. Laura dragged her gaze from Skylar's lips to her eyes, needing her to understand. "I want to be with you."

"As in a relationship?"

"Yes," Laura answered simply. "And I know I come with a past and a history. I know how daunting that can be, especially since I work with my past. I'm around him every day."

"Why?"

Laura stopped her mini rant, turning her head to the side. That was where she should have started, not with what she wanted but with why she wanted it. Breaking Skylar's hold on one hand, Laura curled a strand of hair behind Skylar's ear.

"You irk me, Skylar. I've never met someone who is so damn energetic and serious in the same breath."

"I can't tell if that's a good thing or a bad thing."

"Both and," Laura responded, dropping her hand back down to cover Skylar's. "Before I met you, I didn't even dream of this, not of being with someone again."

The next part was going to be the hardest thing for her to say, but it was true, and Skylar needed to hear it.

"I thought I was broken."

"Laura—"

"Uh-uh." Laura put her finger to Skylar's lips. "Let me get this out before my thirty minutes are up."

The smile reached Skylar's eyes as she nodded.

"I'm not broken. I think I just hadn't found the right key. I've never been with a woman before, and until you, I hadn't even considered it. But you make me think, Skylar. You make me dream in ways I haven't in decades. It's infectious."

Skylar grinned and blushed.

"That isn't a compliment."

"I think it is," Skylar countered, sitting more fully on her knees and in a much more relaxed position.

Laura clenched her jaw to keep from saying anything else.

Here she was pouring her heart out and all Skylar could do was make a joke of it, but it didn't sting. In fact, it felt good. Laura straightened her back, not breaking their hand contact.

"I need to know that you're in this one hundred percent."

"I..."

"Skylar," Laura warned. "Let me speak."

"Go on."

"I don't hedge. When I say I'm doing something, I'm all in, and I need you to understand that. If we do this, I need to know that you're here for everything."

"This sounds like a proposal," Skylar mumbled.

"It is one, of sorts." Laura's nerves had settled at some point through the conversation. She wasn't sure when, but it was so much easier now than it had been before. "I want you to think about this, and I want you to be certain before you tell me. I can wait."

"Can you?" Skylar countered.

Laura wasn't sure how long she'd be able to, but she would have to. She wasn't going into this without eyes wide open. "I'll wait."

"I'm not sure, you know." Skylar couldn't bring her gaze to Laura's, which told her this was exact right decision to have made. "I thought I knew, but the other night—"

"Showed you just how complicated this will be."

"Yeah," Skylar agreed. "I should have known before then."

"I didn't let you in before, not enough for you to make an educated decision." Laura pressed her lips together to keep from saying anything that she might regret beyond that. She'd hidden the problems between her and Rodney for years, and it was so easy to do it most days. It was so easy to hide in her office and not let anyone in. But she didn't want that anymore.

"So what now?"

"Now you go to your lunch meeting, and I go back to work." Laura moved her hands from Skylar's grasp to either side of herself on the couch cushion. She needed the space. She needed the time to think and get herself back together before the rest of the workday continued and before her people came back in to see her.

"I mean what about us?"

"Right now, we're at a standstill. And that's okay. It's right where we should be."

"But it feels so...icky." Skylar wrinkled her nose.

Laura wanted to laugh at the look on her face, wanted to give in and kiss her again, but she held firm in her decision. They needed to start on even ground before they could begin any next steps or no steps.

"I hope I'll see you soon," Laura murmured, keeping her voice soft. Resisting the temptation one more time to lean in and press their lips together, she stood up and walked to the door without looking over her shoulder.

When she settled into her office, she closed her eyes. Fear ricocheted through her chest, from one thing to the next, grasping hold of everything and digging its claws in. What if Skylar rejected her? Hell, what if she didn't? What if she was thrown into the world of a full-blown relationship, completely unprepared?

Taking a deep breath, Laura worked to calm herself down and steady her ranting heart. It had felt amazing to be honest, to be comfortable enough to know that Skylar was going to hear what she had to say, what she needed to get off her chest. Reaching for her pen, her hand didn't shake as much as she thought it would. So much had changed in so little time, but she did know one thing—work wasn't going to be enough for her anymore. She deserved more than what she had. And she was willing to work to get it.

CHAPTER
Thirty-Five

SKYLAR STARED at her ringing phone. They had an agreement. They would only communicate via email and solely for the purpose of the business they were stuck still running together. Skylar didn't want to answer it. Yet the niggling need to find out just what Trina wanted or needed was strong, and she picked up her phone, her thumb hesitating over the button.

She shouldn't do it.

But damn did she want to.

Hitting the button, Skylar brought the phone to her ear. "Hi."

"Hi." Trina's voice was so warm, such a welcome remembrance of how they'd once loved and cared for each other. "How's everything going?"

Confused, Skylar answered in a way she thought was the safest bet. A little information but not too much. "Pretty good."

"Good, good." Trina paused the conversation.

Skylar's heart thudded loudly. She looked around her office, nervous, wanting anything to focus on that wasn't the phone call itself. Why did it seem that exes always had impeccable timing when it came to these kinds of phone calls? She had to stop that thought—she didn't even know what this was about yet. It could be Trina firing her, which would honestly be the best firing she'd ever had.

"How's it going for you?" Skylar awkwardly asked.

"It's going well."

They fell into a silence, Skylar staring at her computer screen, still trying to figure out what the phone call was about. She hated these kinds of conversations, where she wasn't sure where it was going or what shit she was about to step into.

"What's going on, Trina?"

"I wanted to check in about that job."

"What job?" Skylar clenched her jaw.

"The job I got the call about for a reference."

Oh. Skylar's cheeks heated obnoxiously, the conversation she'd had with Laura earlier that day still so fresh in her mind. She never would have gotten as close to Laura as she had without that job and being forced to work together. "I finished it up last week."

"Did it go well?"

"Yes, thank you for asking." She still wasn't sure why Trina had called. She'd never been a reference before since Skylar had specifically not given her name for that. Rodney had certainly done his research to find how the two of them were connected— not that it was hard to find.

"Good, good," she repeated, clearly struggling as much as Skylar to keep the conversation going.

"Is that all you called for?"

"I wanted to check in on you."

"Why? Is everything going well in terms of marketing for you?"

"Yes, it's going really well, I'm looking at scaling the business up, actually."

"Well, I'm ready for it if you are." *Why did I just say that?* Skylar tapped her fingers on the top of her desk. She'd wanted to drop Trina as a client for the last year, but it was good money, good steady income, and increasing that would certainly help her business in the long run.

"I was thinking of hiring someone else."

Skylar's stomach plummeted. Even if it was what she wanted, it still hurt. She took back everything she had thought about it before. She needed that income to survive. Her heart raced, and her hands shook. "I understand."

"I don't want you to think this is me firing you."

That's exactly what it was, though. Skylar had built the business from the ground up. She'd put in countless hours of work before Trina could even pay her. It wasn't that she wanted to be paid back for it, but she'd expected the income to be there as soon as they'd found a steady stream of it.

"Skylar?"

"It's fine, Trina. I get it." They hadn't worked well since they'd broken up. It had been strained at best, and really, they couldn't scale up the business without better communication. Which would mean they either split apart fully now or they figured out how to talk again. Skylar wasn't sure which she wanted.

"I'm still going to give you your part."

"What? What part?"

"You were there from the start, and I want to honor that. So you'll own fifteen percent of the company."

"Fifteen—Trina, what are you talking about?" Now her stomach was doing flip flops.

Trina sighed. "You deserve it. I wouldn't have been able to do it without you, and so I've always considered that you would own part of it when the time came for me to find someone else to do the marketing."

"You never told me."

"I didn't think it would happen a lot of days, so I didn't want to get you excited or to reject it."

"You don't have to do this."

"I know." Trina sounded so confident and sure.

"I don't suppose arguing with you will get me anywhere."

"It won't."

"Well, thank you." Skylar swallowed hard, but her hands still shook.

"You deserve it. I'm just glad I was able to help you get that job."

"Yes, thank you for that. It was an interesting job to say the least." Skylar glanced at the clock on her computer, noting just how late it really was. She had a few more hours of work to get done, and she would need to start making new contacts and landing herself a new contract soon.

"I just wanted to call and let you know that."

"Sure thing. Just let me know who you hire, and I can transfer the admin for everything over to them."

"I'll send you an email when I know."

"Perfect." Skylar ended the call swiftly, sitting at her desk still in a bit of shock from the conversation. Trina had sounded so ready for the next step. Blowing out a breath, Skylar stared at her computer screen again. Relief flooded her, the tension that had been riding in her shoulders for months finally releasing.

It was the right decision to make. She knew it was. She watched Laura struggle with Rodney, with the anger and hurt that still showed up when they least expected it. She didn't want that for her and Trina. They'd found a balance, but it was still fraught with pain.

~

Skylar's back ached. She'd gotten up and made herself tea several times already, but when she found herself standing up twenty minutes after sitting back down, she knew her workday had to come to an end. She'd managed to get some work done, but ever since the phone call with Trina, all she could do was think about Laura.

Laura had come to her, she'd laid her heart out on her sleeve in a way Skylar had never thought would be possible, and then she'd left. She'd up and left with no more explanation other than for Skylar to come to her when and if she was ready.

Falling into her couch, Skylar crossed her legs and held her mug of tea tightly between her hands. She couldn't focus on anything but Laura's eyes as they'd spoken earlier that day. She'd been sincere in everything. She'd been honest. Even though Laura was really good about not talking about what she didn't want to.

She'd left Skylar with a question, however, one that she hadn't managed to find the time to think about yet. At least not with her full focus. *What do I feel for Laura?* It was definitely more than passing interest, that much Skylar knew for certain. It had always been more than that.

Laura wanted a relationship, she wanted to try whatever might be between them, and she wanted to give it her all. *But do I want the same thing?* Going headfirst into a relationship again, especially the one after Trina, the one after the woman she thought she was going to marry. And to be Laura's first same-sex relationship? That was scary as hell.

Skylar sipped her tea, surprised when it was lukewarm instead of hot. How long had she been sitting there thinking? Setting her mug on her desk, Skylar packed up her bag. She could deal with the rest in the morning and clean up from her late night at work.

She was locking up her office when she heard the click of another door. Skylar checked the time on her phone. It was way later than she'd thought it was. Dragging her feet, she made her way to the elevator, intrigued to find Laura already standing there with her jacket on, her purse on her shoulder and her briefcase in her hand.

"You're here late," Skylar said as she rounded the corner.

"So are you," Laura commented with a raised eyebrow.

"I had a lot of work to get done."

"Likewise."

Skylar let Laura enter the elevator first, stepping just to the side of her. Her heart hammered loudly, her nerves on fire.

"My ex fired me today," Skylar started, surprising herself.

Laura spun on her. "What for?"

"She wants to expand the business and thinks it's time to find someone else to work with." Skylar tried to shrug it off like it wasn't a big deal, but it was. It hurt, still, even though she told herself so many times that it shouldn't.

"That's ridiculous. You're perfectly capable—"

"I know I am, and she knows I am." Skylar clenched her jaw. "But she gave me fifteen percent of the company."

"What?" Laura's eyes widened. "Why would she do that?"

"She felt she owed it to me, I guess."

"Very stupid on her part. Very smart on yours depending on what you do with it." Laura shifted her briefcase from one hand to the other, keeping her posture as rigid as ever.

"Right? But I guess it's to my advantage. I'll be a silent partner."

"Yes, but it's also income now instead of a business expense, and if she goes under for doing something stupid you can also be held liable."

Skylar's breath caught. She hadn't thought of any of that. Then again, she had very little experience in this kind of thing, not like Laura would. "Thanks for that advice—gives me a lot to think about."

"Please do. All businesses are a liability."

"True. Maybe it's time we go our separate ways."

Pain flashed across Laura's gaze, and Skylar had to hope that she didn't think Skylar's comment was about her working relationship with Rodney. She and Trina had been working toward this from the beginning of their breakup, and she knew it was going to happen someday. She just didn't want it to be that day.

The elevator dinged, and Skylar followed Laura out. Laura got to the door in the lobby first, holding it open for Skylar. Shivering as soon as the winter air hit her, Skylar waited to walk down the front steps with her. They moved toward Laura's car, Skylar's parked much farther out since she had come back so late after her lunch with a potential client.

"I hope your day was good," Skylar said, trying to keep the conversation going.

"It went well enough." Laura stashed her briefcase in the back seat of her car, crossing her arms as they faced each other again.

Skylar's heart raced. Laura wasn't being cold but there was still a distance between them. Skylar was the cause of it, she knew, and she didn't like it. "You said Mr. Solace apologized?"

"Call him Rodney for Christ's sake. He's not your boss anymore." Laura shuddered. "Yes, he apologized, and he played nice all day. It'll last a few weeks before he starts to slip again."

"I suppose you understand how the patterns of behavior go."

"Hmm." Laura pressed her lips together.

It was so hard to read her face in the shadows in the parking lot. Skylar shoved her hands in her pockets. "I've been thinking about what you said all day."

Laura lifted her gaze to meet Skylar's.

"I can't stop thinking about it, honestly. I've tried." Skylar shifted from one foot to the next, nervous. "I won't claim to understand where you're coming from even half the time."

"I don't expect you to."

"Shut up. You got your chance. This is mine." Skylar stepped in closer, pleased at Laura's surprised look, but as soon as she'd allowed herself to speak, she couldn't stop. "You know, I never even thought this was a possibility when I met you, but I was so damn interested in trying to figure out who you are. And you know what, Laura? I really like what I've found. You're amazingly strong, and you keep everything buried because it's easier, but you're not afraid to confront it either."

"I hardly—"

"Shush, boomer." Skylar grinned, sliding in even closer. "I don't want to hear it. Not right now."

Skylar waited to make sure that Laura wasn't going to interrupt her again, their breath mingling in the frosty air. Skylar slid in closer, grasping Laura's fingers delicately. She stared at their joined hands, her decision solidifying. She'd known it was this the entire time. She just had to get over her own fear at being hurt again.

"Take me home."

"What?" Laura blinked at her in shock.

Skylar stepped in, pushing Laura back into the side of the car, and covered her. Their lips connected firmly, the kiss moving from intense to desperate. Laura moaned, her hands on Skylar's arms, clenching tightly. Skylar pushed her leg between Laura's, leaning in so she would know exactly what Skylar wanted. She ached for Laura to touch her, to be able to freely caress her without the confines of doubts and fears.

Laura nipped her lip, and Skylar grinned as she slid away, a breath of space between them. Laura's eyes were wide as she looked up at Skylar. One last kiss and Skylar would be ready. She made this one quick, needing to get the hell out of the parking lot before she couldn't wait.

"Take me home, Laura."

CHAPTER
Thirty-Six

SKYLAR'S HAND on her thigh was warm. She traced small circles through the fabric of Laura's skirt as Laura drove toward her condo. Anticipation filled her. Skylar tried to make small talk, but Laura's ears buzzed loudly, and she missed most of what was said.

Dropping her hand down, Laura covered Skylar's, threading their fingers together to stop the incessant playing against her skin. She was on fire. Heat pooled between her legs, everything tingling while she imagined repeatedly just what Skylar was going to do to her once they got home.

She parked the car, crooked, but she wasn't about to waste the time to correct it. Laura turned on Skylar, a smile on Skylar's lips, her eyes alight with so much ease. With the decision made, there was no turning back—Laura didn't want to. She wanted everything that was right in front of her and more.

"Are you ready?" Laura asked, double-checking because she had to. It wasn't just for Skylar's answer, but it was for her own.

"Yes. Are you?"

"Yes." Laura lifted Skylar's hand to her mouth, pressing a gentle kiss against the smooth skin on her knuckles. "Yes, I'm ready."

Laura didn't hesitate as she got out of the vehicle. She grabbed her purse and took Skylar's hand as she came around the back side of the car. They walked together inside the building.

The wait for the elevator took forever. Her heart raced, her fingers sweated, and she wasn't sure how much longer she could stand it. She wanted Skylar right then and there, a new experience. She'd never wanted sex this badly. As soon as the elevator arrived, Laura stepped inside and pressed the button for her floor.

Skylar was on her in an instant. Pushed against the wall, Laura struggled to catch a breath. She groaned when Skylar nipped at her lip, when she undid the buttons on Laura's coat, and she had her hands inside, exploring and roaming. Laura threw her head back into the wall. Skylar planted kisses along her neck, down her chest, and back up to her mouth. Their tongues tangled, and Laura gripped the railing on the side of the elevator like her life depended on it.

Skylar coasted her hands down Laura's body, opening her blazer and exploring her belly. She didn't remove any other clothing, not yet. *Fuck, I want her to.* Right here and now Skylar could take her, and Laura would let it happen. The soft fabric of yoga pants against her bare leg was a surprise. The dexterous fingers climbing their way along her outer thigh was even more of a shock.

"Can I touch you?" Skylar asked, voice low and husky.

Groaning, Laura opened her eyes and stared directly into Skylar's. "You better."

Skylar made her way up between Laura's legs and gently rubbed against her clit through the fabric of her thong. Laura sighed into the sensation, the perfect touch that she had longed for. Skylar moved her mouth to Laura's neck, sucking the sensitive skin there.

"Yes," Laura whispered, closing her eyes and feeling only with her body. This was perfect, exactly what she had dreamed of and more. She bucked her hips, wanting Skylar to rub harder, to touch her more, but Skylar didn't give in to her silent demands.

Laura opened her eyes just in time to see the elevator doors open. She gripped Skylar's arm hard to get her attention, both breathing heavily as they stopped all forward momentum and stared at the doors.

"Guess that's our cue," Skylar said with a light laugh. She picked up her backpack that she'd dropped to the floor at some point and took Laura's hand, dragging her forward. "Come on."

Skylar led the way, thankfully. Laura wasn't sure she had the mental capacity to think clearly, not with the feel of Skylar's fingers against her so fresh in her mind, the way she'd teased and rubbed. She fumbled for a moment with the key to the door before she managed to get it unlocked.

"Are you nervous?" Skylar murmured into her ear, tracing the line of it with her tongue.

Skylar was going to torture her, that much Laura knew. She said nothing as she slammed the door shut after Skylar came inside. Laura dropped her purse on the floor, pushing into Skylar right after she dropped her backpack and smooshing her against the door.

Their mouths moved furiously against each other. Laura picked her way against Skylar's jacket, trying to find the damn zipper without looking. As soon as she grabbed hold, she dragged it down and pushed Skylar's jacket off her shoulders so it dropped to the floor, her scent filling her senses. Her heart raced as she reached down to put her hands under the hem of Skylar's shirt, lifting it up and finding gloriously soft and chilled skin.

Skylar had her hand in Laura's hair, holding their mouths together as she skimmed her other hand down Laura's side and behind her back, under the edge of her blazer to pull at her blouse. Laura moved her shoulders and her hands, tugging off her own wool coat and letting it fall wherever it landed. Her blazer followed a second later. Skylar's full body length pressed against her was exactly what she needed.

She wasn't nervous, not at all. Instinct took over, and she did everything by feel and touch, turning her brain off as soon as she could. Breaking the kiss, Laura stepped backward, her hands at the buttons on her blouse as she undid them slowly and one by one, her gaze locked on Skylar's. She kept silent, the echo of her rapid breaths in her ears, wanting to know what Skylar would do, what she would say and think.

Skylar grinned broadly as she took off her tennis shoes and left them with the jackets. She followed Laura's path, hands on her hips as she helped her walk backward toward the bedroom. Laura reached behind her to undo the zipper on her skirt, releasing the fabric around her waist in an instant. They stepped into her bedroom, and she moved out of her shoes just as Skylar came up behind her and pulled off her blouse and skirt.

"You're so damn beautiful," Skylar murmured against Laura's shoulder before nipping at the skin.

Laura's breath caught, and she reached for Skylar's hand, moving it around her waist and down between her legs again. She needed more of that. She needed to find out just what would come of it. Skylar obliged, sliding her hands under the fabric of her thong and brushing the pads of her fingers against Laura's clit, skin to skin.

"Yes," Laura muttered, arching her back into Skylar's front and closing her eyes.

Skylar dipped her fingers lower, teasing her before bringing them back up and racing a pattern against her, the swishing back and forth of her fingers like scissors against her. Laura cried out, clenching her eyes tight at the onslaught of sensation. Skylar wrapped her other hand around Laura's waist and held on tight as she continued to tease.

"Skylar..." Laura lost her breath. She swallowed hard to refocus her brain and her voice. "I'm so close."

"Then feel," Skylar whispered, nipping again at the tender skin right at the base of Laura's neck.

Laura held on to Skylar's arms, keeping her feet on the ground when she felt like she was floating, her orgasm ripping through her. Lights burst behind her closed eyes, and she could barely breathe as Skylar continued to play her fingers against her, continued to drag out the last of her orgasm. The skin along her chest tingled, her nipples pulling tight while the pleasure continued. She wanted to tell her to stop and keep going. Her mind a complete blur.

Eventually, she clenched her hand tight against Skylar's wrist, and Skylar slowed to a stop. The teasing eased up, and Laura found her feet again, able to stand without struggle. Twisting around in Skylar's embrace, Laura pressed their mouths together while reaching behind her to unhook her bra. When she was completely stripped, she leaned forward to pull at Skylar's shirt and lift it over her head.

Skylar was everything Laura wanted. She flitted her fingers across the line of Skylar's bra, taking her time as she explored and touched. Eventually she stepped backward toward the bed, eyeing Skylar with a devious look. "Strip down and join me."

"Yes, ma'am." Skylar giggled and did exactly as she was told before she sat on the edge of the mattress, pulling herself toward the middle.

Laura climbed on, walking on her knees to lean over Skylar's supine form. She bent down, taking Skylar's mouth like she owned it. She kissed her way to Skylar's breasts, teasing her nipples to a point with her tongue. The hard nub brushed against the flat of her tongue, such a contrast to the softness of her breast. She sucked, she teased even more, and Skylar writhed under her. She had dreamed of this as soon as she'd allowed herself the possibility, the weight of Skylar's breast in her palm, the warmth of her skin under her fingertips. She wanted nothing more than to be here in this moment.

Pressing open mouthed kisses down Skylar's belly to her hip,

Laura shifted to sit on her knees in between Skylar's legs. She used her teeth to scrape lightly against the inside of Skylar's thighs, teasing her, drawing everything out as long as she possibly could before she would give in and do exactly what she wanted.

Laura laid down on her belly, running her fingers against the backs of Skylar's legs to her knees. Skylar moaned lightly, her hips rotating, which brought the full scent of Skylar's arousal to her. Laura took in a sharp breath, reveling in the musk with closed eyes. When she glanced up, Skylar's gaze was locked on hers.

"Do it," Skylar whispered. "Do it already."

Laura still took her time. She wanted to drag this out as much as possible. Sucking gently against the smooth skin on Skylar's inner leg, she swirled her tongue, making patterns and designs that she would forget in an instant. Skylar reached up and grabbed the pillow by her head, holding onto it tightly as she tried to stay still. The hair between Skylar's legs was dark brown, curly, coarse, and finely trimmed. Laura moved closer, her cheek brushing against Skylar's swollen clit as she turned to place another purposeful kiss not where Skylar wanted.

Skylar turned into her, and Laura chuckled lowly at her impatience. For someone who was so patient in work, she was absolutely impatient when it came to this. Laura wanted to draw this out as long as possible, tease her into oblivion. But her own temptation to find out exactly what Skylar tasted like, what noises she made, the way she moved overwhelmed her.

"Laura," Skylar whined.

Sliding in closer, Laura nuzzled her nose in. She dipped her tongue out to take a quick taste. Humming her contentment with the salty tang, Laura dove in and slid the full flat of her tongue against Skylar. She gathered everything she could, swallowing as flavor blossomed.

"Laura," Skylar repeated, her back arching upward off the bed.

Laura glanced up, pleased to see the reaction rolling through Skylar. She flicked her tongue hard before soothing with a gentle swipe. Skylar twitched hard, her body jerking as pleasure washed through her. Her fingers clenched into the quilt, tightening as she lifted her hips and pressed them into Laura's waiting mouth.

Pleased with the reaction, Laura did it again. She stayed with the momentum until she changed to sucking and teasing flicks back and forth constantly. Skylar grew louder, her voice reverberating around the room as she rode Laura's mouth. Finally her voice broke as her entire body tensed and her face pinched.

Laura didn't stop, but she did ease back on the amount of pressure and the speed of her movements. She wasn't done yet. She wanted to see Skylar come apart again and again. Skylar gasped in a large breath, and Laura took that as her chance. She pressed back in, sliding a hand under her mouth to insert a finger up to her knuckle.

Skylar cried out. She was so hot inside, her muscles still clenching from the orgasm Laura had just given her. She bucked her hips as Laura curled her finger up and pressed, sliding her finger back and forth as she started in with her mouth again. This was gloriously beautiful. She was so ready for more, to give and to take, to allow them the entire night together to stay in each other's arms.

Before she knew what was happening, Skylar clenched against her again, her hips undulating under Laura's touch. Skylar drew in a ragged breath, her fingers sliding into Laura's hair as she tugged hard. "Enough. Give me a break."

Laura laughed a little as she pulled away, dropping kisses onto the smooth skin on her inner thigh again. She would give Skylar whatever she wanted and needed. That much she knew. Laura moved up the bed to lie against Skylar's side, sliding her leg in between Skylar's as they curled together in a cuddle.

Skylar pressed her forehead against Laura's shoulder, holding on tight as she calmed down from the pleasure raging through her. When Skylar pressed her mouth to Laura's breast, Laura looked down at her curiously.

"Oh did you think we were done?" Skylar winked. "Because we're definitely not finished yet."

Laura brought Skylar's mouth up to hers, kissing her hard. "When did I ever say we were done? We're just getting started."

"My kind of woman," Skylar murmured, kissing her way down to Laura's breasts. "I didn't get enough of these before."

Laura laughed fully, turning onto her back to stare up at her ceiling as Skylar covered her, her weight resting on Laura. This was exactly what she had dreamed of and exactly where they were going to remain for the rest of the night. This was so much better than her dreams.

CHAPTER
Thirty-Seven

THE ALARM GOING off wasn't her usual one. Skylar blinked her eyes open when the mattress under her moved. Laura leaned over, cursing when there was a loud crash. When she finally got the damned thing turned off, she came back to Skylar. Skylar grinned, moving in to press a kiss to Laura's sleep-warm lips.

"Morning."

"Sorry. I don't know how early you wake up, but it's time for me to get ready for work."

"Well, probably not this early." Skylar looked at the window, finding it still dark outside. "What time is it even?"

"Six."

"Jesus," she muttered. "Way too early."

Sliding against Laura, Skylar started teasing her in every place she could reach. The decision to jump into a relationship, while it had seemed impulsive at the time, had been the exact right answer. She'd thought it to death, and it was time to act, to do something other than waffling.

"Can I entice you to stay in bed?" Skylar palmed Laura's breast, massaging gently and teasing her nipple with her thumb. "Because I'm sure I can make it worthwhile."

"Work," Laura groaned.

"You don't have to be there until nine."

"Eight. I work eight to five."

"On what planet?" Skylar furrowed her brow, skimming her hand down to Laura's hip. Just a few more inches and she knew she'd have Laura under her. They hadn't slept much that night but being shoved to the edge of the bed by the woman next to her had been well worth it. "You work way more than eight to five."

"That's when office hours are, and an hour for lunch."

Skylar snorted. "And are you going to take an hour for lunch today?"

"That I can probably be persuaded on."

Skylar bent her head and latched her mouth around Laura's nipple, flicking her tongue wildly against her. Laura gasped, her fingers digging into Skylar's hair in an instant. She giggled when she pulled away and kissed Laura hard again.

"We do have a few hours."

"You have a few hours. I'm much older than you, and while your beauty is there every moment of the day, mine takes a while to find."

Skylar snorted and rolled her eyes. "I totally disagree."

Laura kissed her again, sliding from the bed and walking confidently naked away. *Yeah, age...like that makes a difference.* Skylar watched her until Laura disappeared into the bathroom. Stretching her weary muscles, Skylar stayed on the bed. It was bliss. There was no other word to explain it. Waking up with Laura was nothing like she had dreamed. She'd been shoved to one side of the bed while Laura sprawled over the rest of it, but the entire night, Laura had made physical contact with her in some capacity.

The shower water turned off when Skylar finally dragged her weary ass out of bed. Pulling on her clothes from the day before, Skylar stumbled to the kitchen. Coffee, she needed a good, healthy dose of coffee, and her bet was Laura needed the same.

When she couldn't find anything that resembled coffee,

Skylar found her way back to the bedroom only to discover Laura with a towel wrapped around her chest and her hair thrown up in another one. Her shoulders were pink from the heat of the water, small droplets all along her skin.

"Damn, that's tempting."

Laura canted her head slightly before she fully understood what Skylar had said, then the blush reached her cheeks, and Skylar tumbled even more in love. She stopped cold. She wasn't... was she? No, she couldn't be.

"Did you need something or were you here only to leer?"

Skylar snapped out of her thoughts. "Coffee?"

"I don't have any."

"What?"

"I always buy some on the way into work. My little treat for myself every morning."

Skylar pressed her lips together hard. Not only had they stayed up late, but Laura had woken her up early and now she wasn't even going to give her the elixir that would make her brain something other than mush. It was going to be a long day.

True to her word, Laura stopped by a small coffee shop and ordered them drinks on their way in. Skylar was going to need more than one to make it through the day.

They took the elevator up to the sixth floor together, Skylar giving Laura a quick kiss right before the doors opened. "See you later."

"See you," Laura answered with a huge grin Skylar was sure she'd never seen before.

When she was in her office, she immediately grabbed the fresh set of clothes that she kept there and went to the back room to change. Finally settled, Skylar set out her computer and went to work.

～

"How did you turn her against me?"

"Excuse me?" Skylar narrowed her gaze, spinning around as she came back in from an early lunch with a new client.

"How did you turn her against me?" Rodney stood in the lobby as if he was just leaving, his jacket on, his face set.

"I don't know what you're talking about." Skylar shoved her hands into her pockets.

"Laura, that's who I'm talking about."

Skylar was still unsure of what exactly he was referencing. They hadn't talked since that morning, and none of their conversation had centered on Rodney. Skylar drew in a slow breath, wanting to not be standing in the lobby as people came and went, witnessing everything. Then again, that might be for the best.

"What exactly do you think I did to her?"

"She won't listen to me anymore!"

Skylar clenched her jaw, trying to find a way to delicately step around this.

"You've brainwashed her into thinking we can't work together anymore. That *she* is the boss."

"From my understanding you both own fifty percent of the company, so you're both the boss."

"Exactly!" Rodney's voice rose, echoing through the semi-full room.

Skylar held her position. She and Laura were supposed to meet up for a quick lunch, and if Laura knew she wasn't back yet from her meeting, she could very well come down and find them. She didn't want that.

"You've put all these ideas in her head." He pounded two fingers into his temple. "And now she thinks it's okay not to do her work, not show up on time, and to force me to take over her responsibilities."

Skylar was shocked, trying to hold back any facial reactions to how unhinged he was. She couldn't believe she'd ever thought he was the nice one, the one who had it all together. Holding her tongue, Skylar waited to see where he would go with this and when it would end because she had no idea how to stop it.

"She's not the partner I went into business with, and it's all because of *you*." He pointed his finger at her face.

Cold washed through Skylar. This was going to be more of a confrontation than she had expected, and she wasn't sure she could handle it. The front door to the building opened and closed as the stragglers made their way out. The elevator dinged, signaling someone else was coming down for their lunch.

Skylar shook her head slowly, about to speak when Rodney interrupted her. "You're the cause of all these issues. You're the one who weaseled your way into our business."

"Rodney," Laura's voice was firm, holding with it a scolding Skylar never wanted to be on the receiving end of. "Enough."

He spun around, coming face-to-face with Laura.

"If you want to speak to me privately, you're welcome to, but you won't accost Skylar in the lobby again."

Rodney cut a glare in Skylar's direction. Skylar stood there dumbfounded. She'd never seen this side of her. She'd heard it, down the hall as she'd gone in to see Laura, but she'd never borne the full brunt of it. He was deranged.

"Skylar's done nothing wrong."

"This is an inappropriate relationship," he countered.

"No." Laura stepped forward, getting closer to him. Skylar's heart thundered at what was going to happen next. "You're the one who's being inappropriate, and if you don't stop now, I have no issue taking action. This is unacceptable, and at the very least, Skylar deserves an apology, at the most she deserves your groveling."

Rodney snorted loudly.

Laura put her hand up to stop him before he spoke again. "Not once did I ever treat Jennifer with such disrespect because, while I have issues with what you did, she is still a woman and a person who deserves to be treated well. Both Skylar and I deserve that same respect. Don't you think?"

His cheeks reddened. Skylar still stood, mouth agape, her hands still in her pockets. She hadn't anticipated walking right into this fresh hell, and she had no idea how to escape it. She'd never liked conflict. Listening to her parent's fight had been the worst, and this brought her right back to those moments.

"I'm not your wife anymore, Rodney. You accepted that long ago, so what's this really about? Hmm?" Laura was almost nose-to-nose with him.

"You can't be with her."

"I can be with anyone I damn well please. What's your issue? Her age or the fact she's a woman?"

Rodney paled.

"Ah, that's what I thought. Just because I'm dating a woman doesn't mean my relationship with you was any less valid."

"Laura—"

"No. You can apologize to Skylar now, and then go on your way. I really don't want to hear excuses today."

Rodney was thoroughly scolded. Skylar swallowed hard as he dropped his chin and faced her. "I'm sorry."

"What for, Rodney?" Laura pressed.

He inhaled, deep and shuddering. "I'm sorry for taking my anger out on you. You didn't deserve it, and no, I don't believe anything of what I said. I was trying to hurt you."

"Well... thank you, I suppose." Skylar's voice sounded a whole lot more confident than she actually was. She was impressed with the turn of the situation, but still stunned by the fact that it had happened at all. Skylar continued to stand awkwardly with her back to the wall.

Rodney looked at Laura like a lost little boy. She shooed him on his way, then grabbed Skylar by the arm as soon as they were alone. "I'm so sorry."

"It's not your fault."

"It is, a bit." Laura glanced out the front doors. "Are we still doing lunch?"

"I guess?" Skylar wasn't sure she wanted to.

Laura pinned her with a look, and Skylar knew she had to give an actual answer.

"Sure."

"Come on."

They walked to Laura's car, sliding inside even though Skylar's would still be warm from her early lunch. As soon as the doors were shut and the engine on, Laura let out a huge sigh. "When we got into it the other day, I suspected this was why he was so upset. I didn't anticipate he would come after you, however. I'm so sorry for that."

"It's not your fault."

"I should have talked to him again, made sure he understood that was over the line."

Skylar leaned in and took Laura's hand in hers. "It's not your job to make him behave like a decent person."

"No, but it *is* my job to protect you."

Their eyes locked, a rush running through Skylar at the mere thought that Laura wanted to do that. She threaded their fingers together in a tight squeeze. "It's not."

"From him it is. There's...there's a lot unresolved, and with me being in a new relationship, it's going to shift a lot of those tensions."

Intuitively Skylar knew that. It was impossible not to feel something when an ex she was in love with started dating someone else. That had been partly why she'd broken some of her friendships when she and Trina had split. She wasn't sure she'd be able to handle seeing Trina with someone else, let alone hearing about it.

"I get it," Skylar murmured. "I do."

"Thank you." Laura dropped her gaze to their hands. Her cheeks turned pink. "Thank you so much for last night."

"What for?"

"For everything." Laura's lips curled upward. "I mean that. I really enjoyed it."

Skylar chuckled. "I did, too. So much so that I want to do it again."

"Oh, I hope we will."

"We will. I promise."

"Tomorrow night?"

Skylar nearly choked. "What?"

"Go on a date with me. Tomorrow. I need actual sleep tonight, as much as I'd love a reprise." Laura's cheeks still had that cute flush to them.

Skylar leaned in and kissed her with a grin. "Yes."

"Bistroporium?"

"Sure. Why not try again?"

"Good." This time Laura initiated the kiss, deepening it until Skylar lost all track of time. Laura stopped. "We should probably get something to eat."

"This is better, just saying."

"You're not going to hear any disagreement from me." Laura put the car into gear, and they drove out of the parking lot.

CHAPTER
Thirty-Eight

LAURA GAVE Rodney the rest of the day, but when morning hit the next day, she was ready to confront him. She got to the office before anyone else and left her door open so she could catch him as soon as he came in. When everything was abuzz with work, Rodney stepped to the door of his office.

Laura shot out of her chair and walked right to him, her arms crossed and her face set. "We need to talk."

He winced. Rodney dragged his feet, but he did walk into her office, dropping his briefcase onto the table on the far side of the room.

"Why's it so warm in here?" he pulled at his tie.

"It's not warm." Laura shut the door slowly, having forgotten until that moment that she'd changed the thermostat and hadn't put it back since Skylar was done working for them. She moved to her desk and sat on the edge of it, her hands on either side of her to prop her up.

"I'm sorry about yesterday."

"You should be," she pinned him with her glare. "It was embarrassing."

"I know. I just... I shouldn't have done that."

"And you should apologize to Skylar, again. If you're angry with me, that's one thing. But she has nothing to do with our past."

Rodney nodded, standing in front of her completely still. No doubt he was waiting to be dismissed or chastised again.

"What's got you so upset about this?"

"You've never dated anyone, Laura. Never. Even in college it was just me."

She drew her eyebrows together and cocked her head at him. "I went on a few dates with David, don't you remember?"

Rodney stared at her dumbfounded. "No."

"That's why I wasn't invited to his wedding." She curled her fingers around the edge of the desk. Could he really not remember? "It's why I didn't go to the funeral."

"You two were never really close anyway."

"Because I chose you over him."

Surprise etched its way across Rodney's face. "What?"

"I chose you, and he was always bitter about that, at least to an extent through college. I don't know about later because I never talked to him much."

"Laura, really?"

"That's how I always interpreted it, and honestly, what does it matter if I dated after we divorced? It's my life to live. You started fresh with Jennifer, you have Grayson and a new one on the way, and you shouldn't be so caught up in what I'm doing or not doing."

Rodney winced, his gaze downcast as if he was embarrassed again. "But she's so young."

"She is." Laura agreed. How could she not? There were sixteen years between them, and she wouldn't lie and say that it wasn't a concern of hers, but they had seemed to navigate that fairly well so far.

"What if she wants children?"

Laura jerked her head up at that. Tension rushed through

her, tightening in her chest. She hadn't thought of that. She'd given up on that dream, but she'd always wanted kids. Her heart raced. "What difference would it make? You're fifty and having your second child."

Rodney's mouth flapped like a fish out of water for a second before he shook his head in dismissal.

"We've only just started seeing each other," Laura tried again. "We're not even at the stage of discussing children or marriage."

"But a woman?" At least it didn't sound like a curse or disgust this time.

"Yes, Rodney, a woman. Someone who is passionate, a hard worker, and someone who has her head on straight. I could have done well if I'd chosen someone like her the first time around."

"Ouch." Rodney winced, but Laura wasn't going to dive any more into it.

She meant what she'd said. "Which leads to the second issue we need to talk about. Work."

"What about it?"

"I'm not your bitch to do whatever it is you don't want to do. If you're meeting with a potential new client, you make the portfolio. I'm tired of carrying your weight."

"But you do it so much better than I do."

"Then learn." Laura glared, clenching her jaw. This was something she wasn't going to back down on either. She was beyond tired of pulling extra hours, and it had gotten particularly bad in the last few months. "We have the new year coming up, perhaps you make that as one of your goals. Learn how to work a full day."

"That's harsh."

"But true."

She noticed how he wasn't actually arguing with her. Laura lifted her chin to look at him directly. "I'm leaving on time today. Come five, I'm gone, and I won't have you obstructing me again."

"Understood." Rodney put his hands up in surrender. "Got a hot date?"

Laura pointed at him. "That, we're not doing."

He chuckled and grabbed his briefcase off the table. "Fine. But we will eventually."

"We won't." Laura stood and walked around her desk to get back to work. "And Rodney, I expect you in the office on time from now on."

He grumbled something she didn't quite hear as he left. She smiled to herself as she sat down and started in on the day's work.

~

Laura sat next to Skylar instead of across from her. It was somewhat awkward at first, but the ability to slide her hand along Skylar's thigh and to touch her hand and arm when she wanted was the perfect excuse for it. They'd been there fifteen minutes already, drinks in their hands.

Laura itched to ask Skylar the question that had been on her mind all day, but she wasn't sure they were quite ready for that yet. She wasn't sure she was ready for her hopes to be renewed in that capacity either. Skylar had shown her so much of her dreams that she'd forgotten about, but to dip her toe back into this one might just be too much.

"What are you thinking?" Skylar's curiosity was uncontainable.

Not sure she wanted to answer that, Laura tried to shift the conversation. "I'm glad we're finally getting our date."

"Hmm, I don't think that's really what you were thinking about."

"Why would you say that?"

"Because that's something to be happy about, and you honestly look a little scared."

Laura froze for a moment before setting her drink down, her hands unsteady. "It's nothing we have to talk about tonight."

"What is it?" Skylar touched Laura's leg, offering comfort.

They had grown so very close in the last month, diving into the deep end and not looking back. This was their first date, and Laura didn't want to ruin that with talking about things they shouldn't.

"Laura, if we don't talk about everything, then what's the point of being here?"

Skylar was right, but she still didn't want to talk about it. They should be enjoying their time together, not talking about a future they weren't sure they had.

"It's something Rodney said. Do you think I'm too old to have children?" There, that should satisfy Skylar's curiosity but not bring the actual question itching at her into the conversation just yet.

"No. Isn't he the same age as you? And he's having a kid."

"Yes, but Rodney likes prescribed roles, so it'd be natural for him to think a woman is too old for children while a man isn't."

"Jennifer is your age, isn't she?"

"She's forty."

"Oh." Skylar looked genuinely surprised by that. "I'm not sure I'd want a baby at forty. That seems like a lot of work when I have little energy."

"I can't imagine you without energy," Laura murmured as she reached for her drink.

"That may be true, but I'm not sure that I'd want kids that late in life."

Laura resisted the urge to point out that forty wasn't that far away for Skylar or that Skylar was closer to it that she was herself. Sipping her whiskey, Laura shifted in the chair to lean back. "We can talk about something else."

"No, I mean... this is important dating-type conversation, don't you think? You'd really want a baby at fifty?"

Laura was glad Skylar hadn't said *your age* like she'd anticipated and like it was a curse to be half a century old. Pursing her lips, she glanced in Skylar's direction. "I honestly hadn't thought about it until today."

"And what are your thoughts on it?"

They had managed to find their way to the question without Laura asking it directly. She'd tried once to derail the direction, but that had failed miserably. "I don't know, honestly."

"You have to have some thoughts. You're always thinking."

Skylar was right. Any moment she had that day when she wasn't thinking about work or her date with Skylar, she'd been contemplating that part of her conversation with Rodney. Every time the pull toward children was stronger than any other direction. "I think I would if I found the right person."

"You don't have to be in a relationship with someone to have kids."

Their conversation was interrupted as their food was placed in front of them. Laura hoped that would help them move onto a different topic because the truth of the matter was, she wasn't sure she wanted to do it on her own. She'd been so focused on work and her business that she'd never thought she could do it without someone else. She wanted that support and whatever children she did have deserved two parents, not one who was overworked and overtired. Call it the way she was raised, but it wasn't something Laura had ever been able to get beyond.

"Laura, do you want kids?"

"Yes," she answered before she could stop herself.

"Then what's holding you back?"

"I gave up on that dream years ago." Her heart raced.

"Then what changed?" A line formed in the center of Skylar's forehead.

Laura leaned in and kissed it gently before pulling back slightly. "You."

Skylar's lips curled upward into the beautiful smile she always seemed to be close to. Laura couldn't resist as she pressed their mouths together. She lost herself in Skylar, dashing her tongue out for a taste of the bitter alcohol and the warmth Skylar offered. Laura hummed her pleasure as she moved away. *Why does everything feel so different with her?*

Skylar's cheeks were flushed, and Laura knew that look well by now. She honestly felt the same, though she wasn't sure she was going to tell Skylar that outright—at least not now.

"Laura?" Anna's voice was so curious, but sharp enough that Laura knew Anna had no question as to who she was.

Turning to face her, Laura plastered a pleasant look on her face and tried to hide her annoyance. "Anna, what are you doing on this side of town?"

"I had a business meeting. Who's this?"

Laura's stomach plummeted. She wasn't ready for this kind of reveal, especially with Anna, who would no doubt talk to every single one in their group. "This is Skylar."

"Hi." Skylar perked right up and extended her hand. "It's nice to meet you."

"You, as well, since I haven't heard anything about you." Anna stared directly at Laura. "Seems Laura has been hiding you."

She had been doing nothing of the sort, but Anna wouldn't know that of course, because they probably talked the least of their group. And Anna was the last one she would have wanted to be interrupted by.

"Anna, I'll see you Friday after the New Year, right?"

"Yes, at Maestro's."

"I'll be there." Laura looked at her directly, hoping she would take the dismissal and leave them alone.

Anna, luckily, nodded and stepped away from the table. "I expect to see you there on time."

"I'll be on time. I promise."

"Good." Anna waved at them before she walked toward the entrance.

Laura let out a sigh. "Sorry about that."

"Who is that?"

"One of my college classmates."

"And you still get together?"

"Monthly, except in December." Laura stared down at her plate. How could she have been thinking about having children with Skylar when she didn't even know about Laura's best friends? They were nowhere near ready for that kind of conversation. They needed to get to know each other far better than they did. "There's five of us who lived off campus together. Since we're all still in Denver, it's easy for us to get together."

"What do you do?"

"Dinner, mostly." Laura couldn't bring herself to look at Skylar.

"It's okay if you don't want to talk about it."

As soon as those words were out of Skylar's mouth, Laura knew she had made a misstep. The emotional distance between them increased in a way that was so uncomfortable. Laura panicked. She shook her head and reached for Skylar's hand.

"I struggle with them—that's what this is about."

"What what's about?"

"My hesitation to talk about it." Laura clenched her jaw. She was going to have to dig deep for this one, but she had to make Skylar understand. "They all have families—husbands, children. When we get together for dinner, that's all they want to talk about."

"And you don't." Skylar nailed it.

Laura glanced down at their hands, blinking back the tears that threatened. She didn't want to cry—she never wanted that.

"Are you embarrassed by me?"

"What? No. No. That's not what I meant. I...I was the first one of our group to get divorced, not the last. Anna's been married three times. Lynda's husband died, so she and Camryn are the only ones who haven't been divorced. But I wanted my divorce. We didn't have kids, so it wasn't a long-drawn-out process of a lifetime together."

"But you have a business together."

"We do, but it's not the same." Laura knew she wasn't explaining this well, but she hadn't had time to think it through before the conversation started.

"Laura, I'd think you see Rodney more than any of them see their ex-husbands."

"Probably true." Still her heart thundered. She had to make sure Skylar understood this had nothing to do with her. "I don't complain about Rodney."

"Even to your friends?"

"No."

"I would think that's exactly who you would want to complain to."

"But for what purpose?" Laura tensed with confusion. She wasn't someone who complained in general, but to spend hours being negative about the ones she loved the most was incomprehensible.

"Because sometimes it feels good to just get it off your chest."

Their eyes locked. "I'm not that kind of person, Skylar. I don't complain about Rodney, and I don't have children, so any of those conversations I attempt to join in on are shut down because I'm not a parent."

"I see." Skylar gripped Laura's hand hard. "So you go because you love your friends, and you hope that one day, you'll be able to be friends again."

"That's quite accurate." Laura didn't know how Skylar managed to do that so easily. "I've never had someone say that out loud."

"You should. Sharing things like that is a deep weight off your shoulders."

"Perhaps you're right." Laura grabbed her fork. Little did

Skylar know that was exactly what she was doing with her. She purposely made different decisions than she ever had before. And she wanted to keep that up. "Are you coming over tonight?"

"Do you want me to?" Skylar's voice rose higher.

Every night was on the tip of her tongue, but she held back. "Of course."

"Then yes."

CHAPTER
Thirty-Nine

"ARE YOU IN LOVE?" Brady's voice boomed through Skylar's office, startling her.

"What?" Skylar spun around in her chair, incredulously offended. "What would make you say that?"

"Well, I haven't seen a lick of you in over a week."

Skylar rolled her eyes. "Of course, you have."

"Nope. Pretty sure I haven't." Brady plopped onto the couch and settled his ankle on his knee. "So where have you been?"

"I've been home." She had. It had been for short visits and only a couple nights since most of her time had been spent at Laura's in the last week. It had only been a week, but it was a whirlwind at that.

"You do know Mom and Dad are showing up tonight, right?"

Skylar blanched. She'd completely forgotten. They were going to stay in her old office for the Christmas holiday. Skylar grimaced. She and Laura hadn't talked about the holiday, or whether they would spend any time together. Skylar clenched her jaw. She wanted Laura to meet her family, but she was pretty sure that Laura would flip out over that one.

"You forgot?" Brady looked surprised. "I thought you wanted to talk to them more."

"I do." Skylar winced. "I just...got distracted."

Brady snorted a laugh. "That's one thing to call it. Hence my question."

"Am I in love?" Skylar glanced at the door, imagining she could see Laura through it, sitting in her office and leaning over her desk working.

"That's what I asked."

Skylar fell into silence. She'd been wondering the same thing all week. Laura had been on her mind constantly, since even before that very first kiss in the elevator. *But do I love her?* To the point that she wanted to think about the future, about what the next year that was just around the corner would bring? Skylar wasn't so sure about that. She'd been burned so hard by Trina, by the plans they had made and broken. She'd been hurt horribly, but Laura definitely wasn't Trina. The two couldn't be more different.

"I don't know," Skylar finally answered, her voice a low murmur. "I honestly don't know."

Brady narrowed his gaze at her. "I think you know, but you don't want to admit it."

"What makes you say that?" She was genuinely curious.

"Come on, Sky."

"Come on, what?" Anger gurgled up inside her. She hated being told what she was feeling or doing, but the fact that it was Brady was the only reason she hadn't snapped at him yet.

"Look. What is holding you back from saying it?"

"I don't know what you mean."

"I'm not stupid." Brady pointed at her. "You're holding back."

Skylar hated sometimes that he could read her so damn well. Skylar took the chance she hadn't wanted to take before. She used to use him as a sounding board, so why not now? "There are a lot of complications in our relationship, from our age differ-ence to her jerk of an ex-husband."

"Has he been a jerk to you?"

She saw the instant he went into protective mode and put

her hand up to stop him. She was strong enough to handle it on her own without him, but it was still nice to see her big brother in action. "It's fine. Laura took care of it."

"I don't like this. Men are assholes, most disgusting assholes. I don't like you being in his line of fire."

Skylar pinned him with a serious look. "I can hold my own, and I have with him several times. I worked for him, remember? I know what to expect, and I know how to deal with it."

Brady raised an eyebrow and gave her a stern look. "I don't *know* her."

Which was more the issue than anything, and Skylar realized that the instant he said it. She had met and gotten to know Callie throughout the years, and it would be expected she would do the same with her relationships. "Point taken, I'll set up some time we can all get together."

"You better," Brady said. "But, back to the original question."

Skylar groaned. If she was going to admit that, then she wanted to say it to Laura first.

"What is the block that's holding you up on admitting that you're already in love?"

Skylar's stomach dropped. If Brady could see it, could Laura? Brady knew her so much better than Laura did that she hoped not. She wasn't ready to admit it, but she'd probably been at least a little bit in love with Laura since before the Christmas party. She'd done things for her, put up with some of her antics, and tried harder than she had with anyone else. And still the pesky doubts came back to haunt her.

"Sky, let me say this one thing and I promise I'll drop it, okay?"

"Okay."

"I never saw you this happy with Trina. I know it hasn't been that long for the two of you to figure out who each other are, but you have time for that. Take it."

Skylar stared at him, amazed by how much honesty and truth there was in his words. They did have time. She needed to relish that. They both did, and they both needed to stop pushing things faster than they should go. It hadn't been long enough.

The knock made her jump.

"Skylar, I..." Laura stopped as she stepped into her office. "Sorry, I didn't realize you were with anyone."

Skylar's cheeks heated, and as soon as she locked eyes with Brady, she knew that he knew exactly who was at the door. She wrinkled her nose as she stood up to take Laura's hand firmly. *Well, now is as good a time as any.* "Laura, this is my brother, Brady. Brady, this is my girlfriend, Laura."

Brady's eyes lit up like the Fourth of July, and Skylar knew she was doomed. He was so suave when he stood up and held his hand out, holding the door all the way open for Laura. "It's good to meet you finally."

"You, too." Laura shifted a glance to Skylar, who shrugged. Laura could hold her own, Skylar knew that much. She sat back down in her chair.

"I haven't heard much about you since my sister disappeared last week."

"Likely my fault, I'm afraid." Laura looked directly at Skylar.

"Jesus," Skylar muttered under her breath, her cheeks burning up now.

Both Laura and Brady eyed her. She was doomed. She was absolutely doomed. Laura moved toward the couch, smoothing her skirt under her as she sat down. Brady's lips twitched upward into a smile as he relaxed next to Laura.

"So, you're Laura."

"I am."

At this point, Laura was amused. She had to be. Skylar inwardly cringed.

"I'm curious to find out what you've heard about me." Laura's lips twitched in amusement.

Brady chuckled. "Well, I heard that you're a bit of a bitch and wouldn't give my dear baby sister the time of day for a while there."

Laura's face fell before she looked directly at Skylar. "She wasn't lying when she told you that, but I certainly have noticed her since."

Brady seemed quite pleased with himself. Skylar curled her leg under her and covered her face with her hands. This was not the way she would have planned this.

"I'm glad to see you seem as enamored as my sister is."

"Oh, do I?" Laura once again shifted her gaze from Brady directly to Skylar.

Skylar's stomach flopped. She wasn't sure how much longer she was going to be able to handle this tension. Brady laughed and pointed at Laura while looking at Skylar. "I like her."

"Well, I'm glad you approve." Skylar rolled her eyes, but she was pleased to see he agreed.

"No, I do. She's so much better than Trina."

"Trina? Trina Wilmouth?"

Skylar's stomach dropped. She didn't want to talk about her. "Yeah, my ex-girlfriend."

"She gave you a glowing recommendation when Rodney spoke with her."

Skylar paused, her heart stuttering. She locked eyes with Laura and raised an eyebrow. "Glowing?"

"You deserve it. Without you, she never would have gotten off the ground," Brady butted in.

Skylar's chest tightened and focused on Laura. "She really gave me a glowing recommendation?"

"She did." Laura nodded. "To know she's the one who broke your heart makes it that much stronger."

Skylar hadn't heard it said like that in a long time. She'd thought it many times over, but to have Laura say it didn't have the same impact. It didn't hurt as much as it had months ago or even a year ago.

"So, Laura, what are you doing for Christmas?" Brady kept his bubbly tone.

"Oh. Um...nothing." Laura blushed a little.

"Not going to be with family?"

"No, they don't live around here."

Brady nodded like he already knew and understood it all, and Skylar knew exactly where he was going with the next statement out of his mouth. "Come to my place. Our parents are coming in. Jaz is driving up from the Springs, and Callie's got a couple friends coming over, too. I'm cooking up a big meal tomorrow, which is when we're celebrating since I work all day on Christmas day."

"I..." Laura threw Skylar a look as if she was wanting Skylar to give her the answer. Skylar shrugged slightly, letting Laura know silently that she was fine with the invitation. "I think that'll be very nice. Thank you."

"Can't believe Sky didn't invite you," Brady mumbled and leaned against the back of the couch.

"Don't blame her," Laura stated. "We've been preoccupied with other things."

"I don't need to know that." Brady grimaced. "She's my baby sister."

Laura looked very unapologetic, and Skylar couldn't stop the pride bursting in her chest.

"I think you've tortured her enough," Skylar intervened, standing up and sliding next to Laura on the couch. She settled her hand on Laura's hand, curling their fingers together. She already felt stronger for the move and wished she had done it earlier. Focusing on Laura, Skylar asked, "Did you need something?"

"I was going to ask about tonight."

Brady snickered, and Skylar leaned around Laura. "Shut up. I have more dirt on you and Callie than you would ever care to admit."

He put his hands in the air in surrender.

"Dinner?" Skylar asked.

"Yes, where?"

"Let's eat in." Skylar could tell Brady was holding back the dirty jokes, and she was thankful he had at least put that filter on when Laura had entered the room.

"Okay."

"What's your favorite kind of pie?" Brady jumped in.

Laura shifted her gaze to him. "Sweet potato."

"Really?" Both Skylar and Brady said at the same time.

Laura smiled. "I need to get back to the office. It really was good to meet you, Brady."

Skylar hesitated, but Laura didn't. She moved in and kissed Skylar fully on the lips. When she got off the couch, she smiled slightly at both of them before walking out. Skylar relaxed until Brady slapped her knee roughly.

"Aren't you going to go after her?"

"What? What for?"

"To make sure she wants to come for Christmas before I research all the sweet potato pie recipes out there."

"I'll ask her at dinner tonight. No need to bother her at work for that."

Brady snorted. "I like her. Now that I've met her, finally."

"You met her for all of five minutes."

"Fine, Christmas can be the test if you want, but Sky, I do like her."

"Thanks." Skylar rocked into his side a little. "Are you still going to feed me lunch?"

"Oh my god, yes. Get your shit together."

Brady stood up, ready to go. Skylar followed suit and grabbed her jacket. There was no way she got out of this conversation that easily, and she was pretty sure Brady was going to continue it. Locking up, Skylar resisted the urge to look down the hall at Solace's front doors. It was harder than she anticipated, but she managed. Brady wrapped his arm around her shoulders and tugged her in for a side hug.

"Just so you know, I love that you're in love."

Fuck. He's so right.

CHAPTER
Forty

THE EVENING HAD BEEN LIVELY. Laura had joined them after she was done with work for the day, but Skylar had taken the full day to be with her family. Dinner was fantastic, as always. Brady was such a good cook. It was late when Skylar hooked her arm through Laura's and walked her outside.

"Thank you for coming," Skylar said, her voice raspy from laughing most of the day.

"I enjoyed it." Laura tugged Skylar a little firmer against her side. "Thanks for the invite."

"That was all Brady."

"Well, you can tell him thank you for me."

They stopped at Laura's car, and she leaned in to start the engine to warm it up before standing outside again. Skylar stood awkwardly by, waiting. She wanted to go home with her, spend more time with her. Hell, she wanted to spend every moment she could with Laura, which was probably what Brady had been talking about. She was head over heels in love.

Standing huddled by the car, Skylar shuffled her foot in the light dusting of snow. It may not be a full-blown white Christmas, but at least they had gotten a few flakes, and it looked as though a few more were falling.

"You're welcome to come by tomorrow too," Skylar added. "But we don't do much Christmas day."

"Watch the parade?"

"Maybe I will." Skylar stepped in closer. "Though I'd much rather watch it with you."

Laura hummed, wrapping her arms around Skylar to pull her in closer. "You are always welcome to do that if you want."

Laura pressed a gentle kiss to the corner of Skylar's mouth, and if she didn't know any better, Skylar would say Laura was trying to seduce her. The kiss moved to the line of her jaw. Skylar let out a shuddering breath and dug her fingers into the jacket at Laura's sides.

"It's really tempting."

"I know," Laura answered, full confidence in each word. "But your family is here, and I understand that."

"Only my parents," Skylar whispered when Laura moved to kiss down her neck. "Jaz is driving back tonight."

Laura's tongue against the hollow of her neck was absolutely enticing. Skylar groaned as heat pooled between her legs. It seemed they could never get enough of each other, no matter how much they saw each other. But it wasn't just sex. Some nights they would stay up late talking, laughing, and flirting. It was all still so new, and this side of Laura was so new—she suspected to both of them—and she wanted to revel in that for a bit longer.

"If we stay out here much longer, I might have to sneak you into my bedroom."

Laura's chuckle was low and dangerous, like that suggestion was something she really wanted.

"Laura?"

"Hmm?"

Laura nipped the edge of Skylar's jaw before moving to her ear and tracing the shell of it with her tongue. "Are you trying to undo my resolve?"

"Perhaps."

Skylar hadn't meant it in just the physical way. To finally not be able to hold back on sharing what she was truly feeling would be amazing, but she couldn't, not yet. It was far too soon. In a sudden move, Skylar turned her head and captured Laura's lips with her own, deepening the kiss. She taunted Laura with her tongue, her fingers sliding up and down her body, all around, wherever she could reach.

Laura moaned and gave as good as she got. Skylar focused everything she had on that moment, putting everything she felt she couldn't say into actions and hoping against all hope that Laura would know—somehow that she would understand exactly what Skylar needed in that moment.

When they broke apart, their breath shone in the cold air. Skylar smiled at her. "I'll talk to you tomorrow."

There was a slight pout on Laura's lips, something Skylar swore she would never see, before Laura masked it with a knowing look. "Enjoy the rest of your time with them."

"I will."

Skylar waited until Laura got in her car and pulled away from the curb. Heading back inside, she stopped short when her mother stood with her arms crossed and a stern look on her face. Her heart raced, caught in the act of making out with her girlfriend when she should probably be inside.

"Laura is...?" The question was unmistakable.

Skylar had seriously missed some conversations with her parents in the last few weeks. "Laura is my girlfriend."

Her mother's lips thinned, and she stood ramrod straight.

"I met her at the office building. She owns an actuarial business on the same floor." *Why does this feel like an interrogation?* Her mom wasn't asking any questions, but the entire evening had gone well, and the conversation had flowed so easily.

"She's got a few years on you."

"I know," Skylar answered. She had to remain confident now

because if her mom saw any of her worries about their age difference, she would break down. "We seem to have found a way
around that."

"Have you?"

"Yes."

"Do you love her?"

Why is everyone asking me that? Skylar didn't know how to
answer or get around that one. She wasn't as quick thinking as
Laura was when it came to conversations she didn't want to
have.

"Be honest, Skylar."

"Yes," she finally whispered, her shoulders tightening. She
was going to have to tell Laura soon if the entire world was going
to figure it out before her. She didn't think she was that easy to
read, but apparently she was, especially with her family.

"Then why are you here?"

"What?" Skylar furrowed her brow. "It's Christmas Eve."

"I'm fully aware of that, and Laura doesn't have any family in
town."

"Okay..." Skylar was still lost.

"We'll be fine with Callie here."

Skylar pressed her lips together hard. "What are you saying?
Because I'm not understanding."

"If you want to spend the night with your girlfriend who
doesn't have any family here, then feel free to do that. I like her,
what little I know of her, and I liked seeing the two of you
together tonight."

They had a stare-off. Skylar stood stunned while her mother
stood silently watching the wave of emotions wash through her.

"If you love her, Skylar, then you should be with her for the
big moments. It's important."

"Are you sure?"

"Yes."

Skylar ran straight to her mom, wrapping her arms around
her in a huge hug. "Are you going to tell Daddy?"

"I'll think of something to say to him."

"I love you."

"Love you, too, baby girl." Her mom dropped a kiss into her hair.

Skylar pulled away and grabbed her phone calling Laura immediately. "Hey. Did you hit the highway yet?"

"No."

"Come back." Skylar glanced at her mom. "I'm coming with you."

～

They spent the entire week together, and it wasn't until New Year's that Skylar realized she hadn't seen the inside of her house except to grab clothes. They each had a drink in hand as they sat on Laura's couch, watching the news reels for the big event. Skylar had never really been interested in watching it. Usually she was at some sort of party, except for last year, when she'd stayed home with Callie and wallowed in her own self-pity.

"Are we going to kiss at midnight?" Skylar asked, knowing the answer already, but a little flirting never hurt anyone.

"We don't have to wait until midnight."

Laura sounded so sure of herself. They hadn't waited until midnight, for certain, but that didn't mean that Skylar still didn't want her one special kiss to ring in the new year. Skylar moved in and kissed her lightly.

"That still doesn't answer my question."

"Yes, we'll kiss at midnight."

Grinning, Skylar leaned back into the couch and took a sip of the drink Laura had made her. "So, since you met my family, when do I get to meet yours?"

She cringed as soon as she said it. Laura might not even be thinking about that kind of commitment yet. Skylar was her first relationship after a divorce, and she wasn't even sure she was out with her family yet.

"I'm sorry," Skylar started. "I just... Have you told them about us?"

Laura shifted her gaze slowly to Skylar. "I haven't, but not because I haven't wanted to. I don't talk to them very often, not like you and your family."

Skylar had been better about calling and texting her parents that week, the wake-up reminder that she needed to do that more often.

"We would have to travel to see them," Laura started. "My parents don't fly anymore, and it's easier to see them all at once back home than have them come here one at a time."

Skylar waited for Laura to say more, but she didn't. Gripping her hand, Skylar squeezed tight. "Are you scared about coming out to them?"

"No, actually. I think at this point they'll either accept it or they won't. I think they'll be fine with it."

"Even your parents?"

Laura took a moment before she nodded. "Yes. They're not as with their age as one might think."

"Cool." Skylar wished it had been that easy for her, but even knowing that her parents wouldn't likely kick her out of the house, it had still been an awful build up to the experience.

"What about in the middle of spring. I can find out when the girls have spring break, and we can go that week."

Skylar whipped around to look at Laura. "In the spring?"

"Yes." Laura seemed almost amused as she raised her glass to her lips. "What's wrong with spring?"

"N-nothing is wrong with spring." Skylar just hadn't expected Laura to be so willing to make plans that far in advance, not when they'd only been together three weeks so far. Everything was moving so fast and at the same time, it felt like everything was at a snail's crawl. Skylar wanted it to be spring already. She wanted it to be the next year already.

"Why do you look so surprised?"

"I didn't think this would ever happen to me."

"What would happen?" Laura's hand was so soft against hers. She traced a delicate pattern along the backside of Skylar's hand with her thumb.

That I'd love someone again. She almost said it. She was so close to spilling everything, but again, she resisted. Distracting herself with a kiss seemed like a good opportunity, but Laura kept it simple.

"What didn't you think would happen?"

"That I would find someone again."

Laura's eyes crinkled as she smiled, bringing her hand up to cup Skylar's cheek. "You're so young, Skylar. There are always more opportunities to find someone if you're looking, and even if you're not."

But I don't want to find anyone else. Her heart thudded hard at that thought. It was true, and she knew there was no way to avoid thinking it or saying it for much longer. "Did you think you would find someone?"

"No," Laura whispered. "And to be honest, I think you found me in the damn elevator."

Grinning, Skylar laughed. "Probably true. You never would have talked to me."

"Never," Laura agreed before she leaned in for another kiss. "See? I told you we didn't have to wait until midnight."

Skylar snorted a little as she looked at the television. "Seems it's almost midnight anyway. Get an early start?"

Laura said nothing as she took their glasses and set them on the coffee table. When she came back, Skylar was instantly wrapped up in her. Laura pressed her down into the couch, covering her as their mouths moved against each other. She had become so used to this, the understated passion that Laura had for anything involving physical touch.

Skylar parted her legs, letting Laura settle into the caress of her body. Threading her fingers through Laura's hair, Skylar held on. They would definitely be kissing at midnight still, and Skylar was going to love every moment until then.

CHAPTER
Forty~One

LAURA WAS on time to the restaurant, but she didn't want to be. She'd even tried to convince Skylar to go with her, but she hadn't thought that was a good idea—not yet anyway. Clenching her jaw, Laura gripped onto the strap of her purse for dear life. Lynda had warned her already that she was going to be the hot topic of conversation, which unfortunately meant Anna hadn't kept her mouth shut last month.

Every muscle in her body was tense as she slid into the chair across from her friends. Surprisingly, they were already there. The wine was on the table, but Laura didn't dare drink it. Anna raised her eyebrows, a question in her gaze, but Laura was going to make her work for it.

"How's Skylar?"

"She's well." Laura's answer was terse.

Anna looked to Joni and Camryn before focusing back on Laura. "Want to tell us how you two met?"

In for a penny... Laura flagged down the waiter to order a whiskey sour. She was going to need it. "We met at work. We both rent space in the building."

"How did you two start dating?"

There was no way Laura was going to talk about her upset

and drunken kiss in the elevator. She risked a glance to Lynda and Camryn, wishing one of them would step in and save her from this spectacle she was about to become. "Rodney hired her to work on our company, and by the time her contract was finished, I realized I wasn't. When I asked, Skylar agreed to a date."

"But you're straight!" Joni screeched, her voice far louder than Laura ever wanted it to be. She was sure the entire restaurant had heard her.

"She's not," Lynda murmured.

"What?" Joni strained to hear.

Lynda cleared her throat and spoke louder. "She's not."

"I'm not," Laura confirmed, the words settling in her chest as realization fully hit her. "I'm not straight. In fact, I don't think I ever was."

"What are you talking about? All the boys were falling all over you in school."

Laura grimaced. "They weren't. I don't know how to explain it."

"You're happy," Camryn chimed in. "It's the first time I've seen you happy in decades. I can see it in your eyes."

Laura's lips parted in surprise. She had never expected that. She had found joy, or rather joy had found her in the form of Skylar, but for others to notice was unexpected. "I am."

"She's got to barely be out of college," Anna chimed in. "You all haven't seen her."

"Skylar is in her thirties, yes. She is younger than me, but that doesn't seem to have been an issue so far."

"How could it not be?" Anna grabbed her wine glass and held it to her lips.

Laura sighed in exasperation. "Is this what the entire evening is going to be about?"

They all stared at her expectantly.

"Fine. Yes, she is younger than me, but she's not brand new to adulthood. Skylar owns several businesses, one that is flourishing at the moment and one that she's building up. She's an entrepreneur to the core of her soul."

"You hate entrepreneurs," Camryn tossed into the conversation.

Laura did. She'd even thought as much when she first met Skylar in that damnable elevator. Her lips quirked at that memory, Skylar's enthusiastic energy and her shrouded mood. "I think most will fail, quickly."

"But she won't?"

"She's succeeding so far, but even if she does fail, I'm pretty sure she'll pick right back up somewhere else. She's very resourceful." Laura grabbed her drink as soon as it was set in front of her, thanking the waiter before finally letting the cool liquid slide down her throat and bolster her. "I never knew what it could be like."

"What do you mean?" Lynda leaned in, and Laura was so thankful she was sitting next to her. If anyone was going to be an ally in this conversation, it had to be her.

"Sex." Laura's cheeks heated. They used to talk about sex when they were in college, when they thought it was fun and raunchy, but over the years the conversations had dwindled. She set her drink down heavily, her heart racing. "I never knew I could enjoy it."

"Oh, Laura." The pity that was in Lynda's tone was awful.

"You never enjoyed it?" Joni screeched again, and Laura winced.

"No. I thought... I don't know what I thought, but this is something else entirely. So no, to answer your question, I'm not straight."

They all sat in silence—their eyes riveted on her. Laura straightened her shoulders, moving them side to side. She stared down at the table and then back up.

"I'm not straight, and I'm dating Skylar. She's an amazing woman who is incredibly smart and intuitive in ways I'm not."
And I love her.

Laura left that last part off. Why things hit her so unexpectedly was annoying. Her hand shook as she reached for her glass, but she ignored it and tried to remain the stoically cool Laura she always was with them. The waiter arrived—perfect timing— to take everyone's orders, and Laura was thankful for the break from being the center of focus.

~

Laura pushed open the door to her condo and dropped her keys and purse onto the kitchen table. "Skylar!"

"In the bedroom!"

Laura pulled off her heels and tossed them by the door. She'd had more to drink than she'd wanted, but she'd needed it to survive that disaster of a dinner. Skylar lay propped up on the bed with her laptop on her thighs. Her hair was tousled around her shoulders, her shirt pulled tight over her breasts. Laura groaned.

"I made an absolute fool of myself tonight."

"What?" Skylar frowned, finally focusing on Laura as she stood in the doorway. "What happened?"

"You should have come with me."

"Really?"

"No. That would have been worse. You were right." Laura sighed, not even sure where to start explaining everything. "It was an attack from the start. It turned into picking me apart relationship by relationship to find out where I'd gone wrong."

"I'm so sorry." Skylar shifted her laptop off and settled it onto the floor next to the bed.

"They don't think we should date because you're too young and I'm not gay enough."

"I never understand what that means when people say it."

Skylar padded across the room, coming to stand in front of her. "And I hardly think they can judge anyone's sexuality."

Laura tilted her chin up to look into Skylar's eyes. "It was awful."

"Dinner was?"

"Being the brunt of their bigoted hatred."

"Oh, Laura." Skylar took her by the shoulders and tugged her in.

Laura buried her face in Skylar's shoulder, holding on and breathing in her scent. She'd come to love that, the softness, the gentleness, the sharing again. She couldn't live without it. "Lynda wasn't all bad, but she can't be."

"Why's that?"

"She's dating a woman—Wil—but she hasn't told them that, yet, and after tonight, I doubt she will."

"It was that bad?"

Laura nodded, saying nothing as she took comfort in Skylar's arms. She snorted suddenly and rolled her eyes at herself. "Even Rodney was more supportive once he got over the initial shock."

"Well, maybe you didn't marry a total asshole then."

"Maybe," she muttered. "What am I supposed to do?"

"What do you want to do?"

Laura stepped back and swiped her hands across her cheeks. She wasn't crying, but she was darn near close to it.

"I don't know."

"Well, figure that out, and then we'll go from there."

Skylar's ability to be so confident in life decisions surprised her nearly every time, but she loved it. Brushing her fingers over Skylar's cheek, Laura stared into those wise eyes. "I'm so glad I found you."

Skylar's cheeks reddened. Laura wasn't normally this soft with her, but the moment called for it. Pressing their mouths together in a gentle kiss, Laura held on tight. She wanted this, that much she knew. Whatever was between her and Skylar, she wanted it and more.

"I guess Camryn wasn't awful either."

"See? Maybe they were just surprised."

Laura didn't quite believe that one, especially when it came to Anna. "Anna wasn't surprised. She saw us at Bistroporium, remember?"

"Right."

Laura moved away and started stripping her clothes, wanting to get into something far more comfortable than her work garb. "She's had three weeks to work Joni up over this."

"Work her up?"

"I'm sure that's what she did. The two of them are like two peas in a pod." She dropped her blazer into the laundry basket and pulled at the zipper on her skirt. "They get together nearly every week to complain about everything. I almost hired Joni once, and Rodney put his foot down about it. I'm so glad he did."

"See? Not all asshole." Skylar sat on the edge of the mattress, her gaze glued to Laura as she snagged a loose pair of pants and a shirt.

"I never claimed he was entirely an asshole. Only in some of his decisions."

"True."

Laura flicked the clasp on her bra and ditched it before pulling her shirt on. "But to have to sit there for an entire meal while they quiz me on you and what I'm doing with you—"

"And what are you doing with me?"

Her movements jerked to a stop. Laura stood still, their eyes locking. Embarrassment flooded through her at the thought of what she'd told them at the dinner table. That she liked sex. Though why that was embarrassing was another issue. She should like sex, and the fact it had taken her until she was fifty to figure it out was embarrassing. She hadn't known what she was missing out on for years, hadn't known why Rodney had thought she was so cold every time they made love.

But how do I answer that without telling her I'm completely enam-

ored with her? Laura stepped closer, her bare feet cold on the wood floor as she moved slowly, still trying to work out what to say and do. What was she doing with Skylar?

"I'm loving every minute of being with you." Her voice was husky and low. "I'm so glad you were here when I came home."

Skylar stayed perfectly still on the bed, as if waiting for Laura to let those words slip out of her lips and to change the entire dynamic of their relationship. Laura wanted to do it, but she couldn't. Not just yet, not after the way her *friends* had tainted the night.

"I told them tonight that I'd found joy in you I didn't know existed."

Skylar's eyes widened at that.

Laura didn't hold back her grin, still moving like she had the entire room in her control. "I didn't lie."

"I don't think you ever lie. You're too smart to lie." At Laura's confused expression, Skylar continued, "You can get out of any conversation if you want because you can talk your way around what you don't want to talk about."

"Well, that's true." Laura chuckled a little, finally reaching Skylar. She stood in the space between her knees. "I told them I'm a lesbian."

"So you came out tonight for the second time in your life."

"I suppose."

"And this one didn't go as well."

"No." Laura bent down and kissed Skylar's neck. "No, it didn't."

"And your friends? Will you go out with them again?"

"We'll see." She dashed her tongue across Skylar's smooth skin, twirling the tip right at her pulse point. "They're concerned I'm forcing you to do something you don't want."

"Because I'm younger than you."

"Mm-hmm, but what do you want, Skylar? What are you doing with me?" Laura nipped, expecting the release of breath she had become so familiar with in the last month.

"It's only been a month," Skylar whispered.

"You have more time to live than I do."

"Don't start with that." Skylar wiggled against her. "Are they still your friends?"

"For now. We'll see what happens in the future." Laura kissed Skylar again. "Is there any of that pie left?"

"The sweet potato pie Brady made special just for you?"

"Yes." Laura grinned. Brady had made one for their Christmas dinner, but he'd made her another one, trying to rectify whatever he thought he did wrong with the other one.

Skylar giggled. "It's in the fridge."

"Perfect." Laura kissed her loudly before she set off for the kitchen.

CHAPTER
Forty-Two

SKYLAR DRAGGED her feet as she walked into the condo. The scents in the air hit her hard, taking over her senses and filling her with warmth. Dropping her backpack on the edge of the couch, Skylar stumbled toward the kitchen. Everything ached.

"I don't know how you walk in these damn things every day." She leaned against the counter, lifting one foot to pull off the mere two-inch heels she'd chosen for the day.

"How was the first day?" Laura glanced over at her, eyeing her up and down before turning back to the stove and whatever she was cooking.

"Don't ask." Skylar dropped her shoes by the door and ripped off her blazer. Yoga pants and a T-shirt were so enticing. She made it to the bedroom, carrying her clothes as she stripped them off. A quick toss of the discarded items into the laundry and she was free to slip into something far more comfortable.

"What happened?" Laura leaned against the doorframe with her shoulder, still made up in her outfit from the day, a pencil skirt Skylar had wanted to take off her that morning, and a low-cut blouse.

"I regret taking this contract." Skylar tripped as she pulled on her pants and collided with the mattress. She sighed heavily, sinking into the soft fabric and not even bothering to grab her pants from the floor where they were stuck around one ankle. "Worst decision ever, but I panicked."

Laura hummed, coming over and resting her arm on the foot board. "What happened?"

Shifting her gaze sharply to Laura, Skylar clenched her jaw. If she told Laura everything that had happened, Laura would no doubt be furious, and while angry protective Laura—when not aimed at her—was sexy as hell, she wasn't sure she had the energy for it.

"Skylar." Laura's voice was so firm that she knew she wasn't going to be able to get out of it.

"I don't know why they hired me, honestly. Allen is so misogynistic. Any time I say something, he immediately ignores me. Like what's the point of hiring me to do your marketing if you're not going to listen to me."

Laura pursed her lips. "That's not outright misogyny. What did they say to you?"

Damn you for being so effing smart. "It's little comments, nothing that could get him in trouble."

"What did he say to you?"

Skylar shifted her gaze from Laura's eyes to her hands tightly wrapped together in front of her. "It's the kiddo comments, the little girl comments, the *woman's touch* comments."

Laura shuddered at the last one.

"I wish it was a contract I could break."

"You can always break a contract, especially for something like this."

"I need the income to keep everything afloat."

Laura shook her head slowly, stepping up to the edge of the mattress, her arms crossed as she looked down at Skylar. Had this been any other situation, Skylar would have loved it. She was practically naked in her bra and panties, and Laura looked like the boss ready to go down on her.

"Nothing is worth subjecting yourself to that kind of harassment. Trust me."

"But I need the job."

"No. You don't." Laura leaned in, the fabric of her skirt rough against the inside of Skylar's thighs. It sent a shiver through her, one where she wanted something else entirely to happen. "It's not worth it."

"It could be."

"It won't be. Will you trust me on this?"

Skylar pulled her lower lip between her teeth, trying to think about quitting the job but also not think about how very close Laura was standing to her, the sensation as she moved against her skin, the heat that pooled between her legs.

"Skylar."

Fuck, that tone is back. Skylar swallowed hard, realizing far too late that her gaze had dropped to Laura's breasts, her breathing was rapid, and her heart was thrumming along. Her body was so ready for this. Her mind called for the distraction.

"Ah, I see." Laura glanced toward the door. "It's on simmer."

"What?" Skylar shook the cobwebs from her head, but Laura was so swift as she bent down on top of her, their mouths latched together.

Skylar bucked her hips up. Laura covered her, pushing her into the mattress. The groan reverberated through her chest. Laura dragged the pads of her fingers over Skylar's breasts to her stomach and down to her panty line.

"Laura," Skylar murmured, wiggling underneath her. "What are you doing?"

"I'm showing you that a woman deserves everything."

Skylar's breath hitched. Laura dipped her fingers under the edge of her panties, tangling tenderly with the swatch of hair.

"Because you do deserve everything, Skylar. That includes a good work environment."

"Says the woman who yelled at me on my first day."

Laura chuckled and nipped at Skylar's hip, then sucked hard, leaving a mark. "I didn't say I was perfect."

"You're perfect for me." Skylar clenched the quilt when Laura stopped her descent on her body, eyes locked together. "You are."

They were frozen in time. Skylar couldn't bear to move, wondering if Laura really understood what she was saying, the subtext to the words neither of them had uttered in the two months they'd been together. They'd gotten close, several times, but would this be it?

"I love you." Skylar wasn't even sure she was the one who spoke. Her voice sounded so far away and yet she knew the words had come from her. She'd thought about saying them so often.

Laura grinned, her lips curling upward in the most beautiful and full smile Skylar had ever seen. Her heart filled with joy. Skylar pushed up onto her elbows, ready to say it again, but Laura tilted her chin down and pressed another kiss along her sensitive skin. She twirled her tongue in patterns, moving just under the edge of elastic to tease before dashing it again.

"Oh god." Skylar flopped onto the bed, throwing her hand over her eyes.

Laura dragged her underwear off, her mouth immediately on Skylar's thighs. She was so good at this. Skylar pressed her heels into the edge of the box spring and closed her eyes, focusing on nothing other than the sensations Laura rolled through her with each touch, each brush of her clothes, each puff of air from her mouth.

"Just take me already."

"You're so impatient sometimes."

"Me?" Skylar scoffed. "You're the one who's impatient."

Laura bit her, rather hard, and Skylar squeaked. "You don't have to put up with it, you know."

Skylar had no idea if they were back to talking about the job she'd started that day or the fact that Laura wouldn't put her tongue exactly where she wanted it. "Laura."

"I'm serious, Skylar. You deserve better."

"No one is better than you." She could barely breathe with what Laura was doing to her, pulling her anticipation up every second by not giving her exactly what they both wanted.

"I wasn't talking about us."

Skylar had guessed wrong. Embarrassment flooded her, but just as it fully hit, Laura was between her legs, her tongue sliding against her and circling her clit before she started an insane pace, sucking and teasing.

"Fuck," Skylar muttered, her back arching off the bed. She gripped the quilt tightly to try and keep herself still as her body moved from one conversation to the next action. It was so hard to keep up with everything. Laura wrapped her arms around Skylar's thighs, holding her firmly when she tried to buck up.

"Laura." Her voice broke. "I can't."

She wasn't even sure what she was trying to say anymore. It was all a jumble of pleasure washing through her, wave after wave. Laura's arms were so secure around her. She was completely safe. Laura loved her, she had to at that point. It wasn't a question. Skylar knew it even if Laura hadn't said it. She was secure.

Crashing through her orgasm, Skylar cried out. She clenched her eyes tight, her lips parted as she tried to catch her breath. She was lost in a sea of sensations that skittered across her skin. The soothing fingers on her were the next thing she noticed, the light scrape of nails on her flesh, the brush of hair against her stomach.

"Breathe, Skylar," Laura commanded tenderly.

"Uh-huh."

Laura pulled at her bra, her mouth covering her already hard nipple and teasing it. Skylar was doomed if this was Laura's mood tonight. She wasn't going to survive to morning.

"Skylar," Laura nearly sang her name.

"I'm here."

"Are you?"

"Uh-huh."

Laura's breath was on her chin and neck. "Then kiss me."

Skylar turned toward Laura's voice. Their lips touched in an open-mouthed kiss, their breath mingling. Skylar kept her eyes closed. She loved everything about this woman. From her quick temper to her compassionate heart.

Trying again, Skylar broke the kiss and gazed into Laura's eyes.

Laura spoke first. "You have made me understand love in a different way than I ever did before. I don't think I'd found myself until I met you. Truly."

Skylar clamped her mouth shut, letting Laura speak as she hovered above.

"You opened my eyes to what I was missing. And despite the complications that we come into this with, I think we'll make it."

"We'll make it?" Skylar raised an eyebrow.

Laura pulled away, standing at the edge of the bed again. "Take that thing off already."

Skylar could barely keep up with the swing of the conversation. It took her a second to respond, sitting up to unhook her bra and throw it off the side of the bed. Laura lifted her blouse and pulled it over her head, her hair settling around her shoulders in the soft curls she put in every morning.

When she reached for her skirt, Skylar grabbed her hands to stop her. "Let me."

Laura turned around. Skylar skimmed her hands across the small of Laura's back to her hips, sliding them down before back up. She pulled the tiny zipper, opening the skirt so Laura could step out of it, but Laura's hands on hers stopped her. When she looked up, Laura stared down at her over her shoulder.

"I love you, Skylar."

"Do you really?"

"Oh yes."

Skylar wanted to leap for joy. She wanted to stand up and take Laura right there. She wanted it all.

"Quit the job."

"What?" Skylar shook her head in confusion.

"Quit the job. Trust me that I'll take care of you if you need it."

Skylar wanted to object. She'd never let anyone take care of her, and she didn't want to start now, but Laura had only said if she needed it. Brady would do exactly the same thing. So would her parents.

"I don't want you to be in a position where you're degraded every day just to make a couple of dollars."

"It's more than a couple of dollars."

"You know what I mean. Quit. I won't think any less of you for doing it. In fact, I'll think even more of you for standing up for your convictions."

Skylar turned Laura around, so they faced each other again. "How do you manage to do that every time?"

"Do what?"

"Stun me into silence."

"Must be a gift." Laura's eyes glittered with amusement.

"Must be," Skylar repeated. She moved her hands, letting the skirt drop to the floor. Next, she hooked her thumbs into Laura's thong and dropped that along with the skirt. "You're next."

"But we can't go all night."

"Why not?"

"The soup's on."

Skylar rolled her eyes as she swiftly unhooked Laura's bra. "We can stop for dinner and then get back to it."

"Oh my god."

"Not yet." Skylar tugged hard on Laura's arm, dragging her onto the bed. "But maybe soon."

Laura laughed as she shifted upward to get more comfortable. Skylar didn't play around like Laura did, the call of a good meal too strong. She took small bites as she moved up Laura's thigh right to the crease of her leg and hip. Then she started on the other one. Laura reached up and wrapped her hands around the bars of the headboard. The urge to tie her up was strong, but Skylar would save that for another day or perhaps later that night. They hadn't tried that one yet and the bed was perfect for it.

"God, I love you," Laura whispered.

"Say it again," Skylar demanded. Hearing those words for the rest of her life still wouldn't be enough.

"I love you."

Skylar pressed her tongue against Laura's clit, swirling and flicking as fast as she could. She wanted to give Laura as much as she had received and more. Sliding one finger in up to the knuckle, she upped the pressure of her mouth.

"I love you." Laura's voice sounded wispy.

Skylar kept the pattern, Laura's hips sliding against her in a rhythmic pattern.

"I love you."

Her heart burst with absolute joy. Laura's breath caught, her voice cracking as she tightened around Skylar's finger, her chest lifting off the bed. Skylar teased the last bit out of her before releasing Laura and climbing up to lie next to her.

"I love you, too," Skylar kissed Laura's cheek and neck. "I always will."

CHAPTER
Forty-Three

FIVE MONTHS LATER...

ARM IN ARM they walked out of the restaurant, the beer flavor lingering on Skylar's tongue. She giggled when Laura stepped in to open the car door for her, as if she couldn't do it herself. Instead, Skylar took the opportunity and pressed Laura against the car door, their mouths locked together in a heated kiss.

"Do I get my real birthday present when we get home?"

"And what's that?" Laura asked.

"You know what I want." Skylar nipped Laura's lower lip.

"Yes, we can do that."

"Good."

"Get in the car, Skylar, and sober up a bit on the way home."

Skylar grinned as she slipped into the passenger seat. It had been a wonderful birthday celebration so far. She'd spend the next day with Brady and Callie to celebrate with the rest of the family, Laura included. But she'd wanted tonight just for the two of them.

"I'm glad it's finally warming up outside," Laura said as she slipped behind the wheel.

"Winter's too cold for your liking?"

"Some days," Laura muttered.

"Well, I can always warm you up."

"God, you're flirtatious when you're drunk."

Skylar laughed. "It might be the last time I get to drink for a while, you know. And I'm not drunk. I had one beer."

"I know." Laura suddenly looked serious.

The same worry, fear, and excitement filtered through her, and she had no idea what to do with it all. Skylar tried to lighten the mood on the quick drive home, and by the time they got to the condo, she was successful. Laura took her hand as they stepped into the elevator.

"Remember that time..." Skylar started.

"Yes," Laura cut her off.

"You have no idea what I'm talking about."

Laura cut her a look. "Of course, I do."

"Why so serious?" Skylar pressed into Laura's side. "Do you remember how I almost made you come against this wall?"

Laura shivered, and Skylar inwardly raised her hands in victory. This seduction dance had been going on all day through text messages and dinner. She wasn't about to give it up to save her life. She stayed as close as possible to Laura while they waited for the elevator to deposit them on the right floor.

"I bet you would have loved it."

Laura's cheeks tinged pink. "Next time, it'll be you."

"Now?"

"Next time," Laura reiterated.

"Fine." Skylar pouted as they walked out of the elevator, but to be fair, just the thought of Laura taking her like that was exciting. They pulled off their light jackets as soon as they were inside, damp from the chilly July thunderstorm.

"You need to sober up a bit."

"You keep saying that." Skylar giggled. "But if you want, I'll go take a shower real quick and then I won't drink another drop of alcohol until I've had my real present."

"You do that." Laura kissed her lightly before shooing her on her way.

Skylar sauntered to the bathroom and locked the door behind her. She never did that, but the thought had been weighing on her mind for days now. She wasn't supposed to test yet, not until she went back in for bloodwork, but it had been long enough, hadn't it? Stealing a glance at the door and listening to the noises in the living area, she checked to make sure Laura wasn't coming to talk to her again.

"Okay. I can do this." Skylar dug around in the back of the drawer where she'd stashed the test. She was quick when she ripped it open, but slow as she read the directions twice over just to make sure she didn't screw it up.

Peeing on the stick wasn't as bad as she thought it would be. Capping it, she set it on the bathroom counter, turned the shower on, and stripped. The test said three minutes. She could wait around before getting in to see the results and then have the shower to figure out her emotions. It was perfect. Standing naked, she waited and tried not to dare herself to look, but she couldn't help it.

Skylar bent over the test within the first minute, her eyes wide as the second pink line lit up brightly.

"Fuck."

Her heart raced.

"No way."

Her stomach dropped.

"Shit."

It was their first try. She hadn't thought—with Jaz's problems and Laura's they had just assumed—damnit, what was she going to do? Fear raced through her, her eyes wide as she stared down at the test. Well, the directions had said three to ten minutes. Maybe it would be negative by the time she got out of the shower.

Climbing under the hot spray, Skylar took deep breaths. It was positive. She was pregnant. They were going to have a baby in March. *Holy crap!* Laura was going to flip out, and she could barely even believe it. How was she even going to tell Laura in the first place?

"I'm screwed." Skylar covered her face with her hands and let the hot water seep into her muscles to relax them. She never should have had that beer at dinner. Maybe that was why Laura was so standoff-ish about her being buzzed, because she definitely wasn't drunk. She was happy and flirtatious but not drunk. But now she was dead afraid.

Turning off the water, Skylar stepped out of the shower and wrapped herself in the towel. Immediately she stared at the test. *Shit. It's still positive.* She took slow deep breaths again to settle her stomach and the anxiety that burst upward. They thought it'd take time for this to happen. *Okay. We can do this. We planned for it.*

Skylar pulled on her yoga pants and T-shirt, leaving her bra off. She hung the towel up and put her hand on the doorknob, trying to decide exactly how this was going to happen. She had to tell Laura. There was no way she could make this special because Laura would know in two seconds that something was up. Calming the panic that swelled, Skylar stepped out of the steamy bathroom and into the hallway.

Immediately, she jumped back in, grabbed the test, and shoved it into the waistband of her pants. Swallowing hard, Skylar took her time going to the living room. Laura sat on the sofa with a book in her lap.

"Feel better?"

"Uh...the shower helped, yeah." She couldn't lie and say she felt better because her mind was a racing disaster at the moment.

Sitting next to Laura, completely tense, Skylar tried to ease her mind off everything. Laura kept her book in her lap, but her eyes were locked on Skylar's face.

"Everything okay?"

Skylar pressed her lips together hard, words not forming the way she wanted them to do. Giving in to saying nothing, she reached to her side and pulled out the test, handing it over. Laura tentatively took it.

"You took a test?"

"Yeah." Skylar's voice was so quiet. "I know I wasn't supposed to, and then I thought it'd be negative by the time I got out of the shower, and it wasn't."

Her ears rang with the silence. Laura's eyes hadn't left the test, and Skylar had no idea what to say or do. Her stomach was a mess, her nerves were frayed. She needed some sort of response, anything, because she was one second away from flipping out.

"It's positive."

"Yeah," Skylar confirmed.

"You're pregnant."

Either Laura was completely in shock or something else was going on. Skylar had no idea, but she wanted to know the answer. She tried to read every change in Laura, every hitch in her breath, every twitch in her face, but she was getting nowhere.

"I know I wasn't supposed to take it yet—"

"You're pregnant." This time, Laura's voice lifted up, as if she was excited. Skylar hoped that's what it was because she really needed her stoic Laura back. "It worked."

"It did."

"Skylar." Laura twisted and grabbed Skylar in a hug. "We're going to have a baby."

"Yeah, we are." The panic that had welled up dissipated in a flash. They had wanted this. They'd planned for it, and while it was a shock to happen so quickly, they had expected it. "We're having a baby."

Laura pulled her in for a kiss, joy emanating from every moment they touched and every second they were fused together in each other's arms. Skylar moved away, breathing her relief. Laura stared back down at the test.

"There's so much we have to do. We need a house. There's

not enough room here for a kid. We live in a one-bedroom condo."

"There's time for that, Laura." Skylar covered her hand, squeezing tightly. "There's time."

"I'm going to have to tell Rodney."

"I think he'll be happy for us."

"Maybe. Who knows?"

Laura's cheeks were pale, hollowed out as she worried herself. Skylar recognized the signs in seconds flat. She'd seen it so many times, and the fact that she'd just gone through it all helped her to see it.

"Hey," Skylar whispered. "Take a deep breath for a second."

Laura halfway did as she was told. Skylar had her time in the shower to work through this, and she was thankful for it. Laura was supposed to be her rock and having to be the calm reasonable one took more out of her than she expected.

"We have time to figure that part out. It takes time to have a baby, and who knows if the bugger will even stick. Jaz has miscarriages all the time."

"You're right. I know you're right." Laura flipped her hand over, lacing their fingers.

"Good."

Skylar slid down in the seat and curled against Laura's side. She needed nothing else but to be close to her right then. She needed the comfort, Laura's presence, and the fact that they were in this together to remind her she wasn't alone and that she could do this. She was going to be a mother, and that was scary and thrilling.

After minutes of silence passed, Laura broke it. "Skylar?"

"Hmm?"

"Marry me."

Skylar jerked her head off Laura's shoulder. "Are you serious?"

"When have I not been?"

"Why? Why do you want to marry me?"

"I love you." Laura curled her fingers around Skylar's cheek.

"I want to be with you, and I want our baby—" she dropped her hand to Skylar's abdomen "—to have exactly what they deserve, just like I want you to have what you deserve."

Skylar covered Laura's hand, warmth filling her as the moment sunk in. They'd already done so much together, moved in, decided to have a child, what more was marriage? Raising her gaze slowly to Laura's, Skylar said the only thing she could. "Yes."

"Really?"

"Yeah." Moving in, Skylar stole Laura's lips in a heated kiss. She never wanted this moment to end. The joy and nerves were endless, but with the two combined, they led to a beautifully perfect moment together, one that Skylar never wanted to be done with.

This was what they had both always wanted, and it had taken a stupid elevator ride when she couldn't keep her mouth shut to get there. Laura pulled back, searching Skylar for something.

"What is it?"

"I don't have a ring."

Skylar snorted. "We're not exactly a traditional couple."

"I know that."

"So I don't need a ring for a proposal." Skylar was tickled that Laura would even think of it though.

Laura pursed her lips, a line forming in the center of her forehead. Skylar was pretty sure she knew exactly what Laura was thinking. Kissing her quickly, Skylar leaned back. "I want you to have one."

"That's fine, but I don't *need* one."

Laura grabbed Skylar's hands, her look serious. Skylar's heart swelled with joy, overwhelmed by everything that had changed in the last few months. "We'll get you one," Laura insisted.

"And you. If I get one, you get one."

"Fine, but I've done this before."

"But not like this." Skylar settled into the thought, the weight of the momentous decision they had made so readily alighting in her heart.

"No, not like this," Laura agreed.

Skylar took in a deep breath and pressed their foreheads together. She closed her eyes and let everything in the last few minutes wash over her. "Some birthday."

Laura laughed lightly. "I suppose you like your gift, then."

"Most of it. I'd still like another drink."

"Can't have it now. Well, maybe a sip or two tomorrow to hide it from your family."

"I know." Skylar couldn't stop smiling. As much as she wanted to, she couldn't. Laura rested her head against Skylar's shoulder as they cuddled on the couch.

"I guess I'm not too old to have a baby."

Laughing, Skylar shook her head. "Whoever called you old?"

"You did."

Rolling her eyes in an exaggerated manner, Skylar grinned. "Okay, boomer. If you say so."

"For the record, Skylar, have I mentioned that I'm not actually a boomer?"

Skylar hesitated, moving to look into Laura's eyes.

"I'm Gen X."

Skylar wrinkled her nose. "I know, but where's the fun in teasing a generation that doesn't exist."

Laura slapped Skylar's leg lightly. "I love you some days."

"You love that I tease you some days."

"Every day," Laura whispered. "Don't ever stop."

"Just so long as you don't give up your dreams."

"With you in them? Never."

About the Author

Adrian J. Smith has been publishing since 2013 but has been writing nearly her entire life. With a focus on women loving women fiction, AJ jumps genres from action-packed police procedurals to the seedier life of vampires and witches to sweet romances with a May-December twist. She loves writing and reading about women in the midst of the ordinariness of life.

AJ currently lives in Cheyenne, WY, although she moves often and has lived all over the United States. She loves to travel to different countries and places. She currently plays the roles of author, wife, and mother to two rambunctious youngsters, occasional handy-woman. Connect with her on Facebook, Twitter, or her blog.

facebook.com/adrianjsmithbooks

twitter.com/adrianajsmith

instagram.com/adrianjsmithbooks

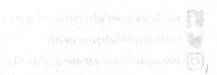

Love Me At My Worst

Three... Two... One... BOO!

Isla Walsh is a prankster, and her favorite person to pull one over on has to be her principal, Andry Murphey. But Isla isn't all fun and games, and her sixth grade students will attest to that. Behind every prank Isla plays hides a secret she hasn't shared since she moved to Cheyenne. She's not the happy person she seems to be. In fact, she's pretty certain everyone will leave her.

Andry Murphey moved to Cheyenne because of a woman, and two years after her marriage ended, she hasn't found who she is other than a principal. For two years all she could handle was the basics of life, until her favorite teacher ups the ante on the pranks. In each trick, she finds joy again, and Andry wonders what it would be like if she could fall in love again.

Follow two broken hearts in this sensual age gap romance as Isla and Andry rediscover themselves and what it means to love others through their worst.

Let the prank wars commence!

Coming June 2023

Also by Adrian J. Smith

Romance

Memoir in the Making

OBlique

Love Burns

About Time

Admissible Affair

Daring Truth

Indigo: Blues (Indigo B&B #1)

Indigo: Nights (Indigo B&B #2)

Indigo: Three (Indigo B&B #3)

Indigo: Storm (Indigo B&B #4)

Indigo: Law (Indigo B&B #5)

When the Past Finds You

Crime/Mystery/Thriller

For by Grace (Spirit of Grace #1)

Fallen from Grace (Spirit of Grace #2)

Grace through Redemption (Spirit of Grace #3)

Lost & Forsaken (Missing Persons #1)

Broken & Weary (Missing Persons #2)

Young & Old (Missing Persons #3)

Alone & Lonely (Missing Persons #4)

Stone's Mistake (Agent Morgan Stone #1)

Stone's Homefront (Agent Morgan Stone #2)

Urban Fantasy/Science Fiction

CPSIA information can be obtained
at www.ICGtesting.com
Printed in the USA
BVHW030810250423
663000BV00013B/920

9 781960 221070